WYLDLING SNARE

Book One of the Wyldling Dream Series

By: A.R. Grimes

A Cycle of Tehara novel

Library of Congress Control Number: 2022913936

Printed in the United States of America: First Printing, 2022

ISBN 978-1-958718-00-1 (ebook)
ISBN 978-1-958718-01-8 (paperback)

http://cycleoftehara.com

Developmental Editor: Huckleberry Rahr
Copy/Line Editor: Wes Imrisek
Cover Art: GetCovers.com
Formatter: R. L. Davennor

Map designed using Inkarnate software (inkarnate.com)
Lilac Grove and the Darkenwood Forest

Happy 19th birthday, Gabriel.
Although I began this saga for myself, I finished it
with you in mind.

For Papa, who said I could.

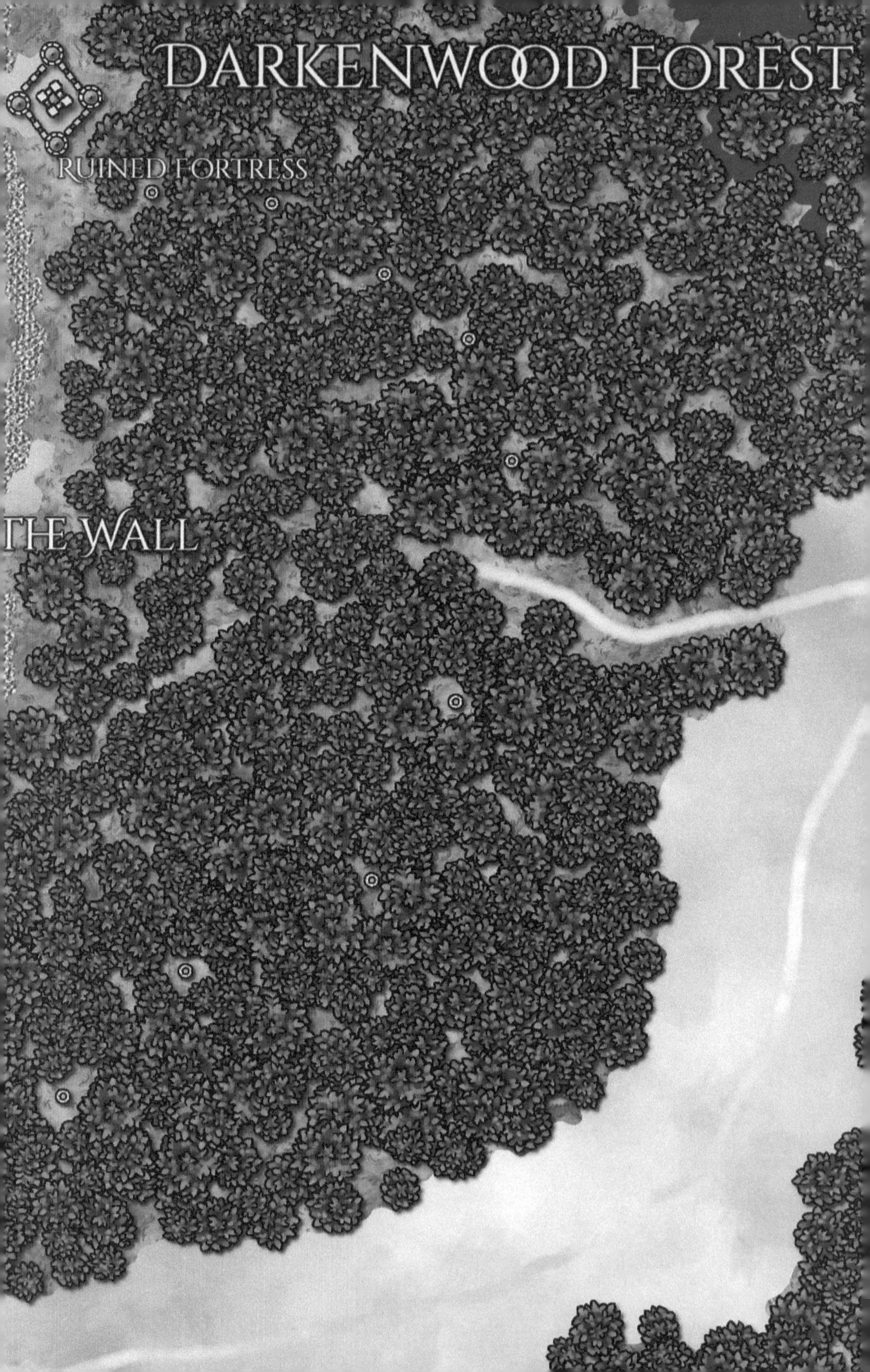

DARKENWOOD FOREST
RUINED FORTRESS
THE WALL

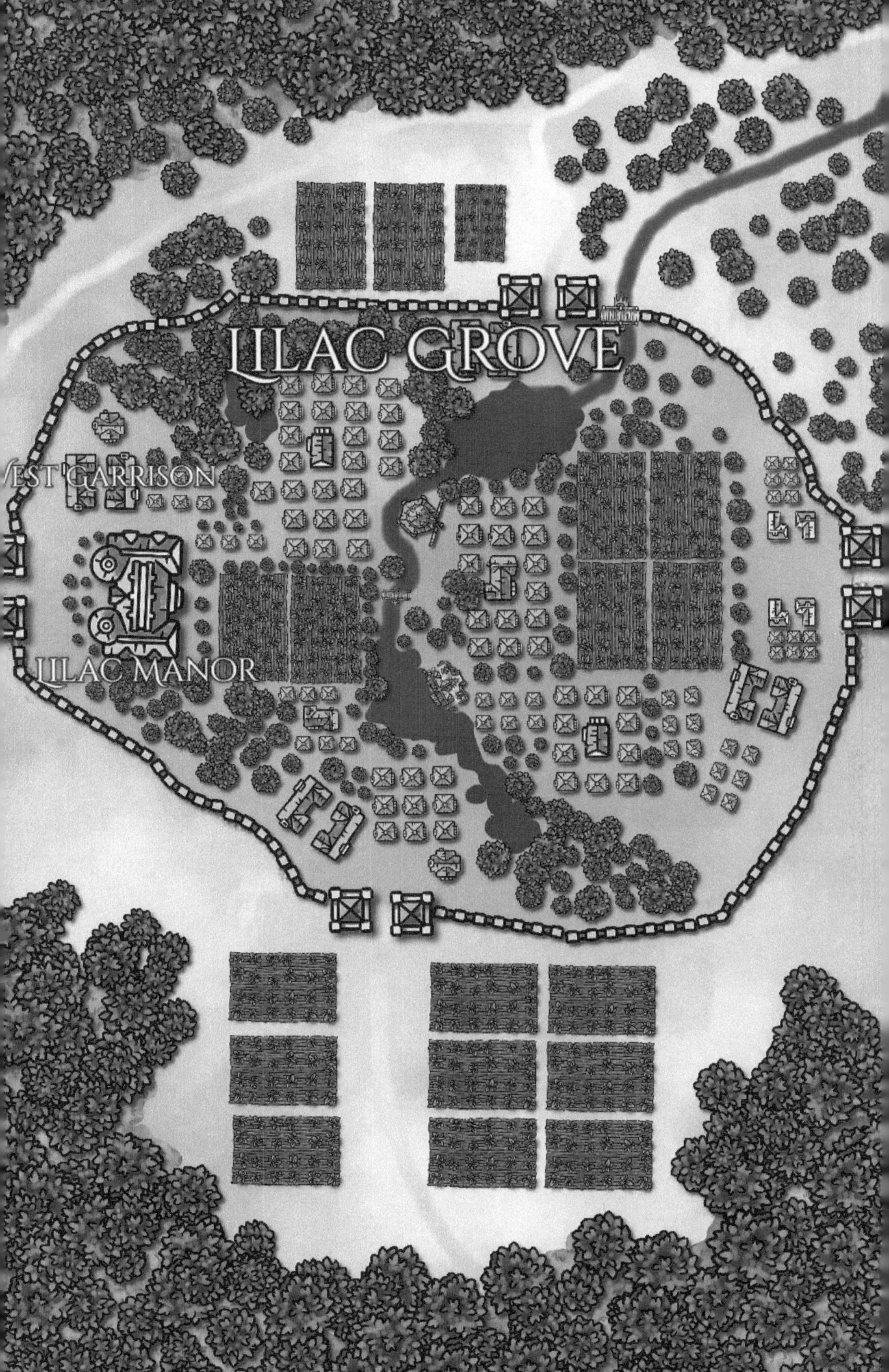

LILAC GROVE
WEST GARRISON
LILAC MANOR

ONE MOON AGO

SWORD DANCE

"I love learning about unknown places," said the maiden in dark blue armor. She traced the curved outline of the map in his book. "What is this world called?"

"Tehara. It's where I live."

Wind gusted through the training grounds, damp and chill. Winter was reluctant to release its hold on the Northern Marches. Enoch Northward shivered as an icy tendril of air slipped around his neck, driving away thoughts of dream conversations with maidens in dark blue armor. Sweat coated his torso underneath his tunic and leather breastplate. On either side and behind him, uniformed men posed in their own private bubbles of perdition.

The baron-knight called out, "Wind of Death." He swung his body into a loose, wide stance using fluid, sweeping movements. He ended with one leg back, his sword raised and angled to the left.

Around Enoch, cloth rippled, and men groaned or sighed as they moved. None of them counted sweating while freezing in the chilly wind amongst their favorite activities, but Enoch wanted to impress his guardian. He must endure, just as the grown men did. He'd be sixteen in another moon and eligible for knighthood within a Cycle—if he mastered all the sword-forms and performed according to the Baron-Knight's Code. Then he'd help Sir Rick and Sir Thomas govern the Northern Marches.

He changed his stance from the eighth to the ninth sword-form, mirroring his guardian. *Too beggaring slow*, he groused, eyeing the others, who snapped into the last position two seconds ahead of him. Every muscle burned from holding eight different stances for three minutes apiece. Sir Rick ran the drills because Commander Storm was off somewhere in the Eastern Marches. *Praise Yshua; Commander Storm would've insisted I hold each stance for at least five minutes.* His arms trembled, and he scrunched his nose to prevent his spectacles from sliding. He must make it through the entire drill. If he couldn't, he'd never be a true warrior.

"Sentinel's Rest," Sir Rick announced. He set his feet shoulder-width apart, sword hilt clasped with both hands in front, blade pointing downward. The others mimicked him. *Final stance*, Enoch thought. *Praise Yshua.* He tried not to slam the sword-tip into the earth between his feet. Three minutes dragged by. A drop of sweat traced its way down his back.

Sir Rick stood like a statue in front, eyes fixed on a point beyond the troopers. At length, his expression relaxed. "At ease," he said. "Well done, men." They saluted him with a fist held against their chest. "Dismissed. Enoch? Walk with me." The baron-knight smiled and beckoned him.

With a sigh, Enoch slid his sword into its scabbard and staggered over to his guardian. His limbs still felt wobbly. Enoch's best friend, Simon Halloway, waved at him as the troopers filed out of the arena for wall patrol duty. Grateful to stretch his muscles, Enoch returned the wave and then fell in step beside his guardian. A cool breeze brought him the scent of thawing earth.

Enoch glanced at his guardian's face, the sepia skin weather-beaten into leather above his salt and pepper beard. Brown eyes crinkled at the corners when he smiled. "How was it this time?"

He glanced at his boots and concentrated on not stumbling. "I can't keep up with the others." Bitterness crept into his tone. "I'm too small."

Sir Rick raised his eyebrows. "I don't believe that'll be a problem forever; you've not reached your full growth yet." He patted Enoch's shoulder. "You're coming along well, lad. I notice how hard you work."

Enoch cracked a smile. "Thank you, sir."

"So… tomorrow, you and Raeden leave for Treehome." Sir Rick lifted his face to the clear sky and breathed deeply. "It's bound to be a pleasant day—the first since the equinox. I've excused you from the rest of your duties; I reckon you have plans?"

Enoch grinned. "Yes, sir." He fished a piece of paperboard out of his belt-pouch and handed it to his guardian. "The Maidens Three have extended their customary picnic invitation."

The baron-knight examined the invitation and hummed. "Miss Cartwright's calligraphy is improving," he noted with a smile. "And Miss Jolson draws a very fine picnic tableau." He snorted. "What's this, now? 'Join us, Enoch, or be forever sundered from our company.' Miss Pines has mastered the art of hyperbole quite nicely." He chuckled and returned the invitation to Enoch. "You youngsters have been doing this since you were twelve, over four Turnings, now. I hope to see this tradition continue; it's good for you to stay connected to the crofterfolk."

Enoch frowned. Why in Tehara wouldn't he? The knights frequently mingled with the crofterfolk while executing their duties. He opened his mouth to ask, but before he got his question out, his stomach growled.

Sir Rick threw back his head and laughed, a rich and carefree, booming sound that rolled through the grounds. He pulled a packet wrapped in butcher's paper out of his satchel. "Here, Enoch. This should tide you over for another hour."

Sheepishly, Enoch stuffed the invitation in his belt-pouch. "I won't take your breakfast, Sir. I'll scrounge through the kitchens. Patsy will give me something."

Sir Rick pulled out a similarly wrapped package, his eyes dancing. "I came prepared. You have no excuse now; take it."

Enoch needed no further prompting. He and his guardian munched their sausage rolls in companionable silence. When they reached the Manor, Sir Rick clapped a hand on Enoch's shoulder. "Clean up and then go enjoy yourself, lad. There're several troopers who served Sir Nicholas transferring here and I have paperwork to wrangle." He sighed and scrubbed a hand over his face to hide the grief. "Nick was a good man; Lord Yshua rest his soul. He didn't deserve to fall to base treachery." He shook his head. "I pray Commander Storm's investigations yield fruit."

The last lump of food stuck in Enoch's throat, and he swallowed. Sorrow swept through him like the icy breeze. Sir Nicholas and many of his elite warriors had died trying to suppress an uprising in the Eastern Marches. "Praise Yshua; we don't have those sorts of troubles here, Sir Rick. I don't know what we'd do without you."

I don't know what I'd do without you—the only father I've ever known.

His guardian smiled and drew Enoch into a one-armed hug, shaking him. "Carry on as usual, I'd imagine." He pushed Enoch away and winked. "Now, lad, what have I told you to do, always, whatever challenges may come?"

Sunslight broke through the clouds. Enoch grinned as he shaded his eyes. *This is easier than sword forms.* "Like I'd ever forget. Seek justice, show mercy, walk humbly with Lord Yshua."

THE APPRENTICE'S TOWER

"Burning suns, I dare you to do your worst."

Framed in his tower's window and naked to the waist, William spread his arms, tilted back his head, and closed his eyes. The last bit of winter's chill in the air invigorated him as he bared his teeth in defiance. Master Tenebris claimed the three suns—Klotho, Lachesis, and Atropos—would blind or even set ablaze any nehmwights foolish enough to wander abroad during the day. So far, despite his constant challenging, this hadn't happened to him.

Apparently, even considering my mixed parentage, I'm a freak.

William scowled. He dropped his arms and eyed the ebony tattoos twining down his arms from his shoulders. They prickled like gooseflesh and shimmered wherever the suns' rays struck them. When William attained the second level a season earlier, his master inked the arkhabala after carving the design into his flesh. William glowed with pride and yet… Tenebris claimed his training was a full Turning behind schedule because of his impure blood.

"Yet another obstacle between me and full mastery of the Arkhabadh. Or so Tenebris says." He snorted. "If Tenebris had his way, I'd remain his apprentice and slave forever."

A delicious thrill ran through him at omitting his mentor's title. Master Tenebris slept far below in the fortress's basement and couldn't backhand him for insubordination.

Upon their arrival at the abandoned outpost five days ago, Master Tenebris designated the crumbling fortress on the fringes of the Darkenwood Forest as their base. Moss and climbing ivy covered its battlements as the forest sought to reclaim its territory. Hardwood saplings took root between the cracked flagstones in the courtyard and then sprouted to grow into fine trees; one in the center possessed an impressive girth.

Although the sorcerer's will held sway over the deep interior where cold stone protected a nehmwight from the sunslight, the exterior remained William's domain during the daylight hours. Four towers graced the cardinal points of the ruined castle. A long-ago battle destroyed three, but the East-facing one escaped the ravages of war and time, mostly intact.

And now it's my secret kingdom.

William made an obscene gesture at the heavens and then ducked inside the round room. Along with half of the roof, much of the tower's infrastructure had collapsed. Over the past few days, he was familiar with the dangers and avoided them.

He shrugged into his burkheld—the gray-brown robe every Arkhadahn and their students wore—and sat on a large piece of rubble placed before a small drafting table. Removing a roll of parchment from his satchel, he unrolled it and pinned the corners to the tabletop. Sunslight filtered through the gaps in the ceiling to bathe the parchment until it glowed creamy and pink. William gazed at it for a moment, then brought out the rest of his tools. The equations and formulae stood in neatly scribed rows, stark black figures like armored soldiers upon a snowy field prior to a twilight skirmish. Less than a moon ago, he'd watched one such from the battlements of the Dreadlord's keep, far away and to the West.

He recalled the bite of winter air freezing his nostrils and the weight of the items the Dreadlord placed in his hands, the silkiness of the soft leather cover of the treatise and the chill of the metal scroll tube. As always, the Dreadlord's violet eyes pierced him. Knowing him.

"A parting gift, William," the Dreadlord had said. "The treatise is from my wife, who sends her love. The scroll is from me. I advise you to study both when you find time by yourself."

William smirked. Another way of saying Tenebris wouldn't approve. *I suppose there's no time like the present to crack open the scroll.*

He studied the parchment for a moment longer, and then reached under a pile of rubble to pull out his other treasure, the scroll-tube from the Dreadlord, encased in waterproof sealskin. Tiny precious stones and faceted bits of metal—ruby, silver, emerald, gold, sapphire, opal, and amethyst—winked in the sunslight from their settings in the scroll-tube when he unwrapped it. He grasped each end of the cylinder and twisted it open. Inside lay a curled parchment, yellowed with age but still supple. He unrolled it far enough to see its title, scribed in the Dreadlord's own hand: *Concerning Wyldlings and the Sages' Artifacts of Power.*

William chuckled. Vortawd's carbuncles, this was rich! No wonder the Dreadlord insisted he study this by himself; Tenebris would flay him if he caught him reading about something as unclean as the Aethyr.

"There is great power in knowledge and even greater power in its careful application," the Dreadlord had told him. "A keen mind like yours is a terrible thing to waste on nehmwight sorcery." His lip curled up on the last few words, but then he smiled and clapped a hand on William's shoulder. "I sense great things in store for you."

There are, indeed. But I'll not cast aside any path to power, thank you very much.

William unrolled the scroll and began to read.

LEGENDARY TALES

A shadow fell across the page. "What're you reading? It looks old."

Enoch glanced up from his book. A girl with merry green eyes and russet hair in an untidy braid stood before him, hands thrust into the large front pocket of her apron. Her pale blue skirts swirled as she shifted her weight from one foot to the other. For as long as he'd known her, Janet Pines never could keep still.

She wrinkled her nose at him. "Please tell me it's not one of those stuffy old tomes about laws the magistrates decorate their shelves with."

Enoch grinned. "Praise Yshua, no." He stuck the invitation between the pages to mark his place and then held up the leather-bound volume for her inspection. He tapped a finger on the embossed title. "See? Here,

10

it says: *Fortulles Evaingynon Seprima.*"

Janet squinted at the book, and then at him. Her skirt-swirling movements slowed. "The who, the what now? Is that High Dwelfnic? You know we crofterfolk aren't taught fancy languages in school, Enoch! Looks like boring old law to me." She scowled, stamping a foot. "You promised you'd bring a story-book."

Enoch shook his head, chuckling at Janet's mercurial temper. "No, it's not a book about laws. And I kept my promise. This book is *Legendary Tales of the Sages*, translated into Tradespeak alongside the original text. And you're right, it's in High Dwelfnic," he added.

Her face brightened. "Why didn't you say so? Or are you trying to impress someone with your fancy dwelfnim talk?" She smirked, plopping beside him. "Someone like, oh… Rebecca Cartwright. You know, Lil' Becky Rosa. Your favorite dancing partner."

Enoch's cheeks flared with warmth. "Let it rest, Jan. So what if Becky and I danced together at the Festival of Lights? That's what people do at festivals. No reason to read anything into it. She's my friend, same as you and Sally. And Simon," he added as though an afterthought, hoping she'd rise to the bait. He caught a flicker of movement in the trees; two female forms, one in green and the other in blue.

Janet's eyes glittered with mirth, and she shook a finger at him. "Nuh-uh. Not like me and Sally." Her voice grew breathy as she added, "Or Simon." She turned away with a studied air of nonchalance. "Oh, look. Here they come, now. Becky! Sally!" Janet rocked to her feet. She hopped up and down, one hand remaining in her apron pocket as she waved at two other girls—one brunette, the other blonde—approaching from the footpath. "We're over here," she called

The blonde girl scurried ahead of the other, pale green skirts flying. A wicker basket dangled from an arm and her two plaits bounced around her shoulders. "Oh, I hope we aren't late; Jan's already here. Hurry, Becky!"

The brunette, carrying another wicker basket, picked up her pace. "We're perfectly punctual. Jan's always early. You know that, Sal."

"Because I can never wait," Janet replied, laughing as she ran up to them, one hand still in her pocket. "Everyone knows that. Did you bring one of your cream cheeses, Sal?"

"Of course I did; it's Enoch's favorite."

Enoch set aside the book and jumped up to lighten their burdens, grabbing a basket handle in each hand. The maidens thanked him and then spread out an enormous old quilt for their picnic. Despite himself, his gaze fastened on the dark-haired girl like steel to a magnet. Her cheeks glowed rosy, and her brown eyes shone from the exercise. Until the Light of the World Festival three moons ago, he hadn't noticed. Becky finished spreading out a blanket on the ground and caught his eye, smiling at him. He found it difficult to swallow.

Janet nudged him, grinning. "You can put the baskets down now. And shut your mouth before the flies buzz in."

Enoch set down the baskets. Becky smiled at him again. He glanced away, rubbing the back of his neck.

"There aren't any flies yet," Sally said, eyes on the basket she rummaged in, pulling out a sealed carafe, linen napkins, and utensils. She flipped one of her flaxen plaits over her shoulder. "It's still too cold at night for insects. Aha!" She pulled out a small ceramic tub. "Here's the cream cheese. Did you bring the lavender honey, Jan?"

One hand still in her apron pocket, a confused and vapid expression spread across Janet's face. She spoke in a sing-song tone. "What is this lavender honey you speak of?"

Sally froze, her eyes widening with disappointment and chagrin. Becky threw a rolled linen napkin at Janet, her laughter ringing like bells.

"She's jesting with us, Sal. The jar's in her apron, see?"

"I don't know what you're talking about," Janet replied in a spooky-sounding voice, spinning in place with both hands thrust in her apron pocket to hide the telltale bulge of the jar. "I must consult the caaaaards."

Sally bit her lip. "I don't like it when you play-act Miss Morton. Enoch, make her stop."

Enoch stepped over to Janet, holding out a hand. "As a keeper of the peace, Miss Pines, it is my duty to relieve you of the item in question."

With a rueful grin, Janet slapped the jar into his palm. "Here you go, *Constable* Northward. Don't lose it, now. I fought off a horde of angry bees just to collect it." She faced the other two maidens, hunching up her shoulders. "I'm sorry, Sally," she said. "I meant it in fun, but I got carried away."

"You're forgiven," Sally replied, setting out the tubs containing cream cheese and freshly churned butter alongside the carafe of milk. She'd made the cheese and butter herself. "And you're lying about the bees. You put them to sleep with smoke first."

Becky smiled and shook her head at their friend. "Just let it go, Sal. Some folks are incorrigible." She added a jug of apple cider, a small filet of smoked salmon on butcher's paper, and a dozen warm rolls to the spread.

Janet flopped down between Sally and Becky, her unkempt russet hair flopping along with her. She took a butter knife out of her apron pocket and tossed it on the pile of utensils. Sally moved it over by the butter crock.

Enoch sat cross-legged on the quilt and placed the jar of honey beside the rolls. The aroma set his stomach to growling. "Those rolls and salmon look delicious, Becky," he said, and then glanced at the rest of the food. He amended, "Everything looks delicious. I can't wait to try the cream cheese."

Becky took his right hand, and his heart leaped into his throat. But Sally took his left hand, and then Janet joined, so they formed a ring. Three pairs of eyes stared at Enoch expectantly—blue-gray, green, and warm brown, like pools of—Oh, right. The blessing. He cleared his throat and spoke the words of the table prayer.

"Amen," they said together when he finished.

After they finished eating, Becky gestured at the leather-bound book he'd left on the log. She arched a dark eyebrow. "So, what are we studying this season?"

"Enoch brought us a good one," Janet put in before he stammered out his awkward reply. "An old tome from ages past. The realest, truest legends about the Sages and the welder... the wild... something. Oh, whatever they were," she finished, waving a hand in dismissal. "I can't remember how to say it."

Sally's eyes gleamed. "You mean the wyldlings. Weeld-lings," she said, drawing out the long vowel. She turned to Enoch. "Oh, can we please read a story about them? Nobody ever talks about wyldlings, and the one time I asked Vicar Taggert, he crossed himself and made me recite Psalm thirty-six *three times*."

He laughed and retrieved the book. "Well, it is your turn to choose." He and Becky both shot a glare at Janet when she opened her mouth to object. Nonplussed, Janet shrugged. With a pointed look at Enoch, she scooped up the last dollop of cream cheese in the crock.

Enoch suppressed a smile as he showed Sally the table of contents. While the maiden deliberated, Becky moved in close. The scent of roses filled his nostrils. A lock of dark brown hair tickled his hand when she bent her head to study the book. She pointed at a line of writing. "I think you'd enjoy the first one, Sal. It's about Gideon, the Sevenfold-blessed. The best of the wyldling heroes."

Not that there were very many of those.

Janet perked up. "Wasn't he the king who went on quests for the

Sages and they gave him magical artifacts? From what I recall, the full story the adults tell is absolutely horrid. There's all manner of carnage, romance, and betrayal in that story." She grinned. "I've always pictured Gideon looking a bit like Simon Halloway."

Sally clapped her hands over her mouth to stifle the giggles bubbling forth.

Becky sat up straight, her fragrance retreating along with her. She tilted her head to one side, gazing thoughtfully at Janet. "That's interesting," she said, "because when I imagine Gideon, he looks like Enoch." And then she busied herself in tidying up, but not before Enoch glimpsed a blush spreading on her cheek. His heart raced. Had Becky compared him to the legendary figure Gideon?

He suppressed an urge to squirm. *I'm just an orphaned youth whom Sir Rick was kind enough to take in. Nobody special. Not a king like Gideon.*

Recovered from her fit of mirth, Sally read aloud the signature words opening each tale: "In ages past, before the East was sundered from the West and the world fell into forgetfulness, the seven Sages sojourned amongst the kingdoms of men. They often counseled those rulers who possessed the wisdom to listen to their advice, but there were many in the noble ranks who were fools and scorned the words of the enlightened. Now, the Sages were equally renowned for their valor in battle and for their supernal wisdom. There came a time when a dispute escalated beyond what mere words could soothe and then folk begged the Sages for their aid in quelling disaster. One such man who sought the Sages' counsel was King Gideon…"

MEANWHILE, ON EARTH

The clarinet honked like a goose mating with a moose. Annabelle pulled the instrument away from her mouth with a groan. "Sorry, Kensi."

The other girl shook her head. "Don't worry about it."

From across the band classroom, Neal MacReady caught her eye and then looked away, smirking. Annabelle's cheeks warmed. She glared at him, but he'd bent over his physics textbook with an innocent expression on his face.

Jerk. Why doesn't he study somewhere else? She turned her music stand and faced Kensi instead of the band classroom at large.

Kensi raised her eyebrows and held her flute up to her lips. "Take four. From the top, Ann?"

Annabelle grinned ruefully. "Only if you allow me to lead, like I should." She formed her lips into the proper embouchure and blew into her mouthpiece, tonguing the reed in the correct places, fingers pressing the keys as she tapped her foot to set the tempo. She and Kensi plowed through the entire piece. It still ended up sounding mushy to her ears and not the clarinet part of the duet she'd heard so beautifully played on the cassette tape. But at least she didn't squawk this time, and Kensi didn't get lost after the fifteenth measure.

"Cheer up," her friend said later as they cleaned and put away their instruments. "We just got the music on Monday. I think we're already improving."

Hard not to sound any worse. Annabelle snorted, but chose her words with care. "Yeah, we might even be ready for Solo and Ensemble in a few months." She smiled. "You sounded pretty good, at least."

Kensi shrugged. She shot a glance at Neal, frowning, and leaned closer. "You're extra distracted today. Has he been more annoying than usual?"

Annabelle tucked the music sheets into her folder. She sighed. "No. It's my dreams. I can't stop thinking about them; they're so odd. Different from my normal weird dreams."

Her friend's eyes sparkled. "You mean no aliens or tornadoes? Please share."

Annabelle shot a glance at Neal; he'd buried his nose in his textbook. She bit her lower lip. "I keep dreaming about a guy in silver armor. He's a knight, I think."

Kensi grinned. "Oh, a knight in shining armor! Is he cute? Does he rescue you from a fire-breathing dragon? You should totally use the dream for your Writing Unlimited class."

"Maybe. Miss Smith said we can write about anything." Annabelle examined her nails and squirmed in her seat. Bitten to the quick, as usual. "Just so you know, it's not a romantic type of dream, Kensi. And—sadly—no dragons. It would be cool, though." She chuckled. "The knight's armor has shiny silver bits, though. He seems familiar, like he's family, but I don't remember his name. I'm also wearing armor. Like his, only dark blue. But the weird thing is, even though we're wearing armor, there's no fighting." She toyed with the frayed end of her backpack strap. "We just do normal things. Kid stuff. Playing pickup sticks. Catching frogs or fireflies. Sitting on a log reading books."

Kensi's eyes widened. "That's way different from your normal weirdness. I still think you should write a short story. Miss Smith loves your writing; she'd for sure give you an 'A.'" She tilted her head to the side. "What kind of books are you reading in the dream?"

"A history book, I think. Except it's actually interesting because it's the history of someplace other than here."

Her friend laughed. "Dreams sure are weird. I don't see how any kind of history would be interesting." She tucked a lock of dark hair behind one ear. "Did the book say what this place was?"

Annabelle gazed past Kensi, envisioning another world. "Yeah. Now you mention it, I remember. It's about someplace called Tehara."

AN ILL WIND

DEATH FROM ABOVE

The soot panther fell upon them in utter silence.

One moment, Enoch led his riding deer along the trail, digging in his belt-pouch for mint leaves, and the next, a dark-furred predator dropped from the branches above onto the back of his companion's mount.

Enoch gasped. "Red, behind you!"

The Lord Seneschal, Raeden von Bleistaff, dropped the bridle and whirled around, staff in hand. His emerald eyes, wide and wild, stood out in stark contrast to his white-furred face. "Stay back, Enoch!"

Enoch stumbled backward, fumbling for his sword. The contents of his belt-pouch spilled and his mount trampled it, struggling to escape from the fanged menace. The pungent scent of mint filled the air. His mount dragged him from the trail before jerking her bridle from his hands. Enoch let her go; his stomach, upset from traveling through the waystone, lurched. He choked back the bile rising in his throat and ripped the sword from its sheath, scanning the forest for other threats.

I let down my guard. Should've known better; the Caravan Route is outside the Veil. Good thing I have Red with me.

Red jabbed at the soot panther. The wily beast dug its claws into its prey and flung itself to one side, putting the mount's bulk between itself and Red. Squealing, the riding deer bucked to dislodge the predator. The soot panther clamped its powerful jaws on the riding deer's neck. *Crack.* The mount went limp and collapsed on the trail. The limber feline twisted to avoid entanglement with its limbs. It fixed Red in its amber gaze and crouched, preparing to spring.

Quicker than thought, Red spun and slammed the iron-shod butt of his staff against the soot panther's head. Stunned, the beast dropped like a stone. Red stabbed it at the base of its skull with his sky-iron hunting knife and severed the spine. Enoch flinched.

Bloody knife in one hand, staff in the other, Red backed away from his kill with black-tipped ears raised and his tail rigid. He licked the blood from the blade while scanning the edges of the trail and the canopy above.

Enoch sheathed his sword and joined his friend, skirting the dead mount. He hunkered beside the slain beast. The soot panther appeared less formidable with its fierce amber eyes glazed in death, but the bared fangs were the length of a man's finger. Gingerly, he rested a hand upon its dark gray flank.

How could a vicious animal have soft fur?

Red slid his hunting knife into its sheath on his belt. "Enoch. One scents nothing, but others may soon come for the dead."

"Soot panthers are tricky and scary fast." He chuckled past the unease in his gut. "No way I could ever move fast enough to kill one. I'm glad you're on my side, Red."

Red bowed his head, his ears drooping. "Forgiveness. Your servant should have moved faster; he suffers from the Waystone sickness, but this is no excuse."

Enoch smiled and patted his arm. "Don't worry, we'll be more careful in the future. Everything will be better when we get home."

Enoch tugged on the halter of his lame mount, encouraging her to pick up the pace. The riding deer shook her head, snorting, and then trotted along behind him. He didn't dare ride her—not after she'd sprained her fetlock trying to flee while the soot panther killed her mate. Instead, he'd placed the pack containing the gifts for his friends from Treehome on her back. A much lighter burden than an adolescent boy's weight.

He scanned the trees along the road. Leaves unfolded from their buds now that winter had gone to its grave. However, the fresh growth made it even easier for soot panthers to ambush unwary travelers.

We have seen none since. Praise Yshua.

The first sun, Klotho, had set, and Lachesis was soon to join her, but the heat of late spring lingered. He wiped the sheen of sweat from his forehead with a handkerchief damp from frequent use. The sweet, heavy scent of peonies grew cloying in his nostrils.

"Wow," he remarked. "If the flowers smell strong to me, then they must be overwhelming you, Red. Are they giving you a headache yet?" No response. "Red?" With a frown, he turned around to check on his companion.

Despite the perils lurking in the surrounding woods, Red had stopped. Ears raised to their fullest extent, he stared into the canopy. His black nose twitched as he scented the air.

"Um, Red?" Enoch scanned the surrounding woods for signs of danger. He licked his lips and tasted salt. "Is it another soot panther?"

"No." Red swiveled his ears toward the Northeast. Toward Lilac Grove. Home. "Someone is coming, Enoch," he replied, rolling his staff between his hands and creating a divot in the trail.

"Who?"

"A syrax messenger." Red's whiskers twitched as he scowled. "For goodness' sake," he muttered in his native tongue. "They have sent Peter. He is…" He closed his eyes. "He is like…" Grimacing, he dug his nails into the wood of his staff. "He is like the wind blowing sickness upon everything it touches."

Enoch gaped at him for a moment. And then he laughed aloud, slapping his thighs. "That's a new one. Nice try, Red. Did you mean to say: 'An ill wind that blows no good'?"

Red nodded. "Yes, Enoch. Those words describe Peter to perfection."

Enoch huffed out a brief laugh. "But, Red, that isn't fair! You can't say Peter always brings bad news. There was one time—" He paused, listening to the faint sound of approaching wingbeats. He cupped his hands around his mouth and shouted: "Peter, we're down here."

A piercing cry answered his call and a creature with a ten-foot wingspan plummeted through a gap in the branches to alight in front of them. Enoch hopped back. If it weren't for the brazen pink color of his feathered, aquiline forequarters and furred, feline hindquarters—and his brown eyes filled with friendly, gleeful mischief—Peter would be downright terrifying.

Presently, he displayed none of his usual spunk and humor. Ears drooped, the syrax panted with his tongue dangling from his orange beak. The pink feathers of his front half were disarrayed after plunging through clutching branches and several drifted lazily to the ground. Having caught his breath, he shook his wings and then furled them.

"Lawks," Peter exclaimed, eyes wide and tail lashing. "Eenie, you're a hard person to find! I'm about done in. I've been lookin' for you and the Senny-shall for ever and ever!"

Red bristled as he stalked up to the messenger. "Peter! Have you a message from Sir Frederick? Report it to this one, at present!"

The syrax hunkered and stared up at the kaenhir with his ears laid back and eyes round and glistening. Unease slithered inside Enoch. What in Tehara could render the normally garrulous Peter speechless?

Peter's orange beak opened and closed several times before words came out. "Not from Sir Rick," he gabbled, unsheathing, and then sheathing his talons. "Can't be from Sir Rick. Can't be. Cappy sent me. I hafta find Sir Thomas first, but I can't find him; he's gone, gone, gone. I'm supposta find you next… only I didn't know if you all're still at Treehome or if—"

Red cuffed him. "Arrive at the peak!"

Peter squawked and hunkered until his belly touched the ground. "Eenie," he whimpered. "Eenie, what's he mean? What's he mean?"

Enoch rubbed the back of his neck. "He means you should get to the point, Peter." He crouched beside the syrax and patted his feathery mane in what he hoped was a reassuring manner. "Just breathe, slow down, and tell me the message."

Peter glanced from one to the other, his eyes brimming with tears. "Okay, Eenie. But it's bad news. Real bad." He curled in his talons and tucked his front paws under his chest, shuffling his feline hindquarters under his belly and then curling his tail against his torso.

"Bad news?" The chill of foreboding crept up his spine like a stalking soot panther. He'd never seen Peter so upset. What cruel tidings did he bring? Had a storm destroyed the crofterfolks' homes? Were the newly sprouted crops ruined? Did a roving pack of lykharim breach the Veil? Or worse: had the nehmwights invaded the Northern Marches?

Enoch gulped, recalling every horrific, spine-tingling story he'd ever heard about the belligerent race dwelling far to the North in the Icemountain Wastes. "Are we at war with the nehmwights, Peter?" He looked at the seneschal. Red gazed back at him with his mouth set in a grim line, gripping his staff in both his hands.

Eyes wide, Peter blurted out, "Eenie, you and the Senny-shall better come home quick. We can't find Sir Thomas and Sir Rick is dead!"

CLOAK AND DAGGER

Wind soughed through branches overhead and William froze, straining his senses in the near-darkness of the Darkenwood Forest. He was no night-blind kadorei; a little light filtering from the stars ensured he saw as well as a soot panther. He cast nervous glances around the wood as he leaned against the trunk of a gnarled old oak. Vervon's hammer, there'd better not be any of those suns-cursed beasts around. He primed his arkhabala to launch a defense, but he'd rather not waste a spell on a hungry feline. Better to save his energy for a much worse predator.

William licked his lips. *It's only been three days. Tenebris's elixir should hold the assassin steady for another week. Speaking of elixirs, I could use another drink.*

He reached inside his robes, drew out his flask of whiskey, and took a quick pull. He grimaced at the harsh taste. Until fresh supplies came, he couldn't get his hands on the good stuff; his flask contained the dregs of a rot-gut brew. *Besides, there are no soot panthers to blistering worry about. Sagebinder's Veil keeps out the wildest, fiercest beasties.* A flicker of movement caught his attention as a tall, bipedal figure slipped out of the deepest shadows and prowled toward him like one of the aforementioned felines. *Mostly,* he amended, watching as the other approached.

He slipped the flask into his robes and stood up straight, concentrating. A faint grayish light surrounded the dark form, extruding wispy, vaporous tendrils to undulate in an unseen wind. Recently, he'd begun seeing auras around people. The scroll on Aethyr informed him these auras were "kythim" and varied in color and size based on many things, such as health, mood, and potential ability with aspects of the Aethyr.

Something Tenebris doesn't need to know about. William shifted his weight from one foot to the other.

The assassin stopped a few feet away and bowed. Yellow eyes gleamed from under a conical hat woven from tough grasses. When he spoke, his voice possessed a pleasant accent, like music. "Good evening, Dull-seeber. You are late."

William scowled. The assassin delighted in taunting him with the surname since Tenebris revealed that the Count of Mirrors, Fitzwillis Dulciber, was William's supposed sire.

"I'm not late, Zakaar; you're early. Where's your talisman? Don't tell me you've burned out the blistering thing already." He grumbled under his breath. "Blazing magic-resistant harkhurz."

Yellow eyes narrowed. Reddish sparks popped in his kythim. "I am what I am, Dull-seeber. The talismans, they burn out so quickly. I save them for when it is most needed."

William squared his shoulders and bared his teeth. "Put on your talisman, harkhurz. I'll make sure it's functional. If not, I have another one. Tenebris will have you on the rack again if you can't maintain your disguise."

Or maybe he'll do us a favor and eliminate you.

While grumbling something in his native tongue, the assassin removed a necklace from his belt-pouch. He took off his hat and tucked it under one arm. For a moment, large furry ears broke up the outline of his head, but then disappeared when he fastened the thong around his throat. His eyes no longer gleamed amber. He donned the hat. "The talisman still works, Dull-seeber." He leaned back on his heels and crossed his arms. "Hurry, state the master's orders. You come later than usual, and my shift begins soon. Until now, I have given the kadorei no reason to suspect me."

No reason to suspect you, huh? After everything you've done to them, I sure as perdition hope not. There better not be any more bloody corpses for me to clean up.

A fetid, copper stench briefly assaulted his nostrils. Waxen faces and filmy eyes. Aching stiffness in his arms from shifting stones to conceal them. A memory of death. William swallowed back a sudden urge to vomit and forced himself back into the present. It was Tenebris's fault he'd arrived late to this meeting. Tenebris and his burning need to lecture William and berate him for making mistakes.

The assassin stood as still as a statue with his arms crossed. His kythim boiled like storm clouds with crimson lightning flickering inside them.

Not good. He'll need the elixir sooner rather than later.

William cleared his throat. "The Dreadlord summoned Master Tenebris to the Farspeaker this afternoon. We have a new target."

The assassin leaned forward, eyes gleaming. "Who?"

William turned and spat to one side. "Master Tenebris didn't give me a name." He shook his head, frowning. "All I know for certain is our next task doesn't require moving on to another barony. Not yet. So, it has to be someone living in this region." He raised his eyebrows and met his companion's gaze. "However, Master Tenebris said you're to continue your observations. No killing until you're given the order this time." The assassin stirred, growling. William held up a finger. "No complaints, harkhurz. You've done enough damage."

The assassin raised his chin and his teeth flashed. "As have you, Dull-seeber. It was not I who could not kill when commanded to. It was not I who let the prisoner escape."

How dare you! William balled his hands into fists.

The assassin dropped his hands to his sides, near the hilts of his blades. His kythim flared with dangerous colors.

Arkhabala prickling, William's anger demanded he release the prepared defensive spell. The shield would hold the harkhurz for a few minutes, but after that… He leashed his temper. Tenebris said an Arkhadahn who lost control of himself was an Arkhadahn who did not live long. Especially around a harkhurz already consumed by the Blood Rage, half-maddened and ready to snap.

Eyes fixed on his companion, William shook out his fingers. His heart hammered against his ribs so hard he feared the harkhurz heard it. The assassin's hands fell away from his weapons. However, the lines of his body and his kythim betrayed his agitation. Suns burn it; he'd need another dose of elixir before the week ended, or there'd be perdition to pay. More dead bodies to bury, at the very least.

He wasn't like this—not this bloodthirsty—before the Eastern Marches.

William suppressed the urge to lick his lips. And reach for his whiskey again. He must not show weakness. "You have your orders: wait and observe." In imitation of his master, he narrowed his eyes and raised an admonitory finger. "Let there be no misunderstanding. Do not disappoint us."

BAD NEWS

There must be a horrible misunderstanding.

Numbly, Enoch reached for the courier-tube attached to Peter's harness. His fingers fumbled at the clasp; he didn't want to touch the scroll. He didn't want to read the message. If he refused, it wouldn't be true. Sir Rick still lived, just as he had over twenty days ago—before Enoch and the Lord Seneschal departed for the Resurrection Festival in Treehome.

Was there something wrong with his spectacles? The shape of the lacquered wooden tube wavered before his burning eyes. Vicious claws squeezed his throat to keep him from speaking.

Red spoke his native tongue. "Sir Enoch." A hand fell upon his shoulder—a rare display of his companion's affection. "Young knight, allow your servant to read the message."

An irrational desire seized Enoch: to rip the tube off Peter's harness and smash it upon the packed earth of the caravan road. "Don't call me that, Red. It's not me. If… if Sir Rick is dead, then Sir Thomas should be the 'young knight'. Not me," he added, fiercely. "Not me!"

I'm not ready.

"But Eenie," the pink chimera whined. "Didn'tcha hear me? I told you… I couldn't find that Thomas fella anywhere. And I looked. I swears it. I looked, and I looked, and I looked—"

"Quiet!" Red grabbed Peter's beak and held it closed. "You make it all worse with your noise. You will bring the predators."

"Mmm. Mmmph!" Growling, Peter jerked his head away, and Red let him go. The syrax allowed the seneschal to remove the message tube, glaring at him the entire time.

Red extracted the parchment scroll. He unrolled and then scanned the message, his lip lifting to reveal fangs. Joints popped and fingernails lengthened into claws to dimple the missive.

Enoch clenched his hands into fists. "Just tear it up! Rip it to shreds!"

He thought Red would obey, his canid visage twisted in anger, but then the moment passed. The feral creature returned to the self-controlled and proper seneschal, his expression wooden as he rolled up the scroll and slid it into the message tube.

"This one cannot," he said, tucking the lacquered tube into a pocket inside his vest. "For you must read what Doctor Fourtier and Captain Faulkner have written about the baron-knight's death when you are ready, young knight."

The kaenhir's words struck him, hard. *It's real,* he thought, his heart plummeting like an arrow-pierced hawk. *Red never tells lies. Sir Rick is dead.*

Enoch's anger rushed out of him, leaving him slack and empty. He lowered his head and a stray tear escaped to trickle down his cheek. "What do I do now?" he said, feeling hollow inside.

A whisper echoed in the wind, the old baron-knight's oft-repeated mantra: "*Seek justice. Show mercy. Walk humbly with Lord Yshua. The innocent must be protected.*"

Red rested a hand on his shoulder. "On this day of trouble, you must pray for guidance and strength from the Almighty. And then you must go in great quickness. The roads are not safe. Peter must take you home."

Home. How could home be home, ever again, without Sir Rick there?

Enoch bowed his head. "Oh, Lord Yshua," he prayed. "I don't know what to do. Grant me wisdom. Do not allow anxiety and dread to overpower me. Strengthen me for the trials I face and bring us safely home."

Enoch settled on Peter's back. He used Peter as a mount only at great need. Not counting his wings, the syrax was half the size of a riding deer. Well-rested, Peter could bear a youth his size over short distances. He hoped Peter had enough energy after searching for Sir Thomas to carry him the rest of the way home.

Luckily, I'm 'small for my age'. He grimaced at the old barb. The prospect of flying with Peter usually filled Enoch with excitement, but now his insides churned like storm clouds. He clung to Peter's ruff as the syrax launched himself into the air. Wind whipped against his face in a fury as they hurtled Northeast. Under the setting glare of the third sun, Atropos, the world around him appeared drenched in blood, the trees ebony in the twilight.

Like a hunting hawk, Enoch's mind circled the idea of Sir Rick's demise. *I can't believe it.* Sir Rick seemed fine when he and the seneschal left for the Resurrection Festival—a hale and hearty man.

Why did Sir Rick have to die? Enoch's grip tightened on Peter's mane as he choked back a sob. He couldn't imagine life without his guardian. As a man, Sir Rick was everything Enoch aspired to be, the closest thing to a father he'd ever known. What would he do without him? And then he shivered as a horrible realization crept over him with insectile claws.

With Sir Rick gone and Sir Thomas missing, nobody stood between Enoch and Commander Storm.

In his mind's eye loomed the statuesque figure of the commander, his gray eyes as pitiless as basalt with a rugged countenance as soft as granite. "*Cease your dad-rotted puling,*" the gruff voice spoke from his memory. "*A true warrior sheds no tears. A true warrior does not fret or bemoan the vicissitudes of fate. He acts. You have a duty to fulfill, lad. Stop your dad-rotted whining and do it!*"

Enoch tasted bitter grief. That's what the commander would tell him now. By Kaspar's silvery wings! Even when Commander Storm wasn't here, he was giving Enoch blustering orders. No doubt he'd put down the insurrection in the Eastern Marches and was on his way back to "mentor" him.

Enoch shuddered at the thought of the implacable commander returning to Lilac Grove several moons early to supervise him in his new role. His grip tightened on Peter's ruff. *I don't want to be the baron-knight! My training's nowhere near complete; I'm not supposed to be knighted until my nineteenth Name-day.*

Enoch glared into the twilight without seeing the forest unfolding beneath him in dark, rumpled folds like a quilt wrinkled by a restless sleeper. In Sir Rick's absence, Sir Thomas should have filled the breach. Once more, his throat thickened, and his eyes stung—and not only because of the wind in his face.

It's not fair. Why did Sir Thomas have to choose right now to vanish?

A skin-tingling sensation startled Enoch out of his dark musings as they passed over the uppermost reaches of the Veil—the invisible barrier running through the wilderness below. The tops of trees beneath him appeared as dark clumps of wool in the red twilight. To save time, Peter flew over the Darkenwood Forest and straight for the Westgate.

Peter began his descent a few miles short of their target through an opening in the forest canopy. As they descended, Enoch spied a longer gap in the trees that might be a road. The messenger's breath rattled in his lungs. The feverish trembling of overworked muscles quivered against Enoch's legs. He bent against the syrax's body and braced himself for a rough landing.

He scooted off Peter's back as soon as they landed in a patch of springy bracken ferns. The pink syrax collapsed, gasping for breath, and not even bothering to furl his wings. He stretched out his forelegs and toes, unsheathing his talons. "You better git, Eenie," he said, jerking his beak toward the Westgate garrison of Lilac Grove before lowering his head to the ground with an exhausted sigh.

Enoch spared another moment to scratch Peter along his crest and behind his triangular ears. The weary syrax purred. He flicked his tongue against the youth's shoulder and the sand-papery rasp briefly caught on his tunic. "Now, git yerself home," he murmured, closing his eyes. "They're es-spect-er-ling you."

Enoch's heart beat like a hammer against his breastbone. Despite its proximity to his home, he'd never ventured this far into the Darkenwood

Forest. Commander Storm declared the region out of bounds to him. This struck him as odd, because the Veil surrounding the Lilac Grove district had always served as a formidable protection against most wild beasts. The deepest part of the forest—which they'd passed over—was warded against human incursion. It should be even less perilous than the region between the Middlemarch Waystone and the Darkenwood, where the soot panther had killed Red's mount.

Seems I'm about to find out for myself whether it's true.

He turned his back on Peter and adjusted his scabbard to keep it from tangling in his legs or the undergrowth. He kept one hand on the pommel. Even with the Veil's protection against dangerous animals, human predators could still lurk in the unwarded part of the forest. He drew a deep breath and concentrated on the air, employing a secret knack for listening as he exhaled.

He'd discovered this ability one day the previous autumn while stalking rabbits. Every sound possessed its own signature, a jagged silver line in sharp relief against a backdrop of dark gray silence. He sorted through them, but nothing stood out to him as dangerous. Just small animals scampering through the undergrowth and birds settling in their nests for the night.

Blessing the absent seneschal for training him in woods-wisdom, he moved toward where the road might be, careful of his footing in the deepening twilight. It felt an eternity, but he reached a path before Atropos sank beneath the Eastern horizon. Enoch set out at a trooper's steady jog. He suppressed a pang of sorrow at a memory of Sir Rick observing from deer-back as he ran with the garrison soldiers in a circuit of the grounds.

Enoch lengthened his stride, pushing himself until sweat trickled down his face and soaked his tunic. He tried to think of nothing. This proved impossible; his mind seethed in a tempest of noise and chaos, a frantic voice yammering about his worst fears. He breathed in deeply to calm himself, and a glowing, silvery mist suffused his vision.

What's this? Either something was wrong with my spectacles, or his eyes were playing tricks on him. He took off the spectacles and squinted through the argent film. No, not his spectacles. He put them back on and picked up the pace. Up ahead, the forest thinned, the trees falling back as the road broadened and then split into three. Two branches of the road led either North or South, while the third branch cut straight ahead through an expanse of cleared ground toward the fortifications surrounding Lilac Grove. Lanterns glowed atop the Westgate walls, a string of gleaming pearls in the distance. A friendly beacon. *Nearly home.*

Something struck him on the left side and sent him crashing to the ground. Enoch's training took over, and he rolled away. *Schict! Schict!* Blades plummeted into the patch of dirt where he'd first fallen.

Bandit! And he's devilish fast.

Enoch flung himself to his feet. His hand darted to the hilt of his sword and tore it out of its scabbard. The silver mist intensified, imbuing objects in his surroundings with dim outlines. He sensed blades cutting through the air, faster and more furious than even Commander Storm during a sparring bout. Enoch swung into the sword dance. Steel rang out as he parried a blow, and then a second.

Remember—two blades.

He hopped backward and slashed with his sword at a hulking shadow outlined by the silver mist. Contact! He felt resistance as his blade cut into flesh and yanked it back, ready to defend. A man's voice snarled, and the shadow reeled, favoring his left side. Silver light glinted off the blades as he raised them again.

Praise Yshua. Enoch grinned as hot blood sizzled through his veins.

The yellow-bellied worm must not be wearing any armor.

Growling, the larger man came at him again, relentless, his blades slashing.

"Honorless dog," Enoch said, blocking his assailant's first blade and then ducking as the bandit sliced at his throat with the other. "Ambushing a lone traveler at nightfall is the lowest form of cowardice."

And stupidity, so near Westgate. He heard men shouting and booted feet and deer hooves pounding against the road as troopers approached from the East. The guardsmen were coming.

To his astonishment, the bandit did not flee. Instead, he pressed his attack. Amber eyes flashed from a bearded visage. The eldritch silver mist limning everything faded away. Bone-tired, Enoch blocked and parried blows, but couldn't go on the offensive. His opponent was a burly man, twice his size and fighting as one infuriated beyond reason. Although wounded—perhaps even seriously, for Enoch had cut him good—the brute seemed determined to put Enoch into the ground.

"Help!" he cried out. "In the name of Lord Yshua," he pleaded, striking out desperately when he tripped over a fallen tree branch and lost his footing. "I'm not your enemy. I'm Enoch Northward of Lilac Grove."

The bladed onslaught ceased as abruptly as it had begun. Vociferous curses in a foreign language filled the air as the bandit backed away and sheathed his long knives. A squad of garrison soldiers rode up on antlered mounts with their own blades bared. One rider carried a lantern on a pole. The man carrying the lantern was Sergeant Matlock. Two others covered him from either side: Deputy Trask on his right and Corporal Dwight on his left. But the faces of the three troopers behind them remained in shadow.

The deputy dismounted. "Back off, Sergeant Ravenos. That's Acting Baron-Knight Enoch Northward. He's the fellow we've been waiting for." He scowled. "And what in perdition are you doing so far away from your post?"

Enoch stepped back, blinking. *Sergeant Ravenos?* The lantern-light revealed the uniform of a gatekeeper sergeant. *Not a bandit… this vicious cur was one of their troopers?*

The large man clutched his side, wheezing. He replied in accented Tradespeak. "I saw something fall from the sky, Deputy. I felt it best to investigate. And I find an interloper…"

"Sir Enoch," called one guard in the rear, dismounting. "Are you all right?" A jolt of surprise and relief ran through Enoch at hearing the familiar voice.

"Yeah," he gasped, taking advantage of the reprieve to catch his breath. "Hi, Simon. Don't… call me… sir."

Baring his teeth, the sergeant glared at him.

A thread of fear tickled his spine. *I've made an enemy of this Ravenos fellow. Not that I'd have reacted differently. I defended myself. If this gatekeeper is stupid enough to leave his post and then attack someone for no blustering reason, it's no fault of mine.*

"Honorless dog," he muttered again.

Dark eyes flashed with rage. Left hand clasped against his wound, the gatekeeper went for a weapon. Simon jumped between Enoch and the man, raising his sword to block an attack.

"Stand down, Ravenos," said Trask, his voice hard. "You're already facing demotion. Another hostile move toward our baron-knight and I'll have you drummed out of the corps."

Good. Enoch stepped to one side for a better view. *Attack me, you cowardly beggar.*

But the bearded man obeyed. He removed his hand from his weapon. "Yes, Deputy." He made a fist with his right hand and slammed it against the left side of his chest in a trooper's salute, wincing. "I am most apologetic, sir."

The smooth cadence of the brute's speech rippled like a song. Repugnance swept over Enoch. The melodious accent did not fit the ruffian standing before him.

"I am thinking he is an enemy scout for bandits," the man continued. "This is… an unfortunate accident. I was mistaken. I wish only to serve our baron-knight with honor." He bowed his head to the officer—after casting another furtive glare in Enoch's direction.

'Our baron-knight' Nether perdition. This is already getting tiresome. His hand shook as he sheathed his sword. Trask asked him another question regarding his well-being, which Enoch answered vaguely enough to cause concern.

"Halloway," Trask said, the command implicit in his tone.

"Already on it, sir," Simon replied, sheathing his sword. "I'll escort him home." He led his mount over and insisted Enoch take the deer. He accepted after offering only token resistance, too tired, shaken, and grief-stricken to argue. Simon studied him in the lantern-light while he climbed up into the saddle. Enoch avoided his gaze and cast a glance over his shoulder, wary of the gatekeeper he'd stung with his blade.

Sergeant Matlock handed off his lantern-pole to Rook and took charge of Ravenos. "Sharkness," he called. "He's wounded."

Predators… don't want to attract predators. Enoch recalled one of Sir Rick's lessons. *"Dangerous beasts can cross the Veil when they're young and small. It happens occasionally. Even within the Veil's protection, it's best to maintain strict discipline out in the wilds."*

One of the other two soldiers, sitting sentinel on his deer, dismounted, and hurried over. They saluted him. Enoch blinked. How had he missed Sharky amongst them? And the other soldier must be Bart Ainsley, another of his friends.

The medic tended to the gatekeeper's injury in a business-like fashion. He wasn't gentle; the gatekeeper tensed and grunted. Apparently, the troopers were not over-fond of this Ravenos fellow, either. Matlock and Rook took charge of the gatekeeper. Sharkness and Ainsley—it *was* Bart—took up the rearguard.

Meanwhile, Trask laced into Ravenos with a harsh reprimand of his behavior, promising an inquiry led by Captain Faulkner when they returned to the garrison. The gatekeeper responded tersely, yet respectfully. He'd seen suspicious movement in the forest—a pink monstrosity plummeting from the sky—and left Rook on guard while he investigated.

"This is why there are always two gatekeepers on duty, no? Surely, there is no need for an inquiry. I repent of my… error."

Enoch imagined his attacker's eyes burning like hot coals into his back, belying the mild tone of his voice. He shivered despite the sultry evening. The thread of fear thickened into a cord. He couldn't shake the feeling something was just plain *wrong* with the man. Childishly, he hoped Ravenos bled to death walking back to the garrison infirmary. Served him right for abandoning his post. Not to mention attacking a lone traveler for no reason. What kind of person *did* something like that?

Simon's voice, hushed in the gathering darkness, brought him back to the present. "Where is his lordship, sir? He should have been traveling with you."

Huh? Oh. He's talking to me.

Dull-voiced, Enoch replied, "Red's on his way and should be here… soonish." He calculated distances in his head, annoyed at his mind—sluggish as a wagon rolling through molasses. "He'll arrive in the wee hours if another soot panther doesn't delay him. One killed his mount and hurt mine, so he's leading her."

Finished berating Ravenos, the deputy left him in the charge of the other troopers. Trask maneuvered his mount over beside Enoch's. "Halloway. Go back and keep your eye on the miscreant." Once Simon dropped back and they were alone, the deputy regarded Enoch. "What's become of the lord seneschal, sir?"

Enoch repeated what he told Simon, adding, "Peter brought me over the trees. Could you send a squad back to check on him? I left him about half-a-mile back, on the North side of the road. He's knackered, so send a medic, too."

"Understood, sir." Deputy Trask hollered for Sharkness. Enoch started. His friend's mount trotted up to parallel their course. They left the confines of the forest and lights bobbed alongside them. More troopers had joined them and four of them carried lanterns.

Was he so far gone that he hadn't notice their arrival? Now his head felt stuffed with wool on top of molasses. Bemused, Enoch watched the deputy confer with the medic. Trask sent Sharkness and Ainsley riding back toward Peter's last known location, one of them carrying a shielded lantern.

"Thank you," Enoch whispered. He wanted nothing more than to crawl into his bed and sleep for a week, then wake to discover the past few hours were a horrible nightmare. Something still bothered him, though. "Deputy," he said, forcing crispness into his tone. "What happened to Sir Thomas?" He couldn't bear to ask about Sir Rick. Not yet.

Trask stared straight ahead. "You'll have to speak with Captain Faulkner, sir. Relating such intelligence is above my paygrade."

"Please, Trask." The man was normally straight-forward. Enoch frowned. *Something awful must have happened.* "Come on, man. Troopers gossip worse than dairymaids and kitchen scullions. Surely, you've heard a tidbit. When we left for the festival, Sir Thomas was stationed in the Eastern Sector. How come Peter didn't find him?"

Deputy Trask sighed. "Truth is, Sir Rick summoned him to investigate a series of disappearances here in Lilac Grove; he'd already taken ill at that point and was fading fast. Sir Thomas arrived four days ago. The day before Sir Rick… passed, with Sir Rick's blessing, he took up the torc of command. And then, two days ago, he left—without a patrol. Gate log states his purpose as searching for the missing folk. Here. In the Darkenwood." He hesitated. "Nobody's seen him since."

"What?" Enoch tugged back on the reins. His mount rattled his antlers and snorted. "Sorry, boy," he murmured, patting the beast's neck. He turned back to the deputy. "What do you mean, disappearances? Who else is missing?"

Deputy Trask was on the point of speaking, but then he shook his head. "Sir, perhaps this can wait until you've had a bite to eat. You should speak to the captain. He'll want to brief you."

No. This will not do. I'll go insane trying to guess. Heart pounding, he said, "Just tell me now, Trask. Who else is missing?"

"This is difficult for me to say, and it will be harder for you to hear." Expression grim, the deputy told him three names.

They hit Enoch like punches in the stomach. Shoulders hunched and head bowed, he stared at his hands, twisting the reins around his fingers. His insides felt as frozen and barren as the winds howling across the Icemountain wastes.

"Almighty Threefold One," he prayed aloud. "Protect your lost lambs. Give me the strength to find them. Grant me the wisdom to serve this barony." His dry throat clicked when he swallowed. Claws choked off his voice. The reins and his fingers went swimmy in his vision. He shut his eyes and continued his prayer in silence.

Please, Yshua. There must be a better choice for baron-knight than me. I'm not ready! Please… help me find Sir Thomas.

THE WIND IN THE VOID

WOODLAND DREAM

I'm so thirsty. Please, God, let there be a creek or something in these woods.

Annabelle licked her lips. This forest bore little similarity to her grandfather's land. The trees looked different from species native to central Wisconsin. An eerie silence hung in the air; no birds sang, no squirrels scolded her. She hesitated, placing her hand on the smooth, gray bark of a towering tree, and scanned the mist-shrouded forest. A sourceless light illuminated the landscape, coloring the mist with a violet tinge. Harp music—or maybe it was a mandolin—broke the silence from somewhere ahead of her. If she found the musician, perhaps they'd tell her where to locate potable water.

She continued walking, the mist fading to reveal the scant

undergrowth and last autumn's detritus collected in hollows between trees. The mist was deceiving; she felt no moisture against her face. Chitinous, dark blue armor covered the rest of her body, supple and fitting like a second skin. Shod in mid-calf boots of the same material, her feet crunched over leaf skeletons and dry twigs. No way she'd ever win in a stealth contest. She kept her eyes on the ground, watching out for hidden divots or hummocks.

I'll probably still trip over something. Maybe I'll get lucky and fall right into a stream. At least then I can have a drink.

Annabelle wove around massive trees resembling oaks but with smooth bark like aspen. Such immense trees required a lot of water. *Where are you, water? Buried deep under the ground?* Maybe she should dig. She snorted. Too bad she didn't have a shovel. She picked up the pace; so did the tempo of the music. The melody changed to a rising and falling theme that mimicked the sound of rain. Annabelle pushed through tall ferns. Beyond them, she heard running water. *How fortuitous,* she mused. *And here we are.*

She emerged into a moss-carpeted clearing bounded by ferns, tall trees, and scattered boulders of various sizes. A large, oval pool built of stones at its center. Water burbled from a natural spring on the far end, a cleft in a tall, dark gray rock free of moss and lichen. Saplings ringed the pool, their roots forcing their way into crevices between stones. She took it in and then rushed around the pool to the spring, her boots squelching in the moss. She cupped her hands under the tiny stream and gathered enough for a mouthful of ice-cold water. It tasted of minerals and a single mouthful quenched her thirst. She stared at the spring, dabbling her fingers in the crystalline trickle, and recalled what Jesus said to the Samaritan woman at the well in Sychar.

She whispered, "If you knew the gift of God and who asks you for a drink, you would have asked him, and he would have given you living water."

A resonant male voice interrupted her musing. "And now, Ahdmerel, having drunk the living waters of Tehara, you belong to her ever after."

Annabelle whirled around, one hand fluttering over her chest. "Cripes, you nearly gave me a heart attack!"

On top of a rounded boulder at the edge of the clearing perched a figure in a dark cloak, his face hidden by a deep cowl. He held an instrument in his hands, but his fingers were still.

Seems I've found the mysterious minstrel. Or, rather, he's found me.

"My apologies." The cowled head dipped toward her. "Greetings, Ahdmerel."

She smoothed her hands over the slickness of her armor. "Sorry, sir; I think you've got me confused with someone else. My name's Annabelle. And you are?"

The cloaked man slid from the boulder to the ground and straightened. Annabelle's eyes widened. The guy met the NBA height requirement and had broad shoulders, too. He was… big. And he had a delightful voice. She wondered what his face looked like.

Instead of answering her question, the cloaked musician gazed at something beyond her. "Ah," he said. "Excellent. Skelsdaran has deigned to join us." He plucked out a mocking little ditty on his instrument and then launched into a new song.

Annabelle spun around yet again. She met the wide-eyed gaze of a young man clad in silver-chased armor standing on the opposite side of the pool. He possessed a soldier's bearing. Relief flooded her; she knew him. The youth was a friend, even if his name escaped her.

The world lurched beneath her feet, and he stood right in front of her, blinking. His blue eyes and almond-brown skin were an odd combination. "Wow. How did you do that, my lady?"

He hadn't moved. Somehow, she'd crossed the pool to join him. Mist began filling in the glade. "I don't know. It just happened." She studied him, her brow wrinkling. "Sorry; we've met before, but I can't remember your name. I think of you as the Silver Knight."

He laughed, his military posture relaxing. "Oh, am I glad to hear you say that, my lady; I couldn't remember yours, either, and felt a horrible cad. My name is Enoch Northward." He bowed and slapped his right fist against his chest.

She held out a hand. "Hi, Enoch, I'm Annabelle Leigh Wells. But you can call me Ann."

Enoch glanced at the proffered hand with a puzzled look on his face, took it and then, bowing, raised her hand and pressed the knuckles to his forehead. "I am at your service, Milady Ann." He released her hand and stood at parade rest.

Blushing, Annabelle burst out laughing. "Oh, my gosh. Déjà vu all over again. We've gone through this before, haven't we, Enoch? And it's just plain 'Ann,' please. Or Annabelle."

Enoch grinned. His blue eyes gleamed with humor, and he tilted his head. "But never 'Annie,' right? Or there'll be perdition to pay."

She returned his grin. "You *do* know me." As she drummed her fingers against her thighs, she examined the lamellae of her armor. "So, what's the deal with these costumes? I mean, they're cool, but what's the purpose—are we supposed to be knights?"

Enoch ran his hands over the silver-lined plates he wore, frowning. "So far as I can tell, this is functional armor. Not a costume." He jogged a few steps in place, twisted at the waist, and bent to touch his toes. "Beggaring good stuff, too. Exceptional flexibility. Hmmm. I've read legends about armor with special properties called 'sourekghar,' and I think that's what this is."

Annabelle chewed on her lower lip. "But I've never read your legends, Enoch. Why would I be wearing this… soo-reck-gahar?" She sounded out the foreign word as she glanced over her shoulder. Her eyes widened. The pool had vanished.

They stood on a road paved with a grayish stone similar to concrete, cracked and crumbling on the margins. Tiny flowers opened white, pink, and yellow mouths along vines growing from the cracks. Mist coiled between the dark-leaved trees and amid the undergrowth; combined with the sourceless light, it made the woodland appear ethereal, like something out of a fairy tale.

The harp music from before drifted in, encircling them like threads from an invisible spider's web. Annabelle suppressed the urge to brush phantom gossamers off her face. She rubbed her arms instead, sliding her hands along the slickness of the armor. "Enoch, where are we now? What happened to the spring-fed pool? I don't recognize these woods… this place." She stomped and the impact rang against the pavement. Not concrete, then.

Enoch moved in close and touched her shoulder. The solid comfort of contact calmed her nervous fidgets. He replied, his voice subdued. "I know where we are, Annabelle. We're in the Darkenwood Forest."

She glanced at him, but he was scanning the surroundings, expression intent. His right hand clenched and unclenched beside his hip, as if accustomed to gripping something that normally rested there.

"Is there something we need to worry about?"

"No," he replied, his face clearing as he smiled. Reflexively, Annabelle smiled back.

Enoch patted her shoulder. "We should be fine. If we turn around, the road leads straight to Westgate, to Lilac Grove. My home." She glanced at him; there'd been sorrow in his tone. He entwined his fingers with hers and averted his eyes. "Shall we go, my lady?"

Annabelle's smile faded. "Sure," she said. "I'd love to see your home."

They turned. A tall, black-cloaked figure limned in violet light stood blocking their path. Her fingers squeezed Enoch's; she felt him tighten his grip and then let go.

Enoch stepped in front of her. He squared his shoulders and stiffened his spine, as if straining for every bit of height he could garner. The hand hovering near his hip closed in a fist. "Sir, please stand aside. The lady and I wish to pass."

The minstrel's deep chuckle caused the hair to rise on the back of Annabelle's neck. "Assuredly, Ahdmerel will visit your home in time, but not presently. Your task in the Darkenwood Forest is not yet complete, Skelsdaran. Those you seek lie within. You must complete this mission alone."

Enoch grunted, staggering back a half step as if someone had struck him.

Annabelle darted up beside Enoch and grabbed his hand. His lips trembled, but otherwise, he seemed unharmed. What had the strange man done to him? A fierce protectiveness swept over her like a wave, washing away her fear of conflict. Heart pounding against her ribs, she narrowed her eyes and raised her chin. "Hey, mister, you never introduced yourself. Who the heck are you, and why do you keep calling us by the wrong names?"

Except, those weird names aren't precisely wrong. Just… ill-fitting, like clothes we need to grow into.

In response, the mysterious minstrel's cloak parted, revealing the mandolin-harp-thing. His fingers slashed across the strings in violent motion, and he cried out in harmony with the jangling chord. The sound morphed into a steady *beep, beep, beep*. Enoch's fingers slipped away. Darkness descended as a black wing, and she sped away through a tunnel streaked with sapphire and silver light.

Enoch's scream followed her.

"Annabelle!"

Beep, beep, beep.

Her eyes flew open, and she flung her arm up. She slapped a button on her clock radio to silence the alarm. Stupid thing; the details of her dream were already fading. She sat up and took a few deep, measured breaths, trying to slow her racing heart. One groping hand switched on her lamp while the other fell on the notebook she kept on her bedside table—the dream journal Kensi suggested she keep. She yanked the pen free of the spiral and furiously began to write.

OBJECT LESSON

The reed pen scratched over the parchment. William scrawled calculations to accompany his diagram of a highly efficient spellform. It integrated clockwork mechanisms with Arkhabadh procedures. Just one more equation and he'd be—

The chamber door burst open, booming as it struck the adjacent wall. His master roared, "William, you blithering imbecile, you've gone and mucked up the surveillance net again."

Heart racing, William scrambled to hide the parchment on his lap under the table.

A tall, dark-bearded man with a thin face and pointed ears stalked across the laboratory, wagging a finger. "I assign you tasks—which you can't accomplish satisfactorily—and here you are, cooling your heels. I've spent an hour fixing your mistakes." He loomed over the table and glowered at William. "Are you hiding something? What sort of idle foolishness are you mucking about with now?"

"N-nothing, Master. I was calculating… preparing the spellform for a Seeker's Web."

"Seeker's Web? Ha! You muck up a simple Watchman Spell and you expect me to believe you're capable of higher-level conjuring?"

Despite himself, he flinched at Tenebris's fearsome expression and knocked a jar of ink off the worktable. It shattered, ink spraying everywhere and splotching them both with interesting patterns. Tenebris froze, looked at the indigo splatters marring his silk robes, and then fixed him with a glare. William grimaced and braced himself for the punitive strike.

Suns burn me to ash!

While boxing William's ears to punctuate every word, Tenebris snarled, "I am surrounded by clumsy, incompetent fools." William cringed away, even though physical blows didn't hurt as much as his master's Pain Hex or Nettle-sweep. Disturbed by his movements, the parchment drifted to the floor. Tenebris snatched it. Orange eyes smoldering, he scanned its contents. "Clumsy, incompetent fools who cannot even construct a plausible lie," he muttered. "What is this… thing? Another clockwork toy? More kadorei rubbish." Scoffing, he wadded up the parchment and threw it into the brazier.

William gasped. *No! I spent hours on that!* He half-rose from his chair, one hand extended toward his lost diagram. Parchment edges were curled and blackening. Hours of work, gone up in ash and smoke. Something hot and acidic bubbled in his throat.

Tenebris grabbed a fistful of William's robes and hauled him the rest of the way out of his seat. "Now that you're no longer distracted by mechanical idiocy, it's time we had a little talk. Come along, William." He jerked his head toward the door. "You can clean up your mess when we're through."

William swallowed his resentment and followed Tenebris into his study, closing the door on the laboratory.

His master spoke while perusing several scrolls on his desk. "With the baron-knight dead, no doubt the kadorei filth sent a messenger to summon their commander. We must be ready to seize the opportunity when it arises, before the suns-cursed evainghir arrives. His presence will complicate our plans, even ruin them."

Fear dragged an icy finger down William's spine. "The evainghir," he repeated. Shivering, he tangled his fingers in his burkheld to still their trembling. He tried not to think about his whiskey flask. "You mean the commander of the combined military might of the four baronies and the dwelfnim? That evainghir? As in, the warrior personally responsible for single-handedly slaughtering Warlord Dunkelnost and his hand-picked Golorum in the Battle of Nervashi over thirteen winters ago? *That* evainghir?"

Tenebris sighed, shaking his head. "Only dunces resort to redundancy." He looked up from his scrolls. "Yes, William, *that* evainghir. I wasn't aware of another in existence on the continent. Even a master Arkhadahn needs his wits about him simply to survive an encounter with him." With his hands tucked into opposite sleeves, he arched an eyebrow. "Do you see why we must accelerate our plans?"

William took a steadying breath. "But, master, if we go after the next target now, then it moves the timetable up drastically. I told the harkhurz he must wait and observe."

Tenebris closed his eyes and spoke through clenched jaws. "I don't mean *right now*, you ninny. I meant within the week." He yanked his hands from his sleeves and fussed with the scrolls again. "Suns burn the harkhurz; we can't trust him to not muck everything up. Capturing even a novice wyldling requires an Arkhadahn's finesse. I'd planned on doing it myself, but the Dreadlord believes it should be entrusted to you." His master scowled. "You have a rapport with the harkhurz; use it to restrain him."

Capture a wyldling? And the Dreadlord wants me to do the job? Elation burst into William's heart. This almost compensated for his lost diagram. A wyldling, just like in the scroll! But it didn't help to crow. If he knew of it, Tenebris would confiscate the scroll on Aethyr the Dreadlord had given them.

William shook his head and feigned ignorance. "Master, are you saying our next target is a wyldling? I thought Warlord Dunkelnost wiped them out at Nervashi. Isn't that the reason the evainghir killed the warlord?"

Tenebris's scowl deepened. "Dunkelnost was a fool—like every warrior in his faction. He saw those of the Aethyr as a threat, and rightly so. But he also feared the Arkhadahns. His own people. Our numbers have dwindled to a mere handful because of his purges. His elite warriors, the Vorkyr Golorum, hunted down and killed more Arkhadahns than even the evainghir destroyed. Had Dunkelnost survived, William, you and I wouldn't be here, having this conversation."

We owe the old reptile a modicum of gratitude for our lives. Struck by the irony of it, William stifled a smile. "If our target's a wyldling, then no wonder the Dreadlord wants him," he mused aloud. "But, master, how are we supposed to contain a wyldling? I heard they can kill people with their minds."

Perhaps the very reason Tenebris is allowing you the honor of the task. He suppressed the urge to squirm.

Tenebris stroked his beard, smirking. "Have no fear on that front, William. I won't throw you to the lykharim without the means to protect yourself. For the past moon—since my last meeting with him at Grivvensfel—I've possessed the one tool necessary for nullifying a wyldling's link to the Aethyr. Of course, the harkhurz cannot touch it, let alone activate it; however, your success mixing the Hesperidion Dust for his mission has convinced me. Together, you and the harkhurz might have the wherewithal for this challenge."

William's eyes widened. *Did Tenebris just praise me?*

His master snorted. "Even if you cannot eliminate one nosy, meddling kadorei soldier after I brought him right to death's door for you."

William deflated. "But it was an accident, Master Tenebris. I meant to dispatch him with the Bloodfire Cantrip, but I lost focus. He made me so angry, calling me a little to—"

"Do you know why I did not flay you for this error, apprentice?"

William grimaced; he hated it when Tenebris stressed his inferior status. "Um," he ventured. "Because it means you wasted your precious time in training me, master?"

Tenebris's eyes flashed. "Insolent wretch. Yes, that's part of it. What you did, the transformation… it should have been beyond your level of training. Far beyond. You've had ample time to ponder since I asked the first time; any protests of ignorance now will bring another object lesson." His eyes narrowed. "Tell me, where did you learn the transformation spell?"

William rose from his seat, his insides quivering. Anger and fear made for a nauseating mixture. "I didn't learn it, Tenebris. It just ha—"

William never saw his master move. One moment, Tenebris glared at him from across the room. The next, William hung suspended, his feet dangling a foot above the floor, with Tenebris's fingers around his neck. Pressure built inside William's head like an oversized melon about to burst.

Tenebris growled. "How. Do. You. Address. Me." His orange eyes burned. Teeth bared, the sorcerer shook him, and William's dark locks flopped around his face. Still gripping the youth's neck, Tenebris charged across the chamber and slammed him against the door. Stars exploded in William's head.

When his vision returned, Tenebris held him up against the door with one hand around William's throat and his other arm flung back and to the side. The long sleeve of his robe hung, a raven's wing poised to beat at him. Arkhabala writhed along the skin of his neck like worms in torment. Twin gates into the nether perditions burned in his eyes. William wheezed and struggled against the wall.

A season of searing agony passed before steel fingers loosened their grip. William dropped to his hands and knees at his master's feet.

"How," Tenebris said, "do you address me?"

William swallowed the bile at the back of his throat. He'd not improve his situation by vomiting. He stared at his master's boots, massaging his abused throat. Even after four Cycles under the man's tutelage, Tenebris's speed and physical strength still amazed him. He could only dream of achieving the Arkhadahn's level of skill. *Burning suns!* Too shaken to embrace the pain, he mumbled the cantrip to suppress it. The agony faded to an echo.

Tenebris planted a boot against his shoulder. "What was that? Don't mumble, fool. Enunciate. And look at me when you speak!"

William braced himself with his hands upon his thighs, staring up with wide eyes into his master's face. His heart hammered against his breastbone so hard he wondered why Tenebris did not remark on it.

I know what you want. But I don't want to give it to you. Not this time. You destroyed my diagram.

Tenebris narrowed his eyes. "Now," he said in a calm voice. "Who am I, apprentice?" His out-flung arm moved, the enchanted sleeve twitching in readiness.

Despite his resolve to be stoic, William flinched. Not the Nettle-sweep again. His skin will itch and burn for days. He sat, quivering with outrage. The words tumbled out: "Master Yvres Tenebris, Arkhadahn of the Thirteenth Order."

"Look at me, wretch!" The sorcerer seized his hair and yanked his head up to face smoldering eyes and prickling arkhabala. Darkness danced in William's vision and gathered into a whispering voice that only wine and whiskey could silence. "And who are you, foul fruit of a woman's womb?"

"I… I…" William's voice caught in his throat, every mote of him resisting speech.

I will not say it this time.

"Answer me, impertinent wretch."

The master's hand connected. Normally, William could endure physical pain, but the Pain Hex overcame such conditioning. The heavy slap struck him like a thunderbolt. William howled. He refused to say it, but if he persisted, Tenebris would then switch to intangible forms of torture. "William D-Dulciber, apprentice Arkhadahn of the Second Order." He grimaced as a horrible pressure seized upon his mind and twisted. And then—as if they were being forcibly extracted from him like shameful ores from the darkest depths of the earth—the words fell from his traitorous lips. "Bastard child of a woman taken as a slave by the kadorei filth, Count Dulciber."

The unwelcome thoughts came to whisper in the darkness behind his eyes, the sordid history his master had told him over a Cycle earlier. His mother escaped captivity, but she abandoned him because of his mixed parentage. The priests would've sacrificed him to Varkrav the Unclean if Tenebris hadn't sensed the spark of ability in him.

A tear leaked from one eye. It stung where the angry imprint of Tenebris's palm remained. William pushed the shameful memory down deep. It still hurt, a pain he could neither embrace nor dismiss with a cantrip, branded into his flesh more indelibly than the arkhabala tattooed across his back and shoulders.

His mother hadn't wanted him, the natural son of kadorei filth.

Tenebris spoke gently, now, as a father might reason with a wayward son. "Now what is important about that, William?" Candlelight returned to the room, and Tenebris appeared nothing more than a tall, dark-haired man with fierce eyes and a shark-like smile.

William took a shuddering breath. "I am the apprentice, y-your s-sl—" he clenched his jaw. It didn't matter what his mother was—*I won't burning say it!* "Servant," he continued, feeling a flicker of triumph at this minor victory. He sighed and finished: "You are my master."

Tenebris beamed at him. William allowed himself to relax. Doubtless, he believed William had absorbed the object lesson. Tenebris glided toward the door leading into his private chamber, his silken robes rippling. He paused with his hand on the latch. "Oh, and William? Don't forget to clean up your mess in the laboratory." The door closed behind him with a grim finality.

William sat on the floor in the flickering candlelight, staring at the place where Tenebris had been. Once assured his master wouldn't return, he rose with a grunt and lurched to the other door. Firstdawn was imminent; William felt the characteristic hum within his bones. No doubt his master, sensing the same, sought his bed.

William scowled. *Just you wait, Tenebris. Someday I will cast aside this mask of subservience and my fear. Someday, I will have power. And then, there will be a reckoning.*

In the meantime, his whiskey flask required refilling.

INTO THE DARKENWOOD

The silvery-white rumor of firstdawn glowed along the western horizon. With one forearm braced against the frame of his bedroom window, Enoch stared out into the new day. Beyond the garrison walls, over the green expanse of distant trees, the sky was cloudless. Perfect weather in which to conduct a search for missing people.

The Threefold One couldn't have sent a more definite sign that He approves of my venture. Enoch mouthed a silent prayer of gratitude and then traced the sign of the cross over his chest. He pondered his strange dream about the forbidden wood. He'd seen the maiden in the dark blue armor and someone else—the shadow-cloaked stranger who stopped him from leaving.

I have a mission in the Darkenwood Forest.

Heart heavy, he turned away from the window and completed his morning ablutions in the toilet alcove. His mind churned over the events of yesterday. Icy claws constricted his throat.

Sir Rick's memorial service.

Afterwards, he had made a pledge to the assembled mourners—the pledge installing him as the Acting Baron-Knight of the Northern Marches. He accepted the service oaths of the Lilac Grove garrison soldiers and the three marshals who commanded the other sectors.

Again, he saw the tear-streaked faces of Mrs. Cartwright, Mrs. Jolson, and Mrs. Pines as they begged him to find their daughters and bring them home. He shut his eyes against the prickling of tears and took a deep breath to steady himself.

Becky. Janet. Sally. Less than a moon ago, we were laughing over a picnic lunch. And now you're gone. Please, Lord Yshua, help me keep the promise I made to their families. Help me find my friends.

Out in the hallway, the clock struck the hour and brought him back into the present.

Hare Watch had begun. *I must leave now. Otherwise, Red'll drag me off to go over the Manor accounts. That's certain to take all morning, and then there are the garrison reports to read, the daily drills to run, and tomorrow is Chapelday. Now is the best time to go.*

He was the acting baron-knight. People were counting on him.

A sense of urgency crackled through his body. He dressed in his well-worn homespun clothing and donned leather armor like a second skin. He buckled his sword-belt with quick, assured motions and threw his satchel over his shoulder. As an afterthought, he grabbed his spectacles off the writing desk as he swept past it and settled them over his eyes.

Enoch strode out the door and went down the West hall corridor.

He took his preferred shortcut through the servants' corridor and tried to ignore the startled, sympathetic glances and hasty genuflections of the maids—who wore sable bands of mourning tied around their sleeves.

Stop it, he wanted to say. *A moon ago, you paid me no mind when I came this way.*

Less than a moon ago…

He swallowed the sudden thickness in his throat and slipped through a door, swinging on well-oiled hinges. Freshly baked bread, cinnamon, apples, stimulant tea, and honey—the aromas that meant home—tickled his nostrils. Tears stung his eyes as he wended his way through the organized chaos and babble of the cooking staff. Careful not to meet anyone's gaze, he kept his eyes fixed on the door leading out into the primary courtyard. Beside the door stood a cabinet with an insulated tureen of hot tea prepared for the guard shift change.

Enoch drew himself a cup of tea. Plain and black, the way a garrison trooper drank it. The way his friends drank it.

The way Sir Rick used to drink it.

Enoch blew steam from his cup and leaned against the wall by the door, observing the kitchen staff at work. The cheerful voices of the women and clatter of dishes should have been comforting to in his ears, but this morning the clamor held a harsh and brittle note. The mourning bands—slashes of darkness against the starched whiteness of their sleeves—ruined the illusion of familiarity. He sampled the hot beverage and grimaced at the bitter taste. Furtively, he added a dollop of honey and a splash of cream to his tea before taking another sip.

That's more like it.

Enoch's stomach chose this moment to gurgle and remind him he'd not yet broken his fast. Right on cue, gray-haired Patsy sailed by with a tray laden with steaming sweet-buns. He snagged two pastries with a deftness born from long practice, wrapped them in a handkerchief, and tucked his spoils into his satchel.

Patsy placed the tray on the counter and caught his gaze. Her dark eyes glittered with amusement even as she shook her head at him. "Still up to your old tricks, dartling jay? You'll ruin your breakfast," she admonished, standing akimbo. Patsy, one of several women in Lilac Grove who helped mother him, often seemed to forget he was old enough to shave. This morning, he welcomed her use of the old pet-name.

Enoch shrugged and grinned sheepishly at the woman. "This *is* my breakfast, Patsy," he replied. "Dartling jays eat on the wing, you know."

She raised her eyebrows. "Too busy to sit down like civilized folk, then?"

"Duty calls." Enoch straightened his spine to gain a few precious knuckles of height. He nodded to her, a gesture of acknowledgment and dismissal. "May Lord Yshua bless your day."

"Yours as well, milord Enoch!" Patsy smiled and curtseyed before rushing off to attend to a fresh tray of sweet-buns.

Milord Enoch? He winced. *That's not me! I don't want it to be me.* He wished to correct Patsy, but the words stuck in his throat as if he'd already swallowed a bite of the honeyed pastry. His lips tightened, trying to deflect the sharp splinter of sorrow slicing into his heart.

I need to leave before someone else 'sirs' or 'milords' me.

Enoch slipped out the door and inhaled the lilac-scented morning breeze and then strode off to the furry warmth of the main stable. The good fortune of Kaspar Windchaser was with him; too busy mucking out a stall while belting out a trooper's marching tune, the groom on duty didn't pay any attention to him. Soldiers had taken most of the deer to aid in the search effort for Sir Thomas and the girls, but his favorite mount, Tinker, awaited him in his stall.

Enoch saddled Tinker and took care not to touch his mount's velvet-encased antlers when he adjusted the headstall and bridle. Lachesis's warm golden rays mingled with Klotho's steel-white glare on the western horizon as he led the deer across the courtyard and toward the Westgate. The next step was the trickiest. He adjusted his leather-scale war cap and fidgeted with his spectacles, devising a statement for the gatekeeper.

He didn't want to lie. But he couldn't tell him the whole truth. It must be a plausible reason, though; the gatekeepers weren't supposed to lift the gates on a whim. Even baron-knights needed to follow the proper protocol.

Enoch halted several strides away from the gatekeeper's booth. The day-watch gatekeeper, Corporal Higgins, leaned against the side of the narrow building, talking to his partner on gate-duty, Trooper Gilmore. Two women were with them, one in a gray dress covered by an apron with many pockets, the other in dairymaid white. Enoch recognized Jessica Morton, the village herbalist, and Frannie Pines, the dairymaid. They looked up as he approached. Frannie's eyes were red-rimmed but filled with a dawning hope as she met his gaze. An icicle plunged into his heart. Her sister, Janet, was one of the missing girls. Trooper Gilmore's cousin, Sally Jolson, was another. It seemed everyone in Lilac Grove was related either by blood or marriage.

Everyone, except me.

Enoch stiffened his spine and raised his hand in an awkward wave. "Good morrow," he said, glancing away from Frannie. "How are the search parties deployed this morning, Higgins? I want to help. Who's in charge of the proximal Darkenwood Forest contingent?"

The day-watch gatekeeper touched Frannie's arm as he stepped out onto the path. "Just fifteen minutes ago, Deputy Trask led his cohort to the Northwest, sir, to search the fringes of the forest. If we hurry, we'll catch up to them."

Enoch's face flushed hot as the man dashed over to the gatekeeper's booth to write a note in the ledger. He had no desire for company. He stretched to his full height. "No need for you to accompany me, Higgins. I can spot a cohort of men traveling the caravan route just fine by myself." He faced the dairymaid. "I promise I'll find your sister, Frannie. And your cousin," he told the soldier. He raised his voice. "Open the gate, Higgins."

Enoch climbed up into the saddle. He sighed in relief when Higgins obeyed. After the corporal raised the Westgate portcullis, he urged his mount into a brisk trot. "May the Almighty Threefold One bless your day," he cast back over his shoulder as he rode through the open gate. Behind him, Higgins cranked the winch in the opposite direction and the portcullis slid along well-oiled grooves in the stone walls.

Enoch stifled a twinge of shame for his indirect falsehood and took a swig from his waterskin to drown it.

Miss Morton called after him: "Take care, Sir Enoch. Watch out for evil sorcerers."

Tinker sneezed.

"Yeah, that's my opinion of Jessica Morton, too," Enoch said, urging his mount on. "Simon claims she's touched in the head."

He patted Tinker, although the beast required no soothing. He took several long breaths and felt his nervous distraction fade with each exhalation. *"Good air in. Bad air out."* His guardian's voice was clear in his mind; he recalled the old man's lessons more clearly and often.

"A deep breath cleanses the soul and prepares the mind for the next task," he spoke aloud, past the lump forming in his throat. One of Tinker's ears swiveled back at the sound of his voice. Enoch patted his mount's neck again. "Besides, it's not as if I *lied* to Higgins," he told Tinker. "I just said I didn't need his help to find the patrol." He might run into Deputy Trask's patrol sometime during the morning, but he had no desire go out of his way and search for them.

The dense wood hid the evidence of thirddawn—when the bloated, red sun Atropos joined her celestial sisters, Klotho and Lachesis, in the summer sky—but his empty stomach alerted him to time's passage. With half an ear on the avian chatter in the forest canopy, he pulled out his pilfered breakfast and ate while scanning the pathway and the undergrowth for signs of Sir Thomas or the missing girls.

The morning progressed inexorably toward firstnoon, and the still, humid air beneath the heavy boughs of ancient trees grew warm. Perspiration beaded on Enoch's face and under his war cap and leathers. He wiped his forehead with a handkerchief as he scanned his surroundings. The road's breadth dwindled the further West they went. Several times during the growing season, the garrison troopers escorted a crew of stoneworkers who cared for the caravan route leading to the Waystone, but Enoch saw no evidence of such maintenance here. He did not like how the colony bushes grew up right next to the road; they provided perfect staging points for an ambush.

I must talk with Captain Faulkner about this oversight before Commander Storm conducts the midsummer inspection.

"I wonder," he murmured aloud, "how long has it been since patrols swept this area for bandits and robbers?" He reined in his deer. Tinker slowed to a walk. "Maybe I should have let Higgins attend me," he whispered to the deer.

Enoch breathed deeply, concentrated, and engaged his special listening skill. Silver mist imbued his vision. However, birdsong and squirrel-chatter were the only sounds he heard for miles. Flickering shafts of sunslight penetrating the thick canopy of brooding trees to dapple the forest floor. Everything seemed peaceful, a typical late spring day in a normal forest.

Enoch dismissed his talent and the silver mist faded away. If anything dangerous lurked in the vicinity, Tinker would've been on the alert. As it was, the deer ambled along at his master's pleasure, his dilated nostrils twitching as he scented the air.

Before long, the dirt road—not worthy to be called a road now—petered out entirely. The forest encroached on either side of the narrow track remaining, determined to obliterate man-made progress.

Enoch clicked his tongue and his mount halted. He rummaged in the satchel for the map he'd brought along and found it buried under his journal, writing supplies, a cloth-wrapped packet containing his provisions, a spare knife, and a hoard of interesting rocks and bird feathers he'd collected on previous excursions and then neglected to remove. The roll of parchment had become creased and dented at the bottom of his satchel.

He grimaced. *Should've put it in a scroll-tube.* Red would chide him for his carelessness. He alternately examined it and the environs for several moments, and then nodded. He rolled up the map again and stowed it in a separate satchel pocket.

"End of the road," he remarked to Tinker as he dismounted. "We may as well take a break, boy. Intrepid scouts need to eat lunch."

While Tinker nibbled on the tender shoots of a young colony bush, Enoch sat upon a fallen tree trunk and scarfed most of the food in his satchel. Periodically, he monitored his mount's behavior, which continued placid and unconcerned. No predators.

He drank some water to wash down the last bite of his meal and then stretched out stiffened muscles. To his pleasure, a faint breeze stirred the stagnant air. He tilted his head back and closed his eyes to luxuriate in the coolness. A shadow fell over him, and he fancied he heard the rustling of pinions settling, the scrape of a pen-point against parchment, and a human voice whispering in a language he almost understood.

Skelsdaran…

Tinker nuzzled his shoulder. Enoch scrunched his face. *Now I'm hearing voices? I must've been imagining things.*

"Thirsty, boy?" He removed his war cap, raked back bedraggled locks of hair, and enjoyed fresh wind fanning his sweaty forehead. A faint sound—the distant flapping of large wings—tickled his ears once again. But when he looked up, he saw no trace of any bird in the canopy. He sighed as he poured a measure of water into the tough leather cap.

After the deer drank his fill, Enoch grasped Tinker's reins. He led his mount along the game trail, winding westward around the fallen tree. The deer balked at first; an alder bush branch partially obstructed the head of the trail, and his velvet-covered antlers were sensitive. In the end, he held aside the branch and coaxed the beast past the obstacle.

"C'mon, Tinker," he insisted. "Daylight's a-wasting, and we've still miles of this forest to scout. There's a nice lump of sugar in it for you when we get home. Maybe we'll even find some arborcress deeper in these woods."

Tinker followed him into the depths of the forest. The game trail meandered first one way, and then another, joining up with other paths or fading. Even though his mount could find the way home, he left signs at these junctions just as Red had taught him: cutting into the bark of trees, piling up small cairns of stones, and bending twigs. Wood-craft signals were not strictly necessary, but creating the signs lent an official flavor to his foray into the forbidden wood, as if he blazed a trail into uncharted wilderness—an intrepid soul on an adventure.

The Darkenwood Forest sure is peaceful. It's nothing like the Bloodwood Forest to the south or Les Koshmarov beyond Northgate.

He'd ridden twenty miles along this path, and no one and nothing had attacked him. There were no vicious predators. No bloodthirsty bandits. No sign of an evil sorcerer—or even a rogue skraeling shaman—taking up residence in this forest.

"Perhaps the sight of a mighty warrior scout has frightened them into hiding," he suggested to his mount, and then laughed bitterly. Since his twelfth winter, he'd prayed every night to the Threefold One for a growth spurt, but over a Cycle later he was still shorter than every garrison soldier. But nobody teased him about his height since he'd returned from Treehome. Not even Sergeant Matlock.

Enoch forced himself to focus on the people he sought: Janet Pines, Sally Jolson, Becky Cartwright, and Sir Thomas.

The three maidens had been his playfellows. His friends. Spirited away by the machinations of an evil sorcerer, according to the lead rumormonger, Jessica Morton. Simon scoffed at her claims when she accosted them at the memorial service. "Sorcerers? Bah! Commander Storm and Sir Rick put paid to their ilk Cycles ago." And then every trooper raised a glass of sherry and toasted the memory of Sir Rick.

Enoch blinked. Sir Rick died in the course of his duty, and now he must pick up where his guardian had left off. His eyes burned with suppressed tears. In his memory, he heard Commander Storm say: *A man does not weep. He acts.*

Sir Thomas wasted no time with tears. Sir Thomas acted. When Sir Rick fell ill, he came at once from the East Sector. Under his final dictated orders, Sir Thomas vanished in the Darkenwood Forest while out searching for the missing girls.

Enoch sighed. "I wish Sir Thomas was here now, to be the baron-knight," he told Tinker. "He'd tell me what I should do. I'd give anything to have things back the way they were, when Sergeant Matlock called me 'Runt' and Patsy pinched my cheek, if only…"

The memory of Sir Rick's voice intruded. *"Life is what it is. Many things are beyond our control and there's naught complaining's ever done to change it. Leave the whining to small children and lazy fools, Enoch. Get to work changing the things that can be changed."*

Commander Storm would be even more direct: *"Cease your dad-rotted puling, or I'll wallop you into the next fortnight."*

Remembering those past rebukes was a slap in the face. Commander Storm would certainly disapprove of his current activities.

He checked the draw of his sword from its sheath. "I've been trained for this sort of thing," he told Tinker. "I don't need Red or anyone here to hold my hand. No matter what the commander says, it's been two winters since I outgrew the need for a minder. Besides, I'll attain my majority in two Turnings."

Enoch steeled his resolve and continued putting one foot in front of the other, unable to explain why he chose the trails and paths he did. He followed a route first charted in half-forgotten dreams. Several times, he climbed up an obliging, sprawling-limbed tree to orient himself by the suns, as well as taking care to mark his progress on the map he carried. As he ducked and dodged the jabbing boughs of thorn bushes and small saplings with his reluctant mount in tow, he envisioned himself as one of the seven Sages in one of Lord Evanrudhe's stories, out to discover new lands and bring the Way of Yshua to the unenlightened folk who lived there.

Or he could be a valiant hero on a quest to rescue a hapless damsel—or three, in this case—from dire bondage in slavery to be returned safely to the bosom of their families. He drifted into a reverie involving him fighting off at least twenty ruffians guarding an enormous tower—the residence of a powerful sorcerer and the three maidens he held captive. After outwitting the sorcerer and infiltrating the tower, he sundered the enchantment around Sally, Janet, and Becky with a mighty blow of his sword. He imagined rosy-cheeked Becky smiling at him. She'd say, breathless and overcome with admiration: "You're a hero, just like Gideon the Sevenfold-blessed."

"And then," he muttered, "I'll free Sir Thomas from the sorcerer's dungeon and he'll be so impressed, he rewards—"

Enoch was so intrigued by his own imaginings he almost tripped over the immense toad crouching in his path.

"Hey!" croaked the toad, its icy eyes glittering. "Watch it, kid!"

Enoch swore: "Kaspar's Wings!" He backpedaled into Tinker, who grunted at the impact.

Nether perditions, that's one gigantic toad! I've seen smaller tomcats. Wait... did the thing just talk? *Wake up, Enoch Northward. How would Sir Rick or the commander handle this?*

Eyes fastened on the creature, he drew his sword with trembling hands and assumed a defensive posture. The toad flinched and then froze, glaring at him and poised to leap. Behind Enoch, the stag snorted, stepped aside, and started nibbling on a nearby patch of herbs.

After a moment of bated breath, the toad spoke again. It sounded male. "Are you gonna stick me with that thing, or what?"

"You can talk," Enoch said aloud.

"Congratulations, kid," the creature replied, rolling his bulbous eyes. "Your grasp of the obvious is mind-blowing. Did you want a medal or a chest to pin it on?"

Enoch blinked. He raised his eyebrows, incredulous. "I almost stepped on you."

"And that would've really ticked me off."

"I'm sorry; I didn't see you down there."

The toad glared at him. "Then you must be blind, kid. And deaf," he muttered when Enoch did not respond. "Or dumb as a sack of hammers."

Enoch opened his mouth to berate the creature for its impertinent tone, but the look in his eyes deflated him. Commander Storm often stared at him in the same way. After fumbling with his sword and scabbard, Enoch sheathed the weapon.

His face heated. "Sorry," he said in a sullen tone.

Pale blue eyes seemed to appraise Enoch's ability with the weapon and willingness to use it. The oversized amphibian puffed up; doubtless he thought he looked more threatening. "Take your sorry and stuff it, kid!"

Kid? Enoch scowled. "I'm a warrior—not a baby goat! I'm was just walk—"

With a smirk, the toad interrupted him. "Head in the clouds. Space cadet."

How can a toad smirk? And what's a space cadet?

"Look, I didn't mean to offend you. Or step on you." And then he laughed as the irony hit him. "It's not as if I expected to run into a talking toad who insults me when—"

The cantankerous creature inflated his throat sac. "I am not a talking toad."

Enoch snorted. "Sure looks like it to me."

"I am not a talking toad."

Enoch lifted his chin and placed his hand upon the pommel of his sword. "Then what in festering perditions are you?" *Balthazar's blades; I sound like Commander Storm. Even when he isn't here, his way dictates my life.*

The creature opened his mouth and then closed it again. He shifted in the dust, his eyes clouded. "Why can't I remember anything?" He shook his head. Louder, he said, "Never mind, kid. What you should be—"

Enoch spoke over the toad. "I am on a mission of utmost importance, seeking people who've gone missing from my village. I refuse to be detained by annoying talking animals—"

The toad's pale eyes flashed ice-cold. Its voice cracked like a whip. "Don't you dare call me that, kid. I. Am not. An animal."

Enoch reeled back at the note of command in the creature's voice and the rage behind its wintery gaze. His irritation vanished like smoke in a breeze as he frowned. The toad reminded him of somebody, but he couldn't think of whom. For some inexplicable reason, though, he wanted to trust him.

Enoch rapped a fist against his chest and bowed his head. Politeness may bring the irascible creature around. "Truly, sir, I offer my apologies for offending you. My name's Enoch Northward."

The toad snorted. A glint of humor replaced the blazing anger in the pale eyes. "'Sir?' I'm no 'sir' of anything, kid."

"What should I call you, then?"

"Gone," the creature retorted, shuffling its warty body around until it faced away from him. "Because I'm out of here. I've got far more important things to deal with than babysitting your sorry self, kid."

Despite himself, Enoch laughed. "If you won't tell me your actual name, then I'll have to call you 'Toad.'"

The creature smirked again. "Very creative. Fine by me, kid. I suppose 'Toad' is as good a name as any, and more fitting than most. Now we've settled the all-important name issue, it's time for me to make like a tree and leave." Toad swiveled around and hopped away.

Enoch's heart fluttered behind his breastbone, a bird in a cage. He'd promised to find the girls. This toad might have seen something. "Wait. Please."

Toad hesitated.

Enoch cleared his throat and spoke. "Where are you going that's so important?"

"Someplace you're not." Toad hastened his pace. Oddly, he continued to hop along the path instead of veering off into the bracken ferns like one of its smaller cousins might have done.

Why must the toad be so difficult? He sucked in air through his teeth and prayed for patience. Sir Rick always warned him nothing worth doing was ever easy. He snatched Tinker's lead and chased after the amphibian. "Toad, wait up."

Toad halted, muttering to himself. "Jiminy cricket, first amnesia, and now this clown shows up. Can't a guy catch a friggin' break?" He sighed. "Okay, what do you want?"

"I just wanted to ask some questions. Before you go, will you at least tell me if you've seen anything unusual around here?"

Toad eyed him sidelong. "Unusual how?"

"Anything out of the ordinary. Like people wandering around, lost."

The toad inflated his throat sac, eyes thoughtful. "Oh, like you? No, you're the first idiot I've encountered wandering around lost in these woods, so long as I can remember."

"I'm not lost."

Toad narrowed its bulbous eyes at him. "Uh-huh. Sure, kid. And do you know where this path leads?"

"Of course, I…" He paused, his eyes widening. He yanked open his satchel and frantically rooted through it. He pulled out the map.

Toad watched him, annoyance warring with amusement in his gaze. "For the record, I'm not in the mood to entertain stupid kids who've got themselves lost in the woods."

"I'm not lost, Toad!" Enoch knelt to unroll the map on the ground and weighed down the edges of the map with several rocks. Tinker sidled off the path to graze upon a nearby patch of clover. "Just because I don't know exactly where I am doesn't mean I'm lost."

His companion scoffed. "Kid, that's the definition of lost. So, you're searching for missing folks. It looks to me as if someone sent you on some sort of wild goose chase."

Unable to help himself, Enoch retorted, "Nobody sent me anywhere. I took the initiative and came out here because it's the right thing to do."

Toad stared at him. "If you say so, kid. Unless you give me more details, this'll turn into a friggin' clown parade."

This is blustering ridiculous. The stress of the past few days came crashing home. Enoch collapsed to his knees and burst out laughing. Tinker raised his head and regarded his young master in gentle astonishment, clover stems dangling from his muzzle.

"Laughing boy," the toad said, raising his eyes to heaven.

Enoch sobered, recalling his reason for being in the Darkenwood. *I made a promise to those girls' families. Come icy tempest or fiery perdition, as acting baron-knight, I am bound by my word to honor it—even if it means asking talking toads for directions.*

While Tinker filled his rumen with grasses and forbs, Enoch explained his mission. Toad listened without further sarcastic commentary and confirmed he'd seen neither girls nor baron-knights. Enoch rolled up his map and stuffed it into his satchel. He retrieved his war cap and rose. He should have known better, but he'd been so certain. It felt right to follow this path, as if the Darkenwood Forest contained what he sought. And he wasn't going to admit he had second thoughts around the toad.

Toad's eyes gleamed. "This is a pretty big forest, kid. If you're looking for someone else lost in the woods, then chances are small you'll stumble upon them by wandering around aimlessly yourself. You have a map, but do you have a plan?"

Enoch shrugged. "I was going to keep walking and see where this path leads—for a start." He clicked his tongue at Tinker. With a resigned grunt, the stag swallowed his last mouthful of greenery and came to him.

Toad groaned, cursing. "That's the way I'm going. But I guess I can't stop you from tagging along."

Enoch stared at an impenetrable tangle of burr-weed, colony bushes, and trees.

Toad glared at him. "Road ends here, kid."

Enoch straightened his spine. "Not for me, Toad. I think there's something beyond this thicket." *Of course, the way I intended to go is overgrown. Beggar it; those bushes are over twenty feet tall if they're an inch.*

Toad snorted and muttered something under his breath.

Enoch investigated the bushes. No way would Tinker go in there—not with his new antlers still in velvet. Enoch sighed and took out his map. He estimated the distance traveled, marked it on the map, and then led his mount to the edge of the thicket. He took out his handkerchief and tied it to a shoulder-high branch of the nearest colony bush.

Pointing to the handkerchief, he commanded: "Tinker, stay!" Tinker folded up his long legs and sank to the ground. He exhaled noisily.

"I'll be back. I'll try to find some nice, juicy arborcress for you."

The stag flicked an ear at him and settled to chew his cud. Enoch crouched, seeking an opening in the dense brush large enough to admit him. At the base of the colony bushes were snarls of burr-weed, ground ivy vines, and a black-barred, silver feather the length of his hand—a pinion from a dartling jay's wing. He tucked it into his belt-pouch.

Toad crawled up beside Enoch. He rolled his eyes and croaked. "Wait, kid. There's a way to get through. Seeing as I live around here,

I'm familiar with this line of bushes. If you're so hot and bothered about discovering what's on the other side, then follow me." He shoved bracken fern aside and slipped beneath the arching limbs of the lush colony bush, complaining under his breath about the stubborn idiocy of adolescents.

Enoch hesitated. And then a nagging sense of anticipation compelled him to follow into the dense tangle of bushes. He peered into the undergrowth. *I hope there isn't any itchweed in there. The last thing I need is to wake up with a rash tomorrow morning.* He spent several seconds struggling through tightly woven branches before he gave up and crawled after Toad, using his knees and elbows to drag himself onward.

Enoch's sword banged against his leg and slowed him until he hitched his belt around, so his weapon lay along his backside. *Praise Yshua, there's no itchweed.* He discovered a few sprigs of the promised arborcress for Tinker's treat and tucked them into a belt-pouch alongside the feather.

Sweat drenched Enoch within a moment. The dense foliage of the brush tinted the sunslight shining through a warm yellow-green, and the musty scent of crushed fungi made him sneeze. To distract his mind from his physical discomfort, Enoch imagined himself as a caterpillar inching his way along a tunnel toward another world. His stomach growled to alert him of missing a meal; for a moment, he wished he *was* a caterpillar so he could munch upon the leaves slapping against his face.

The worst part is the spiders. He grimaced as he brushed cobwebs and scuttling arachnids from his clothing. *They won't bother Toad; he can eat them.* Fleetingly, he wondered if Sir Thomas could have fit through the tunnel. The girls could have if the spiders had not deterred them, but he did not find any sign of human passage.

Toad abruptly disappeared as the trail curved to the West. "It's not far now," he called back to Enoch. Above them, a squirrel chattered and squeaked, no doubt scolding them for disturbing the peace. Enoch adjusted his spectacles, which were sliding down his sweat-slicked nose again, before crawling round the bend. Ahead shone a bright circle of light and Toad's bumpy silhouette bobbing up to break it. His heart throbbed faster with anticipation. For no reason he discerned—tired, sweaty, and uncomfortable as he was—excitement beat like a second heart deep within him.

It's very near. Whatever I've been looking for, it's on the other side of these bushes.

Toad called out again, but the thunder of rushing blood in Enoch's ears and the raspy noise of his own ragged breathing drowned out the gravelly voice. His world narrowed to the widening circle of silvery light at the end of the tunnel. To whatever was pulling him forward. When he emerged into the daylight, he raising a hand to block the glare of the suns and knocked off his spectacles. But he didn't need them to see something vast and dark gray ahead cutting through the forest like a massive knife.

It was a wall.

"What in Tehara is that?"

Enoch picked up the spectacles and settled them on his face without removing his eyes from the soot-colored edifice. He'd smudged one lens, but he was too busy gawking at the barrier looming over him to do anything about it.

Toad made a gulping noise in his throat. "From its general wall-shapedness, I'd venture to guess it's a wall, such as it is. There's nothing on the other side to justify its existence. I'm not sure how far south it goes, but to the North of this clearing it just sort of… ends. You wanted 'unusual,' kid. Voila. Here it is."

This is what's been calling me. This… Wall. Oh, Lord Yshua. Almighty Threefold One, be with me now.

Enoch stood, his heart palpitating. For no discernible reason, he felt as if he'd come home. With reverent languor, as a man moves in a dream, he approached the Wall, which ran the entire length of the glade and curved away into green depths of the forest in either direction. Until, presumably, it ended, as Toad said. It stood fifteen feet high and was constructed from dark gray stone, crumbled and broken-looking in places at the top. He reached out a hand.

"I wouldn't!"

Enoch ignored Toad's cry of alarm and touched the cool, rough surface. Something prickled and hummed for an instant against his palm. A sudden pressure built in his sinuses and then, abruptly, the sensation disappeared. From a distance came a series of pops resembling isolated cracks of thunder. He braced himself for the Wall to suck him within its chill grayness like quicksand—where he'd be trapped for eternity—but this did not happen. The Wall was a barrier, nothing more.

He shook his head, swallowing past the icy claws grasping his throat. *I must be imagining things. There's no way Sir Thomas or those girls could've passed through solid stone.* Maybe he grasped at straws, thinking this strange Wall had anything to do with the disappearances.

"Hello, what's this?"

A recessed, window-like opening in the Wall beckoned him. Covered with a polished metallic sheen reflecting the sunlight, the lower rim lay just above the crown of his head. He tapped the surface of the oval aperture with one finger. It felt solid and cool to the touch, like glass. Enoch grunted thoughtfully. The Wall had a window. Unable to resist, he pressed his fingers against the surface. It grew warm under his skin. He frowned. What was the purpose of such windows? Yet another puzzle.

Perhaps the dwelfnim knew. They possessed an entire library dedicated to ancient lore long forgotten by the other races of humanity. If the library failed to yield results, no doubt the First Councilor and eldest of the dwelfnim, Lord Evanrudhe, would prove a treasure trove of information. He knew so much history and legends about everything. This Wall could feature in a legend of the Seven Sages; he vaguely recalled a huge, impenetrable wall mentioned in one of the adventure stories he'd heard as a very young child. He'd ask the First Councilor about the Wall at the next opportunity. There were many questions.

Who built it, and for what reason?

Did the gloomy edifice attract him, or was it something else?

Why am I drawn here? he asked the unnatural barrier.

"To be made whole," a voice whispered.

Enoch's eyes widened. That wasn't Toad's voice; it came from inside his own head. Had the Threefold One spoken to him?

A tingling energy ran through his body and up his arm. Silver mist flooded his vision. The Window's glass grew warm and pliant beneath his fingers, which leaked silver vapors. His arm trembled. Without losing contact, his hand slid, and—as if he'd dragged the entire thing down—the Window hovered before his face, gleaming and swirling like molten metal. The surface engulfed his hand. Silver light poured out, the whispering noise of the wind caressing him. He gasped, frozen in place, as the wind fanned his sweaty face and ruffled loose strands of hair. The glowing quicksilver rotated, his buried hand serving as its axis until the liquid metal spun away, the Window clearing to reveal blackness studded with bright points of light.

Were those stars?

He was falling into the blackness through a tunnel streaked with lines of silver and sapphire blue. Wind roared in his ears. He reeled away from Toad and the glade like a kite caught in a thunderstorm.

SILVER AND SAPPHIRE

Pillow tucked under her arms, Annabelle sprawled on her stomach across her bed, reading *A Wind in the Door* by Madeleine L'Engle. Some stories never grow stale, she mused, even the third time through. She gleaned more enjoyment from it each time. The description of Proginoskes was fascinating; she imagined what it would be like to meet cherubim in real life.

Probably every bit as terrifying as it was for Meg, and then some. Ezekiel paints a decent picture of cherubim in his prophetic visions. Very weird. She tucked a bookmark into the novel and reached for her Bible on the nightstand. Cool air caressed her cheek. She froze, her hand on the black cover.

A draft? Improbable. Nobody in Wisconsin with half a brain left windows open during February with the furnace running. A real wind in her door? No. She'd closed her bedroom door to keep out her younger siblings. Even buried in a book, the creak of hinges would've alerted her. Wind tickled her face again. She turned to check, and her eyes widened. Her door remained shut, but something else captured her gaze—the mirror hanging on the wall the door shared. Or where her mirror used to be. An oval of glowing, molten silver, or mercury—like the villain from *Terminator 2*—swirled in its place.

She murmured, "Holy cow." Heart pounding, she rose and approached the anomaly. The color of the light looked the same as the boy's armor from her dream. Could she be dreaming now? *If I dreamed about pinching myself, would it wake me? Not the time to worry about dream pinches, Annabelle.*

She pinched herself and winced. *Apparently, I'm awake.* Wind traced invisible fingers over her face, no longer cold, but gentle and warm. She raised her hand, hesitating. A voice spoke in her head, sounding like her mother's: *You know better, Annabelle. Walk away now, before you get hurt.* She bit her lip and stared into the gleaming depths. *Can I walk away? Can I, really?* Even after her arguing and angst, Meg Murry didn't walk away. She plunged straight into danger to save her brother.

Warmth enfolded her outstretched hand as she touched the surface.

Before she exhaled, her bedroom disappeared. Silent darkness enveloped her. She blinked. Blackness dotted with hard, bright points of light surrounded her. Sapphire ribbons spreading from her body undulated like seaweed in an ocean's current. The threads were a part of her; she'd become a discorporate being made of blue light.

Ahead, the streaks of blue light condensed into a glowing silver sphere. A white dwarf star? Vapor of the same color extended from its surface, contracting into strands of silver light, whipping threads on an unseen wind. Another being of light. Strands like glowing, metallic wires extended toward her.

Annabelle reached for the silver strands. Instead of two arms ending in hands and fingers, many thin blue threads shot out from her core. They met the silver wires and tangled together, holding fast like roots in soil. Someone spoke directly into her mind using a familiar, masculine voice. The voice of the boy in the weird silver-chased armor from her dreams.

"Colored threads and strands? So, this is what a person's kythim looks like!"

Kythim? Why does that term seem familiar?

Annabelle gasped. Her blue strands were slipping away from the silver wires. The other being's strands—his kythim—wound tighter around hers. She matched his efforts with her own, weaving ribbons together until she couldn't tell where the silver ended and sapphire began.

Awe and curiosity radiated from the silver orb. "Are we speaking aloud or using thought-speech, as the dwelfnim sometimes do?"

Excitement jolted through her, and the blue strands flashed. Dwelfnim, kythim and thought-speech. *Not sure what dwelfnim is, but… Ah, yes, kythim sounds like kything, the weird communication thing the characters do in my book.* Coincidence? Had she been wrong about being lost in a dream?

Annabelle shook her head, or whatever passed as the head of the sapphire star-form she possessed in the strange, celestial, void place. If she'd dreamed up this place, she might as well go along with it. She asked, "Are you the Silver Knight? Where are you from?"

The silver being flared bright and drew nearer. "I'm Enoch Northward, from Lilac Grove, in the Northern Marches."

Enoch. Recognition flashed through her. *It's him—the boy from my dream!* Confusion followed, swirled in shifting bright and dim patches along her ribbons. "Northern Marches? Where is that? It's not anywhere on planet Earth, is it?"

"Earth? No. I live on a planet called Tehara."

Tehara! Annabelle shivered. Just like in her dreams. However, this time she had more conscious control over the situation. She wished she could check her dream journal.

"And you, my lady? You seem familiar. How are you called?"

Is she even human?

She laughed; amusement pulsed like blue Christmas lights along the kythim strands. "My name is Annabelle Leigh Wells. And yes, I'm human. Aren't you?"

The Enoch-star sparkled. *She read my thoughts.*

Giggles shook her, and blue light spread out in ripples. "Of course I did; how else are we communicating without sound?"

Silver light rippling with laughter, he replied, "You got me there. And yes, I'm a human being, too. A kadorei man, just as the Threefold One created me." A sense of awe, followed by a stray thought. *Yes, this is the same maiden from my dreams.*

Annabelle thought for a moment. "What did you mean, 'kadorei?' Is that a different language? The Threefold One—is that your god? Oh! I can see it in your mind now. Kadorei means a human being. I guess that means I'm kadorei, too. And the Threefold One…"

How do I convey this?

She concentrated, envisioning a triangular symbol with intricately knotted vertices flashed across the mind's eye of both. "Your Threefold One is a different way of referring to the Trinity." She thought of a cupped hand, and then replaced it with an eye inside a triangle, rays of light streaming outward. "God, the Father."

Recognition pulsed from Enoch, and she sent another picture, this time a stylized flame, followed by a bright and shining dove descending from the heavens. "God, the Holy Spirit."

Divine Wind. The Counselor. The Converting Fire.

Annabelle flickered, impressed by his choice of words. "Exactly. And, last but definitely not least—God the Son, Jesus Christ."

She concentrated, sending a series of images: a baby lying in an animal's feeding trough, a kind-eyed man in rough attire speaking to a crowd, healing them with words and power, the same man dying on a cross with a crown of thorns cutting into his head, blood dripping… and then, she showed an empty tomb and the man leaving it after rising from the dead.

Enoch's kythim flashed, triumphant. *That's Lord Yshua, our Redeemer.*

Annabelle quivered. "This is wonderful! Your 'Lord Yshua' is the same as my Jesus Christ. How cool is this? Even though we're from different worlds, we have the same faith."

Excitement crackled like lightning between them. Annabelle marveled that their entwined kythim allowed for an effortless, swift, and silent exchange of imagery and ideas.

"These kythim thingies must give us telepathy," she said. "Or something like it. Kythim are the tendrils of our thoughts. Thought-tendrils." She pulsed with amusement again, and then an effusion of something warmer. "Oh, I'm so glad to meet you, Enoch. It's weird, but I feel as if I've always known you."

Maybe it's these dreams we've been sharing. Determination rose in her like water filling a cup. *I don't want this to stop.*

Enoch glowed steadily, emanating the same warmth. "I feel like I've always known you, too. After everything that's happened, this is an unexpected… pleasure."

An understatement; Annabelle read his mind like a book. He likened meeting her to coming out of the snow after a hard day's training and basking in the warmth of the Lilac Manor kitchen's hearth, drinking chocolatl or hot cider with Simon and the other young troopers. Or curling up in his bed, listening to a thunderstorm rage while he lay snug and safe inside, listening to Verbena Fourtier read a bedtime story by candlelight and watching the familiar shadows dancing across the walls. Or even studying baronial law in Sir Rick's office while his guardian went over the ledgers, looking up to relate an amusing anecdote from his own childhood.

Annabelle observed these thought-images, musing to herself. *Those people… I want to meet them. I wish I could visit his world.*

Enoch did not respond to her idle thought. He dimmed, pushing the memories away. "Those times are past and gone. As Commander Storm would say, I can't afford to indulge in sentiment. Not when I have my duty to accomplish. Not even in this strange, in-between place of star-crazed blackness and glowing thought-tendrils."

Annabelle sent a ripple of sympathy, reassuring him with her presence. "Don't shut down. You're so sad. I can tell something's wrong. Is there anything I can do to help?"

Enoch flickered, dark patches roiling over the glowing orb of his presence. He showed her, in glimpses, his original purpose in entering the Darkenwood Forest before he'd contacted her. He sought four missing people. Silently, he framed questions and pictured each of them in his mind. First came three girls, his playmates and friends, whom he'd known for as long as he remembered, as far back as his childhood memories extended. Becky, Janet, and Sally—she saw them, and how much he cared for them. Like sisters, except for Becky, for whom he'd felt something different; Annabelle suppressed a knowing smile. *Enoch has a crush on the pretty, dark-haired girl.*

Sir Thomas was another matter; difficult to envision because Enoch barely knew the man. His entire recollection of Sir Thomas was the way the knight's unsettling gaze—his eyes a pale blue as distant as the winter sky—pierced him when they met.

Annabelle understood. "No," she replied, the pulsing of her blue kythim subdued. "I'm so sorry, Enoch, but I haven't seen those three girls, or a guy with cold eyes."

She frowned; something pulled her away. She felt her grip slipping again, despite the woven tapestry of their kythim. A vast gulf yawned, dark and terrible, separating their corporeal beings. The bright orb shrank into a tiny silver dot, a single star among billions scattered across the heavens. Sapphire light surrounded her as she plummeted backward through an impossibly glowing tube with white streaks like star-lines when the Millennium Falcon went into hyper-drive. *A wormhole?*

Her stomach lurched. Fear crystallized her insides. Where was she going now? *Oh, crap, this isn't a dream, it's all really real—*

Enoch howled from across the void. "Annabelle, come back!"

She reached for him, but he was gone. Gasping for breath, head spinning, she sat on the floor propped against her bed and stared at her mirror. It reflected the ceiling and nothing more.

Enoch howled into the void. "Annabelle, come back!"

But she was gone. Again.

The ground shifted beneath his feet, and he stumbled, falling on his backside with a pained grunt. He blinked away the reversed afterimages of lights floating across his vision and stared at the blank, gray expanse of the Wall. His head reeled. What had happened to him?

"Kid!"

Startled, he flung up his arm in a defensive gesture—but it was only Toad, who hunkered under a large blue mushroom. The amphibian's pale eyes bulged out farther than usual. He stammered a blistering oath.

Enoch winced. "Wow, Toad. I hope you don't kiss your mother with that mouth. What's your problem?"

Toad closed his eyes and sighed. "After standing there and staring for hours into that glowing thing, not hearing a friggin' word I say, the kid asks me what my problem is."

Enoch frowned. "What do you mean? I went someplace else. You weren't—" He cut himself off, eyes widening as they took in the sky. "Wait, did you say *hours*?" The quality of light had changed since his journey to the starry void where he'd met Annabelle. Klotho had set, Lachesis had slipped behind the trees, and the bloody disk of Atropos had slid toward the Eastern horizon.

"Blood and offal. Is it that late already?"

Toad cast him a long-suffering look.

"Perdition and bloody offal!" Enoch cursed again.

Toad smirked. "Wow, kid. Do you kiss your mother with that mouth?"

Enoch dove into the passage underneath the colony bushes. "Sorry, Toad, can't talk now. I've got to go!"

Tinker lurched up on his hooves with a grunt, harness bells jingling, just as Enoch burst out of the thicket. His large ears pricked and he snuffled at his master's belt-pouch. Enoch pulled out the drooping sprigs of the herb he'd gathered and fed them to his mount. Still reeling from his experience with the Wall and Window, he reattached the reins with shaking hands after Tinker swallowed his treat and then clambered up into the saddle.

"*Home*, Tinker. Go home!"

The stag pranced for a moment, sniffed the air, swiveling his ears. He seemed spooked, but not enough to flee in panic. Had Tinker scented or heard something odd?

Enoch drew in a calming breath and shut his eyes. He employed the trick he'd discovered several moons ago: his knack for hearing far-off sounds. But the gloaming lament of the nightingales and whippoorwills flooded his senses.

He grit his teeth, held the reins slack, and waited for Tinker to gain his bearings. He trusted his mount; the wensallen-kaenim who'd bred him had trained him well. If any real peril lurked in the vicinity, his mount would react.

After a moment of stamping with nothing attacking them, Tinker set off along the trail back the way they'd come. Before long, the well-rested stag bounded East along the packed dirt road beneath the shadowy canopy of tall trees.

His mind full of excitement and unanswered questions, Enoch clung to his mount the entire way home, the breath of the dying day whipping with the force of a gale into his face.

A BIT OF CONJURING

As soon as the young man and his stag were out of earshot, William puffed out a sigh of relief. He released his death-grip on the talisman hanging from his neck. *That was close.* Burning suns above! If the beast scented him even through his arkhabala's camouflage, it would have given everything away. His master would flay him alive if he mucked this up.

One hand braced against the tree, he rose to his feet. *It's too blazing hot for cloaks.* He pushed back the hood to peer more closely at the tangled brush. The other young man had emerged from under the bush and then fled on his mount.

But not in fear. No jagged, bright yellow lines sparked from the youth's kythim, only orange spirals twirling in the glowing silver aura. He'd merely been eager to leave, as if late for an appointment.

How very interesting. A glowing silver aura. Could the youth be a wyldling? William smirked. The scroll the Dreadlord gave him concerning the Aethyr had proven quite useful.

William stepped forward and met with a mild resistance as the avoidance field of the ward-spell pressed against his body. The tension grew much stronger if he approached whatever lay beyond the dense stand of bushes. It wouldn't allow him to get close enough to see anything of genuine interest; the field may become an impregnable wall, or it could allow some progress and then expel him. It might even harm him, or at least cause great discomfort. Even now, his skin prickled, itching as if unseen insects crawled over him.

No matter what it did to him, William must try to penetrate the warding field. Otherwise, he'd be punished for shirking. Or perhaps malingering. His master's reasons for the discipline he meted out were often vague.

William rubbed his long-fingered hands over his arms and considered his options. His master ordered him to discover the reason behind the sudden diminishment of the impenetrable ward-spell enveloping much of the Darkenwood Forest and—if possible—whatever the ward-spell concealed. He dared not return to his master without something substantial to report, not so soon following his previous muck-up.

He rolled his eyes. "Yes, Master Tenebris," he said in falsetto. "I saw a boy riding away on a courier beast. No, I don't know how, in the blistering blazes, he penetrated the field. I didn't ask him. Please, please don't whip me again!"

Sneering, William drew a flask out from underneath his cloak and took a swig. Pungent liquor burned pleasantly down his throat. Thus fortified, he took another step forward. His nose plastered against an unseen force. He retreated and rubbed the offended organ. That answered his question. The warding hadn't collapsed. Its boundary had shrunk.

Vurkhelli's hairy ears! He'd need to set up another series of telltale alarms. But first, he had another idea to test.

He patted his robes. Yes, he kept everything he needed secreted away inside the pockets of his sakkhelt, the linen sash every Arkhadahn wore under his robe containing charm and spell components. With a cry of triumph, he extracted a spool of thin twine. He gathered up a small pile of branches and stones and then tied the loose end of the twine around one stone.

Nausea roiled his stomach as he sliced the pad of his thumb with a blade fashioned from a human thigh bone. He used his blood as ink to scribe symbols on the forest detritus he'd chosen to serve as his proxies. As he intoned a guttural phrase, he daubing a rune on his forehead with his bloody thumb. Energy hummed through his arkhabala and snapped into place.

William unraveled a length of twine from the spool and swung his missile around and around, gathering momentum until he let it fly toward the invisible barrier. The stone struck the ward in a flare of bright orange light and then rebounded to strike his forehead while still containing all the force with which he'd swung it.

William blinked up at the red-streaked sky and wondered how he'd ended up lying on the ground with his cloak puddled around him. Pain lanced through his skull. He groaned, fingers fumbling in the folds of his cloak until they met his flask. This time, he took a hearty gulp. *Burning, blistering suns, that blazing hurt.* Gingerly, he probed the knot forming on his forehead. The stone had broken neither his skull nor his skin. With eyes closed, he muttered an incantation—one of the very first he'd learned—to bury pain and nausea. His proxy spell hadn't worked and he didn't care to repeat the violent results.

William smiled. He needed to try something else; use a method he'd developed on the sly. His master definitely wouldn't approve.

Even more reason to employ it. How the blazes would he even know I did it? There's no one else here to tattle on me.

He clenched his jaw against the pain he no longer felt and sat up, crossing his legs tailor-fashion in front of him. As he lurched upright, a sloshing, woozy sensation trembled in his skull, but it soon passed. He rooted through his pockets until he found a tiny pouch no larger than his thumb. It was full of kaiber powder. He trickled a line of the dark, gritty powder on the back of his left hand and then snorted it up one nostril.

His mind spun, rising above the haze of pain until it stilled. He peered out into a world filled with violet mist, shadows, and movement. He called it the shadow realm, and it showed him the happenings of the past several hours. The silver image of Northward left his mount, ducked, and crawled beneath a bush. William pursued him, latching on to the shadow-form of the boy. He met with resistance, but pushed through until he stood in a clearing, staring up at a soot-gray wall. It seemed more solid than anything else in the shadow realm. He looked into an abyss of sooty grayness, and then tore his eyes away before he spun off into oblivion—or before something looked back at him.

Threads of silver and blue lights swirling together without mixing spiraled into a gaping maw of blackness in the dark wall. He watched as a glowing violet thread burst from his shadow-form and plunged into the black pit. *Well, that's decidedly odd.*

Two disparate forces tugged him in opposite directions; the violet thread dragged him forward into the swirling pit while something else repelled him. His blood boiled.

It blistering *hurt*.

William swallowed an agonized scream, tore himself away from the vision, and fell out of the shadow realm. He lay on the ground, watching the world spin around him. He promptly turned on his side and vomited, missing his clothing with the precision of practice. With a moan, he rolled away from the mess he'd made and shut his eyes. Physical pain he could handle, either by embracing it or conjuring it away. However, the pain he'd just experienced had been something else.

Night descended while William recovered. Darkness held no concerns for him. After a fashion, he could see. He clutched at his head, throbbing in time with his heartbeat. He embraced the pain of his headache, as his master had taught him. Baring his teeth in a rictus of ecstasy, he picked up the remnants of his backfired spell. He scattered the stones he'd gathered along the perimeter of the warding. Tenebris would approve—not that he'd bother to leave his basement laboratory and examine his apprentice's work.

After further searching, William found the blood-encrusted rock and twine. He tucked them into his cloak. The other stones he marked should collect information for him in his absence. With the effects of the kaiber powder wearing off, he felt too ill to construct a reliable telltale to alert him to a human presence. He'd return on the morrow to do so after he rested himself and restored the energies in his arkhabala. It would be a prudent course of action. His master expected no less of him, especially considering what he'd winkled out.

Why had kadorei youth ventured into the warded glade—and how had he been able to enter? And what in blazes was that wall?

William glanced to the East, where the bloated third sun sank behind the trees. A smile spread across his face. "I mean to find out. He'll be back. And so shall I."

RETURN TO LILAC MANOR

Atropos hovered above the Eastern horizon when Tinker dashed through the Westgate. The calm evening breeze ruffled Enoch's hair, bringing him the cool, pleasant scent of lilacs flanking the courtyard.

Enoch reined in Tinker and his gasping mount skidded to a halt. He frowned. *Why is the portcullis raised?* And then, a voice hailed him in a pleasant-sounding tongue like a ruby-throated lyreling's rippling notes.

Shock ripped through Enoch, chased by cold fear. His heart pounded against his breastbone. He spun toward the gatekeeper's booth. Framed by the doorway, Lance-sergeant Ravenos stood at attention, his uniform impeccable. A feral glint in the man's eyes set the hairs on the back of Enoch's neck to prickling. He'd not seen the man since their altercation on the caravan route two evenings ago. Ravenos made his skin crawl.

Enoch wanted nothing more than to get away from the penetrating gaze, but he couldn't run off like a scared little boy. He sat up taller. *I'm the acting baron-knight.* He tried to speak nonchalantly, but the words came out harsh and brittle. "Why does the gate stand open? And where is the other gatekeeper?"

Ravenos saluted stiffly, ugly emotion flitting across his countenance. "I opened it only moments ago in the hopes of your return, sir. Sergeant Matlock, he attends to a call of nature, sir. Something he ate, it disagrees with his belly."

Well, that explains it, then. But Enoch couldn't shake his uneasiness. He grasped the reins so tight his knuckles turned white. He bit off an order. "Close the gate, soldier."

He watched as the gatekeeper busied himself with lowering the portcullis against the falling night, waiting until the man was engaged with his task before sliding out of the saddle. *Doubtless, the man's wound still smarts and he chafes because of his demotion, nothing more.* But his suspicion remained that pure hatred burned inside Ravenos.

In the kitchen, women lay waiting in ambush like soot panthers. Verbena Fourtier, the doctor's assistant, and Marilla Mulgrove, the housekeeper, jumped up from the tea-table to pounce on him the moment he came through the door. The head cook, Nancy Tellyson, was only a step behind them.

Tears streamed from red-rimmed eyes as the housekeeper clasped his face between her hands. "Praise Yshua, you're alive! You've been gone all day; we've been so worried. Jude Higgins is in deep disgrace for letting you out of the gate unescorted and the seneschal's still out looking for you. Land sakes! You must be starving, Enoch. I'll have Nancy whip up something for you—"

"He's too old for that, Marilla," Verbena said, tugging on the other woman's arm. "And call him 'sir'; he's the master, now." But the brightness in her eyes and trembling in her gentle voice betrayed her concern.

"Nonsense. He'll always be our little dartling jay—"

His cheeks burning under her palms, Enoch blurted out, "Yes, Mrs. Mulgrove. Food would be appreciated. Thank you."

Mrs. Mulgrove turned to issue orders, but Nancy already danced around the kitchen gathering ingredients to prepare something suitable for a baron-knight's dinner.

"Bread and cheese is fine," he called to her, but she ignored him. The other two women fussed over him, making him sit at the table despite his protests.

Enoch smoothed a scowl from his forehead. What good was it being a baron-knight if nobody listened to you? He'd wager Sir Rick never needed to put up with this. And now, Higgins was in disgrace on his account.

Verbena prepared a cup of tea him while Mrs. Mulgrove rattled on concerning the woes that could have befallen "her dartling jay" and how glad she was—praise Yshua again and again—he'd come home safe and unscathed. Beige cheeks darkening, Verbena tried to hush the other woman. She stirred in a splash of cream and a generous dollop of lavender honey and handed it to him.

Enoch sipped; the tea tasted bittersweet. The honey jar was stamped with the Pines family mark. *What would Janet think of your efforts to find her today?*

He wanted to swallow his guilt with the tea, but it burned like gall in his throat. He cleared his throat. "No, Mrs. Mulgrove," he interjected, striving for the calm, measured tone of authority Sir Rick used. He never had trouble quelling the garrulous housekeeper. "Everything was fine. I didn't encounter any bandits, evil sorcerers, or sinkhole sands in the Darkenwood Forest. No lykharim or soot panthers from beyond the Veil, either. There wasn't even any itchweed." He took a drink. Hungry or not, he needed to get away from them. "Now, ladies, if you'd please excuse me, there are important matters I must attend to—" And then, his stomach decided to growl.

Mrs. Mulgrove adopted a no-nonsense look. "Dartling—excuse me—Sir Enoch, it's best you eat something and then take yourself to bed. Verbena, don't you agree it's best?" Nodding, the other women looked into her tea with a wry smile. "Yes, I'll have Sylvie bring a tray up to you for supper, once Nancy—ah! Never mind, here it is." Nancy slid a steaming plate in front of Enoch and, smiling apologetically, handed him a napkin.

"And then," the housekeeper continued, "you should get some shut-eye. Almighty willing, things will look brighter in the morning." Her tone softened, and she patted his hand. "They always do."

Enoch managed a smile. *Oh, please, Lord Yshua, let her shut up so I can eat in peace.*

Mrs. Mulgrove opened her mouth to launch into another stream of platitudes, but Verbena cleared her throat. "Marilla, dear," she said, placing a hand on her wrist. "Before he retires, I must assess our baron-knight's health. If you could please grant us some privacy?"

"Oh, dearie me, yes," the housekeeper replied. "I just remembered; Sylvie needs to be trained to clean the baths. If you will excuse me, Dart—I mean, Sir Enoch?"

Enoch nodded. "Good night, Mrs. Mulgrove. And good night," he added to the cook, who stood beside them awaiting further orders. She bobbed a curtsy and left through the servants' door. He held his breath until Mrs. Mulgrove curtsied and then bustled out the swinging doors leading into the Manor's dining hall.

Verbena raised a hand to cover her grin. "Go on, dear, eat. My 'assessment' can wait; I'll not come between a hungry adolescent and his food."

Enoch breathed a brief prayer of thanksgiving and tucked into his meal—a warm pastry crust filled with onions, sausage bits, scrambled eggs, and cream cheese. One of Sally's cream cheeses? He envisioned her round face, lit up with an expectant smile as he sampled her hard work from the dairy. His grip tightened on his fork.

I didn't find them. I must try harder tomorrow.

Tears filled his eyes and spilled over, dripping off his nose. Salt to season the crumbs left on his plate. Furiously, he wiped his face with the napkin, and then pulled it away to look at it more closely. There, in one corner, the weaver had stitched her symbol. A cart's wheel.

Becky wove the linen for these napkins. Lil' Becky Rosa, with yellow roses in her hair, her dark eyes shining in the torchlight. Dancing. Would she still believe he resembled King Gideon if she saw him now?

Enoch shuddered; the napkin crumpled in his hand. *I will find you—I promise!*

A warm hand rubbed his shoulder. Verbena's low voice said, "It's all right." She put an arm around him. Turning, he buried his face in her apron smocking, and inhaled through his nose. His nose filled with the sharp scent of healing herbs.

His throat grew thick as the icy claws tightened. "Oh, little mother," he choked out. Despite the tea he'd drunk, his throat felt scratchy and dry.

Verbena's arms drew him close, but they seemed smaller and frailer than when he was a child. He clung to her anyway. "It's all right," she crooned. "Everything will be all right."

CHASING AFTER THE WIND

ENOCH VERSUS THE TORNADO

Enoch smiled; everything was as it should be. The comforting clutter of Sir Rick's office surrounded him. Through the blinds, Klotho's light cast everything in a silver-white glow. Violet tinged the sunslight. The aging warrior sat behind his cherry-wood desk, looking just as he remembered. Enoch's heart filled with joy. Sir Rick was alive! He suppressed the urge to throw his arms around the man.

I'm too old for such childish displays.

The baron-knight bent over his marshals' reports on the realm's readiness for war. Enoch blinked in confusion. *The Northern Marches aren't at war with anyone.*

Still perusing the document, Sir Rick said in his gruff voice, "Don't go borrowing trouble, lad. Concentrate on the task in front of you."

"What task is that, sir?"

The baron-knight glanced up from a parchment written in Marshal Ventrude's heavy-handed scrawl. He looked weary and haggard. For an instant, his eyes flashed with violet light before returning to their familiar warm brown color.

"Cross the Void-Bridge. Bring back the Weaver of Water. Tehara's future depends on it."

"Void-Bridge. Weaver of Water. Got it, sir." He frowned, puzzled. "Wait. What're those?" But the details of the room and his guardian were fading away. The violet glow intensified. The liquid music of harpstrings rippled around him, cool as springtime rain. *Where is the music coming from—and where is Sir Rick? Is any of this real?*

"Wait!" Enoch hated the panicked, reedy quality of his voice. Tears stung his eyes as he reached out for the vapor-thin image of his guardian. "Sir, come back, please! I miss you. Sir Thomas is gone, and I don't understand what you want me to do."

The old knight's voice lingered, a ghostly whisper. "Cross the Void-Bridge. Bring the Weaver of Water." A pause. "What is the ultimate duty of a baron-knight?"

Icy claws grasped Enoch's throat as he responded. "The innocent must be protected."

"And how," prompted the fading remnant of the beloved voice, "does one do this?"

"By seeking justice. Showing mercy. And walking humbly with Lord Yshua."

Enoch stood before the Wall, wiping tears from his eyes. An oval portal whirled and shimmered, molten silver in a heated crucible. It solidified, forming layered ridges like flower petals closed into a bud.

Argent light burned through the cracks. And then the petals burst open into sword blades swirling out from a center of blazing light.

Is this the Void-Bridge?

Enoch plunged through the gap created by the steel flower's opening petals. There was a blue light shining in the distance as he sped along the tunnel. He must reach the source of the sapphire gleam before it was too late.

He lurched sickeningly. The tunnel with the blue light at the end of it warped, stretched like warm taffy, and then skittered out of view. Blinded, he fell into a darkness beyond darkness. Strands like thin, muscular ropes seized him, entangling his limbs and torso.

Enoch struggled against the tendrils ensnaring him. One wrapped around his neck, icy as death. He gasped for breath. They tightened around his body and dragged him down…

Lord Yshua, save me!

Behind his breastbone, a steel flower spread open serrated petals to present a tall pistil shining with a harsh, argent glare. He reached inside his chest and grasped the hilt of a silvery sword. It burned with the deep cold of the Icemountain Wastes and the blistering heat of the suns. He pulled it out, screaming in agony. The blade flared bright in his hand, cutting away the void, slicing through the strands like a hot knife through butter. His bonds disappeared. Something gave voice to a brassy wail and then receded, disappearing into an incalculable distance.

Sword in hand, Enoch plunged through the shining tunnel. The silver light shifted to blue and brightened. He shut his eyes to avoid being blinded. When he opened them, he stood in a field filled with tall grass up to his knees. A glowing purple mist lurked beneath a row of birch and poplar trees. Beneath their boughs, a cloaked man played a stringed instrument. The silver sword pulsed in rhythm with the music.

This is so strange. Am I dreaming?

Enoch spun in a slow circle, taking in his surroundings. An amber twilight lay across the rest of the land. The yellow-green stalks of the grass stood upright and motionless in stark contrast to the dark and swollen underbellies of storm clouds churning overhead.

"Dream or not, I don't like the looks of those clouds," he murmured aloud. His sword thrummed an uneasy chord of agreement.

Enoch completed his circle and blinked. Nearby, a female figure stood with her back to him. Her face tilted toward the turbulent sky and golden hair plaited in a long tail tumbled past her waist. She turned as Enoch approached. Like him, she wore spectacles over her blue eyes. Her skin was pale as milk. Dimples formed on her cheeks and her pleasant features lit up when she smiled. The tension inside him eased.

It's her. Annabelle.

Wind roared in his ears. Lightning forked across the purple-gray sky and thunder cracked. The darkness above rotated counterclockwise in time with a sickening, tugging sensation in Enoch's gut. Behind him, the music's tempo grew frenetic and wild. Contempt built in the clouds even as the atmospheric pressure dropped.

He concentrated. Armor of molten jet and silver flowed over his clothing and a war cap of the same material covered his head. The sword vibrated in his hand in time with the music, but with a hungry edge. It wanted to hack and slash.

The funnel cloud came corkscrewing from the sky like a dirty gray snake. It reached for the girl. Smile fading to slack-jawed horror, she stared at the descending cyclone as if mesmerized. Her braid lifted above her head. Dust and stalks of grass spiraled around her. Although the wind's noise should have drowned it out, her voice screamed, clear as day, in his mind. "Tornado!"

No, you will not take her!

Enoch was already moving, blowing like a gale across the field, the grass bowing before him. His heart fluttered madly; a bird caged against its will. Armor and sword blazing with silver light, he vaulted into the air and flew at the twisting column of vapor and wind. The tempest's disgust for Annabelle's weakness writhed in his stomach.

It will destroy her if I don't beat it.

He whispered a prayer: "Almighty Threefold One, grant me the strength to defeat the storm and protect Annabelle."

Distracted from its intended prey, the tempest roared, winds snatching at Enoch. It tried to rip the sword from his hand, to beat it from his grasp, but the silver blade refused to surrender. Fluid and effortless, the sword seemed to move of its own accord, slashing through the funnel as Enoch circled around it in a clockwise direction.

I need to sever the main updraft, the largest airstream; that should kill it.

The tempest rumbled its frustration—as if it divined his plan—but the grasping winds couldn't touch him in his own isolated airstream. He ascended, his blade slicing up the cloud while his flying disrupted the cyclone's updraft, starving it of energy. The cyclone died away with a sulky growl. The dark clouds vented their wrath in a downpour of water.

Enoch ducked his head with a cry of disgust to keep his spectacles from getting wet as raindrops hammered against his armor. Below him, Annabelle skipped around in a circle, sodden braid bouncing. Dark blue armor of a style similar to his own now covered her clothing. Lines of sapphire light danced in swirling patterns across the armor plating. Unperturbed by the soaking, she sang a child's rhyme. "Rain, rain, go away, come again some other day." The deluge slackened to a sprinkling and then ceased altogether. So did the lights in her armor. She looked up at him and waved, her smile like the suns coming out after a rainstorm.

Still aloft, Enoch waved back, grinning. The storm was over. *It's wonderful up amongst the clouds. This is where I belong.* "Now, to make sure this cloud's not able to cause further mayhem." He darted like a damselfly, dissecting the thunderhead. It collapsed into quivering pale gray mounds that looked like soiled sheep. Shafts of buttery sunlight broke through the overcast.

Enoch frowned, hovering with his arms akimbo. "I think I'd prefer a sunny day to this gloom. Let's send this flock to a more distant pasture!" He sucked in a deep breath and then exhaled a great wind to drive the rest of the clouds away. While the fleecy masses sped away, he examined his sword. The blade hummed with satisfaction, its double edges gleaming.

"You're an excellent sword," he said. "And an excellent sword needs a name. I think I'll call you Windblade." The hilt thrummed happily against his palm and then went silent. Enoch smiled. "Glad you approve. Now, how and where do I sheathe you?" In response, Windblade disappeared. He laughed, wiping his empty hands together. "Problem solved."

Enoch retracted his helm. He stretched his arms over his head and scanned the heavens. A single yellow sun shone. *That's odd*, he thought. *Lachesis is never alone. Where are Klotho and Atropos?*

Annabelle laughed. "You won't find them here. Earth only has one sun."

One moment, Enoch was in the air, and the next, he stood in the field near the young woman. Soft music drifted from the direction of the trees.

Eyes bright, she ran up to him. "Wow, that's incredible! You really are a knight in shining armor. My Silver Knight. Thank you for saving me. I know this is only a dream, and I've had lots of dreams about tornados before, but I've never been close to one." Chattering away, she brushed dead leaves off a pauldron and plucked a twig out of his hair—how did it get through his helm? The top of her head only came up to his chin.

It's nice to find someone shorter than me, even if she speaks of strange things.

Annabelle gestured at the sky. "I didn't know a tornado could be stopped. It must be cool to fly. I wonder if I can do it, too?"

"I suppose anything is possible in dreams," he said, rubbing the back of his neck. He felt the collar of his jacket and realized his armor had gone the way of Windblade. "And the rain was rather chilly until you put a stop to it. We make a good team."

Annabelle flashed a shy grin at him. "Yeah, we do. It's so awesome to be here, in the sun, with you and away from the blah wintertime. I believe I can fly," she sang, spinning. She ran a few paces and then sprang into the air. She rose several feet, but then at once descended. As her feet touched the ground, her armor changed back into her previous clothing and her golden hair lay dry on her back. She laughed; her cheeks flushed. "Too bad. Probably just as well. I'm afraid of heights. I guess I'll leave the flying to you, Enoch."

He watched her antics, smiling. Annabelle was different from the few girls he'd known growing up in Lilac Grove. Where her peculiarities because of the dream or because she came from another world? He shook his head and replied, "And I'll leave stopping the rain to you."

"Speaking of the weather," she said, "now it's cleared up, we should go for a walk." She took his hand, and his fingers interlocked with hers, as naturally as their kythim had twined together in the starry void place. Enoch hadn't held a girl's hand since he'd danced with Becky Cartwright at the Light of the World Festival. Unlike then, he wasn't on fire and quivering inside. Not around Annabelle.

Images and thoughts flowed like water from Annabelle's mind into his. The field they walked through belonged to her maternal grandfather. He saw the man through her mind's eye, followed by her maternal grandmother, and then her paternal grandparents—all four still alive— as well as the rest of her extended family, singly and in groups, portraits speeding by and then fading into mist; a veritable clan! Annabelle sat with her parents and two younger siblings in the last portrait. Enoch's heart clenched painfully around the empty place where his own forgotten family should be.

Where Sir Rick had been.

"Oh, Enoch," she murmured, tears in her eyes. "He was like your dad, wasn't he? I'm so sorry for your loss. It's okay to cry. You need to mourn."

She's right. She knew what he needed. Unable to thank her aloud—the claws squeezed his throat again—he sensed she understood. Because they were together in the dream, she understood everything.

Minor strains of string music rolled over him in a melancholy fog. Once more, Peter told him of Sir Rick's death. The seneschal read the parchment from the message tube, his claws digging into it. Enoch remembered telling him to tear the message apart because facing the news in print was unbearable, Red insisting he must read it soon. He curled up under pine trees on a carpet of orange needles, weeping. Annabelle knelt beside him and put her arms around his shoulders.

If his mentor, Commander Storm, could only see him now. Crying like a baby in a maiden's arms. Enoch would never live it down; the commander claimed a true warrior never shed tears for the fallen. Women and children wept; baron-knights did not. Sir Rick had always been steady—solid as a rock. Surely, he'd never cried like Enoch did now.

Once he returned from the Eastern Marches, Commander Storm would knock such maudlin nonsense right out of him. He'd work Enoch to the bone and keep him too busy to grieve for his dead guardian, wonder about his lost family, or think about girls from Earth. Agonized shock spread like hoarfrost throughout his insides. If Commander Storm had his way, then he'd never see Annabelle again!

She rested her forehead against his and he breathed in the warm scent of her tears. "It's okay," she said, her voice quavering. Her arms tightened around him. "It's okay for men to cry. Even Jesus wept, sometimes."

Enoch clung to her, tears stinging his cheeks. Once more, he saw the parchment in Red's hands, the anger in the seneschal's expression. "But I feel so lost, Annabelle. Why did Sir Rick have to die? I still need him. He's the closest thing to family I had."

"I'm here. I'll always be here for you. If you need a family, then I will be your sister."

Enoch sniffled. "Always wanted a sister. Felt wrong, growing up without one."

Annabelle chuckled through her tears. "And I always wanted a brother who wasn't an annoying brat." She leaned back and wiped her nose on her sleeve. "What's that paper you keep picturing in your mind? I understand it's a message associated with Sir Rick and you dread it, but what does it say?"

Shame swept over his face in a scalding rush. "I don't know. Red wanted me to look at it then, but I couldn't. I'm still afraid to find out."

Annabelle stared off into space, biting at her lower lip. "It's a painful reminder, so you've been avoiding it. I totally understand that. But if you want my advice, I'd tell you to bite the bullet and read the darn thing. It's probably important stuff you need to know to do your job. Sir Rick is already dead and you're the baron-knight now. Whatever's written is in the past. At this point, what's the worst thing it can say?"

Enoch sat up and leaned against the tree. He tipped his head back and closed his eyes. For a moment he comprehended Red's confusion concerning Tradespeak idioms: he'd no idea what a bullet was or why anyone wanted to bite one. Oh well; he figured Annabelle knew best.

"Of course, I know best," Annabelle teased. "I'm the smart one."

Enoch chuckled. "You certainly are. All right, I'll read it." He felt much better, lighter, having resolved to read the message. The distant music changed from a funeral dirge to something in a major key. He hummed along to the tune.

Annabelle took his hands and pulled him up to his feet. They danced under the dark green boughs of the pine trees, their feet silent against the thick carpet of dead pine needles. And then they were floating off the ground, shooting into the canopy. Annabelle's grip tightened and apprehension flashed across her face.

"Trust me," Enoch said, pulling her close against his side, one arm around her waist. "I won't let you fall. There's no reason to be scared; this is a dream, remember?"

Annabelle offered a wan smile and wrapped her arms around him as he carried them over the treetops. "Okay, just don't go up too high. Does everyone from Tehara know how to fly?"

Enoch paused in midair, taken aback. "Um, no. Not as such. So far as I know, only the seven Sages in the legendary tales could fly. And a few wyldlings."

He resumed his flight but held himself back out of concern for Annabelle. Otherwise, he'd be zipping around and pushing himself to find his limits. He swooped down over the field, buzzing the tallest grass, and then reascended. Annabelle clung tighter but made no other sign of distress.

"What's a weeld-ling?" she asked, sounding it out. "Is that what you call a person with superpowers in Tehara?"

Enoch considered her question as he touched down in the middle of the field. Fortunately, their interwoven kythim allowed him to discern her meaning more clearly. "According to the books I've read," he replied, "wyldlings were powerful. Lord Evanrudhe says wyldlings were kadorei who tapped into the seven aspects of Aethyr: air, water, fire, stone, flesh, mind, and void. They cropped up now and then throughout history, but there's none around anymore. Only the dwelfnim still have Aethyric abilities, but those are relatively weak. I've heard bards sing great ballads about their deeds and exploits; I'm uncertain how much is fact and how much is fancy." He chuckled. "However, this is a dream, so we'll pretend we have powers like the wyldlings of legend." Was he forgetting something about wyldlings? No problem. Surely it didn't matter.

"Right," Annabelle said, smiling wryly. "But I still can't fly. Not even in a dream."

"You made the rain stop, though," Enoch pointed out. "I couldn't do it."

Hand in hand, they walked through the field, grass swishing around their legs. Grasshoppers sprang up into the warm air, and they chased the cloud of insects whirring toward the stand of birch and poplars, whooping and laughing. The sun sank behind the trees and the day grew old. A purple twilight spread in a mist across the land from beneath the row of trees, where the cloaked figure still strummed his instrument in the shadows. The grasshoppers disappeared into the violet mist. Everything beyond the line of trees grew dim and indistinct. Enoch and Annabelle staggered to a halt before the mysterious musician.

"That looks like a mandolin," Annabelle said in an absent tone. "But it's too big, bigger than an acoustic guitar."

The tall, cloaked figure turned to them, his fingers dancing over the strings. The violet glow suffusing the mist illuminated a broad smile gleaming like a crescent moon on a handsome, masculine face. "Greetings, children," he said in a deep, pleasant voice. "This instrument is called a lytarra. Her name is Lyrica, and my mother possessed her before she became mine. Would you like to hear a ballad about three wyldlings who crossed the Void-Bridge? It is my composition and completely true, I promise. I, myself, am eager to discover how it ends."

Enoch stepped between Annabelle and the man, who seemed

familiar. Where had he seen him before? He squared his shoulders. "Who are you and what are you doing in our dream?"

The man threw back his head and laughed. "Dear children, do you think the dreamscape belongs only to you? Hardly."

Enoch summoned Windblade. The sword thrummed dangerously in his hand. "Who are you?" he repeated, more firmly. "And why are you here?"

The man smiled. "Did my war-minded brother never see fit to warn you of me? I suppose he thought of protecting you. He always did play with his cards close to the chest. Pity." He flung off his cloak to reveal himself: a tall, handsome man with dark hair and lavender-gray eyes. Violet lights danced in their depths and sparked along the lines in his soot-colored, lamellar armor.

"I am the traveler of dreams," he proclaimed, "the questor of nightmares, the wandering bard who never leaves his prison. Now, attend, children. I shall sing you a lullaby to send you safely back to your beds." He sang a single, pure note of heart-rending beauty and then struck a dissonant chord on his lytarra. The instrument keened again like a girl weeping in pain. Annabelle fell away from Enoch, and everything dissolved into silver light.

STONE CIRCLES

William stood looking out the west-facing window of his tower as firstdawn broke. Silver light spread and Klotho sprang over the western horizon. The quickest of the three celestial sisters, one could observe the small white sun racing across the sky. As a lesson set for him by the Dreadlord, William had done this in the past for each of the three suns— noting the variations of their paths across the sky depending on the season.

But such isn't my business today. Tenebris insists I measure damage to the ward-spell rings. He grimaced, imagining the distance he must trek through the forest. Miles and miles. He wished his master would let him steal a mount from the kadorei garrison. It shouldn't be too difficult. Burning suns! Kadorei were stupid and unobservant; blistering easy to fool with a spell.

Tenebris, allow such an extravagance for his apprentice? Outer Darkness forfend! If William mucked up a disguising spell, they risked discovery. Never mind that William mastered a seventh order level glamourye in concealing the bloodthirsty assassin's trail of murder; Tenebris remained dissatisfied. And so, William must walk the entire circuit of ward-spell rings. Fortunately, his master didn't require him to complete the onerous task in one day.

Tenebris's response to his report about the boy in the glade was to send him out on this errand. "I don't care about a silly pile of rock, William," he'd said. "Indeed, as you say, this development makes our task easier. You have done well to bring me this information and shall be rewarded for your labors. However, we must know the extent of the barrier's failure, lest we be caught unawares if it replenishes itself and traps us before we complete our mission."

"Suns burn it to ash," William grumbled. "The reward of hard work is even more and harder work." After securing a rucksack containing needful items on his back, he descended from his tower and set out for the nearest ward-spell ring—a two-hour walk.

Upon reaching his goal, he wiped sweat from his brow and sighed. Twelve oblong, weathered, soot-gray stones festooned with lush green moss stood in a ring. A shiny, soot-stained puddle like dirty ice covered the ground in the center. A chilly frisson of unease quivered along William's spine at the sight of the rock formation.

He dropped the pack and hunkered beside one of the standing stones. He ran a fingertip along a vitreous streak. *The texture's similar to glass.* And then he grinned. *Must be the remains of the shattered spell crystal.*

Aside from this, the ward-spell stone circle resembled the waystone ring he and his master used in traveling to the Northern Marches from the Dreadlord's Fastness. He'd studied a scroll concerning waystones;

how they activated portals based on the positions of celestial objects. It also claimed an adept could open a way, but hadn't explained what type of adept. After reading *Concerning Wyldlings and the Sages' Artifacts of Power*, William ventured a guess—a wyldling.

William rose, brushing off the detritus clinging to his robes. *I'd wager the kadorei fool I saw yesterday hasn't the slightest inkling of what he is or what he can do.* Now, William would show Tenebris what he could do. If he'd calculated accurately, he won't need to walk the whole blistering circuit of the ward-spell rings.

He placed both hands on the stone and concentrated. *Yes!* Beneath the chill, energy tingled against his palms. Power. He grinned as sensations ran through him. His arkhabala rippled like a beast stretching after a nap. Power remained in the Aethyric gems embedded within the standing stones despite the central focus crystal's destruction.

Of course. Why wouldn't there be? It's similar enough to the waystone rings, which don't even have a central focus gem... William's eyes fluttered open. *Can it be?* Heart racing, he delved in deeper. Pressure built inside his skull and heat sizzled along his arkhabala. No stranger to pain, he pushed, insistent.

Suns burn you to perdition, Aethyr! I'm going to ferret out your secrets. Show Tenebris I'm not a useless apprentice.

Pain rose to a crescendo until white flashed across his vision. His arkhabala spasmed, then subsided into quivering. *The way out is through.* He pressed on. Something tore, and he went through, floating like a cloud and untethered from pain's immediacy. He gazed at the colorful patterns displayed before him in a jeweled tapestry. Strands of light reminiscent of kythim connected to incandescent nodes of power.

Yes! As he suspected, the ward-spell was a small-scale version of the waystone spell—but inverted to repel sentient beings instead of forming conduits between linked circles. The linkages were intact. Each stone circle still communicated with its neighbor to either side—albeit weakly—an echo of the fallen barrier.

Specialized circles of focus crystals, linked in a series…

William hovered over the bejeweled landscape, exploring how the Aethyr connection spell functioned. Simple enough, if different from an Arkhabadh spell. He saw how to use the defunct ward-spell rings; by tapping into the link connecting them, he could examine the damage to every stone circles at once.

Certainly, it would be nice to not have to walk the breadth of the entire forest and still provide a satisfying report for his master. However, William sensed further potential residing in the spell-rings. He wanted to adapt them for his own purpose.

Too bad I can't set up a large-scale surveillance spell like the linked ward-spell circles.

The idea came to him in a flash, jostling him loose from his heightened awareness. He could! Dare he—a nehmwight and trained in the ways of the Arkhabadh—meddle with constructs built from the Aethyr? He steadied himself, weighing the costs and benefits.

Tenebris wanted a report. Well, he'll give him his burning report, but he wasn't traipsing all over the blistering forest like Tenebris intended him to. No, as the Dreadlord always said, one must accomplish one's goal in the most efficient manner possible.

William stooped like a hawk and tangled the colorful skeins of his spell-thread prey in his talons. Energy pulsed through his arkhabala, overloading it, and scalding him. *Is this what sunslight feels like to a normal nehmwight?* With a soundless scream, he impressed his desires on the jeweled tapestry. It seemed the correct thing to do. Pain, pain, and more pain. And then, everything went violet. He drifted, marveling as the violet light outlined features of the spell.

His voice echoed across the glowing tapestry. "It doesn't hurt anymore."

William spun, examining his adjustments. Elation filled him; his changes melded seamlessly with the workings of the original spell. Now, he should test the results. As he completed his circuit, he tugged a violet strand connecting him to the bright nodes of power.

Pain exploded, and the violet-limned vista disappeared. He collapsed against the monolith in the forest clearing, his arkhabala prickling pins and needles. The roughness of his robe scratched his skin as he convulsed. When the fit subsided, he slumped, exhausted, a gnawing hunger hollowing out his gut.

Birds twittered overhead, louder than usual, and the bright sunslight penetrating the canopy stabbed his eyes. The melange of late spring forest odors assaulted his nostrils. He triggered a cantrip to suppress an urge to vomit. His arkhabala throbbed, igniting fire across his shoulders, but his nausea vanished.

Muttering curses, William squinted against the glare and dug through his pack for the food he'd brought. He breathed in the appetizing scent of bacon before devouring the meat.

He was halfway through bolting his meal when the realization came to him. Eyes widening, he froze mid-chew. Not once did the spell require the use of his blooding knife. Not once had he tapped into the Arkhabadh for strength. It should be impossible for a nehmwight, and yet… he woven a spell using the Aethyr.

FRIENDLY ARGUMENT

The aroma of breakfast tea, sweet rolls, and bacon roused Enoch from the murky depths of sleep. An insistent voice and jostling motion hastened his awakening. His eyelids lifted. A white-furred hand on his chest shook him.

Enoch brushed the hand away, wishing himself back in the dream with Annabelle, where he could fly. He yawned and sat up, rubbing sleep-grit from his eyes. "G' morrow, Red."

The seneschal dipped his head and saluted Enoch with his right fist against his chest. In the early morning light, the monocle sitting over his left eye glinted. the kaenhir had opened the drapes before rousing him from his slumber. He replied in his native tongue. "Good morrow, young knight." With his eyebrows raised, he plucked a watch on a silver chain out of his waistcoat pocket and added, "It is half-past six of the clock. Your servant has brought your breakfast."

Enoch grunted, emerging from the dissipating fog of the dream. He blinked at his companion. "Huh?" And then he fastened on to Red's last comment. "Breakfast?"

"Yes. The tray is on your writing desk."

Red stood at attention beside his bed with a leather document case tucked under his left arm. As befitted the seneschal of the realm, he wore coal-dark trousers, a dove-tailed jacket, and a black silk waistcoat over his starched, collared tunic. A white neckcloth at his throat was knotted thrice in a simple pattern with the ends tucked into his waistcoat.

Red's wearing a cravat. It must be Chapelday. Or "Cravat-day," as Simon calls it. Blood and offal! I hate wearing cravats.

Red regarded him sternly, his eyes hard as emeralds. "The Chapel service begins at half-past seven. Rise now, or you will be late. Tardiness is of the devil."

With a groan, Enoch pushed away the bedclothes and rolled out of bed. He staggered over to the desk and attacked his breakfast. He grimaced at the bitterness of tea deficient in the honey and cream department, but he choked it down. A man needed his wits about him, and his head swirled with dream vapor remnants. As he chomped crispy bacon, he wondered why Red acted so extraordinarily disapproving and grave.

Chapelday's his favorite day of the week. Has somebody misplaced the employment records again, or have I forgotten another of his silly appointments? Oh, no...

He choked on his sweet roll as memories of yesterday's events slammed home with the force and subtlety of one of the commander's roundhouse blows. His venture into the Darkenwood Forest. Higgins's disgrace because of Enoch's dishonesty. The unsettling confrontation with Ravenos and the bloom of fear in his gut.

Chagrin and faint stirrings of anger filled him—a sour combination. Scowling, he muttered. "What else am I forgetting?"

Red tsked and shook his head. He drummed his nails against the document case. "Yesterday, at one of the clock, you were to speak with your servant about the ledgers." His accent grew thicker. "This one has been saying before, Enoch: you must make greater efforts to remember your duties."

What's he saying—I don't know my responsibilities? Angry heat rose, replacing his chagrin. Enoch shot to his feet. "That's what I was doing. Those lost girls won't find themselves! Sir Rick used to lead patrols into the Darkenwood Forest whenever there were reports of bandit activity."

Eyes narrowed, the seneschal raised a hand, extending two fingers and the thumb. "Three facts your servant feels compelled to point out." He responded, folding one of his fingers. "First fact: Sir Frederick was a grown man. Lord Commander did not give the explicit order to the baron-knight that he never step foot within the Darkenwood Forest until he deemed him ready to face its perils." Red folded another finger. "Second fact: Sir Frederick told his servant where and when he was going someplace. He knew the schedule to fulfill his many obligations." Red folded in the thumb to form a fist; Enoch understood the symbolism. "And the last fact: Sir Frederick never ventured into such a dangerous place alone without a proper escort."

Enoch averted his gaze. "I wasn't alone. I had Tinker."

Red furrowed his brow. "Your mount is not sufficient protection. You said these words yourself: The baron-knight 'used to lead patrols into the Darkenwood.' In the case your memory is deficient, Enoch, a patrol is always a group of warriors—no matter the language one speaks."

Enoch stalked past Red and snatched his spectacles from the top of the bureau. "I have two points to match your three facts. In the first place, I can defend myself. In the second, I saw nothing even remotely dangerous out there—no bandits, lykharim, or soot panthers. Not even itchweed." He crammed the spectacles onto his face and spun, hands fisted at his sides, to yell at Red's back. "And—and—besides, what baron-knight beggaring cares about the silly ledgers when there's people missing who're supposed to be under his protection?"

A ringing silence followed. Chin raised, the seneschal stiffened and clasped his hands behind his back. He did not turn.

Enoch froze and held his breath. Had he gone too far? He stared at Red's fingers, tightly curled above a tail standing out rigid and quivering. Even the copper-colored queue tied with black ribbons and hanging down his back seemed to bristle.

It's not too long since Red last switched my bottom for such impertinence.

The seneschal laid his ears back. He spoke softly, but distinctly, in Tradespeak. "Your servant recalls this: along with Sir Thomas, it is your dear friends who are missing. You are stretched out and wrung over from the worries for them." He pivoted on his heel and pierced Enoch with his emerald glare. "Therefore, he chooses to forgive you—as Lord Yshua does—for your rudeness."

Shame flared as burning embers against his skin, but he held the seneschal's gaze. "I apologize," he blurted. "I spoke from the seat of anger instead of reason. Thank you for being so gracious with me." He took a deep breath. "I've also wronged you by forgetting our appointment. And I shouldn't call the ledgers silly. And not including you in my, um, decisions yesterday. It won't happen again." He traced the sign of the cross over his heart.

In the pregnant silence that followed, the seneschal stood still and watched him without expression. At length, his whiskers twitched, and he smiled in the kadorei fashion, although he took care not to bare his teeth for longer than an eye-blink. He tapped his free hand in a fist against his chest again and dipped his head in a slight bow of acknowledgement.

"Very good. You have well learnt the lesson of honor. Know you, this one is forgiving you, Enoch, for any wrong you have done him."

Tension flowed out of him and he sighed in relief. "Thank you, Red."

The seneschal bowed. "You are most welcome, young knight. Of course, one would appreciate knowing about the great important thing in the Darkenwood Forest that displaced your duties here." He raised his eyebrows. "Perhaps your servant can assist you with the garments as you speak."

Grief stabbed Enoch with needle-thin blades. Before his investiture as the lord seneschal, Red served as the late baron-knight's valet, and Sir Rick upheld cravats and fancy jackets as part of the daily uniform. And, since Red agreed with Sir Rick in most everything…

Oh, well. I suppose this is my life, now—even if cravats are better repurposed as napkins or tea-towels.

Enoch sighed and ran a hand through his hair. "Okay, fine. I'll tell you. But it's strange. And, please, Red, remember: nothing terrible happened to me."

His lie of omission to Higgins haunting him, Enoch told Red everything he recalled of his adventures yesterday. Best to tell the truth; Red could sense when someone lied. He began with his original purpose of finding Sir Thomas and the girls. Certain Red wouldn't respond favorably to Toad or his experience beyond the Wall in the strange void place, he tried to paint everything with a palette of cheerful colors. He explained how the maiden he met in the void place, Annabelle, comforted him in his dream. He stressed her belief in the Threefold One—with Red, this should be a point in her favor.

The seneschal picked out a suitable jacket and helped Enoch tie his cravat. His canid visage gave away little of what he thought. "Very good, young master. After the Chapel service, your servant will have the matter of this wall and maidens from beyond the void investigated to his own satisfaction. He will go with you into the Darkenwood Forest."

As he entered the Chapel narthex, Enoch's gaze drifted toward the massive book resting upon a plinth. It contained records of every birth, marriage, baptism, and funeral service occurring within its hallowed walls, dating back before there had even been baron-knights of the Lilac Order. He recalled paging through it as a young child, searching for a mention of his family, but he'd never known the surname.

Sir Rick tried to help, but it's unlikely anyone documented my family in the book.

Only Commander Storm might have known who his parents were, but he claimed he found Enoch alone in the ruins of Nervashi—a garrison town at the foot of the Icemountain Wastes—too little to remember anything. Everyone else was dead.

Enoch's throat tightened. He glanced away from the book, only to meet the sympathetic gaze of Vicar Taggert, who stood at the door, greeting people.

Enoch forced a tight smile on his face as he nodded to the vicar, and they exchanged "good morrows." As soon as was polite, however, Enoch averted his gaze and stepped toward the sanctuary with the seneschal close behind him. *I should have arrived earlier and stood there beside the vicar, greeting everyone. Sir Rick would've done. Too late, now.*

As he hesitated on the threshold, Enoch noted everyone in the Manor had already arrived. A sea of voices murmured in the chamber and folks turned back to face the door. He fought back a flurry of anxiety. All those pairs of eyes locked upon him…

The old knight's voice whispered in his memory. *"Remember who and what you represent. Folks look to the man in authority to set the example."*

He heard the echo of his childish voice ask: "How do I set the example, sir?"

"Seek justice," the baron-knight said. "Show mercy. Walk humbly with Lord Yshua."

Yes. Time, now, to worship. With chin lifted and eyes fixed straight ahead at the altar and the crucifix, Enoch strode toward the empty pew in front of the chancel, reserved for the baron-knight, his immediate family, and any squires or apprentices.

He sat by himself now that Sir Rick was gone.

Enoch slid into the front-most pew, then sat with his back straight and his eyes fixed on the crucifix without seeing it. His mind drifted. A throat cleared, breaking the fog of his musings. He blinked and focused on the front of the chancel, where the vicar stood at the proclaimer station, hands clasped before him. The man swept his gaze around the sanctuary, no doubt assuring himself everyone was present and accounted for before he began. As if Sir Frederick jes Ursanovir still sat on the front-most bench beside Enoch, the vicar opened the service in the way he always did.

"Good morrow, my dear friends. In the name of the Almighty, the Threefold One: Father, the Son, and the Holy Counselor, amen."

After confessing his sins, Enoch went through the motions of worship, mouthing the responses by rote, his thoughts drifting far away. Caught upon a silver hook, they swirled in the wind deep into the Darkenwood Forest, through the tangled brush, and into the glade beyond. To the sooty gray Wall. There, the gleaming silver portal awaited him, and the star-streaked tunnel through the blackness where he'd met Annabelle.

Enoch's mind raced through everything she'd said, both in the void place and in their shared dream. He remembered her holding him while he wept, telling him he needed to confront… something.

Someone poked him. "Young knight," Red hissed into his ear. He jabbed his shoulder again for emphasis. "The Sacrament."

While his mind gathered wool, the worship service went on. The altar assistants stood on the chancel floor. The vicar beckoned him up to the altar railing for the Agape Feast. Everyone else waited on him—the baron-knight's heir—to lead the way. His cheeks mantled with scarlet flames, Enoch scurried to his place at the rail.

Please forgive me, Lord Yshua. I owe my life and salvation to you, and here I can't even pay attention when the vicar preaches your Word.

Red and the housekeeper knelt on either side of him. The assistants distributed the unleavened bread, followed by the wine, and the vicar spoke the words of institution over both. Vicar Taggert touched his shoulder before he passed down the line. Enoch tried to focus on the scripture verses; relief swept through him when they recessed to make room for the next wave of communicants.

Back in his pew, Enoch cast a surreptitious glance over his shoulder to gauge Red's reaction to his shameful behavior, but the seneschal had already moved to the rear of the sanctuary. He stood beside the door with his head bowed in prayer.

The lyrist struck a C-chord. Enoch started. *I've missed the benediction.* As the notes reverberated throughout the sanctuary, Red bowed to the vicar and slipped out. As soon as they shut, Vicar Taggert led the congregation in a hymn to close the worship service.

Ah, yes, the sound of singing voices overwhelms Red; I wish I could leave, too.

Enoch flinched at this uncharitable thought. *Sorry, Lord Yshua.*

Despite his own love of music and song, his lips hardly moved as the voices of the others surged around him in praise of the Almighty Threefold One. Since hearing of his guardian's death, he couldn't sing a note. The clawed fist of grief squeezed his voice into nothingness. Stricken, he stared at the crucifix with hands clasped tight and bloodless in his lap. He prayed while the others sang. "Lord Yshua, something is broken inside me. I can't praise you as I ought. Please, will you mend it?"

The musicians ceased to play, and the household staff filed out, but Enoch scarcely noticed. Tears dripped onto his white-knuckled hands, tracing lines of silver on his skin.

"Enoch, my boy."

A warm hand rested on his shoulder. Enoch glanced up through the silver haze and into a pair of kind brown eyes. The sanctuary was quiet and empty, save for the vicar and himself.

"You carry a heavy burden. Please, come and speak with me, and we'll see what we can do about lightening it."

In his closet-like office, Vicar Taggert gestured toward a pair of wooden armchairs with lilac-embroidered cushions facing each other. Enoch chose the one with a view of the doorway; Commander Storm told him never to sit with his back to an open door.

The vicar hung up his alb, settled into the other chair, and then offered a tray of fruit tarts to Enoch. Not wishing to speak right away, Enoch thanked him and selected a tart. He bit into it, and a melange of sweet and sour flavors exploded on his tongue. He devoured it. The vicar smiled as he ate, commenting wryly that Patsy included the tarts as part of her weekly offering.

"She makes great pastries," Enoch agreed, his mouth still full.

Vicar Taggert set the tray on the little table serving as his desk and gave his full attention to the youth. He crossed his left leg, resting the ankle against his right knee, and folded his hands over his belly. "I will dispense with the polite nothings and empty platitudes; you know I am a plain-speaking man who prefers to delve to the heart of the matter." Vicar Taggert leaned forward. "You are hurting, sir. Please, tell me what is on your mind."

Enoch winced. Less than two winters ago, this man confirmed him in the Khristosian faith so he could partake of the sacrament. And not long before, he'd rebuked Enoch in front of Sir Rick for neglecting his catechism studies in favor of reading legendary tales in the Manor library. Now, Vicar Taggert spoke to him with respect, as one adult to another.

He opened his mouth, but no sound came out past the icy claws, so he closed it again. The vicar waited, his brown eyes serious but kind. A pressure built up inside Enoch, and at once the frozen dam burst. A stream of words flowed out of him: how he worried for the lost maidens and his promise to find them. How he feared he'd end up breaking the promise and let down everyone. That no matter how hard he strove to do his duty, he'd never measure up as the Acting Baron-Knight, and then Commander Storm would refuse to raise him to full baron-knight status. "I am afraid I'll fail in my duty to the folks of Lilac Grove, let alone the entire Northern Marches," he concluded.

"These feelings are only natural," Vicar Taggert replied. "You are inexperienced. However, remember what the Threefold One said to Joshua when he installed him as a leader: 'be strong and courageous. Do not be afraid; do not be discouraged, for the Almighty will be with you wherever you go.' Rely on the Threefold One. Read his scriptures and pray for guidance. It will come."

Enoch fidgeted in his chair. Guilt prickled over him like stinging nettles. He was being childish and ungrateful, but the root-spring of his grief and anger spilled out of him. "Vicar, I know everything that happens turns out for the good of those who love Lord Yshua, but what good comes for the rest of us out of Sir Rick dying? Why did The Threefold One have to take him away from us… from me?"

Vicar Taggert sighed and sank back into his chair. Suddenly, he looked older, the lines around his mouth deeper as he frowned. "If I could answer those sorts of questions, Sir Enoch, then I'd surely be a prophet." He shook his head. "No, it is not for us to question the Threefold One's wisdom. As painful as this is for you to hear—and for me to say—we must submit to his will and trust him. He is faithful and has never lied to us."

Enoch found himself unable to meet the vicar's gaze anymore. He stared at his boots, feeling the heat of his shame rising into his cheeks. A scuff marred the toe of his left boot, and the laces of his right boot were an untidy tangle because of his hasty tying. He'd have to fix it. At length, he said, "I wish I could say the same."

The vicar sighed. "Sir Enoch, this morning we confessed our wrongdoings and received forgiveness for our sins through the sacrament. What remains to trouble your conscience?"

"Yesterday," Enoch began, and then needed to stop because the claws squeezed his throat again. He tugged on his cravat, pulling the knot away from his neck. "You may already know this, but yesterday, I went into the Darkenwood Forest without an escort, without even telling anyone where I planned to go." He licked his lips and then continued, more slowly. "I deceived Jude Higgins. On purpose. I didn't lie, exactly, but I made it seem as if I planned to join Deputy Trask's search party. And now Higgins is in disgrace." Enoch cleared his throat. "I feel awful; I wish I'd done things differently, but I don't regret going into the forest alone." He went silent, reluctant to mention Toad and his experience in the starry void place with Annabelle to the vicar for reasons he couldn't explain.

Vicar Taggert spoke after a moment's hesitation. "If I may suggest, Sir Enoch? Speak with Captain Faulkner. You are now in a position to intercede for one who might be wrongfully accused of dereliction of duty. And then, apologize to the wronged parties."

Enoch stared at his boots. He swallowed past the lump in his throat. "I am sorry."

Vicar Taggert reached out to trace the sign of the cross over Enoch and then placed his hand on the crown of his bowed head. "By the authority vested in me, accept Lord Yshua's forgiveness, Sir Enoch Northward. You are loved more than you'll ever know."

Even with the vicar's hand still on his head, Enoch felt the weight pressing on him lessen. "Thank you, Vicar."

Vicar Taggert beamed. "Sir Frederick would be proud of you."

He shook his head and examined his boots. The intricate tangle of laces seemed a fascinating puzzle. "I still feel as if I'm letting him down."

Wood creaked as Vicar Taggert shifted in his chair. "Please remind me, what is the baron-knight's ultimate duty?"

Enoch raised his head and met the vicar's gaze, a bittersweet smile curving his lips. "That's easy. Sir Rick mentioned it all the time; it was his mantra. 'Seek justice. Show mercy. Walk humbly with Lord Yshua.'"

"Do this and there shall be no disappointment when you are reunited in Heaven."

DIRE PORTENTS

Shoulders back, Enoch strode through the Lilac Hedge Maze with his ears tuned to the murmur of running water. The man he sought often visited the fountain in the maze's center on Chapeldays after the worship service. He nodded to gardeners, returned to their work following the service, weeding flower beds, or applying fresh mulch to the myriad lilac bushes. Many clusters of the purple blossoms drenched the environs with the heady scent of home.

Enoch rounded a bend and found himself at the center of the maze. Water jetted from leaping stone fish mouths, sparkling in the sunslight. He hesitated. Two men in uniform stood in earnest conversation on the far side of the fountain, one tall with graying hair and a tawny complexion, the other medium height with close-cropped sable hair and warm umber skin. Neither appeared to have seen him.

Well, there's Captain Faulkner. I wonder what he and Benjy are talking about?

Enoch inhaled lilac-scented air. He concentrated, exhaled, and the quality of light grew brighter and harsher. Tendrils of silvery, glowing mist whipped around his body like feather-tree leaves in the wind.

How incredible! And different from before. Now, how do I make it—oh, there it goes. He grinned, watching one mist-tendril curl out and extend across the courtyard to the two men. Their voices jumped into his ears.

"—Darkenwood," the captain said. "I want your cohort focusing on the Northeastern quadrant this afternoon."

"Yes, sir," Trask replied, rapping a fist over his heart. "There's little hope left for Sir Thomas or the girls, but we'll keep looking until—Threefold One willing—we find something."

Good man, Benjy. I'm not quitting until I find them, either. I made a promise. But, "first things first," as Sir Rick would say. I need to right a wrong.

Enoch relaxed his focus and the sunslight returned to normal. His vision of the silver mist receded. Deputy Trask being here expedited matters, but he'd hoped to speak with the captain alone. *Oh, well, there's nothing for it; I need to face the music. Red insists Yshua's Will is done, regardless.* He suppressed a chuckle. Probably he'd make up a malaprop like "looking at the song," or something to that effect.

Back straight, Enoch strode toward the two men. They both stiffened to attention, saluting. Enoch gestured for them to be at ease as he approached. They greeted one another.

Captain Faulkner's eyes crinkled at the corners as he smiled. "Sir, we're discussing our next move regarding the search. Which one of us do you need?"

Enoch stood feet shoulder-width apart with his hands clutched behind his back to keep from fidgeting. "Both, actually." He glanced from the captain's amused face to the deputy's more serious one. He swallowed. "It's about Corporal Higgins."

Trask's expression darkened. "He's on probation, sir. He knows his duty, and he should've escorted you to the nearest patrol yesterday."

Enoch frowned. *This will be more difficult than I thought.*

"But I ordered him not to." He suppressed an urge to duck his head. "Captain, I recommend you lift the probation on Jude Higgins. He wouldn't be in trouble if I hadn't deceived him."

A faint smile cracked Deputy Trask's façade and warmth crept into his reddish-brown eyes. He mouthed the words, "Rule number one" and rapped his knuckles against his chest.

Eyes twinkling, Captain Faulkner smiled at their byplay. "That's fair of you, Sir Enoch." And then, his expression sobered, his face haggard and unshaven from harried days with little rest. "You have a tough row to hoe here, now Sir Rick has passed. Indeed. It's often hard enough for a man to admit to himself and to the Almighty when he's in the wrong, let alone to others under his authority. Rest assured; I'll lift Jude's probation. And I'll tell him it's owing to your liberality, sir."

Enoch broke his stance and rubbed the back of his neck, stammering. "Just following Rule Number One, Captain."

Trask grinned outright. Everyone knew about his rules.

Rule Number One: "Never leave a comrade behind."

Captain Faulkner chuckled. "Right of you, Sir Enoch." He glanced at Trask. "Looks to me as if you've taught him well, Benjy."

Still grinning, Trask shook his head. "I did my best, sir. But others have had a large hand in it, as well—including yourself, Captain." He met Enoch's gaze and saluted him a third time. "I'm proud of you, Sir.

And I'm here to serve."

Captain Faulkner nodded. "You've grown by leaps and bounds from the boy who used to tear about the village with Simon Halloway and his squad. You rascals have grown up into fine young men, each in his own way." He smiled, his hazel eyes crinkling at the corners.

Trask's eyes gleamed. He stiffened to attention. "Sir and sir. Permission to share the good news with Corporal Higgins?"

Captain Faulkner lifted his eyebrows.

Enoch grinned. An enormous weight lifted from his shoulders, just as the vicar had told him. "Permission granted, Deputy. Dismissed."

Trask saluted both of them and jogged off, whistling. The captain followed him with his gaze. He nodded. "Good man, there. He'll make a fine garrison captain someday." He turned back to Enoch. "And now, sir, I think it best to assign a guard detail to you, for your own protection, you understand?"

Enoch's heart plummeted, and his face must have fallen to match it, because the captain's lips twitched. "I have the names of fifteen men who volunteered for the honor just this morning before they deployed for the search patrols. I picked out seven of them for you to approve. When the commander arrives, he'll either validate our decision or make his own recommendations, but I rather think he'd be pleased with my choices."

Enoch crossed his arms and snorted. Captain Faulkner hyperbolized; nothing ever pleased Commander Storm. He decided not to argue the point. "Who are the men?"

Captain Faulkner grinned outright. "Bart Ainsley, James Guffin, James Tellyson, and Tad Marsh. Levi Quent offered the services of himself and his hounds. On the grounds you'll need a medic, Philip Sharkness put himself forward for consideration."

Enoch tensed. Six names, young men with whom he'd gotten up to mischief in the past. He considered them his. Enoch flattered himself they were fond of him despite their age difference. However, the name he most wanted to hear was significant in its absence.

"They're great troopers, but none of them ranks above corporal. Who will lead them?" he asked, his heart in his throat.

The captain furrowed his brow. His eyes danced with merriment, though. "Yes, sir, it is a problem. We need a sergeant. Alan Matlock put himself up; he'd be a prime choice, but I know he rubs you the wrong way."

Enoch started. *Matlock volunteered to be in my guard?*

"Benjy Trask wanted to do it, but I told him he's earned his rank as deputy and I'd rather he served in this capacity."

Me, too, thought Enoch. *Faulkner's right; after he retires his commission, Benjy's the best candidate in the garrison for captaincy.* Agitation churned in his gut. Who else volunteered? One more name. Why did the captain not mention the one nearest Enoch's heart?

"Among others, Jude Higgins also put his name in the helm," the captain added, "but I believe a consequence for his negligence should forgo the honor, for now. I suppose I'll have to promote somebody to sergeant." His expression brightened. "And Simon Halloway is our man."

Despite himself, Enoch jumped and whooped in excitement.

Up on the widow's walk, Enoch tilted his head back and feasted his eyes on a blue sky unblemished by clouds. Days like this were rare in the Northern Barony during late springtime, when rain showers were frequent and thunderstorms common. A cool breeze buffeted him. He drew in lilac-scented air.

Ever since I remember, I've wanted to soar and race around in the sky—just like a dartling jay or a spearhawk. I wish to fly as I did in my dream.

In the dream, he'd conquered the cyclone and saved Annabelle from its ferocious winds. He imagined Windblade's hilt in his hand again, the sword humming as he sliced away airstreams and vapor. Fleetingly, he wished a storm would come.

I wonder… can I replicate in the waking world the things I did in my dream?

On a whim, he held out his right hand and concentrated, in much the same way he did when using his listening talent. He pictured the sword as he saw it in his dream, the double-edged blade gleaming silver. He more than half-expected nothing to happen. Silver light flickered in his vision. And then—just like at the Wall—a tingling sensation rushed through his body from his core and into his arm. The air over his palm swirled and quivered, thickening to form a misty outline of a silver hilt. Astonishment shattered his focus. The silver light winked out. Air whooshed out in every direction from his hand as the sword's cloudy image disappeared.

Enoch's heart fluttered against his ribs like the wings of a caged dartling jay. He'd summoned Windblade, the sword from his dream. Did this mean everything in his dream was real? Could he fly? The legends claimed only the seven Sages and wyldlings flew. And he definitely wasn't a Sage.

His breath caught in his throat. "Could I be a wyldling?"

When he gave voice to the question, it sounded foolish. Wyldlings were rare even back in the Epochs following the Oblivion Wars. In the past seven generations—the Epoch preceding the present—no records existed of any wyldlings. He'd said as much to Annabelle in the dream: wyldlings were more stories and legends than historical fact.

Enoch's cheeks puffed out as he exhaled. *I'm glad I said nothing of the dream or my listening talent to Vicar Taggert; as generous as the man is with dispensing forgiveness, he'd frown upon anything that distracts me from my faith and my duties to the realm.*

From below came the clock's ringing chimes. Enoch gripped the railing. Wren Watch. *Too bad I can't fly right now; I'm late for my appointment with Red.*

The seneschal worked in the small antechamber of the baron-knight's study, a place Enoch took care to avoid as much as possible since his return from the Resurrection Festival. There was too much memory associated with Sir Rick's untidy office. Enoch felt uncomfortable in this room, even though he need not sit behind the master's monstrous cherry-wood desk. His own chair and a small worktable were tucked away in the room's corner nearest the adjoining library. Over the past two Turnings, Sir Rick had taught him more and more concerning various aspects of a baron-knight's responsibilities.

The seneschal had suggested Enoch use the late baron-knight's desk, now his by right as the Acting Baron-Knight. He refused for two reasons: first, for Enoch to use the desk made everything more official, the final nail in Sir Rick's coffin, so to speak; second, the chair was meant for a man of Sir Frederick's statuesque proportions, not a half-grown adolescent boy who had always been, and probably always would be, something of a runt.

He'd appear a child playing at being the baron-knight if he sat behind the desk. No one would take him seriously. Better to sign and seal the realm's paperwork in the library, where the chairs fit him.

Enoch had just raised his hand to knock on the office door when Red opened it. The seneschal flicked his ears back but made no other sign of displeasure at his tardiness. The latch clicked as he locked the door behind Enoch. While Red fetched the documents of interest from the safe hidden in the office, he glanced around the long, narrow room.

Red's desk faced the entrance and a lamp stood beside it. Mounted on the wall was a huge bas-relief carving of the seal of the Baron-Knight of the Northern Marches. An arched opening cut into the back wall on the right communicated into the late knight's office. Daylight streamed in through the floor to ceiling casement windows of the larger room. No door or curtain separated the rooms. It was—had been—one duty of the staff in the antechamber to guard the master's privacy while he worked in his study.

As befitted any seneschal, Red was a tidy and regimented person. He organized the ledgers and scrolls in his office on long shelves running from floor to ceiling on either side of the door. The seneschal could locate any file in short order on demand. He himself had little need for the meticulous records, but he kept them, as he said, for the "betterment" of others.

As usual, there were no personal or decorative items in evidence. Red kept only necessary items on his desk. Sometimes this included a tea service brought by a footmen, but only the hallowed schedule book, a bottle of indigo ink, a heavy silver pen in its holder, and the blotter graced its polished surface now.

Enoch looked up as the seneschal swept into the antechamber, which smelled faintly of the kaenhir's peppery musk. Gooseflesh pebbled his skin at the sight of a familiar scroll-tube in Red's hand. He sank into the chair in front of the small and utilitarian desk and Red took his own seat, a backless stool. He placed the message tube in the center of the blotter.

Enoch stared at it with trepidation, as if it was a venomous adder poised to strike.

Red tapped the scroll-tube, his sharp nails clicking on the lacquered surface. "Please, young knight. It is time for you to see what is written. Very much past time, but your servant thought it best not to distract you from adjustment to your new duties." He fixed Enoch with a gaze fraught with meaning.

Heart pounding, Enoch recalled the dream-Annabelle encouraging him to confront the message on the parchment. Whether she'd been real, her support strengthened him. "You're right. It is time to read it."

Ears and eyebrows lifted in surprise, the seneschal nudged the lacquered scroll-tube with an index finger. The tube rocked in Enoch's direction. He picked it up, hefting its weight.

So small and light a thing, to convey such dire portents.

The two halves of cylinder screwed together in the middle and fashioned from butternut wood and lacquered to prevent rot. Enoch held the tube on either end and twisted the halves in opposite directions, pulling it apart to reveal a small roll of beige parchment. He extracted the parchment roll and then glanced at Red. The kaenhir sat silently, his fingers steepled. His eyes fixed on Enoch, he nodded.

Enoch sighed and unrolled the parchment. He read what Doctor Fourtier wrote regarding the death of Sir Frederick. Mere fragments and phrases were enough to summon the icy specter's grasp on his heart, squeezing until he felt breathless.

"A foreign agent in the blood…"

Annabelle was mistaken. Knowledge of the message's contents could make things worse. To read the scroll was to lose his guardian over again.

Sir Rick had not died of natural causes. Someone had poisoned him.

WIND OF HIS PASSAGE

FOOLS RUSH IN

Shields crashed as they slammed together. Wooden swords clacked and men sweated while sergeants bawled insults. Soldiers chanted in cadence as they ran laps. Even on Chapelday, Commander Storm expected troopers to drill for at least four hours. Enoch was halfway to the arena before he remembered that baron-knights were exempt from the strict training schedule. They held other, far weightier responsibilities. He stood on the edge of the garrison training yard, breathing in the familiar sounds. The clamor should have reassured him following the eerie silence of the past evening, but it rang hollow after his conversation with the seneschal.

Who would want to poison Sir Rick?

No, he mustn't think of it now. Enoch shoved his grief down, hard. The contents of the messenger scroll—and everything it meant—could wait until he returned from the forest. Duty pressed him like a sack full of stones on his back. Like a mountain of stones.

Hooves clicked against cobblestones. The seneschal approached with two riding deer in tow; a doe called Clover and Enoch's favorite mount, Tinker. Enoch patted the stag's neck. "Ready?" he asked.

"Of course," Red replied. He slid his wooden staff through the loops meant to secure it to his mount. The seneschal had exchanged his pristine blouse, waistcoat, and formal suit for garb better suited for excursions into the woods: a black leather wrap-around vest and dark buckskin trousers. A pair of knee-length, well-worn riding boots, into which he tucked his trousers, replaced the polished black shoes. He'd secured his long queue in a pouch at the nape of his neck. Incongruously, Red still wore his monocle. A serviceable hunting knife with a bone handle and sky-iron blade attached to his belt instead of a sword. Although Red knew every sword form, he did not own a sword and never used a real one when he sparred with the commander, only his staff or a stave.

Red scratched his mount's ears and then vaulted up into the saddle in a single bound.

Enoch snorted. "I wish I could just leap into the saddle."

"Can you not learn to do so?" Red glanced at him; eyebrows raised.

Obviously not, Enoch mused as he climbed into the saddle, *or I'd have managed it by now.* To cheer himself up, he thought instead about his near success in summoning the sword from his dreams. Windblade was real, so perhaps, one day, he'd fly and not need a mount.

As the deer trotted toward the Westgate, Enoch experienced a jolt from his conscience. Corporal Higgins was on gate-duty. Frannie Pines visited with him, of course, keeping him company after finishing her milking shift; the two were affianced. Commander Storm would put a stop to these visits, but Enoch hadn't the heart to deny them. Officially, Sir Rick allowed it only on Chapeldays but turned a blind eye so long as they upheld moral propriety.

"Hey, Higgins." Enoch rode up to the gatekeeper's booth and reined in his mount. Tinker clattered to a halt, snorting as he rattled his velveted antlers. The seneschal muttered a prayer for patience as he drew level and reined his own mount in close alongside him.

The day-watch gatekeeper stiffened to attention and saluted the young knight, his expression bland and neutral. A trooper's face. "Sir Enoch. Milord Seneschal." Frannie ducked her head and bobbed in the briefest of curtsies, muttering a polite greeting. She refused to meet his eyes.

Enoch swallowed. He resolved to apologize. *Why is this so hard?*

"For the gate records, Corporal Higgins," Red announced, before anyone else spoke. "You will make a record. Sir Enoch goes to continue his search. He will join Sergeant Matlock's patrol in the Darkenwood Forest. This one escorts him."

"Yes, sir." Corporal Higgins saluted them both again, his motions stiff. He spun on his heel and marched into the gatekeeper's booth to jot down the entry in the Westgate logbook.

Enoch remembered Corporal Higgins volunteered to be in his personal guard but had been denied. *Because of my deceit.* That loosened his tongue. "Higgins, I'm sorry!"

Frannie stared at him, open mouthed.

Higgins emerged from the booth, hesitant. "Come again, sir?" Trooper Gilmore, standing beside the winch to raise the portcullis, stared at Enoch as if he'd sprouted a second head.

Blushing, Enoch tugged on the reins. Tinker shifted beneath him, twitching his ears in mute reproof. He cleared his throat. "I'm sorry my deceit landed you in the cook-pot, Higgins. It won't happen again. Forgive me?"

Frannie's slack jaw firmed into a bright smile. She spread her skirts and dipped into a proper curtsy due a baron-knight.

"Why, thank you, sir!" Higgins replied. "That means a lot to me. Of course, I forgive you. Wasn't too long ago I got up to mischief, too." Frannie elbowed him. "I mean, not that you were up to mischief, sir," he added, his own face coloring. "Sure as spit, you were doing important baron-knight things out there in the woods."

Frannie patted her fiancé's arm. "What Jude means, sir, is he accepts your apology. May the Threefold One bless you, Sir Enoch."

Enoch silently thanked the Threefold One when Trooper Gilmore chose that moment to crank open the portcullis. Red insisted on riding out first, no doubt to make sure no danger awaited them.

"Lord Yshua go with you," Gilmore said. Enoch returned the greeting with every bit of decorum and self-control he could muster.

Higgins saluted. "Keep him safe, Milord Seneschal!" Frannie curtsied again, her smile for Enoch.

From outside the gate, the kaenhir nodded. "One intends to."

Gilmore lowered the portcullis. Enoch faced forward and rode stiffly in the saddle, trying not to squirm like a child.

"That was honorably done, young knight. Your servant is proud of you."

Enoch shrugged. He mopped his face with a handkerchief. *It's still early but the day's already too beggaring warm.* When they entered the Darkenwood, he spurred his mount into a ground-eating gallop along the sun-dappled forest road. The cool breeze of his passage fanned the embarrassed heat from his face.

Ten miles later, Enoch reined in Tinker to a steady canter. Behind him, Red did the same. The seneschal seemed content to follow him without breaking the silence, even though they had much to discuss after perusing the contents of the scroll. Prior to Sir Rick's death, Enoch would have filled the silent void by giving voice to his ruminations as they traveled. Now, he didn't wish to pollute the fresh air by voicing dark thoughts about poison and the wrongful death of his late guardian.

By the time Klotho reached her zenith, the travelers arrived at the spot Enoch had marked on his map. They paused for an early luncheon. The deer foraged a few mouthfuls of the grass and forbs they favored. Red and Enoch both ate in a pensive hush, broken only when Red voiced surprise they'd not yet encountered a barrier to their progress. Enoch shrugged in response; the probable placement of ward-spells was not his area of expertise. Commander Storm presumably knew many things about them, and waystones, too. The kaenhir lapsed into silence and ate his share while monitoring their environs.

Enoch eyed his companion sidelong. "I don't know why you bother," he said. "Tinker and Clover are calm. There's no danger here from either beast or bandit."

Red sighed, brushing crumbs from his vest. "How quickly you forget the lessons your servant taught. The one who fails to set his own guard while the birds sing places his life in the hands of fools."

Enoch frowned. Wensallen-kaen proverbs rarely translated into intelligible Tradespeak. "What do you mean?" he asked, still searching the canopy above for suspicious looking birds.

Red narrowed his eyes. "It is not wise to drop the watch and rely solely upon the instincts of one's mount. Or the efforts of others, when one is capable. As the Lord Commander says to you: 'constant vigilance, lad.'"

Enoch winced at the credible facsimile of his mentor's deep voice from Red's throat. Only a syrax mimicked voices better than a wensallen-kaen. But the seneschal's proficiency was borne of long acquaintance with Commander Storm.

"All right," he said. "You've made your point. I'll keep a better watch from now on."

Red raised a finger, whiskers twitching. "This is the beginning of wisdom."

After finishing the meal, Red consulted Enoch's map—muttering that Enoch ought to have stored it in a tube—and located the markers he'd left the previous day. The two remounted and directed the deer along the trail at a slow jog.

Enoch took a deep breath and employed his listening talent. Nothing but leaves rustling and birdsong. Something tugged him toward the Wall. He stifled a gasp. Distracted, his enhanced hearing returned to normal, and the tension lessened. Enoch braced himself and tried again. Yes; his awareness sped to the same destination. *Very curious.*

He decided not to experiment anymore, lest Red grow suspicious of his preoccupation. Enoch didn't wish to discuss his weird new talent or aspirations toward flight with the kaenhir. Red often claimed all power led to the devil; he always pointed to the darker side of the legends and wyldling tales. Temptation, tyranny, and the abuse of power.

But I won't abuse my power. I'm not a tyrant like Kaiselle of Abaddon, or a thief like Josiah Horn. I'll always remember my abilities come from the Threefold One. They made mistakes and I can learn from them; do better. Can't I?

Enoch watched for Toad as they traveled, but didn't see him. Perhaps he stayed near the Wall and expected to meet Enoch there. He'd need to introduce him to Red when they arrived. Enoch wondered what they'd think of one another.

Hopefully, Red won't see Toad as a threat and kill him.

Before long, they reached the clearing where the path forked. The two slid out of their saddles. The kaenhir placed a hand on Enoch's shoulder when he moved toward the tangle of colony bushes. "Wait, Enoch. As is right and prudent, your servant must assure no danger lurks hereabouts. Only fools rush in where the Almighty's angels counsel discretion."

Enoch fidgeted with his satchel as Red prowled along the boundary of the thick brush in a fluid, loose-limbed gait with his ears raised to catch every sound. Every few steps, he paused, and his black nostrils flared to sample the air. He'd not gone very far before he stopped and turned to face Enoch with a grim expression.

"Your servant has scented something here," the kaenhir said. "It worries him, for he cannot identify it. The trace is very faint. However, he must investigate further."

"Oh, great." Enoch rolled his eyes as soon as Red turned away. He removed his spectacles and wiped the sweat from his face. Then he tied the handkerchief to the same twig he'd used for this purpose the day before and both deer knelt. Enoch smiled and scratched them both behind the ears. He left them with a pot of water to share and a handful of dried corn each before crouching to find the opening in the underbrush.

"Over here, Red," he murmured, just loud enough for the kaenhir to hear him.

Enoch dove beneath the branches of the colony bush and crawled toward the Wall. Like spent storm clouds drifting beyond the horizon, his concerns about the missing girls and the results of his late guardian's autopsy receded.

He'd prove to Red no threat existed here. And see Annabelle again.

Enoch's entire being crackled with heady excitement as he crawled through the green-tinted gloom of the tunnel and emerged into the narrow clearing. He blinked rapidly as his eyesight adjusted to the full glare of the three suns.

The sooty, gray expanse of the Wall loomed over him and reached toward the heavens. Surely, someone else must have stumbled upon it in the past. He wondered again why he had found no records concerning the Wall in the Manor library. He'd search more thoroughly when he returned.

And don't forget to seek any practical information about wyldlings. Not just stories.

He stood with his gaze fixed on the Wall. When he moved toward it, a firm hand grasped his shoulder.

Startled, Enoch pulled away. "Let me go. I need to touch it."

Red held up a finger. "After one moment more, young knight. Patience. Your servant has not yet examined this Wall. In the event you have forgotten to mention a thing. Once he is satisfied there is no threat, you may approach."

"There's nothing to worry about. I was safe here yesterday."

Red's flat tone brooked no argument. "That was yesterday. Today is a different day."

Enoch sighed. "All right. I'll wait. But only for a minute." He recalled how swiftly the hours marched past yesterday while he'd been in the void place. They planned to join the proximal Darkenwood search party by Klotho-set, which left only a few hours for Enoch to contact Annabelle. If he could.

The kaenhir thanked him. He regarded the soot-gray barrier. Warily, Red approached the Wall with his weapon angled in front of him. He tapped the stone several times with the end of his staff. When nothing happened, he placed his left palm against the Wall and then slid it toward the mirror-like aperture Enoch called the Oval Window.

Jealousy coiled, a restless serpent in his stomach as Enoch stomped toward the Wall. What if Red contacted Annabelle before he did? "That's enough." He paused next to a large blue mushroom. "You've completed your recon. Are you satisfied?"

Nonplussed, Red withdrew his hand before it touched the Oval Window and turned to regard his young friend. "No. Each place has danger for the unwary." He stepped back from the Wall and bowed. His whiskers twitched, and a slight grin revealed his prominent cuspids. "But your servant shall keep watch, and perhaps danger will not find you here today, yes?"

"If it makes you feel better, Red, go ahead and stand vigil."

The kaenhir's brow furrowed in confusion. "Go ahead where? Your servant was beneath the stamp he would remain here."

Enoch laughed and his tension melted away. "I think you meant 'under the impression.' We will stay here," he added, clapping a hand against his friend's arm. "I meant you should stand watch while I show you what the Wall does."

Red's back-tipped ears rose in astonishment. "You speak wisdom."

"Don't sound so surprised. I haven't lost my senses completely, you know."

Whiskers twitching, the seneschal stood with his hands clasped behind his back. "Then your servant will also keep watch for the parts of your senses that are lost."

Enoch chuckled and shook his head at his friend's attempt at a joke. He drew his palm across the mirror-like surface of the ovate aperture. In it, he saw his reflection and everything behind him, including the seneschal, who scrutinized him.

Had the Window sat this low on the Wall yesterday? It felt slick and cool, despite the suns' rays beating against it. The tugging sensation had subsided. Enoch's hopes sank. He shut his eyes and rested his forehead against the glass.

Please, please let me in.

Red exclaimed in his native language.

Enoch opened his eyes. The quicksilver surface of the Oval Window swirled, distorting the images it once reflected so clearly. Behind him, a gale-force wind turned tree branches into flailing whips. He touched the slick surface. It gave beneath his palm, silver ripples spreading. His worries and cares flew away like birds on the wing. He laughed with delight.

"This is what I told you about. Just wait and see, Red."

He felt Red grab his arm. A vibration ran through his body, and then the pressure on his arm vanished. He heard the seneschal howling. Or was it the wind rushing in his ears? Silver light flashed, wind roared… and then Enoch floated in the silent, star-crazed expanse of the void place. Worries regarding the missing girls and his grief fell away as he gazed in awe at the silent beauty surrounding him.

"Wow," he said in a reverent whisper. "It worked. See, Red? Like I said: nothing to worry about."

The seneschal did not answer him. Enoch shifted, the kythim flaring out around him in silver tendrils. Eyes wide, he gasped. Red hadn't accompanied him.

THROUGH THE WORMHOLE

As usual, her little sister slammed the door behind her so hard every dish in the kitchen cupboards rattled. Annabelle winced. *Kid doesn't know her own strength; someday, the darn house will collapse.* Muffled by intervening walls, her mother's voice rose to a peevish pitch out in the garage; no doubt she scolded Amy to that effect. Annabelle snorted and returned to spreading peanut butter and honey on slices of whole wheat bread.

A chill swept over her body in an icy wind, pebbling it with gooseflesh. She shivered and hugged herself. *Who left a window open? It's freaking winter. Darn kids; it was probably Drew, shooting his stupid Nerf darts at squirrels again.*

She picked up her plate and traced the draft to the foot of the stairs.

And stopped. Her eyes widened, and she nearly dropped her sandwich. "What the… f-f-fudge?"

A transparent, silvery stream descended from above. It swept around her in a cool breeze, caressing her face and ruffling her hair. Its touch filled her with warmth. It glowed, like something out of her dream.

The silver knight who destroyed a tornado. Enoch.

Annabelle's heart hammered against her breastbone, and she drew in shaky breaths. Placing one foot in front of the other, she ascended the stairs; the light intensifying the entire way. She followed the shining stream of silvery air to her bedroom. It ended at a vortex of shining quicksilver in the wall where her mirror had been.

What is that? It looks like the wormhole from the movie Stargate.

Her eyes never leaving the swirling disk, she set the plate on her desk. She crept toward it, whispering, "Enoch, are you there?"

A voice answered her. "Annabelle."

She gasped; like ribbons, sapphire strands extended from a blue aura surrounding her and undulated toward the portal. Blue light swirled alongside the silver in a crazy pinwheel. Silver tendrils emerged from the quicksilver pool to wrap around her blue ribbons. Fear shot through her, and the blue ribbons trembled.

"Annabelle, are you well?"

The silver light intensified, and a comforting warmth of another presence surrounded her. She sucked in a breath and reached out into the syrupy swirl of blue-silver light. The warmth of the silver presence deepened. Another pair of human hands met her grasp. Real hands with real warmth and strong fingers.

A gasp of relief escaped her. "Oh, praise God! You're real. Hold on, Enoch."

She gripped the hands, leaned back, and pulled. He shot out like greased lightning. She glimpsed wide, blue eyes behind spectacles on an almond-brown face and then backpedaled until she hit the opposite wall, the boy stumbling along after her. He drew to a halt just before he crashed into her, still gripping her hands, swaying on his feet. He stood taller than her by several inches and wore brown leather a shade darker than his skin.

Disheveled golden-brown hair obscured half of his face from view. A few strands puffed out from his mouth as he exhaled a pent-up breath. "Annabelle?" He squeezed her hands before letting go and swiped the hair out of his eyes.

She had the same idea; her hands bumped into his. "Oops, sorry," she giggled, at the same time he said: "Pardon me!"

Awkwardly, he withdrew his hands and a wide grin split his face. "Kaspar's wings! I made it to the other side." His grin softened into a smile as he stared at her.

She smiled back. "You're really here. My silver knight."

"In the flesh, my sapphire lady!" Enoch stepped back and sketched an awkward bow. They both burst into giggles. Half-laughing, he said, "I can't tell you how happy I am to see you. I was afraid I imagined everything."

She grinned back. "Me, too. I thought I'd gone over the deep end." She tapped his nose. "Meep. Feel that? We're real enough."

He tapped her nose. "Yeah, I'd say so." He frowned. "Should I have said 'meep,' too?"

Annabelle covered her mouth with her hands, laughing. "No, that's just me being silly." She recovered from her mirth and peered over his shoulder. "Wow, Enoch! My mirror has turned into a wormhole. A real wormhole leading to my room. Through outer space. Just like the one in *Stargate*!"

Enoch furrowed his brow and tipped his head to one side. "Worm… hole? Star… gate?" And then he raised his eyebrows. "Ah. You mean, the Void-Bridge."

"Void-Bridge?" Annabelle smiled slyly. "I suppose that's as good a description as any I ever heard for an instantaneous portal transecting the spacetime continuum."

He opened his mouth to respond, and then the light behind him winked out. Annabelle's eyes widened. Nothing remained but a blank white wall and a mirror. The portal was gone.

Enoch turned. His body tense, he looked at her with a sickly expression.

Annabelle clapped her hands over her mouth. "Oh no, Enoch. How will you get back home?"

KALUBRIDAHN

William scarcely noticed the miles as he jogged back to the ruined fortress. Strange how the place felt like home. His mind bubbled with excited thoughts at what he'd discovered, and he was eager to work out the ramifications of hybrid spells. The sight of a burly figure leaning against the arched gateway on the Eastern side of the castle sent a fiery jolt of shock through him.

Veychekh's poisoned arrows! What's he doing here?

William halted a stone's throw away from the arch. He mopped his brow, panting. The assassin uncoiled from his lounging position. He wore a green jacket with brown trousers tucked into the tops of high leather boots and a wide-brimmed, conical hat woven from sawgrass. A pair of yellow eyes gleamed out from underneath the hat's brim. William's elation from the successful use of his new watcher's spell drained away as he met those eyes. His skin crawled at the madness peering back at him.

He's getting worse.

Burn it, but he needed a drink. His hands shook; he hid one in his sash while the other dipped under the collar of his robes for his flask. He relished the whiskey as it blazed a pleasant path down his throat and squinted at the visage under the hat. "Your talisman must not be functioning correctly."

Zakaar bared his fangs in a parody of a grin. "As you see, it is not. I felt the power waning. I come to ask Milord to amend the talisman, for I am on duty tonight."

William snorted. "Smart choice. One look at your ugly mug and this entire operation becomes a full-fledged muck-up."

"I am not ugly. In fact, I am accounted one of the most handsome men in my clan."

"Who cares? You left your clan. Here, you're just a bug-ugly harkhurz." He waved a hand as if to dismiss the insult. "Never mind. The talisman just needs to be revitalized. Come on, then." Silently, William raged. Suns burn the assassin and his blistering resistance to the Arkhabadh! The illusion would've lasted another fortnight if the assassin wasn't a harkhurz. "You know the drill," he said aloud. "Leave your weapons."

Zakaar bared his teeth. "You fear me? The 'bug-ugly harkhurz?'" He unbuckled and removed his sword-belt and the two blades attached to it. Still grinning in an unsettling fashion, he rolled them up and handed the resulting packet to William.

"As if," William muttered, suppressing the urge to roll his eyes. He placed the items in a niche hollowed out of the wall for this purpose. "You burning well know my shield won't allow you inside with weapons in your possession."

The assassin shook his head. "This is not complete truth, William. You let me inside when I, myself, *am* a weapon." With a toothy grin, he tugged on the hem of his dirty jacket with filth ground into the fabric in places.

Filthy beast, William thought, creating a brief opening in the shield for them both to pass through. "While you're here, do you have anything new to report?" He wrinkled his nose as the brute slipped past him. "Ugh! Have you been rolling in carrion? You need a bath. Master Tenebris will not be pleased to smell you in close quarters, let me tell you!"

The assassin spoke in his native dialect, which William understood from necessity, working closely alongside the assassin for over a Cycle. "I am closer, William. But I need the talisman working for my mission to succeed; I am not accustomed to taking prey alive. And I need the elixir from Milord," he added, flexing his fingers. His joints popped and crackled. "I try to fight it, but I feel it. The crimson madness will soon come over me again."

Despite himself, William tensed. What was Tenebris playing at? The "elixir" only seemed to make Zakaar's blood rage condition worse. It wouldn't be long before he became a slavering wreck and was no longer competent. A liability fit only to be dispatched. Not to mention a danger to them. If Tenebris believed his pet assassin had outlived his usefulness and wanted him dead, then why not just kill him? William experienced a pang of sorrow at the impending cessation of their partnership. Maybe he should develop a true elixir to extend his colleague's usefulness. Even Tenebris admitted this harkhurz was by far the best assassin he'd ever employed—and he'd employed a few good ones, to be sure. The Dreadlord always said they should never waste good talent. William's fingers traced the lump of the medallion hidden under his robes.

The main hold's roof blocked out much of the sunslight. A chill sank into William's flesh as they approached the stairwell leading into the dungeons where the master held sway. He crossed the threshold without stopping, but Zakaar hesitated. William turned to glare at him. Zakaar muttered to himself, something about regaining his honor, and grimacing into the shadows of the stairwell as if he smelled something rotten.

As if he had any right to complain about smells, reeking of carrion as he did!

William beckoned impatiently. "Vystralied's flaming bullocks! I've got my own stuff to do today, and I want to get back to doing it." Not that Tenebris would let him work on the scroll of equations the Dreadlord's wife gave him. No doubt his master had a plethora of meaningless drudge work for his apprentice.

Zakaar sneered at him. "You want only to be drinking the spirits-of-fire until you are besotted. Milord might not be pleased with me, but I am thinking, William, that Milord will not be much pleased with *you*, either."

"Shut up, Zakaar! Less talking, more walking." Insane or not, his sly colleague still knew the best way to get under his skin. He only drank whiskey to bolster his confidence, or until the pain inside went numb. Never to the point of incapacitation. Never in his master's presence.

Scowling, William conjured a little orange ball of werelight, providing just enough illumination to prevent him from tripping over hidden cracks and plunging through gaping holes in the wall. He sent the tiny, feebly glowing ball bobbing ahead of them like an inebriated firefly. It was a simple enough spell, one of the very first he'd mastered during his apprenticeship. Summoning a werelight didn't require him to shed blood. This was fortunate; he must not show his weakness in front of the assassin.

Zakaar remained silent as they descended the uneven stone steps. William restrained himself from looking back. He grew even more aware of the noise he made: every panting breath of effort, the scuff of his boots against stone, the rustle of his clothing, even the beating of his heart sounded loud to his straining ears. A trickle of sweat traced its way down the groove of his spine. With trembling hands, he pulled out his flask.

A *crackle-hiss* came from close behind him.

William paused as he tucked away the flask. *Great, now the blistering harkhurz is laughing at me.* Despite Zakaar's derision, he took another hearty swig to prepare himself for the approaching confrontation with his master.

Both the apprentice and the assassin hesitated when they arrived at the heavy oaken door of the laboratory. Neither wished to be the first to alert the master to their presence. The two glanced at one another, united in their fear of the man in the chamber beyond. William grimaced. They would settle this in the usual way: kalubridahn. He raised his hand, made a fist with his thumb toward the ceiling, then opened his hand so his fingers remained curved into a hook, and then straightened them out to form a plane parallel to the door. The harkhurz nodded his agreement.

They both held out their right hands, clenched into fists, knuckles toward the ceiling. William counted to three, and then rotated his hand, leaving it clenched in a fist, the hand-symbol for the cudgel. Simultaneously, Zakaar uncurled his fingers halfway into the hand-symbol for the whip.

William mouthed a furious curse. The whip always bested the cudgel.

The assassin gestured toward the door with one of his clawed hands, his meaning unmistakable. William sighed and rolled his eyes. He took another hasty nip from his flask and then grasped the iron ring serving as the door knocker.

A resonant voice boomed around them. "Enter, you idiots! You've been standing out there long enough to calcify into stalagmites."

William started and Zakaar's tail went rigid behind him. The ball of werelight flared for an instant before dimming again. William hastily adjusted his outer robe to cover the pocket where he hid his whiskey flask. His companion tugged on the brim of his hat and shifted to one side, muttering something about honor in his native language.

William sighed with disgust. *Burning coward, I'm sure he cheated.* Icy dread filled his stomach, but he hesitated only a moment before pushing the door open.

HOT COCOA

Enoch wrapped his hands around the steaming mug, its warmth seeping into his cold fingers. A clever person had painted a colorful pattern on the mug's glazed surface. White pellets bobbed in the heavenly-smelling brown liquid. Annabelle called it "cocoa." The white sugary puffs slowly dissolving into the hot liquid were marshmallows. He stared into the depths of the cocoa and ignored the food on the plate Annabelle set before him—a "peanut butter sandwich" that smelled delicious. But he'd partaken of neither. How could he eat? A ball of ice filled his stomach.

Despite the marvels he'd witnessed in Annabelle's world, the moment he sat, the ramifications of the portal's disappearance slammed home. Once again, the Northern Marches lacked its baron-knight.

"I'm sorry."

Annabelle sat across the table with one hand half-extended toward him. Her lips trembled and eyes shimmered with unshed tears.

Sir Rick would be ashamed if he saw me sitting here feeling sorry for myself… making a lady cry. I need to get a hold of myself.

Enoch shook his head. "No need for apologies. This isn't your fault." He straightened his shoulders and forced a smile as he took her hand and squeezed it. "The Threefold One brought us together for a purpose. Let's see how this plays out. In the meantime…" He raised the mug in a salute and then took a sip.

His eyes widened as warm nectar, sweet with an underlying bitterness, flowed over his tongue. It brought back memories from the Festival of Lights when he drank chocolatl, a beverage similar to this "cocoa," albeit less sweet and with a peppery heat. It came from an exotic land farther south even than the Southern Marches.

Is Annabelle's world any less exotic? I admit, I prefer cocoa to chocolatl. It's sweeter.

Enoch sipped the warm beverage. "Thank you. It's the best drink I've ever tasted." He felt rewarded when she smiled. He took another sip. "We have something like this—but more bitter—to drink during the Festival of Lights, in the winter when the nights are longest. There's dancing and a banquet." He smiled as he described the last feast to Annabelle. He faltered, feeling a pang, remembering Becky with yellow roses in her hair. The soft warmth of her hands in his. Her carefree laughter, her brown eyes reflecting the candlelight…

Annabelle stared at him. "Enoch?"

He took another drink to give himself time to compose his face. "And then," he continued with forced joviality, "everyone walks around in circles and in rows, holding candles to chase away the darkness while singing praises to the Almighty. We commemorate the first coming of Lord Yshua and looking forward to his return as our king."

Annabelle's eyes glowed. "Oh! We celebrate a similar holiday. Only, we call it Christmas." She continued, describing how the people of her realm decorated an evergreen tree with lights and ornaments and then wrapped presents to place beneath its boughs. Enoch wondered what putting gifts under a tree had to do with Lord Yshua's birth—and how they put lights on a tree without burning it—but before he asked, she mentioned family gatherings, cookies, music, and the worship services.

Similar to how we celebrate back home.

He closed his eyes, envisioning it. "It sounds wonderful."

Annabelle smiled. "Yes. Christmas is a wonderful time of year." She sighed, and her smile faded like clouds covering the suns. "Unfortunately, there's an awful lot of winter without Christmas in it. It gets to be so 'blah' after a while." Turning the mug in her hands, she scrunched up her nose. "And now we're in the blah-est month of all. February. The only good thing about it is my birthday's coming up soon." She grinned. "I'll be sweet sixteen. My friends are all coming over to celebrate. When's your birthday? Do you have birthday parties, too?"

Caught off-guard by her questions, Enoch choked on the chocolatl. *No—cocoa. She called it cocoa.* He wiped dribbles off his chin, frowning. "My birthday? And… parties? Do you mean 'party,' as in a group of people?"

Annabelle stared into her mug, then looked up, nodding. "Actually, yeah, I do. In a manner of speaking. A birthday party is when a bunch of people come over and celebrate the anniversary of your birth." She laughed. "Words can have so many nuances. Isn't language fun?"

Enoch gave her a wan smile. *Not really; in certain company, using the wrong word could get you killed.* "Sometimes," he replied, wishing to keep the smile on her face and the light in her eyes. "To answer your first question… it's strange, but I, too, will be sixteen soon." He titled his head and furrowed his brow. "Five days from now. As for your second question, we don't celebrate the anniversary of someone's birth. Our Name-day, the anniversary of our baptism, is how we track how old we are—at least, that's how we do it in the Northern Marches. And there's no 'party,' as such." He shrugged. "More often than not, birth and baptism both happen on the same day."

Annabelle stared at him. "Enoch… we share the same birthday. That's so cool!"

What does the temperature have to do with anything? Enoch raised his eyebrows. "Cool?"

She smiled, looking sheepish. "Sorry, it's slang; I should've known better. I meant, sharing a birthday is… interesting. And good. It links us together." Eyes shining, she grabbed his arm. "Oooh. Like, we could be twins! *Cosmic* twins!"

Enoch laughed, infected by her excitement. *I'm not sure what she's talking about, but I won't dissuade her.* She reminded him of Sally and Janet, both of whom he viewed as sisters. He told her so, his merriment dying away. *I must find them, somehow.*

Annabelle stopped giggling. Her expression grew intent, concerned. "Those are two of your missing friends, aren't they?"

He nodded, staring into the foamy dregs of his cup. When had he finished the cocoa?

Annabelle scooted her chair over until she sat right beside him. She touched his hand, her voice soft. "I'm sorry. I want to help you. Oh!" She brightened. "Sometimes, when I'm stuck with a problem, I think about something else for a while; distract my brain until it offers a solution out of nowhere." Her fingers curled around his, warm and comforting. "Tell me about your friends, Enoch. Who knows? Maybe the wormhole will appear, and you can return home."

"Okay." He managed a smile. *Vicar Taggert would say the Threefold One has a purpose in this... somehow. Everything will be fine.* For her, he'd pretend his life wasn't falling apart. He began with Sir Rick. For a mercy, his voice didn't shake when he spoke of his late guardian. Annabelle's fingers tightened on his, and her eyes brimmed with tears. He moved on to the other people in his life.

Annabelle interrupted him before he could describe Red. "What happened to your mom and dad?" she asked. "I realize Sir Rick was your guardian—and your friends sound great—but you don't mention your family."

Enoch grimaced and rolled his shoulders. "I don't have any. I'm an orphan. A ward of the Northern Marches. That's why my surname is 'Northward'; nobody knows about my family, my bloodline. Commander Storm found me in the wreckage of a garrison town after a battle." He looked into his empty cup as if it held the answers. "He told me I was the only survivor."

Annabelle looked down, shaking her head. "It must have been hard growing up without a mother."

Enoch chuckled. "Oh, I lacked for nothing. All the women in Lilac Manor had a hand in mothering me. Especially Verbena." He rubbed the back of his neck, embarrassed. "I called her my 'little mother' because she insisted she hadn't the right to claim me as her son."

Annabelle opened her mouth to speak, but a loud double tone rang and drowned out whatever she meant to say. Enoch leaped to his feet and Annabelle came up with him. His hand went for his sword... it wasn't there. He glanced around wildly.

Annabelle hugged his arm and burst out laughing. "Oh, Enoch! You should see your face. That's the doorbell. I'm sorry; I forgot about Kensi coming over to practice with me."

He followed her to the door and hung back when she opened it. He shivered as freezing air swept inside. "Enoch, this is my best friend, Kensi Cooper-Jones. Kensi, this is Enoch Northward, the guy from my dreams."

Enoch bowed to the tall, dark-haired maiden standing in the doorway. Mist puffed from her mouth as she laughed and stepped inside. "How chivalrous! Nice to meet you. Ann and I've been best friends since kindergarten." Annabelle closed the door against the winter chill and took a slender black case from her friend. The other maiden doffed a knitted red cap, scarf, and a puffy red coat made of a strange crinkly material and walked into the hallway closet as if she owned the place. Metal jangled and cloth rustled.

She returned without the outer garments, finger-combing her shoulder-length hair, and looked Enoch up and down. "So, Ann, your silver knight's a real person, after all. And kinda cute, too," she commented under her breath. "In a weird, Ren-fair way."

Enoch found himself at a loss for words. He blinked, exchanging a glance with Annabelle. No doubt sensing his discomfort, Annabelle suggested they adjourn to her room. Once there, she seemed subdued in her friend's presence. Annabelle offered him her desk chair, but he shook his head. When he played with the light switch—to witness the miracle of electricity—both maidens laughed at him.

Enoch stood stiffly beside the closet door, feet shoulder-width apart, hands clasped behind his back. Face still burning, he stared at the wall opposite, where Annabelle kept shelves crammed with books. Titles on the spines swam before his eyes, almost decipherable. He did not look at the tall, dark-haired maiden sitting beside Annabelle on her bed, although he sensed her sneaking glances at him. She was pretty, if not as pretty as Becky, but her bold manner made him uneasy.

I wish Kensi would go home, so Annabelle and I were alone again. What if the Void-Bridge doesn't return in the presence of a stranger?

Quietly, the two maidens assembled their musical instruments. Kensi's silver flute came in three parts that she slid together. The five pieces of Annabelle's clarinet and her placement of the reed on the mouthpiece took longer. But instead of playing, they held the instruments in their laps and watched him; Annabelle with concern, her friend with speculation glittering in her eyes.

Kensi broke the silence. "All right, Ann, you've had your fun. Who is he—really? The historical re-enactment nut from your church?" She snorted. "Whoever he is, he enjoys pretending he's a soldier or some kind of military man."

Pretending? I'm not pretending! Enoch clenched his jaw. How would Sir Rick handle this? He took a calming breath and then pivoted to face her, clasping his fingers to keep from fidgeting. "I assure you, Milady Cooper-Jones, I am the person she says I am: Enoch Northward, Baron-Knight of the Northern Marches."

The maiden rolled her eyes. "Seriously… 'Milady?' So medieval."

Annabelle spoke over the top of her friend. "He's from Tehara, like I said." She set aside her clarinet and bounced up to her feet. "And stuck here on Earth. At least, until the wormhole appears again." She stood beside him, biting her lip. "I hope it appears again."

Kensi rolled the flute between her hands, frowning. "Okay, let's say I believe you; he's from another world. What's his plan?"

Annabelle laughed weakly. "Plan? Who said anything about a plan?"

Enoch nodded at Kensi. "She just did. Perhaps she has some ideas about how to bring back the Void-Bridge."

Eyebrows arched, Kensi shook her head. "Void-Bridge?"

"He means the wormhole he came here through," Annabelle said in a rush. "Like the portal in *Stargate*." She fussed with the hem of her shirt, twisting it. "Oh, Mom and Dad are gonna be so mad at me."

Enoch dropped his military poise and touched her shoulder. "Annabelle, I apologize for causing you so much trouble."

Kensi rose and narrowed her eyes at him. "Speaking of trouble, why did you come here, anyway, Enoch? You better not be a con-artist taking advantage of my friend."

He rocked back on his heels and jerked his hand away. "I beg your pardon?" He didn't recognize the term *con-artist*, but he understood the context of Kensi's accusation. *She thinks I mean harm to Annabelle.*

Annabelle squawked. "What?"

Kensi groaned as she tilted her head back. "Lucky for you I'm here, Ann." Locking eyes with Annabelle, she gestured at him with her flute. She jabbed at him as if it were a weapon. "You're far too trusting for your own good. He could be gaining your trust so he can use you in some sort of scheme. I don't want you to get hurt."

Anger flared. Enoch's fingers curled into fists. *How dare she impugn my honor? I'd never hurt Annabelle—or any maiden.*

He suppressed the rage boiling up inside him, not trusting himself to speak. It would disappoint Sir Rick if he snapped at Kensi. *Holy Counselor*, he prayed. *Grant me patience and allay her suspicions. Please, almighty Threefold One. I don't want to cause problems for Annabelle. Bring the Void-Bridge back.*

Annabelle grabbed his arm, jarring him from his prayer. "He's not, Kensi," she protested. "What could he want from me? It's not as if I'm rich or an heiress. He's not a con-artist. He's my friend; my cosmic twin from another planet!"

A line of bright light sprang into existence on the closet door. Kensi's jaw dropped. She backed away and pointed her flute at the light, her hand trembling. "What? How? Is that the…"

The line rotated, at first slowly and then picking up speed, streaks of silver and sapphire following it until a gleaming pool of quicksilver rippled where Annabelle's closet had been.

He gasped. "The Void-Bridge." A great weight lifted from his shoulders.

Annabelle bounced on her feet. She shook his arm. "Holy cow, Enoch—it came back!"

Kensi collapsed into the child-sized armchair by the window, holding the flute against her chest, still staring. White ringed her brown irises. "Oh, gosh, I'm so sorry, Ann. I didn't believe you." She turned to glance at him. "I'm sorry, Enoch. Boys haven't always treated Ann very well, and I just…" She shrugged and stared at the quicksilver pool. "Anyway, I'm sorry."

"It's okay, Kensi," Annabelle said, letting go of his arm and going to her friend. Annabelle helped the taller maiden rise from the awkwardly short chair.

Kensi glanced between him and Annabelle. "Seriously, Ann, 'cosmic twin?' You've been reading too many sci-fi/fantasy books." She giggled. "I can't see you being twins. Your eyes might match, but he's even browner than I tan in the summer."

Enoch stepped toward them and bowed. "I forgive you, Milady Cooper-Jones. You were protecting her, and I can honor that."

"My last name is a mouthful. Call me Kensi." She pointed her flute at the Void-Bridge. The polished surface reflected the flickering light. "You're not planning to take Ann through this creepy thing, are you?"

Enoch opened his mouth and then shut it again. Wasn't that what he wanted?

"Kensi," Annabelle began, but her friend spoke over her.

Kensi's gaze on him hardened. "No it's a terrible idea. A new planet might be cool to explore, but all sorts of things could go wrong." She turned to her friend, rolling the flute between her hands. Her voice quivered. "What if you're trapped over there? What if you don't come back?"

Enoch raised his hands. "I'm not here to take Annabelle away. I tried to bring Red here; prove to him Annabelle was real." He frowned. "But he didn't come through with me."

Annabelle's eyes widened. Light flashed across the lenses of her spectacles as she looked from him to the Void-Bridge. "You didn't mention bringing your friend before."

Enoch shrugged. "So many things happened. I forgot until now." He sighed, shaking his head. "Red's probably upset with me right now and thinking I left him behind on purpose."

Annabelle raised her chin. "I'll go with you, then. Just for a couple minutes to meet your friend." Her gaze flicked to Kensi and then back to the rippling quicksilver pool. "And then I'll come right back home," she added, moving toward the Void-Bridge.

Kensi grabbed her arm. "Hold your horses, Ann. There's got to be a better solution." She turned to Enoch. "You say you need evidence? Would anything from Earth be good enough?"

Relieved, Enoch nodded. *I have no desire to cause any more trouble for Annabelle.* "It needs to be something small enough for me to carry."

Kensi tugged on Annabelle's arm. "Ann? Ann, did you hear? You don't have to go."

Enoch glanced at Kensi's hand gripping Annabelle's arm and then up at Kensi's face. He raised his eyebrows. She let go with a grimace.

Annabelle tore her gaze from the swirling portal. Brow furrowed, she rubbed her forearm. "Like a book? Or I could write a note."

Kensi narrowed her eyes and tapped the flute against her leg. "Ann, why don't you give him a photo of you to take back to wherever he's from."

Annabelle grinned. "Good idea, Kenz; I have recent ones from our last band concert in the album. Enoch, it's right behind you—the thick book with trees on the cover sitting on top of my bookshelf." She pointed, and Enoch found it. He handed it to her.

The two maidens bent over the album as she opened the cover and flipped a few stiff pages, which made a crinkling noise.

Enoch drew closer and peered into the book they held open between them. Four rectangular sections on each page depicted exquisite renderings of people and strange contraptions. Several of the renderings included a tiny Annabelle—very faithful likenesses.   "What are those?" he asked, his tone reverent.

"Photographs," Annabelle said. "They're a kind of portrait."

"They look very lifelike."

"How about this one?" Kensi asked, tapping one portrait. In it, Annabelle sat in a group of young people holding musical instruments. Annabelle made a face. "Ew, no. That one has Neal in it. I'm pretty sure he wouldn't want a picture of *him*."

Kensi smiled and asked sweetly, "If you hate it so much, why keep it?"

Annabelle's cheeks grew rosy. "Moving on," she said breezily and went to turn the page.

Enoch touched her wrist, arresting the movement. "Who is this 'Neal,' that he'd make a portrait objectionable?"

Kensi pointed to the young man sitting beside Annabelle in the portrait and then covered her mouth, snickering.

"A jerk," Annabelle muttered, her color deepening. "We were friends, but now he picks on me."

Enoch leaned closer. "Then he is no gentleman." He examined the portrait. The dark-haired young man next to Annabelle appeared respectable enough, wearing a sort of long, dark cravat over a crisp, white tunic. A large, shiny, bronze instrument lay across his lap; Enoch never before saw the like. Scowling, he added, "He looks as if he needs to be taught the error of his ways. I'll challenge him to a duel."

Kensi snorted behind her hand, and Annabelle laughed. "Oh, Enoch. I'm pretty sure duels are illegal in the United States." She peeled back the transparent, crinkly sheet covering the rectangular portraits—the photographs—and removed a different one from the adhesive securing it to the page.

"Yes," Kensi said, recovered from her fit of mirth. "That's a good picture of you, Ann. You look gorgeous in forest green."

Her cheeks pink, Annabelle closed the album and handed it to Kensi. "I should write something on the back." Before Kensi stopped her, she darted to her desk with the photograph and scribbled on it with a blue stick. She spun around as he approached. "I should give you the pen, too. See? It's retractable. Pretty sure you don't have retractable pens on Tehara—right?" Grinning, she held out the blue stick and the portrait.

Enoch played with the strange pen for a moment, enjoying the *click* as he depressed a plunger on one end just as Annabelle demonstrated. He felt a pang of bittersweet emotion he couldn't identify. "I will cherish this always. Thank you." His eyes widened at a sudden idea, and he dug into his belt-pouch. "Wait, I have something for you, too." He pulled out a dartling jay feather, and then tucked the photograph inside, wrapped with a clean handkerchief, beside the clicky pen.

"Aw, that's sweet," Kensi murmured from behind him.

Annabelle accepted the black-barred silver feather, holding it against her heart. She looked on the verge of tears and her red-rimmed eyes were very blue. "Will you come back?"

"I'll try to come again tomorrow, or the day after." Hopefully, Annabelle's suspicious friend wouldn't be there.

With a faint cry, she threw her arms around him, and he froze. Over Annabelle's head, Kensi narrowed her eyes. *I might not understand maidens, but I know a threat when I see one.* Annabelle squeezed him tight and then pulled away before he moved. "I'll pray for you, that you get home safe, and you find your missing friends in the woods."

Enoch managed a wan smile. "Farewell, for now."

Kensi came to stand beside her friend, smiling, pleased as a cat with a bowl of cream. "It's nice meeting you, Enoch. Sorry I was so snippy."

No, she isn't sorry. That maiden is glad to see the back of me.

Enoch took a deep breath, then stepped through the shimmering silver arch in her wall. He rushed along the light-streaked tunnel toward another silver window, every second increasing its size. It expanded to fill his entire existence.

The air, the very fabric of reality pulsed and then *snapped* as he plunged back into the heat of a summer midafternoon. He shut his eyes, blinded by the commingled glare of three suns' light. The world tilted crazily, spinning off balance until the earth smashed into him like one of the commander's iron-hard fists.

RAVEN WATCH

"Hey, kid. You all right?"

Enoch opened his eyes. Fiery worms burrowed through his skull and guts. He squeezed his eyes shut, groaning, and then opened them again. Had he taken ill? Perhaps he lay curled up in warm bedclothes, snug in his bed at the Lilac Manor.

A man walked toward him, his torso ridged with knife scars, the flat of a massive broadsword resting on one shoulder, his eyes blazing with golden light as dark auburn hair fluttered in the summer breeze…

"Kid?"

He blinked, and the scarred man holding the enormous sword disappeared. Toad crouched a foot away, peering into his face.

With a grimace, Enoch sat up, leaning his head against the Wall. The sky no longer beamed fair and blue; clouds the color of bruises gathered in the southwest. The air felt heavy and close. Thunder rumbled in the distance. A storm was coming.

Enoch buried his face in his hands and groaned. Commander Storm was coming.

"Hey, kid! Are. You. Okay?"

Had there been the slightest bit of concern in his gravelly voice?

Little by little, memories of his experience emerged past the discomfort. *I crossed the Void-Bridge.* He calmed his breathing. The worms gnawing at his brain and stomach died, leaving behind the clean sensation of hunger.

He lowered his hands and offered his friend a bright smile. "Yeah, I'm fine, thanks."

Toad glowered at him. "Spectacular. Wonderful. Glad that's all squared away. Because for a while, you weren't here!"

Enoch scrambled to his feet, scanning the area. Several trees to the North were fallen, and something had decimated the colony bushes, leaving a clear path into Enoch's secret glade. It looked like a cyclone hit the place. "What happened?"

"I was hoping you'd explain," Toad replied waspishly. "There I was, minding my business, hunting slugs in the underbrush, when you come blundering in with your dog-faced buddy and summon a friggin' tornado. Thanks, a whole boatload, kid."

The breath rushed out of him. *Is this mess my fault?* "Merciful Yshua. Where's Red?"

Toad hopped toward the torn-up bushes. "Follow me. He's still alive; I checked. You're welcome."

Heart pounding with dread, Enoch rushed past him. "Red,

where are you?"

A groan drifted from beyond the bushes. He wended his way through splintered stumps and jagged branches. The deer, who sheltered in a copse of oak trees, trotted over, ears raised and eyes rolling. Back by the trail, the kaenhir reclined against a pile of broken branches and shredded foliage, his green eyes blank and unfocused. Miraculously, his monocle was still screwed in over his left eye. Aside from his disheveled clothing, he seemed unharmed. One hand held Enoch's satchel, the strap broken, and the other clutched his sheathed sword. Enoch grasped at his belt; sure enough, the scabbard frogging had ripped free.

Slowly, Red turned his head. He spoke in his native tongue. "Young knight, a great wind and tumult came down from the heavens." He blinked. "You are well?"

Tears stung Enoch's eyes. He knelt beside the seneschal and touched his shoulder. "I'm fine, Red. Are you all right? Did you hit your head? Let me look at it."

Red submitted to his ministrations, his whiskers twitching with amusement. "Yes, a minor bump, but your servant has a hard head. He has recovered." His nostrils flaring, the seneschal leaned closer and inhaled. "What is this scent?" He grabbed Enoch's arm and snuffled along his chest. His ears trembled. "It is like you, only… sweeter."

Enoch pulled away. "Ack! Stop it, Red. You must smell Annabelle. She hugged me before I left." He cleared his throat. "Can you get up? I didn't feel any swelling or cracks."

Although unsteady, Red rose to his feet. He summoned his mount with a clicking sound and then leaned against her. "You cannot deter your servant from the scent; speak more of this maiden you claim to visit, young knight."

Hurriedly, Enoch dug out the photograph and the blue clicky pen.

"Here, she gave these to me. I hope it's enough to prove to anyone I went to another world." He depressed the plunger on the pen several times, grinning at the clicking sound.

Red looked from one object to the other, but made no move to touch them. His ears and eyebrows rose. "What manner of witchcraft is this?" he asked, one hand grasping the crucifix he always wore.

Enoch thrust the photograph at him. "See? It's not witchcraft, Red. This is a portrait of Annabelle, the maiden whose scent is on my armor. And yes, she is very sweet. Not dangerous in the least." Annabelle's friend, Kensi, was another matter; he refrained from mentioning her.

Red hesitated, then took the photograph, gingerly holding it on the edges in both hands. Brow furrowed, he brought it up to his face, sniffed it, and then peered at it intently, his pupils dilating. He closed his eyes and shook his head, grimacing. "Not dangerous, the stripling says," he muttered in his native tongue. "A thing may be sweet and still be dangerous, young knight, through no fault of its own. Very dangerous."

Irritation prickled through Enoch like nettles. He suppressed it; Red was still addled from the windstorm he'd caused. He held out a hand. "Could I please have it back now?"

Ears quivering, Red lowered the photograph as if it was a precious artifact he feared to break. Enoch took it—trying not to snatch—and Red sighed, slumping against his mount.

Enoch frowned. *Poor fellow, he must have hit his head harder than I thought. And I'm to blame for it.*

While Enoch tucked the items into his belt-pouch, Red looked up at the sky and his eyes widened. "What is the time?" He patted at his vest, reaching for an interior pocket, and extracted his silver watch. He flicked it open and blinked at it. "Half-past five of the clock. Raven Watch. Is it tea-time already?"

Right on cue, Enoch's stomach growled. He grinned, sheepishly.

Red's whiskers twitched. "There is time enough to eat before seeking the patrol."

Enoch nodded. "You should take it easy for a little while." The wensallen-kaen people were tough, he thought, pawing hurriedly through the saddlebags. Red would feel better after he ate something. He took the sword and satchel from the seneschal and pressed a bundle containing dried meat, cheese, and a canteen into his hands. While munching on a wedge of cheese, Enoch tied his scabbard to his belt with a thong and stowed his satchel in the half-emptied saddlebag while Red devoured the food.

Crouched by the new opening in the colony bushes, Toad observed everything in silence. The kaenhir finished the last morsel and went still, his nostrils flaring wide. "What scent is this?" he asked in Tradespeak. "It is a very strangish creature."

Toad inflated his throat sac and then exhaled in a loud croak. "No stranger than you, dog-face. What the heck are you supposed to be, some kind of werewolf?"

Red tensed. Enoch stepped between them. "That's Toad," he said. "Don't let him rile you up. He's harmless."

Toad puffed himself up again. "Who's harmless?"

"Mostly harmless," Enoch amended. "Toad, this is Raeden von Bleistaff, the Lord Seneschal of Lilac Manor."

Toad deflated, squinting at the kaenhir. "I thought his name was Red."

Enoch snorted. "No, that's just what I've called him ever since I was little."

Red growled. "A toddler cannot say the name correctly. This one grants a special—how to say it in this cursed tongue—ah, a dispensation, a special dispensation for the young knight. No one else must use it," he added in a warning tone.

"Wouldn't dream of it," Toad muttered.

Red's gaze sharpened, and he looked around, ears twitching. "What has happened here? One does not remember this… destruction."

Heat mantled Enoch's face. "Freak windstorm," he said. *Technically, it's the truth.*

"With the emphasis on 'freak,'" Toad added, rolling his eyes.

Enoch kicked a pebble at him. "Who's a freak, Mr. Talking Toad?"

"Enough, children!" Disgust wrinkled Red's short muzzle. He looked around, ending with a disdainful snort in Toad's direction. "Young knight, if the stomach is content, then it is time to leave. Your servant detects a foul stench in the air."

"Good riddance," Toad said. He swiveled on his hind legs and hopped into what remained of the brush.

THE WIND THAT GRIEVES

THE PERSISTENCE OF MEMORIES

In his master's presence, William's success with the stone circles vanished as if it never existed. He was seven winters old again and failing at the task Tenebris placed before him.

Tenebris bent over a huge, leather-bound tome covering the entire surface of a stone worktable. Guttering tapers perched upright in pockets of their own melted wax surrounded him, the light they provided tumbling down and around the folds of his silky, dark robe like water off a nightswan's wings. His eyes never leaving his master, William leaned against the door until it clicked shut.

Like a harmless scholar, unaware of the visitors in his presence, Tenebris continued to read.

William tucked his hands into opposite sleeves of his burkheld to conceal their trembling. A drop of sweat slid from his hairline and down his forehead. The tumultuous emotions quivering around the assassin were overpowering, palpable, and too chaotic for him to decipher. Even if he wanted to. Which he did not.

The assassin shifted one leg, making a noise. When their master failed to look up from his book, he ventured to clear his throat. "Milord?"

Better you than me, William thought.

Tenebris, sighed, turned from his volume, and regarded them both down his nose, one dark eyebrow raised. "Do you have news to report, harkhurz?"

The assassin flexed his fingers, hands hovering at his hips on either side. "Yes, milord. As instructed, I gather information."

"Good." Tenebris spoke without a trace of emotion in his voice. "Continue."

While the assassin delivered his report on troop disposition and their ongoing search for missing people, William observed his master in the same way a mouse watches a snake. Did he dare trust that calm tone? Perhaps Tenebris was in a decent mood today. Burn it! Reading his master's kythim always presented difficulties. At least he had good news to deliver this time. But how much could he tell without divulging his unorthodox methods? Upon hearing Zakaar mention the kadorei youth, he returned his attention to the conversation.

"The youth is wayward, yet earnest," Tenebris said, one hand stroking his short, spade-shaped beard. His eyes glittered in the candlelight. "Interesting. It seems your... appetites have proven an unexpected boon. Northward's determination to find those girls might lead him directly to us."

Him, along with an entire brigade of soldiers, if he's wise. William shifted uneasily. *The second-worst-case scenario for our plans.*

The assassin stepped closer, licking his lips. "Yes, Milord, he is certain to continue the search in the forest. I take him for you the next time he comes." His amber eyes gleamed out from the darkness under his hat brim. He grinned, saliva dripping from his fangs. "When you are done with him, may I kill and devour him? It is a matter of honor—"

"Silence." With a casual wave of his hand, Tenebris sent the assassin flying into the wall, knocking off his conical hat. The arkhabala tattooed on the master's hands writhed, a tangle of black, spiny worms.

William flinched, watching Zakaar's hat roll across the floor.

Tenebris continued in a soft voice. "When the time comes, you shall work with William to achieve our objective. I do not employ you to be… proactive."

The master's eyes glowed orange and black symbols crawled across ashen skin like angular snakes. He raised a hand and clenched his fingers into a fist. The assassin doubled over, whimpering and groaning.

With a sickened fascination, William watched his body shudder and twitch. *So, that's what it looks like from this side.* His stomach churned as if he'd swallowed poison and he pressed his lips together. *I will not vomit. Why don't I become hardened to this?*

After a moment, the master's face relaxed and his arkhabala went quiescent. The eldritch light faded from his eyes. He uncurled his fingers and lowered his hand. Breath rasping in his throat, the assassin straightened up again. His yellow eyes flashed with a long-burning resentment. Without his hat, the harkhurz's brown-furred visage, pinned ears, bristling whiskers, and bared fangs were visible.

Tenebris narrowed his eyes and muttered a cantrip under his breath. The arkhabala along his jawline stirred. He raised a hand again, but this time he made a curious beckoning gesture. The assassin's irate expression turned to one of horror as his body slid toward Tenebris. With a grunt of disgust, Tenebris jerked his hand up, and a pendant the assassin wore on a leather thong around his neck jumped out from underneath his stained jacket. Tenebris made the beckoning gesture again, and the assassin grunted as the thong tugged against his neck before finally breaking. The pendant shot across the chamber and into Tenebris's waiting hand. He closed his long fingers over the pendant, his eyes never leaving the assassin's.

"This is the order of the Dreadlord," Tenebris murmured. "You are not to molest the youth in any way. Do not disobey me in this. You have caused enough trouble already in indulging your appetites. If you muck this up, there will be a very object lesson in store for you. And it will be the last. Do I make myself clear?"

William choked on the terror and mortified anger radiating from his colleague like a foul stench. Jagged streaks of yellow and broken spirals of rust-red twisted through his kythim.

The assassin nodded. "I am your very obedient servant, milord. I will wait."

Tenebris smiled thinly. "Very good. See that you do." Turning to his workbench, he opened a drawer, dropped the spent pendant inside, and withdrew two items. His smile gone, Tenebris tossed first another pendant and then a small metal flask to the assassin. "Here is a fully charged talisman. And your medicine. Now, leave us." He flicked a hand and the door creaked open behind William.

Zakaar tucked both the new talisman and the potion inside his jacket, snatched his hat off the floor, and scuttled out of the room. The door slammed shut behind him.

William sidled toward his worktable, his eyes never leaving his master. Tenebris stared at the laboratory door with one hand resting on his chin. William eased himself into his chair. The wood creaked, and he winced.

Tenebris stroked his spade-shaped beard. "Our old home, William— do you recall it? The place we lived before entering the Dreadlord's service."

William's brow furrowed. *What in Vorniad's six abysses is he on about now—is this an attempt to trick me into being punished?* He cleared his throat and managed a sickly smile. "Of course, Master. Gangolorum. The greatest nehmwight fortress south of the Nevermelt. We didn't live there very long, before we needed to flee…" His voice died away and he suppressed the scowl forming on his face. *He asks me a question and then doesn't even listen to me.*

Tenebris gazed off into the middle distance. His expression and kythim were both unreadable as he fingered the locket he always wore on a golden chain around his neck. William licked his lips and fussed with his burkheld. What did Tenebris mean by asking him about Gangolorum?

He recalled their first home in flashes, the memories jumbled and often frightening. Some were neutral—even pleasant, if confusing. William running across a courtyard of polished stones toward a patch of sunlight; Tenebris shouting at him to get back in the house. The moonlit garden of pallid, waxy flowers growing on tall stalks, their perfume making him sneeze. A fire crackling merrily in a stark, glossy hearth of obsidian built into the wall. Tenebris on his hands and knees, hair hanging loose and hiding his face, body shaking—was he *weeping*? William's grip on his robes tightened. *Some things, I don't want to remember. Suns burn that stupid locket.*

While they lived in the nehmwight city, William had discovered the locket in a box under his master's bed. He recalled how it looked overly large in his small hands. A fascinating item, out of place amongst an Arkhadahn's possessions. Tenebris came into the room before he opened it. William winced. The way his master's face contorted with rage still gave him nightmares. *That's the first time he beat me—for invading his privacy, he said.* Ever since, his master kept the locket on his person.

His master's orange-eyed gaze sharpened and Tenebris tucked the locket away, under his robes. William leaned back in his chair as his master's glare bored into him. With the image of Tenebris bent and shuddering fresh in his memory, he feared the Arkhadahn read his mind. His words tumbled out like dice from a cup. "Te—I mean, M-master? What—I, uh, I mean, why mention Gangolorum?"

Tenebris narrowed his eyes and sneered at him. "Stand up, William. I never gave you leave to sit. And how many times have I told you to stop mumbling and enunciate?"

More times than I care to count, Tenebris. He rose, speaking without thought. "Do you want me to answer?" Inwardly, he cringed.

Tenebris grunted. "Of course not, fool. It was a rhetorical question." With one eyebrow arched, he leaned forward, bracing himself with his forearms on the table. "Now, you returned earlier than I expected. Tell me about the damage to the warding spells."

William suppressed a relieved sigh; no object lesson for him today. Hopefully. He straightened his burkheld. On the way back to the ruined fortress, he'd debated how much he should reveal. He'd decided on the truth—but not the entire truth.

Unless he specifically asks, I won't tell him how *I assessed the damage. And I won't talk about the surveillance spell.*

He tucked his hands into opposite sleeves to hide their trembling and cleared his throat. "The crystal was shattered in the one I checked. So far as I determined, the wards are decaying at the rate you expected, Master. And there's no sign they'll recover or regenerate—not without a new crystal." He rolled his shoulders back and smiled, thinking of his accomplishment.

Tenebris raised his eyebrows. "You determined this after examining—what? One or two ward-spell rings? You scarcely had time to examine more of them."

William hesitated, searching his mentor's kythim, straining to sense his mood. *Nothing. How does he manage it?*

Tenebris closed his eyes and sighed. "Go on, William. I won't punish you, so long as you explain." He straightened up and folded his arms across his chest. He speared William with a pointed gaze, adding, "Intelligibly."

William swallowed. "The circles are still linked," he replied. "Somehow, even though the blistering spell crystals were obliterated. I tapped into the connection." He went on, describing what he'd done to assess the damage. While he spoke, his master flipped through parchments on his worktable. The man's kythim never flickered.

How does he keep it so tightly controlled?

When William finished his summary, Tenebris frowned. "This confirms the Dreadlord's suspicions," he murmured, as if to himself. He drummed his fingers on the tabletop. And then, he froze. He looked up, his eyes burning embers. His voice grew silky soft. "You tapped into an Aethyric binding, didn't you, William?"

"Only on the surface," he blurted out. "And just long enough to confirm the crystals were gone and the ward was dead." He gripped his forearms, palms clammy, fingernails digging into the skin. "Master, after all you've taught me… I'd never sully myself with the workings of the dwelfnim."

Tenebris held him in his glare for a moment. William held his breath. And then, a shark-like grin split the Arkhadahn's face. "As usual, you misunderstand me, William." Turning to a cabinet, he pulled out a drawer and removed an object wrapped in purple cloth. "I am pleased with you. It is time you attempted the Seeker's Web again—and with a more potent memory anchor. If I can trust you to keep it intact."

William's eyes widened as his master approached him with the bundle cradled gently between his hands as if it was a small animal he feared would escape. *A new memory anchor. What is it?*

He took his hands out of his sleeves to accept the bundle, holding it as carefully as he'd seen his master do. He willed his hands not to shake, and for a mercy, they remained steady. The purple cloth proved to be a silk handkerchief, a design embroidered in a visible corner, but the stitching had been marred beyond recognition. The item it contained felt heavy for its size, the length of his hand and half as wide. He lifted one embroidered corner.

Tenebris touched his wrist and William paused. "Not now," his master said. "Put it away somewhere safe."

William opened his satchel and settled it into a cushioned compartment. He turned back to his master, tucking hands into opposite sleeves again.

Tenebris placed a hand on his shoulder. William forced himself not to flinch away from the intensity of the Arkhadahn's gaze. "I don't think I need to tell you to take care with it. I invested a considerable amount of time and effort into its making."

William gulped. More than a Cycle had passed since he'd broken one of his master's craftings but he still remembered the punishment. "I'll be careful."

The grip on his shoulder tightened to the point of pain. "If you break it—" his master's voice went cold, "—you will suffer for it."

William's hands shook within his sleeves. He dug his fingers into his forearms to still their trembling. *Must not show weakness.* He raised his chin and met his master's gaze. "I won't break it, Master."

Unblinking, they stared at one another. Pressure built inside William's skull. Colorful shapes sprang into existence around his mentor, tendrils waving like smoky pennants.

William's heart pounded. *Am I reading his kythim?*

Tenebris's eyes flared. Gasping, William flinched back. As swiftly as they appeared, the dynamic colors winked out and the Arkhadahn's kythim subsided into its usual flat grayness. He blinked in confusion.

Eyes narrowed, Tenebris leaned in until their noses touched. "You are not strong enough to challenge me, apprentice. Not for many moons yet." He squeezed harder. William's eyes stung with tears.

I won't cry. This is nothing, nothing compared to the pain I endured when I gained my arkhabala. I will not. Blistering. Cry.

Abruptly, Tenebris released his shoulder and stepped back. "Very good," he purred. A smile spread across his face—a rare smile reaching his eyes. The smile wasn't warm, but it approached something akin to warmth. "Join me for a meal. Casting the Seeker's Web will exhaust your arkhabala."

William ventured a smile of his own while surreptitiously massaging his shoulder. "Thank you, Master. I'd like something hot inside to fortify myself."

Lit by the green-blue light of a ferglis-lamp, the subterranean room felt close and smelled of mildew and blood. William's gorge rose at the memories of the last time he worked in the conjuring chamber.

William stepped up to the interrogation table with the knife in his trembling hand. Strapped down and prone on the table lay the flayed man with a golden aura. Blood oozed from the wounds Tenebris had made, running into the channels etched into the surface of the metal. The flayed man sneered and called him names. William's anger ignited. Orange-streaked violet light flashed. The man disappeared, and a creature the size of a tomcat squatted on the blood-soaked table. Tenebris screamed at William to kill it; William retched from the stench of blood filling his nose...

And then, the cursed thing had escaped through a drain. Tenebris made him search the ancient castle's sewer. William spent hours crawling through dank tunnels, to no avail. As he mused on his past failure, he felt the echo of his master's punishment, the Pain Hex, like bits of jagged metal cutting into his skin. A hiss escaped him, and he rolled his shoulders back to relieve the sudden tension. His grip tightened on the satchel slung over his shoulders.

Suns burn it all to ash. Why couldn't he forget about the incident and just move on?

I'll forget when I find the burning snoop. And put an end to it, once and for all.

William clenched his jaw and turned away from the metal table with its limp, dangling straps. He approached the spellform, a twelve-pointed star engraved in a square-shaped, basalt slab three feet across. Twelve radii forming deep grooves bisected each ray and ended beneath a glyph carved above each vertex. Like the clock things the kadorei filth used to tell time. He wanted to get his hands on one of those, take it apart and then tinker with its innards. But enough of that; Tenebris had tasked him to produce a functional Seeker's Web to locate their erstwhile prisoner.

Thus far, William had failed to do so.

William knelt beside the spellform, placed the satchel on the floor, and opened the flap. Each vertex was a station for an anchor-item. He took one of the thirteen objects from within, an oblong item wrapped in cloth. Carefully, he unwound the cloth to reveal a glass statuette of a woman with a crimson inclusion at its heart. *Tenebris will kill me if this breaks.*

His master's voice droned in his memory. *"Each anchor-item must be tied to the Arkhadahn; either a meaningful trinket or something prepared specifically for the ritual. Take care in your selection, William, for these things will serve as a beacon for your roving spirit."*

William stared at the statuette cradled in his hands. A gentle warmth embraced him, an echo of something he'd once known but then forgotten. Comfort and safety. A shadowy face with a soft smile and kind, dark eyes. A gentle voice, singing. And then, the sensation changed to cool glass and emptiness. Tears filled his eyes. He sniffled. Scowling, he bent to wipe his nose on his sleeve.

Vervik's bulging sinews, he needed a drink. But Tenebris could walk in at any moment. Best get on with it before his hands started shaking and he dropped the blistering thing.

He chanted a brief cantrip, touched the figurine to his forehead, and then dabbed it under his eyes, anointing its head with his tears. For memory, tears were as effective as blood. He set it down on the glyph in the first position. Memory, to anchor him to the past. The memory object always came first; after that, it didn't matter what order he set out the anchor items.

William pulled out a fresh sprig of bloodwort fern collected from a plant he nurtured himself. He placed it in the eleventh position, over the glyph for Life. Next came the things representing the four primal aspects: a marble bowl filled with pebbles for earth, an inflated bladder for air, a flask containing water, and a candle stub which he lit to represent fire. Those went in the twelfth, sixth, ninth, and third positions respectively. The other six anchor items represented the senses: a polished mirror for sight, a brass bell for hearing, an ermine's pelt for touch, a small jar of fever-bee honey for taste, a bundle of dried lavender for smell, and a carpenter's level for balance.

Again, he heard his master's voice in his memory. *"The thirteenth object represents the person, place, or thing sought by the Arkhadahn. When seeking a person, it is best to fashion a poppet from twigs, rags, or even clay; the construction material does not matter. However, the one thing a poppet must contain is hair, blood, or saliva from the—are you even listening to me? Pay attention, William!"*

He scowled and rubbed his head, recalling the resulting blow. "I always pay attention, Tenebris," he muttered as he pulled the thirteenth item from his satchel. He set it across the depression at the center of the spellform. The poppet, a man-shaped bundle of twigs covered with clay, had been simple enough to construct. He'd worked strands of reddish-brown hair into the wet clay and a scrap of blood-stained cloth at its center. He swallowed queasiness; there'd been plenty of blood on the grooved table when Tenebris had finished cutting the man.

William made a rude gesture toward his master's study. "Take that, Tenebris," he hissed. "My poppet contains both the hair and blood of the one I seek."

Not that he wanted his master to see his handiwork. It would be a boon if Tenebris delayed checking up on him for another few minutes. He did not want his master present for the next step. He reached for a bone knife on the tray beside the basalt slab. Made of sharkskin, the hilt wrapping kept it from sliding in a hand slick with moisture.

William's eyes traced the spellform's grooves, following channels sloping to the vertices from the raised cup in the center, like the caldera of a volcano, and the poppet resting on the raised edges. He licked his lips. He must fill the little cup. William bared his forearm up to the elbow, held his left arm over the center, and placed the edge of a bone knife against the underside of his left forearm. He drew in a shaky breath. There were plenty of scars; the latest cut had only recently scabbed over. His hand refused to move.

Come on, do it. You've done this before. How else can you achieve mastery of the Arkhabadh? How else will you claim power?

Another memory, this time from a place far in the west, a secret place.

A pair of violet eyes bored into him; ancient eyes filled with knowledge and an assurance beyond even his master's. *"There is always a price for power,"* the Dreadlord said in a resonant voice. *"Are you prepared to pay it, William Dulciber?"*

William clenched his jaw. Yes, he was. He'd seize power by the horns and let it gore him if he must. *Power equals freedom; my favorite equation. I will pay the price to balance it.* His hand jerked, and the knife slashed through his gray skin. Blood welled up from the cut, black in the blue-green light. It stung, but it wasn't the pain bothering him. It was never the pain; he'd grown accustomed to that. *Why can't I get used to the sight of blood?*

He swallowed with an effort, wiping the knife on his robe. He set it on the tray beside the stone slab without taking his eyes off the dark stream trickling down his arm and dripping over the poppet and into the central cup. The little depression filled, embracing the poppet, and then blood crept through the channels of the spellform. He pursed his lips and forced himself to watch. The coppery stench of blood burned in his nostrils.

Don't vomit, don't vomit, don't vomit… He swallowed again.

As soon as sufficient blood filled the grooves, he wrapped the wound and then tied off the bandage with his teeth. He winced. One obstacle surmounted. One more to go. Despite having set up the spell in flawless textbook fashion, he always failed the next step. He curled his fingers into fists to stop their shaking.

Varma's flail, I could really use a drink right now.

William banished his craving and took another deep breath. His hand still trembled as he dipped his index and middle fingers into the shallow pool of blood on either side of the poppet. Again, he recalled his master's voice: *"The seeker's web is a mid-level spell and comprises thirteen blood runes. No, no, attend me, you clumsy oaf! You must draw the lines perfectly straight, or you shall suffer a nasty backlash."* And then, a wicked chuckle echoed in his mind. *"Pain is the best teacher for an apprentice as dim-witted as you."*

Shut up, Tenebris, you old bat.

A delicious thrill ran through William at his mental rebellion. He bent over the spellform and painstakingly traced twelve glyphs on the raised triangles between the channels. While muttering an incantation, he paused to replenish his sanguine ink. Disgust filled him at the warm stickiness. Sweat popped out of his pores and prickled, sliding along the groove of his spine. William clenched his jaw, forcing guttural phrases out through his teeth in choking gasps. *I will not vomit,* he thought as he drew the glyphs. In the blue-green light, the angular figures looked like men frozen in tortuous poses.

He daubed the thirteenth glyph—a broken circle with a line extending from a dot in its center—on his forehead and uttered the thirteenth phrase of power. His skin tingled. Along his back and across his shoulders, the arkhabala pulsed and uncoiled, a many-legged predator waking from sleep. His skin quivered beneath the sticky blood rune on his forehead. Light like heatless embers flared along the channels carved in the basalt slab and filled with his blood; the sullen, orange glow outlined every object in the chamber.

William's eyes widened and his pulse quickened. *I did it. The web's activated!* Shock weakened his concentration. He bit back an oath, tightened his mental hold on the poppet while envisioning it as one with the flayed man from his memories, and cast his mind spiraling out, a falcon on the hunt. Like a hound following a scent.

Seek, seek, seek…

Images flashed before his eyes but refused to resolve into coherent patterns. Damp coolness against his palms. A dartling jay's piercing cry rang in his ears. His nostrils flooded with the dark and spicy smells of earth and vegetable matter. His mouth filled with the taste of slugs and earthworms. Slime coated his tongue.

William gagged. The sensory impressions fled. Fiery whips slashed him along the arkhabala vines tattooed in his flesh and the bloody glyph on his forehead. William bent over, dry heaving, arms clasped over his middle. Nothing came up, praise the Outer Darkness. But he'd lost his trace on the one he sought. *I had him for a moment, though.* Blood roared in his ears like an echo of the wind rushing through tree branches.

For a moment, I succeeded.

A GRAVESITE

A strong breeze shook the branches above them, and the canopy foliage rustled. The hairs on the back of Enoch's neck prickled. He glanced behind them. Nothing. Although his sense of smell lacked the seneschal's acuity, he agreed with Red; something didn't feel right. The deer displayed no sign they detected any threat, but unease made Enoch's scalp tingle. He scanned the bushes along the road, his hand hovering near the hilt of his sword.

Kaspar's wings, what is it?

Nothing appeared amiss.

Should I use my listening knack? He glanced at Red's back and pricked ears; he'd kept his skill secret for moons. After his comment about

Annabelle's portrait being witchcraft—and the tales about wyldlings using their abilities for evil—what would Red think if he caught him at it? He fidgeted with the reins. *Beggar it, either he or the commander are bound to winkle it out. I suppose now's as good a time as any.*

Red's mount halted, and he twisted in the saddle. The doe accommodated him by shifting around until she stood broadside. "Young knight, are you well? Something has your waistcoat in the punch." His emerald eyes glimmered with concern.

Enoch stared at the seneschal. *I don't recognize that one.* He swallowed, his throat dry. "Do you still believe the portrait of Annabelle is witchcraft?"

Red eyed him for several heartbeats and then shook his head. "Your servant would have taken it from you if he did." He tilted his head. "Speak in plainness: what troubles you?"

How much should he reveal? He opened his mouth and then closed it. Reins squeezed in his hands, he blurted out, "I can use the wind to hear things I wouldn't otherwise hear."

Red's expression never changed. His whiskers did not quiver. "It is your servant's observation," he said "that you use the wind for other purposes, as well."

Enoch stiffened and then drooped in the saddle. "You're right, Red. The windstorm in the clearing was my fault. I'm sorry; I never meant to hurt you. And as for why you didn't come along with me to see Annabelle..." He shrugged.

Red relaxed, his whiskers twitching. "You are forgiven. It shall not be spoken of again unless you wish it."

The oppression on Enoch's spirits lifted. "Then you're fine with it? May I show you?"

Red nodded and pricked his ears. "Your servant is very curious."

With one eye on the seneschal, Enoch drew in a breath and concentrated, listening. He accomplished it with much less effort than in the past. Instead of merely amplifying his hearing, this time his consciousness merged with the wind.

Did my journey through the void place to Annabelle's world change me, enhance my "knack" somehow?

He glided around the trees and over dips and ridges in the forest, speeding toward men's voices, hounds snuffling, and shovels plunging into the soil. He saw nothing, but heard a trooper cry out: "Here, this one's hardly buried. Gilgamesh's toenails, it *reeks!*"

It sounded like the voice of Bart Ainsley, whom Captain Faulkner assigned to his personal guard.

Enoch gasped and reeled his senses back. His head spun with vertigo, but the spell passed within a matter of heartbeats. Cautiously, he spooled out his awareness in silver threads, more slowly this time. *Yes, there!* He'd located the path to the search detail.

"Red, I found a shortcut." He rattled off a series of directions.

Red's ears lifted. "You are certain?"

He nodded. "Trust me."

Red bowed. "Of course, young knight." The kaenhir avoided his eyes and his ears quivered, betraying his unease.

Enoch clenched his jaw. *He never said outright he was fine with it.*

They rode along the path and made a turn to a game trail, which they followed until they encountered another faint pathway, where Enoch concentrated again.

"We'll take this trail for another half-mile, then turn right just after the split rock. There's another trail there."

In this manner, Enoch directed him along another game trail for over an hour until they encountered a sentinel, leaning against a tree and chewing on a twig to clean his teeth. The man's eyes widened, and he nearly choked on his twig.

Enoch recognized the garrison soldier: James Guffin, three summers Enoch's senior and one man who'd come forward to be in his personal guard. The young soldier had recently married. Everyone called him Guffie, instead of Jim, because his brother-in-law was also named James.

"Milord!" Guffin saluted the kaenhir, and then his eyes shifted to Enoch behind him. He brightened and saluted the young knight. "Sir Enoch! Dep must be prescient. He set me to watch for you, if you came. Halloway's standing sentinel to the North of the hollow, yonder." He jerked his head to show the direction.

Enoch replied with a ghost of his former humor as he slid out of the saddle. "Hey, Guffie. Guess what? Captain Faulkner told me—"

"Corporal James Guffin," Red interrupted in a clipped tone, his back ramrod straight. His gaze was pointed enough to deflate Enoch's cheer. "Deputy Korr has set you to watch. Did he give leave for you to take in the ease?" The kaenhir slid out of the saddle and after straightening his vest, clasped his hands behind his back and, with eyebrows raised, looked down his nose at the guilty party.

Wide-eyed, Guffin opened and closed his mouth without making a sound. Longtime companion of Corporal Halloway, Guffin enjoyed the same degree of Red's disapproval; with the notable exception of the medic, Philip Sharkness, Enoch's childhood associates still lived in terror of the Lord Seneschal of Lilac Manor.

Enoch sighed. "Never mind Red. Just take us to the others, Guffie."

Guffie tossed his twig aside as he turned to the North and stepped around the tree. "This way, please."

Even without his secret listening knack, Enoch heard the soldiers long before they entered the small, sheltered glade where they labored. The *shuck-shuck* of shovels biting into the loamy earth, the grating noise of canvas dragged across the forest floor, and Sergeant Matlock's voice raised to encourage—or rather, to taunt—one of his underlings to greater efforts.

"Balthazar's Blades, Telly! My bedridden granny can shovel faster than that. Put your back into it, man."

What were they excavating? The men were supposed to be out searching for the girls, not digging holes. A chill ran up Enoch's spine.

Guffie called out, "Deputy. I found 'em! Er, I mean, they found me, sir!"

Enoch smiled, but then sobered upon seeing the grave expressions of Deputy Ignatius Korr and the man with him, Levi Quent. A couple medium-sized sable and tan dogs with sad, rheumy eyes, droopy ears, and pendulous jowls lounged at Quent's feet. *Gog and Magog.* Because of their physiognomy these dogs always looked depressed, even when given treats. Gog and Magog pricked their ears and wagged their tails. Enoch resisted the urge to pet them. Instead, he looked to the men for an explanation.

The deputy and the tracker both saluted him with fists to chests. They nodded to the seneschal, who returned their greeting with his customary flawless composure. But Enoch recognized the tension in his lowered tail, clenched jaw, and quivering ears.

Enoch returned the salute. "What have you found?" he demanded, cold sweat trickling down his back at the bleak look in the men's eyes.

You know already.

"If you please, sir," Deputy Korr replied evenly. "Come with me and I'll show you. Quent and Guffin will watch your mounts." He raised his eyebrows at the two men. "You're on sentry duty."

Quent responded in the twangy drawl of a former Western Marches resident. "Yes, sir."

As they passed, Deputy Korr looked at him with concern. "Sir Enoch? You might wish to prepare yourself. Most folks find this sort of thing very disturbing."

"Forgiveness. One must be certain." The seneschal pushed past them to enter the clearing, his black-splotched tail bushed out.

"Red, wait—"

The rest of his words caught in his throat. Heart hammering, Enoch scanned the little glade. Seven gnarled and massive old trees surrounded it like cowled hags brooding over a cauldron. Their roots humped up out of the ground to produce serpentine ridges surrounding the clearing like a terrace in an amphitheater. Red perched on one of these huge buttress roots, tail still bushed out behind him, hunkered with his left forearm braced upon his thighs while he clutched his crucifix in his right hand. Ears pricked forward, Red observed intently. His whiskers trembled with suppressed emotion as he mouthed a prayer under his breath. He made no sign of acknowledgment when Enoch passed him.

Six troopers worked in the glade under Sergeant Matlock's supervision. One of them was Trooper Tellyson, Guffin's brother-in-law. The sergeant ceased haranguing him and glanced at Enoch as he approached. Enoch raised a hand and shook his head. He didn't want to draw attention to himself. Three of the troopers extracted dead leaves, twigs, and other detritus from natural hollows formed beneath the trees by the junction of multiple roots; Matlock scolded them for their lack of progress. The men had excavated five rectangular holes around the clearing, one each at the base of one of the massive trees, the dirt piled in the middle of the clearing. Two troopers finishing the sixth excavation knelt at the edges to pull something out of it. A third trooper with a handkerchief covering his nose and mouth rooted through a seventh hollow in the junction between two huge roots.

On the ground beside one of the largest holes lay a large oblong bundle of once-white material stained by soil and other effluvia. A giant moth cocoon? No. Cocoons didn't have patterns stitched on them. Bed linens did. He glanced away, his throat tight.

The pattern along a ragged edge of the wrappings resembled one stitched on the bed sheets used in the servants' quarters in the Manor. Or on the troopers' beds in the barracks.

Ice rimed his heart as the men by the sixth hole hauled up another wrapped bundle. It looked as if it contained what once was a person… His lips thinned. No, it's a *moth cocoon*! The sergeant hurried over, his face grim. The two soldiers—Trooper Tellyson and Trooper Ainsley—looked up from brushing off their trousers and saluted.

Mouth dry as ashes, Enoch went toward the man who worked alone, Corporal Philip Sharkness, the cohort's foremost medic and another of Enoch's childhood playmates. He bent over the shallow declivity and smoothed away the loose dirt and detritus.

Another cocoon. Rust-red effluvium stained the material enclosing this object. Enoch held his hand over his mouth. The air was foul and thick with a putrid stench.

"Sharky," Enoch said in a low voice. It came out sounding hoarse.

The dark-haired man jerked around. He blinked once, and then he pulled down his makeshift mask. "Sir Enoch. You made it."

This is the last thing I wanted. "Stop calling me that. I'm not officially raised yet."

The medic bowed his head. "Soon enough and you will be. We should get used to it now."

Red appeared to have regained his composure. He gestured toward the cloth-swathed bundles with one hand while covering his muzzle with a handkerchief he held in the other, his voice nasal and muffled. "This one sees you found bodies here. The number is not—how do you say it? —auspicious, yes. Know you who they are?"

"We just, ah, exhumed them." Sharky rubbed his forehead with the back of his right wrist. "And though the doctor's been training me some in pathology, I'd rather he be the one to examine the remains to determine identities. He should make the call. Right, Sarge?"

"Affirmative." Matlock came over to supervise the soldiers as they pulled the third body out of the declivity. Red nodded. Hackles raised, he crouched beside the swathed figure that Tellyson and Ainsley unearthed. Teeth bared in a silent snarl, the kaenhir stared at the stained linens but did not touch them.

Enoch rubbed his arms, pressing down the rising gooseflesh. Thunder rumbled, still distant, but drawing closer.

"There's a storm coming," Ainsley remarked, resting on the handle of his shovel. He wiped the sweat from his brow.

"Then hustle, soldier," Matlock barked. "Get them on the stretchers and ready to move out. Cover 'em with the tarps."

The men hustled.

Enoch covered his nose and mouth with a handkerchief and swallowed past the lump in his throat. The three bundles were not moth cocoons. They were shaped like people. None large enough to conceal the body of a grown man, but of a size to be the bodies of young girls. He regarded the third cocoon Sharky had pulled out of the shallow declivity.

The linens seemed loose as if someone had unwound and then hastily re-wrapped them. He forced himself to approach it.

"Sharky, I'm sure Dr. Fourtier wouldn't mind if we tried to identify them." He knelt beside his friend. "Whoever they are, we owe it to their families to resolve this. I, um, order you to attempt a preliminary examination of these cocoons, um, remains."

The medic pulled the handkerchief back up to cover the lower half of his face. With only his eyes visible, Sharky looked Turnings younger than his nineteen autumns. He heaved a shuddering sigh. "Aye, Sir."

Gingerly, Sharky peeled the filthy linen away from the corpse's face. He fell back on his rump as if someone pushed him over. "Ah." The medic crossed himself with a trembling hand.

"Balthazar's teeth!" Ainsley swore, eyes wide. The soldier staggered back and tripped over his shovel. Tellyson turned aside and retched.

"Well, lads?" Matlock demanded. "Who is it?" He stepped forward to look and swore. "Sweet Miryam, mother of Yshua! That's—" He glanced aside at the medic.

No time to be squeamish. Do your duty. You owe it to those girls and their families. He leaned in for a closer look. Beside him, Sharky stiffened. He grimaced, averted his gaze, and replaced the rag.

Shock punched Enoch in the gut, driving the air from his lungs. He recognized the lifeless features, despite the lack of luster in the dark eyes and blooming roses on its cheeks. He had seen it often enough, in life.

No, it can't be. Not Becky. I never told her…

Time crystallized around him. The bottom dropped out of his stomach and his head floated away like a balloon untethered from its moorings. He stared at the shrouded corpse. It was hidden now, but he couldn't unsee the tortured, silently screaming face.

Enoch closed his eyes, shaking. *I am so sorry, Becky. I wish Sir Rick were here. What would he say now?*

He touched his friend's shoulder. "I'm sorry, Sharky." *Too little. Far too little; Becky's his favorite cousin.* He swallowed the rest of his words before his voice broke.

Enoch's eyes burned. He gazed at the other two shrouded figures on the stretchers and covered with waterproof tarps. No need for verification, now. He knew whose faces those rust-stained wrappings concealed. His earlier fantasies of rescuing the three maidens from an enchanted tower were ridiculous fancies concocted from the dreams of a puerile fool.

"Sharkness, you need a moment?" Matlock's expression shifted to concern. The other three soldiers gathered nearby, looking troubled and uneasy.

The corporal started as if waking from a dream. He passed a hand over his forehead. "I'm okay, Sarge. I'll be fine."

Enoch squeezed the corporal's shoulder and then let go. What would Sir Rick do? He swallowed his queasiness and turned to face Matlock. "Let him have a break," he said, surprised at how calm and level his voice was. It seemed to come from somebody else's throat, for the grasping claws were gone. Icy numbness had replaced them.

They were gone. Janet, with her untidy hair and laughing eyes. Sally splashing in the pond, lecturing on the proper methods for capturing frogs. Lil' Becky Rosa, dancing with yellow roses in her hair…

Murdered.

Darkness passed before his eyes, but superimposed over it he saw Becky's face, smiling and rosy-cheeked in life, only to transform into the waxen and sunken-eyed horror beneath the stained and filthy rags. He wouldn't get another dance with her.

Sir Rick's face replaced it, stern with disapproval. *"The innocent must be protected."*

Good air in, bad air out, he thought, holding the handkerchief over his face. But here, all the air is bad. Foul with rot. Boughs of trees hung dark and heavy overhead as if the wings of a massive raven loomed over him. The air pressed in on him, laden with moisture and the stench of death. He stumbled out of the hollow, ignoring the voices his men raised in concern. He must leave before the weight of the dead crushed him. Silver light danced among the trees ahead of him, promising freedom. Enoch ran toward it, the trees no longer an obstacle. He gathered speed, and rose above the stuffy forest until the clean, cool wind blasted in his ears.

TRAITOR

Thunder rumbled.

Enoch staggered out from beneath the eaves of the Darkenwood Forest toward the Westgate. He didn't know how he'd arrived there, but very little time had passed since he left the crew in the hollow of death. His mind moved in circles, trapped in a rut like a cart on a city road. The image of Red's stricken face stuck in his mind—the way he stared with disbelief and horror at the linen-wrapped corpses.

Janet, Sally, and Becky. All dead. Murdered.

How could the Threefold One allow this to happen to innocent people? It made no sense.

He'd danced with Becky at the last Harvest Festival; he recalled his awkward, sweaty hands, and her beauty in the light of the bonfires. Yellow roses in her dark hair… Shock seared through him in a bolt of lightning. *I'll never dance with Becky again. I'll never play hide and seek with Janet or hunt polliwogs with Sally either.*

The cycle of memories began anew. Red's horror-struck visage. The waxen-skinned corpses in the hollow. Sir Rick, saying: *"The innocent must be protected."*

As he left the confines of the Darkenwood, the path took him to a clearing between the wilderness and the garrison walls. *Commander Storm calls it the killing ground*, he thought. *There's been too much killing lately*. He wanted to scream, "Why?" But claws tore at his throat and muted him.

Enoch blinked. He stood before the lowered Westgate. Behind him, thunder rumbled again. In the Eastern sky, clear of clouds, Lachesis sank toward the horizon. The rose-tinted sky deepened toward crimson.

He hollered a greeting, and then waited for the gate to open. The portcullis lifted and he trudged through the opening as soon as it rose high enough. Lilac fragrance hung heavy in the quiet, still air. The hush before a storm. He swept his gaze around the courtyard.

The courtyard appeared deserted aside from Lance-Sergeant Ravenos, who lurked beside the winch like a soot panther lying in ambush. The gatekeeper's eyes gleamed underneath the wide brim of a conical hat. His lips tightened between his mustache and beard. One of his hands drifted toward his injured side while the other formed a fist at his hip.

Enoch flexed the fingers of his right hand and placed it upon the pommel of his sword. "Honorless dog," he muttered under his breath as he strode past.

Snarling, Ravenos closed the distance between them, ripping open his jacket. Buttons clinked against the stones.

Enoch whirled. Steel rang as he drew his sword to block Ravenos's attack. His opponent's hirsute hands held a pair of weapons he'd hidden inside his uniform jacket. Enoch glimpsed short, tri-pronged blades—sword-breakers? —just before his blade slid between the prongs. Effortlessly, the fiend wrenched the sword from his grasp.

His sword clattered to the ground. Falling back on his hand-to-hand combat training, Enoch's right arm shielded his throat from the weapons lunging toward him. The gauntlet caught and deflected a blow as he stepped back and to one side, narrowly evading the second thrust.

Kaspar's Wings! His speed is on a level with Red's or the commander's. How can any kadorei man move so blustering fast? Oh, merciful Lord Yshua, please save me!

A silvery glow limned every object in Enoch's vision, announcing his attacker's every movement. He raised his arms to block another pair of thrusts with the tri-pronged weapons; with offensive strikes Ravenos lacked imagination. To Enoch's surprise, he had plenty of time to react to the gatekeeper's attack. There—an opening to disarm his larger opponent and then launch a strike of his own. Ravenos wore no armor on his wrists.

Heart hammering in his ears, Enoch completed the cross-block, and then swiftly brought his arms down in opposite directions, chopping at Ravenos's wrists with the edges of his stiffened hands. Enoch twisted his body to one side to avoid a boot meant to bury itself in his solar plexus. The gatekeeper snarled, dropping one weapon. He maintained his grip on one of them, though; Enoch's left knife-hand strike failed to hit its target squarely.

Ravenos recovered from the loss of one weapon faster than Enoch expected. Reversing his grip on the hilt of his remaining weapon, the gatekeeper countered with a barrage of lightning-fast punches interspersed with twirling roundhouse kicks he found difficult to avoid, even with his mysterious, silver-enhanced vision. Gasping, he raised an arm to deflect a fist or a foot when able but couldn't launch a counterstrike. His opponent bewildered him.

How could a kadorei man be so blustering nimble? And where on Tehara had Ravenos learned the wensallen-kaen style of combat? Red claimed the clans were fiercely protective of their martial arts training; they would never teach an outsider their secrets.

Who is this man?

Ravenos advanced with the implacable fury of a shadowy whirlwind, coat flapping, the metal prongs of the sword-breaker glinting in the sullen twilight as he hopped and spun, lashing out with alternating kicks and punches. Enoch backpedaled as he ducked and weaved to evade silver-outlined blows when he couldn't block.

Desperation sparked in his limbs. *I must call for help. Ravenos is too much for me to handle on my own. A garrison should be filled with soldiers. Where is everyone?*

Enoch dodged under the gatekeeper's sweeping arm and sucked in a deep breath. Warned in time by the silver outline, he evaded the prongs of his opponent's weapon, which Ravenos twisted around in his hand to slash at him. Startled, Enoch released his pent-up breath in a wordless cry of terror. A blast of silver-shining air slammed into the gatekeeper with a plosive sound, arresting his twirling attack and lifting him off the ground. Orange light flared sullenly under his shirt before flickering out like a snuffed candle.

Propelled by the wind, Ravenos flew back several paces, his limbs waving and his eyes comically wide. The gatekeeper lost his grip on his weapon as he landed and the sword-breaker clattered away. The straps securing his hat snapped, the wind tumbling it toward the gate. Ravenos sprang back to his feet with a grace belying his hulking frame. He came prowling toward him.

Enoch trembled with fatigue. He raised his arms to ward off his attacker and staggered, his legs turned to jelly. He opened his mouth, but nothing came out except a mouse's terrified squeak.

"Warlock!"

Ravenos howled like a rabid lykhar as he bore down on him, eyes flaring amber in the lurid, sanguine light. An incredible force plowed into Enoch. His head struck the ground, stars flashing against a field of darkness. His spectacles flew from his face. Enoch grappled with a stinking mass of muscle and coarse hair.

"Warlock!" the gatekeeper howled again, seizing Enoch's wrists, and pinning his arms against the cobblestones. His greater weight settled on top of Enoch, muscular thighs pressing down on his legs. Ravenos screamed vicious threats in his native language, spittle flying from his mouth.

Panic seared hot pain throughout Enoch. He couldn't *breathe*.

Hot saliva splattered on Enoch's face as he twisted, trying in vain to roll out from underneath Ravenos, to fill his lungs with precious air. The fiend's rank breath shrieked unintelligible threats, choking him. Shadowy fireflies flickered in his vision; a memory of the corpses Korr's men unearthed flashed through his mind. He tossed his head, fighting for air, glimpsing long canine teeth and yellow eyes blazing demon fire from the netherworld. Ravenos's snarling and the sound of his own blood rushing in his ears were a roaring tempest.

I must have a concussion, he thought. *I'm seeing impossible things. Weren't his eyes brown? And are those fangs snapping in front of my face?*

"Murderous rogue!"

The gatekeeper jerked to the side and the stone-like pressure of his weight vanished from Enoch's chest. Blessedly cool air fanned his spittle-dampened face. He inhaled; strength flowed through his trembling limbs. Half-blind, head spinning, Enoch rolled up to his feet and into a combat-ready stance.

The endless drilling Commander Storm put me through is good for something.

The twilight world, blurry and less distinct without his spectacles, provided enough light to make out two wiry figures battling near the gatekeeper's booth—one light, the other dark. But his ears worked fine; the snarling and growling of two dogs, interspersed with human speech, echoed around the courtyard.

The dark one howled something in his native tongue.

"Not if this one ends you first, child-killer!"

Men shouted in the courtyard, deer hooves clattered, and boots pounded against the flagstones, approaching the tumult. A hand clapped upon his shoulder to keep him from moving toward the two combatants. With a harsh cry, he twisted and swept his arm out to the side in a knife-hand strike while raising the other to prepare for a hammer blow. His new opponent slipped behind him. Enoch's legs went out from under him. Two muscular arms snaked around his torso and arms, picking him up and restraining him. Crushing him.

He couldn't breathe.

Not again. Never again! Enoch bucked in the other man's grasp.

"Whoa, whoa, whoa, E." Warm breath fanned against his cheek. "Steady now, man, it's just me—your old pal, Simon."

Enoch drew in a deep, shuddering breath. Clean sweat and the sharp scent of mint filled his nose. He gasped in relief. "Simon, put me down."

Halloway set him on his feet, his hands on his shoulders. The tall, fair-haired young man looked him over. "Praise Yshua! You'll live." The corporal released him and stooped to pick something up.

Beyond the altercation near the gatekeeper's booth, large blurry shapes entered the courtyard: more soldiers astride deer coming through the open Westgate. Enoch squinted but he couldn't make out their faces.

Several men rushed from the garrison yard to aid the seneschal and restrain the gatekeeper. Enoch took a step toward them, but once again a hand on his shoulder held him back. This time, he tensed but didn't react.

Simon pulled something out of his belt. "Leave it to them, sir. Between his lordship and our men, we have the situation well in hand." He gave Enoch his spectacles and his sword.

"I'm not a 'sir' yet, Simon," Enoch said. *What just happened here?* He took his spectacles from the taller man, wiped them on his tunic, and put them on. The world sprang into focus. He replaced the sword in its scabbard. It slid home without trouble, but he'd need to check it for damage later.

Simon elbowed him. "Full knight or not, you're still our commanding officer."

I might be a bit rattled, but I can take the hint, Simon. He straightened his back and threw back his shoulders, grimacing at a twinge of pain. Ravenos had done damage. He called out to the two soldiers circling the two grappling figures. "Gilmore! Kettering! Secure Ravenos and take him to the dungeon!"

As if they needed *him* to tell them that!

Detached and floating, Enoch observed through cracked and smudged lenses. Ravenos stiffened, yelped, and fell limp on the ground at Red's knees. Curled on his left side, the brute's right arm whipped out toward the seneschal, throwing something into his face. Red sneezed and sprang away from his adversary, and the soldiers each grabbed one of Ravenos's arms. The man sagged between them like a half-stuffed scarecrow. His greasy black hair hung to conceal his face and dripping blood formed a small, dark puddle on the ground beneath him.

Good. Red must have stabbed the honorless cur with his hunting knife.

Even though both were strong and toughened warriors, Gilmore and Kettering staggered under Ravenos's burly frame. Enoch winced in sympathy, rubbing his chest. He knew how heavy Ravenos was from firsthand experience. Two more soldiers came from the garrison grounds to help Gilmore and Kettering. Another soldier—Corporal Dwight— jogged past them toward the gatehouse, a small hurricane lamp dangling from his hand.

"You want to tell me what happened, sir?" Simon asked in a low, mild tone, never taking his eyes off the prisoner. His hand rested on the pommel of his sword. "I've never liked that Ravenos fellow—always thought there was something shifty about him, no matter what Bulstrode and Fenton said—but I can't imagine what possessed him to attack *you*."

"I don't know. It's all a blur, but I think I might have insulted him, or impugned his honor, somehow."

"Huh," the young corporal snorted. "Then he bloody well overreacted. Even a lance-sergeant ought to have better control of his temper. I'd hoped your first battle would've been over something more meaningful." He grinned, roguishly. "Like a woman."

"Yeah, right." Enoch's face grew hot. His heart beat a drummer's staccato against his ribcage. *My first proper battle, over so quickly. Should I tell Simon about the silver light and the wind? No, he'd say I'm concussed and hallucinating.* A heavy weariness settled upon him despite his hammering heart. He swallowed, grimacing. Why did his throat ache? He didn't remember Ravenos trying to throttle him. He touched his neck. No palpable wounds.

Simon's hazel eyes snapped back to him. "Did he hurt your neck, sir? I didn't see how it started, but I saw him throw you to the ground. That could mean a whiplash injury. You'd better ask Doc or Miss Fourtier to look."

"I'm fine, Simon!" *Aside from feeling as if I ran the full circuit of the West Sector.* He wiped his damp palms against his trouser legs. "And stop calling me 'sir.'"

Red rose to his feet, unsteady and still sneezing. Legs trembling with fatigue, Enoch stared at the dark-haired man propped up between the two laboring soldiers. Why *had* Ravenos attacked him with intent to kill? Surely, he knew such an action only condemned him to prison—even to the gallows. He acted as if a possessing demon drove him to it.

He turned to mention this to Simon when Trooper Gilmore cried out in pain. And then Kettering shouted.

Ravenos wrested free from his captors and darted toward the open gate. He snagged his hat up from the ground on his way, and Enoch caught the full brunt of the dark man's yellow glare of naked loathing just as he slipped through the gap. Two paces behind the fugitive, Red's legs crumpled beneath him as he collapsed.

"Come back, coward!" Red snarled in his native language, hammering at the ground with his fists. He sneezed and then resumed his howling. "Rogue! Murdering rogue!"

"Too slow, Ray-den!" Ravenos's cruel laughter faded. The gathering darkness beyond the Westgate swallowed him up, as if embracing him as its own.

Enoch and the others stared out after the rogue in horrified shock. And then their eyes shifted to the figure scrabbling at the cobblestones.

The furious kaenhir swung around on his hands and knees, his tail raised and bristling. He growled horrible oaths Enoch couldn't translate. Faces pale and trembling with fear at the seneschal's uncharacteristic display of raw anger, the soldiers backed away, Gilmore cradling an injured arm. Kettering knelt on the ground, hunched over and groaning, oblivious. Eyes narrowed and hackles raised, the kaenhir sprang to his feet and stalked after the fleeing soldiers, his plumed tail raised.

A frisson went down Enoch's spine. Red never acted this way.

A viciousness lurked just underneath the seneschal's well-groomed, self-controlled façade. *How much do I truly know about him—one of my oldest friends?*

Simon thrust Enoch behind him and hollered: "Milord!"

Why is the courtyard rocking like the deck of a ship? Enoch raised a hand to his head to steady the tilting of the planet beneath his feet. He must not fall off.

Eyes glittering, Red froze. He drew a shuddering breath and then sneezed three times in succession. Trembling, he lowered his head and wilted like a parched yarrow plant at the height of summer. He placed his long-fingered hands upon his thighs, inhaled deeply, and after a moment released his pent-up breath. But his tremors continued. No one dared to move toward him, not even Halloway, who stood between the seneschal and Enoch, grasping his sword.

Red looked at Enoch. He rasped out words in his native tongue. "Forgiveness, young knight. The rogue poisoned your servant. The rogue… is folken."

Enoch moved toward the kaenhir. Simon grabbed Enoch's arm. Unlike the rest of the world, the soldier's voice held steady. "Milord. With all due respect, what in perdition's flames is going on here?"

"Abomination." His eyes were wide and dark, the pupils dilated. "Young knight, you must hunt down the treacherous rogue and kill him. That rogue—that *fiend*—murdered those unfortunate little ones!" Still staring at Enoch, Red collapsed.

Head spinning, Enoch staggered and fell off the tilted surface of the planet.

"Enoch!" Simon's voice followed him into the silver-lined darkness.

A VENGEFUL WIND

STRANGE ARTIFACTS

Overhead, silver stars twinkled in the inky predawn sky, but William took no opportunity to enjoy the view. He woke earlier than usual, unsettled by a dream of violet mist and shifting shadows. A cloaked man with a lytarra had visited him. He'd taken things.

William shuddered at the memory. He pulled a satchel out of its hiding place and sighed with relief. His prizes were still inside: the engraved silver torc and the strange, twinned artifacts. Could they be wyldling weapons? He'd confiscated all three from the knight who came snooping around the fortress six days ago. William had stood gaping, dazzled by the golden light outlining the man—who would've disemboweled him with his sword if Tenebris hadn't knocked him out.

It had been his first glimpse of kythim. According to the Dreadlord's scroll, only wyldlings possessed kythim of such pure color. Not that William informed Tenebris about his suspicions. Bright aura aside, the man betrayed no eldritch abilities while under his master's bone knife.

William grimaced, pushing aside a sudden onset of nausea at the image of the half-flayed man on the stone table. The coppery stench of spilled blood. The trespasser's hoarse screams echoing in the underground chamber. Sometimes William fancied his ears still rang from those cries—and from Tenebris's brutal beating, afterward, for mucking up the execution.

"But I got him good," he said aloud. "Mouthy, trespassing wyldling. Call me names, will he? I showed him! Now who's the ugly toad, eh?"

Even though the snoop escaped, there was nothing he could do now to thwart their plans—not with the grammerye William laid on him. A fitting punishment, no matter that Tenebris said he should have killed him. William pulled out an oilcloth pouch and removed three items. The silver torc he set aside as a known entity; the knight had been wearing the rigid neckpiece under his armor. Silver and tiny amethysts made it valuable, but the piece of kadorei adornment held nothing mysterious. No spells were set into its flower-like gems or engravings and if the snarling reptilian beasts' heads at the open ends resembled nothing existing in the natural world, neither did they hold any enchantments. A simple matter to conceal the torc's existence from his master, who no doubt would want it for his own purposes.

William wrapped up the torc. "Reason enough to hide it from him," he muttered. "He's taken away enough from *me*. Every clockwork toy I built..." Tenebris called building contraptions a waste of an Arkhadahn's time and destroyed them in front of William. He scowled at the memory and returned the torc to his hiding spot. If nothing else, he'd sell it, so he'd always have money for whiskey and kaiber powder.

His spirits rallied at the sight of the other items in his cache. Even if Tenebris took away his devices, he possessed these interesting artifacts to study, with Tenebris none the wiser. Now, if he could only figure out how to make them work…

His elation faded somewhat as he gazed at the two L-shaped metal devices nestled within custom-fitted leather cases, like knives. But the strange, blunt objects were not knives. Nor were they a type of club, although the objects were large and heavy enough to serve as bludgeons. William didn't know what they were, but they must be weapons, since the man he'd taken them from was a warrior.

He removed one artifact from its sheath. Its metal finish glinted in a stray beam of sunslight as he turned it in his hands. There was a round hole in the end of the long piece. He closed one eye and peered into it with the other. As usual, he saw nothing inside.

William pulled out the other artifact and set them both side by side on his drafting table. He looked from one to another. Aside from a few scuff marks, the two devices were identical. "It's a burning shame," he addressed the metal things, stroking them. "I want to capture that arrogant knight again. I'd make him tell me how these blazing devices work." A vision of the half-flayed, blood-soaked figure presented itself once more, the man sneering at the young apprentice despite the agony he endured. Gorge threatened to rise at the remembrance. "A less messy way to make him talk," William amended.

A prickling sensation danced along his spine like the legs of centipedes. He hissed. *Something's triggered the alarm I set around the edge of the ward-spell barrier.* With trembling hands, he wrapped up his treasures and returned them to their hiding place, and then rushed to the tower stairs, sidling carefully to avoid gaps and crumbling edges.

Once on solid ground, he breathed easier. Zakaar, the harkhurz assassin, had taunted William, claiming eventually he'd tumble to his death while intoxicated. What did the crazy harkhurz know? William snorted; he never drank whiskey in his tower. Up there in his own private domain—with his scrolls, books, and other treasures—he didn't need whiskey.

He closed his eyes and concentrated, measuring the energy he'd siphoned into his arkhabala during evening meditations. The tattoos prickled, crawling along his back and arms. He shrugged away the discomfort, pleased that he'd remembered to energize the inked tendrils before he left. The tingling in his left shoulder, where he stored the alarm spell, told him in which direction the disturbance occurred.

With his cowl pulled over his head, William smiled as he set out. *I hope it's that burning knight.* He fondled the handle of his bone knife. *Should be easy enough to catch him. Then I can figure out how, in all of blazing perdition, my deathspell went awry.*

"I cannot fathom why Tenebris punishes only *me* for mucking things up when you're doing such an exemplary job of it, yourself."

William threw a leather satchel upon the cracked flagstones of the courtyard. He glowered at the hulking figure prowling around the courtyard like a hungry lykhar. "You blundering lummox! Do you have any idea how much burning work I'll have to do to conceal your stinking trail, not to mention eradicate traces of the blood you dripped all over the blistering forest?"

Zakaar laid back his ears and narrowed amber eyes. "More work than the lazy oaf wishes to do. Alas! It takes time away from drinking the spirits-of-fire in his lofty tower when he should practice his lessons in obedience to the master." The assassin winced as he pressed a hand to his side, where blood seeped through wrapped rags under his jacket. He still wore the defunct talisman, nestled like a cracked egg in the thick brown fur covering his chest.

William shook a finger at him. "Don't you dare blame me. Burn your eyes! You're lucky the Dreadlord summoned Tenebris to the farspeaker last night; he has no inkling about what happened. Yet. You really mucked it up this time, harkhurz. The ward-spells are down, so now the entire military might of the Northern Marches is free to come after us— and you've given them a blistering good reason to do so." Flame-colored sprouts of pain twisted in the assassin's kythim. William sneered. "If the slaving little kadorei pinked you again for your troubles, then it blazing well serves you right."

"No." His companion's eyes flashed with contempt, retelling what happened and biting off the words as he spoke.

Unease melted the sneer from William's face. "So, the barbarian's pet harkhurz protector pinked you, then." His ashen complexion paled even further. "Tell me you used the hesperidion powder I gave you."

The assassin nodded. "Yes, William. I threw it in his face. The exiled one is too sick to give us trouble, or he is dead."

William mouthed another oath, this time with grudging gratitude to gods he did not believe in. Tension flowed out of him. "This explains why my spine hasn't been ripped out and I still have both my ears. But it's a blistering good thing I covered your back-trail. Otherwise, we'd be up to our burning ears in kadorei troopers and enraged harkhurz warriors."

Zakaar growled in his native tongue, his amber eyes narrowed to slits, "It does not matter whether anyone follows. Even though I die in the attempt, I shall kill whoever comes." A feral grin revealed pointed fangs as he switched to Tradespeak. "Once I kill the warlock, I will die content."

William glared at the assassin. "Oh, no, you won't. That's not our mission, and you blistering well know it. Now, get your furry tail below to the infirmary so I can stop the bleeding. Varjev knows, I'll be the one dealing with your stinking carcass if you succumb to an injury. Burning suns! The first wound hasn't entirely healed yet."

William led the way into the bowels of the ancient fortress.

"He will pay," the assassin growled. "I want to kill him. I want to kill them all."

William winced at the joint-popping sound of the harkhurz's claws lengthening. *What did the Northward fellow do to set him off? A simple sword cut can't be it, even crazy as he was.* Whatever his problem, William wouldn't let the assassin kill the wyldling. At least, not without the Dreadlord's blessing.

He yanked open the heavy door of a small lamp-lit chamber, where a kettle puffed and hissed over a small fire like an angry cat. "Eliminate his protector if you want, but Tenebris specifically told us Northward is not to be harmed. Killing him would mean harming him and harming him means disobedience to an express command from the master. And disobedience leads to object lessons." He shuddered. "Remember the rack?"

The assassin grunted and made a series of contemptuous gestures before removing his coat and seating himself upon the examination table. "My pain is immaterial, William. My death is immaterial. I shall kill the warlock. The insult to my honor must be redressed."

William frowned. What honor did Zakaar Ravenos have left? He'd drowned his honor in blood time and time again for Tenebris's elixir, bound himself as a slave to the sorcerer until death. Tenebris made blistering certain the assassin had no honor left, save for his name, which he refused to sully. Wait. William paused with his hand on the cabinet handle. A harkhurz—even a half-mad one—never told an untruth and never broke an oath once given.

Not knowingly, at least. He needed to swear an oath to serve that baron-knight the Dreadlord wanted eliminated. I'm fairly sure Zakaar doesn't realize how many people he killed under Tenebris's orders in the Eastern Marches.

His plan took shape while he pulled bandages and ointments out of the cabinet. He poured boiling water over metal instruments in a tray and then cleansed his hands with soap rough enough to make his skin tingle. He schooled his expression to bland pleasantry and turned.

"Oi, Zakaar," William said. "How has the potion been working for you? Still experiencing hours of blackout time and feelings of bloodlust? Cravings for human flesh?"

Naked from the waist up, the assassin froze as he folded his jacket. His urine-yellow eyes glowed in the lamplight. A deep, canine growl rumbled in his chest.

"I'll take that as a yes," William replied, selecting a pair of shears. *Bait set.* He snipped off the filthy bandages on the assassin's torso, which proved to be a blood-stained and torn tunic. With a moue of distaste, he tossed the rags into the fire and then gathered the supplies and implements he'd need to tend to his companion's wound. He cursed, threatening torture when his patient flinched in pain while he shaved away hair, cleaned out the lacerations, and doctored the injuries.

At length, the assassin spoke. "William, why did you ask about the master's potion?" Discomfort crackled like ruby lightning through the harkhurz's kythim and he grunted when William wrapped clean bandages around his hirsute torso and tied off the ends.

Ah, I have him on the hook now. William wiped sweat from his brow. He tried not to smile. "I was just wondering how the current formula's been working for you. Thought you'd be interested; I worked out an improvement on the master's recipe."

Zakaar did not respond. He sat still with his ears upright. His clawed hands remained still in his lap, dug into the folds of his jacket. Bright gold interest sparked around him. He watched William clean up the materials and put them away. William said nothing. The urge to gloat rose in him but he dared not, lest it ruin his plans.

At length, the assassin sighed. He clenched his hands into fists and bowed his head, speaking through gritted teeth. "What do you want, Dull-seeber? Speak it plain."

And he bites!

"Your word, Zakaar Ravenos." William raised his chin to look down his nose at his seated companion. "I want you to swear an oath, by your very name, that you will not kill or incapacitate our target in any way—at least, not until after I no longer have a use for him. And you'd have to wait for an explicit instruction from me that this is the case," he added. The harkhurz was sly and sneaky. He might choose to misinterpret his words. He'd done as much before when it suited him, while keeping to the letter of his promise.

His companion's eyes gleamed. "You say: only your explicit instruction, William? Not our master's?"

"Yes. This is a deal between you and me. Ten—I mean, *Master Tenebris* is not involved."

The assassin tipped his head and gazed into the middle distance. "So, I wait for vengeance until I am told the warlock is fair game. And William Dull-seeber will make a better elixir for me. One to keep the whispering shadows and blood-red mists at bay for a longer time." His gaze sharpened as it settled on William. "How do I know you have made this elixir, the elixir works, and provided the first two are true, that you will continue to supply me? Do you swear by your name it is so?"

This time, William couldn't suppress his smirk as he pulled a flask out of a pocket in his sakkhelt and tossed it to the assassin, who caught it deftly. "Try it for yourself, harkhurz. Yes, I have made it, yes, it works, and yes, I will provide more of it as needed. But I know what you think of me. You wouldn't trust any blazing oath *I* swore, not even on my name."

The former gatekeeper of the Lilac Grove garrison uncorked the flask and sniffed its contents, his whiskers quivering, hackles raised. He poured a drop out on his tongue and tasted it, champing his jaws. After a moment, he shrugged, and then threw back his head to chug the entire contents. Zakaar waited, holding the empty flask in his clawed hand, staring at him. William folded his arms and leaned back against the wall, confident that—for the assassin's desires—his formula was superior to his Master's. *After all, I brewed my potion to help him and cancel out the more deleterious effects of Tenebris's potion. But I won't tell him about it. Not yet.*

A quarter hour passed, and still the harkhurz stared at William. Hands trembling, William pulled his own flask out of the depths of his robes and sipped whiskey. Zakaar's whiskers twitched, and his eyes glittered with amusement. Eyes shining clearer now. Eyes that were *sane.*

At length, the brute closed his eyes and sighed. He retracted his claws and put his hands together. His voice quavered as he murmured a prayer of thanksgiving in his melodious tongue. Tension fled from his frame as he finished. He straightened and slid to the floor, his eyes clear for the first time in moons. "I know this will not last. I know the red mists will return and I will die. But if you give me more elixir until I restore my honor, then it is worth the sacrifice." He slammed his right fist against his chest and went down on one knee. His fierce amber eyes reflected the lamplight and burned with their own inner fire.

"I, Zakaar Ravenos of the Sunrise Clan, swear upon my very name and honor, I shall not kill the warlock, Enoch Northward, or incapacitate him in his body, until William Dulciber releases me from my oath." He stood up and made a slashing motion across his throat and over his heart. And then he grinned, baring his fangs as he held William's gaze with his own. "We have a bargain, my friend."

William suppressed a shiver of unease at the glint in the assassin's amber eyes. *This worked better than I hoped!* Now he'd bound the fiend even more tightly to himself than to Tenebris. The harkhurz even named them *friends*—a concept with many nuances in the nehmwight tongue that did not translate well into other languages. He frowned, disconcerted by a sudden thought. Assuredly, he'd worded the oath without weaselly wriggle room or loopholes for Zakaar to exploit.

So why do I feel like I'm on the losing end of this bargain?

William left the windowless infirmary in favor of his hidden whiskey stash, shakily humming a tune half-remembered from a recent dream. He needed to fortify himself before cleaning up Zakaar's mess.

LITTLE MOTHER

In the cozy, lamp-lit room, someone sang a slow and sweet melody, lulling Enoch into sleep. The sound of the voice reminded him of honeyed milk and yellow-throated violets opening under the warmth of sunshine. He basked in it, safe despite his aching head, sweat-slicked skin, and the blanket trapping his limbs. The familiar and faint sound of repetitive grinding lent rhythm to the lullaby. The sharp, bitter scent of herbs filled the air and tickled his nostrils, comforting him. A word drifted in his memory, nebulous and feathery. Tickling.

He sneezed, expelling the half-formed word like a chick's fluff from his nostrils.

The singing stopped. A cool hand touched his brow. "Praise Yshua," the singer said, a low and soft woman's voice. Her voice, warm as the suns, cradled his soul. That word, her name. What was it? He strained for it, searching.

Fingers stroked damp hair back from his forehead. "The fever has broken," she said. "Well done, little sparrow! You fought off the infection without the touch of my wyld—just as your papa said you would. Let's go tell him before he leaves with the evening patrol."

Arms gathered him up with the blanket still wrapped around him, pressing him against warmth and softness. Lavender soap overlaid the bitter odor of healing herbs. A firm hand cupped the back of his head as the singer rocked him back and forth, humming the melody of the same song.

She spoke again. "Your kythim is sour with exhaustion. Don't worry, sweetie. We'll flush out those nasty poisons."

Poison. Why did this word hold such significance? *Is it the one I seek? No…*

A cool strength flowed throughout his body. He shivered and then relaxed. With a whimper, he wriggled around until his arms were free and then wrapped them around her neck. He nestled his head against her shoulder. The crooning continued. He swayed in her arms in time with the lullaby's rhythm. A wooden door creaked. He opened his eyes to see where she carried him. Despite the torches mounted on the stone walls, everything grew dim and indistinct until he saw nothing at all. The comforting voice faded; soon he no longer felt the warmth and vitality of another body against his own. Only then did the word return to him, full-fledged, on wings of terror.

He cried out: "Mama!"

"Enoch?"

The voice had changed. Once more, a cool hand rested on his brow. His nostrils flared at the familiar scent of bitter healing herbs and stimulant tea.

"Enoch," said a woman's voice, an echo of a forgotten memory. It stirred up a sense of comfort and safety. "There, there. You're all right, dartling jay. It's only a dream."

He groaned. His gummed-up eyelids refused to part. *Where am I?* He rubbed the sleep-grit away. Not in his room; the sounds and smells were different. But familiar.

Enoch opened his eyes. A tiny spirit lamp on a table beside his cot defined his world in a small circle of light. Dark shadows cloaked the rest of the room. The steady, even breathing of sleeping men, broken by the occasional buzzing snore, surrounded him. The garrison dormitory? No. Healing herb smells informed him he lay in the garrison infirmary.

What had happened? He pushed himself up on his elbows and took stock of his condition. Instead of his normal clothes, he wore the long tunic patients wore while convalescing in the infirmary. His body felt tender—like when he lost a sparring match. No broken bones, however. So, not a surprise, armed-assailant training session with Commander Storm. Cloth rustling behind him drew his attention.

Verbena Fourtier, the doctor's trusted assistant, sat on a stool at his bedside with her hands folded in her lap. She'd pulled back her medium brown hair into a neat bun. The well-worn, multi-pouched apron she wore over her starched white blouse and gray skirt only accentuated her plainness, but her intelligent brown eyes glowed with a warmth to help put patients at ease. Despite his confusion and concern at finding himself in the infirmary, Enoch smiled at the sight of her.

"Good morrow, little mother," he said, using his old nickname for the woman who most often took care of him as a very young child. "I mean, Miss Fourtier."

He frowned at the rasp in his voice and soreness in his throat. Had a fever had laid him low? He was sore, but not weak. He sat up and rearranged his tunic. His stomach tightened around a ball of ice as dark memories stirred: the flash of amber eyes and slashing fangs in the sanguine gloaming. He bit back a whimper.

Without a word, the woman took a steaming mug from the table beside his cot and handed it to him. He blew on the hot contents of the mug and then sipped. One never knew what sort of concoction the doctor or his daughter might brew up to dose him with. This time, it tasted like the stimulant tea the soldiers drank, its bitterness dulled by cream and sweetened with honey, just the way he liked it.

She smiled, her eyes crinkling at the corners. "Yes, I added honey and cream." She patted his hand, adding, "To ensure you drank it, dear."

"Thank you, Miss Fourtier," he said, slurping. The tea warmed the cold hollow in the pit of his stomach but failed to dispel his unease. "What happened? I feel sore, but other than that nothing seems to be wrong with me."

"You don't remember?" Concern drew lines across her brow. She reached out to examine his head. "Corporal Halloway said you struck your head on the pavement when you fell, but other than slight bruising, I didn't find any damage. Praise Yshua you were wearing a helmet when that man attacked you."

Amber eyes flashed with hatred. He winced. *Ravenos.*

Enoch jerked his head away with more force than he intended as an epiphany sank sharp claws of terror into his viscera. "Balthazar's Blades!" He scrambled out of the cot with the half-empty mug, sloshing its contents on the sheets. *This is no time to lounge about in bed sipping tea.* "What Watch is it? Did Korr make it back from the Darkenwood? Where's Red? Is he okay? What happened with the autopsy? If you please," he added more respectfully, seeing the consternation on the woman's face.

Verbena dabbed at the spilled tea with a napkin. "It's a quarter hour shy of Frog Watch. Yes, the deputy and his men came home safe; they made it inside the gate before the storm hit. As for the seneschal, he's sleeping off the effects of the powder that man threw into his face." She frowned. "My father identified it as Hesperidion Dust, a lethal poison if swallowed, but we got the antidote into him. Praise Yshua! Commander Storm insists we keep it on hand at all times. We expect His Lordship to make a full recovery within the next twenty-four hours."

Verbena patted the bed and Enoch sat. She sighed. "As for the girls' remains, my father completed a preliminary examination the evening before. He'll make his formal report as soon as we finish the full autopsy of each corpse, which may take the entire day." She pursed her lips and smoothed a hand back over her hair.

When Enoch pressed her for details, Verbena did not mince her words. The results of the doctor's preliminary examination were even more gruesome than Enoch at first surmised.

Not only had the murderer slaughtered the girls like lambs but then he'd gnawed on their carcasses. Bile burned at the back of Enoch's throat.

"There," Verbena said reproachfully. "Now, you realize why I didn't want to tell you."

He swallowed back the bitter, burning sensation. "You aren't doing me any favors in trying to shield me from facts, little mother."

"I know." She slumped in her chair. As she stared off into the middle distance, she looked every day of her thirty-seven winters. "But I prayed you'd remain a child longer."

"The Threefold One doesn't always answer our prayers," Enoch said, caustic as lye.

Verbena sat up straight, her mild features filled with alarm. "Of course, he does, Enoch. He always answers our prayers. Just not in the way we expect or wish. But he always works things out for our good."

Enoch toyed with the mug in his hands, refusing to meet her eyes. "He has a funny way of doing it. I wonder if Sally thought he worked things out for her good while a monster ripped into her flesh." Tears thickened his voice. "Did you know, she told me once she feared the dark because there were monsters. I told her to pray every night and the Almighty would keep monsters away. Well, he didn't stop one from getting her."

The mattress sagged. Verbena put her arm around his hunched shoulders. "Oh, Enoch. This is too much for you to bear on your own. I don't know how to counsel you; I'm a physician of the body, not the soul. Please, allow me to send for Vicar Taggert."

"I'll talk to him later after I catch the beggaring son of a goat that killed my friends."

Verbena hugged him. Her voice shook. "I never thought I'd say this, but I'm so glad Commander Storm is arriving later today. He might not trust in Yshua, but he will guide you in matters of leadership. He will help you set things to right."

Enoch stiffened. "What did you say? The commander'll be here… today?"

Verbena recoiled. "Yes. The messenger returned this morning. He brought tidings of the commander. In fact, Peter's waiting outside the infirmary right now. He wanted to see you as soon as you woke up. I tried to put him off—"

"I want to see him." A hurt look flashed in her eyes, and he hastened to add, "please, little mother." She didn't deserve such a nasty tone from him. It wasn't her fault Commander Storm would soon be here to direct Enoch's every little movement.

She sighed. "Yes, so long as you meet him up front. I won't have him disturbing my other patients." She patted his knee. "I'll bring you some breakfast."

"Thank you."

Verbena hugged him again. He sat there, staring into the middle distance. The mattress rose and her footfalls padded away.

Enoch listened to the slow and even respiration of the seneschal and the two injured soldiers sleeping in their cots. He envied them their blissful ignorance.

Just as he left the ward, a ruckus erupted at the infirmary's main entrance. Verbena's voice raised in admonishment to "be quiet." And then, the door burst open. A flurry of iridescent pink feathers and sleek, leonine grace bounded into the room. Hazel eyes sparkled with mischievous glee, and the orange hooked beak opened in a squawk, "Hey, Eenie, Eenie, Eenie, I'm baaaack." The syrax rubbed his cheek against Enoch's face, purring.

Laughing, Enoch shoved Peter's head away after a moment. "All right. I'm pleased to see you, too."

Simon arrived, carrying a rucksack, followed by Sharky, and Verbena brought a breakfast tray from the pantry. She looked disgruntled as she placed the tray on a folding table beside a chair. "Please try to keep quiet. This is an infirmary, not a carnival."

Peter eyed the tray with interest. "Mebbe you should start chargin' admission t' keep out the riff raff."

Verbena snapped a towel at his beak, and he jerked his head back. "That's Enoch's breakfast," she said. The soldiers hung back against the wall, pretending to cough behind their hands. "Sounds like you boys have a cold. I'll mix up a tisane. Stop by my worktable before you go," she said with a faint smile as she left the room.

"Don't worry too much about noise," Sharky said as soon as the door closed. "Gil and Kett were sedated last night when Doc and I patched them up. They won't be waking up for another five hours."

"What happened to them?" Enoch asked. "I mean, I was there, but I recall little."

"Oooh, I love stories. Please tell." Peter rattled his pinions, furled his wings, and sat on his haunches. He tucked his paws and talons under his belly. Enoch smiled; Peter resembled a pink loaf of bread with wings.

Sharky described the troopers' injuries using dry, medical terminology Enoch couldn't follow. Muttering "this isn't a very good story," Peter's eyes glazed over and narrowed to slits.

Simon frowned at the syrax. "Why are you here, Peter? I heard Captain Faulkner sent you out to find the commander."

Peter's eyelids flicked open like window shades. The crest of feathers between his ears flared. "Dukey's 'bout six to eight hours behind me if he makes the waystone crossing. Left him chargin' along the East Caravan Road in high dudgeon, I did."

"That's nothing new. Commander Storm is *always* in high dudgeon." Simon frowned, puzzled. "Is there even such a thing as a 'low' dudgeon?"

"Not in Commander Storm's case." Sharky glared at the syrax. "You'd best tame your tongue, Peter. You know the commander hates to be reminded of his noble rank. He also won't abide mockery of it."

"Why would he hate it? He *is* a duke. It's what being commander of the Enlightened Faction's army means. If Dukey don't want 'is title no more, I'll take it off him." Peter fluffed up his feathered crest. "I hear ladies fancy a gent with *qual-hit-tee*."

Sharky shook his head, the ghost of a smile on his lips. "You're incorrigible."

Peter cackled. "No, thank you, Fill-up Philip. I hates porridge."

Sharky groaned with exasperation and leaned up against the wall.

Simon shoved a bowl of hot farina at Enoch. "Speaking of

porridge, E: eat up."

Honey, butter, and cinnamon tickled his nostrils. Enoch licked his lips. "How can I refuse?" He dug in. A rasher of bacon accompanied the cereal. He tossed a small piece to an appreciative Peter. Finishing, he drained the mug of mint herbal tea. Afterward, he felt better.

Simon folded his arms and scowled at him. "Captain Faulkner raised me to sergeant. I understand I have you to thank for it, E. I mean, sir."

Enoch set his empty dishes on the tray. Sorrow lingered like salt on his tongue. "I didn't ask for my promotion either, Simon."

Sharky bent to scratch Peter's ear tufts. "Don't listen to him, sir," he said. "Simon's just kidding. He's tickled you approved his promotion." Despite the light tone, there were dark hollows under the young medic's red-rimmed eyes and weariness in his movements.

The young sergeant's hazel eyes widened. "Balthazar's Blades, Enoch, I apologize for the flippant remark. My joke was in poor taste. Sharky's right: I'm grateful, sir."

Enoch shrugged and attempted a smile. "You're forgiven, Sergeant. It would've made me laugh any other day." He folded the napkin. "Has Captain Faulkner arranged for a manhunt yet?"

The two men exchanged a glance. "That's part of the reason we came to see you, sir," Simon said. "Deputy Trask is leading a cohort into the Darkenwood in an hour. Captain figured you'd want to be involved, but only if you feel up to it. I told him you would, sir," he added, heading off Enoch's indignant protest.

Sharky rubbed Peter's ears. The syrax's eyes closed with a blissful expression on his aquiline visage. "Pending a medical examination," he put in. "And as the team's medic, I deem you fit for duty, sir." He smiled grimly. "That should override Miss Fourtier's opinion. And Doc's too busy with some bull-goose fool who broke his leg jumping out of a tree to say otherwise."

Enoch frowned. "Who broke their leg?"

"Jedediah Pines," Simon said. "He was roaring, raving drunk."

Sharky scrubbed a hand down his face. "He heard about Janet and… the others." His voice caught and he averted his eyes.

Sally, Janet, and Becky. I failed them…

Guilt and anger swept over Enoch, stabbing like a heated blast of wind off the Losaridos Desert. "Who's been talking? I should've been the one to bring the tidings. And weregild for their loss."

Simon ran a hand back through his close-cropped hair. "People talk, Enoch. Ill news has the swiftest wings, as my mother always says. Whoever talked probably meant well. Nobody heard about it from the seven of us." When Enoch gave him a puzzled look, he added with a lop-sided grin, "Your personal bodyguard: yours truly, Sharky, Guffie, Bart, Jim, Tad, and Levi."

Enoch sprang up to his feet. "Let's stop dawdling and go, then. It's just as Paul wrote in his letters: 'Make the most of your time, because the days are evil.' Now, where are my clothes? And my sword and armor?" He grimaced. "And my beggaring specs?"

Simon handed him the rucksack. "Already thought of it, sir. Your boots are right outside the door."

Sharky added, "Unfortunately, your specs broke last night. I sent them to the oculist for repair."

Enoch sighed. As much as he disliked them, he needed those spectacles. But it couldn't be helped; he'd have to adjust to their loss until the oculist repaired them. Within the rucksack, he found his sword and belt on top of the pile of leather armor and clothing. His sword had new frogging. His eyes moistened. "Thanks, both of you."

Simon snatched up the sword. "I'll just hang on to this for you." The two guardsmen turned their backs to allow him privacy while he dressed.

Peter's eyes remained closed, light snores bubbling from his nostrils.

His back still to Enoch, Simon held up the sword, wriggling it from side to side. "This part comes with a price, sir."

Enoch paused as he pulled on clean small-clothes. "Huh?"

"Tell us how you made it back to the garrison so fast. Without your mount."

Sharky added, "And what you found in the Darkenwood Forest."

SEEKING THE PATH

"*Death can come for a man from above as easily as it comes from the ground.*"

Or so Commander Storm claimed.

As he searched the trees, Enoch glimpsed nothing more dangerous than the late spring foliage hanging limp from brush and tree limbs alike, as if the effort of growing under the weight of humidity wore them out. A gray squirrel scampered along the bough above his head. He wiped stinging sweat from his eyes.

Birds sang, their voices oppressed in the soupy, summer heat. Sweat darkened the troopers' uniforms and dripped from their faces. Their mounts plodded on doggedly, ears flicking away flies and gnats. To the

East, the chortling rasp of myriad chorus frogs drifted from a small, hidden pond or a marshy seep.

At least someone's enjoying this muggy weather, Enoch mused. *I wonder if Toad's keeping vigil by the Wall, waiting for me to return.*

Annabelle waited for him, across the Void-Bridge.

Concentrate, Enoch Northward, he told himself. *You're hunting for a dangerous fugitive. You can't afford to let your mind wander.* He glanced side-long at Simon and felt a pang of guilt. He hadn't told his friends everything. Not exactly. His memories of the previous day were still jumbled, mixed up with nightmares of Ravenos attacking him. Had he flown away from the exhumed bodies, free as a bird, just as he'd always dreamed? He recalled looking down at treetops and an impression he'd traversed thirty miles in an eye-blink.

Simon and Sharky didn't know. He claimed not to remember how he got home.

Not a lie. Not really.

As soon as they reached the gravesite, Levi set Gog and Magog to work. Gog snuffled around the Eastern end of the hollow while his sister concentrated at the opposite end. The enormous trees ringing the declivity of overturned earth still reminded Enoch of evil hags crouching over the desecrated bones of the gatekeeper's slain victims. Despite the earliness of the hour, the day seemed dim—as if the suns were reluctant to shine upon the gravesite.

"My faith!" Thad said, falling back on his Southern Barony dialect. "A man never believes someone could commit such vile crimes so close to his home. It is the sort of thing you hear told in tales of far-off places, not happening here, so near to Lilac Grove."

Bart grunted wordless agreement as he peered up into the canopy, no doubt monitoring the sky and keeping watch for the renegade gatekeeper. "The weather's likely brewing itself a thunderstorm," he remarked to Simon, sotto voce.

"Now you mention it, Thad," Guffie chattered over him, his delivery rapid-fire and nervous, "my cousin Bill—he's in the medical corps out East in Fulcrum County—wrote the family here a while back and said there was folks, mostly maidens but also a few men, as went missing and then found buried in a place sorta like this over in the Eastern Marches. You know, corpses dug up again and again with pieces missing, bones cracked with the marrow sucked out and whatnot. It's so grisly it stuck in my head, but I dunno why I didn't think to say anything earlier. Cousin Bill always said—"

Jim rolled his eyes. "Balthazar's Blades! *Again*, with your horde of cousins. How many cousins do you have, Guffie?"

Before Guffie responded, Simon raised a hand and clenched it into a fist. The men fell silent and scanned their surroundings, their crossbows at the ready.

But the sergeant made a quelling gesture and watched Enoch. "Sir, Faulkner didn't tell you about the murders in the Eastern Marches yet, but he briefed me this morning just after my promotion. What Guffie said is true, but why his cousin told him about it is beyond my ken!" When Guffie opened his mouth, Simon gave him a look, and he shut it again. "I didn't make the connection before," Simon continued, "but Cap must've done. Still, it isn't a coincidence, sir; you should know: Ravenos served as a deputy under Sir Nicholas just before Fulcrum fell to the Insurrection."

Sharky stirred, his dark eyes still scanning the forest, crossbow ready at hand. "How many people has the evil son of a beggar murdered? We have to catch him. Justice will be served. For Becky... for all of them."

Enoch nodded, grief welling up inside him. "For Becky. And Janet. And Sally."

Magog whimpered, dancing around a spot beside a tree on the western end of the gravesite. Levi said, "I think she's found the fugitive's trail." He snapped his fingers to summon her brother. Gog bounded over and showed the same interest. Both dogs cast about the hollow, drawing farther away, noses to the ground and tails wagging. Levi smiled grimly. "That confirms it. They've found his scent. It's old trace, but thickly layered. He's been back here often."

Guffie bowed his head and made the sign of the cross over his chest. "'As the dog returneth to its vomit,' and so on, as the good book says."

Fierce exultation rose above Enoch's grief. He looked at Simon, whose eyes shone. "We've got him, now. Let's go."

They followed Levi and his hounds West. Their surroundings grew more and more familiar. Levi called attention to the trail markers Enoch set up earlier. How dare Ravenos come this way! Anger seized Enoch with silver hooks. Heedless of his companions, he spurred Tinker into a canter.

Simon maneuvered his mount to block Enoch's advance. "Balthazar's blades, E! What are you thinking, man? You'll trample Levi and the dogs."

Enoch adjusted his balance when Tinker shied. Heat flared, mantling his face. "Sorry," he mumbled. "I… I got carried away."

"Sir?" Bart spoke, but the others gathered around him, too. "What's the problem?" Jim asked, and Guffie said, "Should we call Levi back?"

In response, Simon mimicked the call of a gaffling warbler. Gog and Magog stopped in their tracks, although they quivered with eagerness to continue. Levi turned around with an inquiring expression on his face.

"Stay here," the sergeant said, his expression stern. Taken aback at his friend's unwonted authoritative manner, Enoch swallowed his eagerness and allowed Bart to take his reins.

"Sorry, sir," Bart whispered, watching his squad leader confer with the tracker. Levi, nodding at Simon, knelt to fasten a lead on Magog's collar and another on Gog's. The male dog whined and danced on his paws, eager to be off again.

"Don't worry about it, Bart." Enoch felt foolish. Of course, he should have known Simon would prevent him from rushing off on his own.

The mantle of obligation and responsibility weighed like a sack of stones on his back.

Now, he reflected bitterly, *we must set aside childish things and grow up.* He sighed; Simon shot him a questioning look. *It's time I told the others about the Wall. And Annabelle.* Enoch beckoned to his friend and the tracker using Battle Sign.

Simon brought his mount close beside him. "Sir." His quiet, worried tone sounded unnaturally loud in the heavy hush of the early afternoon "I hope you don't mind, but I told Levi where we're headed. Did you want me to inform the others?"

Enoch's lips twitched; it was uncanny how well Simon knew him. He licked his lips. "No, I'll do it." He beckoned the others closer and explained the Wall, Toad, the silvery Void-Bridge portal, and Annabelle, leaving out the part about the wind. He showed them the photograph and pen. After gaping at him in astonishment and uttering disbelieving curses along with the others over the artifacts, Simon and Sharky exchanged a look.

Simon grinned as he handed back the photograph. "Knew there must be a maiden involved in it, E. Pay up, Sharky."

Thad chuckled, mopping sweat from his face with a handkerchief. "Now I can guess why we brought the axes. Fortunately, I'm wise enough not to lay a wager on it."

Grumbling, the medic pulled a silver rondel from his belt-pouch and tossed it to Simon.

They continued along the beaten path. As it narrowed, Bart, Thad, and Guffie veered off the trail and let their mounts choose a way through the undergrowth on a parallel track. Jim rode point, just behind Levi and the dogs, while Sharky fell back to guard their rear. Simon flanked Enoch. Idly, the young sergeant waved away a green fly droning around his head and then stuck a toothpick in his mouth.

Enoch's knuckles whitened as he clutched the reins. Despite his desire to capture the fugitive, his being strained toward the Wall. Toward Annabelle.

Levi slowed to join Enoch and Simon. "We'll catch him, sir. The scent's fainter than I'd wish. Maybe Ravenos came through here last night, but I can't say for sure. There's no blood."

Simon frowned. "His Lordship wounded him pretty bad, so he couldn't have made it very far. It won't be long 'til we track him to his lair." Both men looked at Enoch.

Ravenos's lair better not be near the Wall!

Enoch wiped sweat from his face. "We'll leave no stone unturned. Search the area." His gaze riveted to the hounds and their handler trotting ahead of them. The hushed gloom of woodlands conjured memories of the Lilac Grove mausoleum. The troopers spoke seldom and then only in murmurs. Trees and brush crowded in close around them. Other than the flies and gnats, the forest fauna kept a low profile.

Pressure built up inside him, urging him to hurry, hurry. He took a deep breath and strained to listen to what lay ahead, but the heavy air was sluggish, relaying little information. A susurrus like the rustling of feathers tickled his ears even though no birds flew nearby. He shook his head.

"Fly buzz into your ear?" Simon asked. "They sure are annoying today."

"Um, yeah." Enoch rubbed at the offended organ.

The hounds led them to the divergence. Enoch took out his handkerchief and wiped his dripping face. He wished for fresh air once they reached the thin place in the canopy, but no wind blew. The sky grew more overcast. He hoped to see Annabelle again and convince her to cross the Void-Bridge before the commander arrived. Before the storm broke.

Gog and Magog, chasing the faint scent of their quarry, showed puzzlement. With anxious whines, the dogs veered away from the left-hand path and the destruction wrought by the freak windstorm the previous day. After a moment of confused sniffling and snorting, Gog found the scent again and, with his sister close behind him, dragged Levi toward a copse of hardwoods, where both hounds returned to questing for their prey.

Enoch heaved a sigh of relief; Ravenos had not entered his secret glade.

The hounds milled around the hardwood copse, but their excitement soon turned to bewilderment. Levi brought them back to the divergence to retrace the scent. The hounds followed it into the copse once more, where they displayed the same confusion. The soldiers scanned their surroundings with crossbows armed and ready, pretending not to watch as Levi tried again, and yet again. He even climbed one tree in which Gog and Magog showed interest. Exasperation writ large across his features, the tracker signaled to the sergeant after he led the hounds in a fruitless search around the copse for the fifth time.

Simon turned aside to speak with Levi, who brought Gog and Magog over to sniff along the broken colony bush barrier. "I don't get it. How can a scent just vanish?"

"Another scent must be throwin' them off," Levi explained. "Has to be something potent. Or real big to get this kind of confusion, though. Real big."

"Big like a puma, or big like a lykhar?"

Levi snorted. "Not hardly. Hounds behave differently for different scents. Gog and Magog would be growling and rarin' to go if it were a varmint. Not that we've found any trace in the Darkenwood of large animals so far. Now, some kinds of powders or vapors can cause such an aversion." Levi rattled off a list of chemical names Enoch didn't recognize.

"But those'll make them sneeze and howl, at the least," Sharky argued, "not act as if the boogeyman's hiding in the bushes."

Jim chuckled. "There's no such thing as boogeymen, Sharky. They're just a story your mama told to keep you in line."

"Or maybe," Guffie whispered hoarsely. "Maybe it's something else. Jim… Phil… what if there is a sorcerer in these woods, as Jessie the herbalist's been saying?"

Thad laughed. "You listen to her nonsense? The commander and the baron-knights wiped out the sorcerers Cycles ago!"

Guffie persisted. "But what if they only *thought* they got all of 'em? Maybe one heard about Sir Rick's death and decided to set up shop here in the Darkenwood. Someone had to've cast a spell on that false gatekeeper, so's the dogs can't sniff him out."

Enoch flinched and then turned to give Guffie a probing look.

Did an evil sorcerer erase the trail?

"It just doesn't make any beggared sense!" Sharky snapped. He glanced around, gripping his crossbow. "How could the dogs have lost the murdering son of a goat's trail? Scents don't just magically vanish!"

Thad, mopping his brow with a handkerchief, interjected with an edge to his voice. "Oh? How would you know? Have you suddenly become the tracking expert, Sharky?"

Simon raised his hands. "All right, boys. Put a lid on it and simmer down. We're all sweaty and tired. And bloody frustrated. So, how's the weather forecast coming along, Bart?"

Bart looked up at the overcast sky with a concerned frown. "Sarge, I can't guarantee anything, but it looks—and feels—as if we have four to six hours before we have to worry about getting soaked. Only the

Threefold One knows for sure if it'll turn to something worse, but it's looking to be another whopper of a storm."

Simon grimaced and spat out his toothpick. "Perdition's flames! I could stand a shower but a heavy downpour would wipe out the trail for sure." He turned to Enoch. "Your orders, sir?"

Enoch's nerves itched with the desire to enter the glade. He squeezed his reins. "The murderer might have gone by the Wall I told you about. We need to investigate."

"Yes, sir." Simon turned to the others, raising his voice. "Bart, Guffie, Jim, Thad—it's time to put those axes to work. I want this opening widened out enough for two to walk abreast. Chop, chop!"

While the four troopers cut the damaged brush, Levi walked the line of intact colony bushes with Gog and Magog. Simon and Enoch cleared out cut branches and limbs, stacking the harvested wood in piles off to one side. Sharky settled the deer near a stand of flowering elderberries and stood watch. Simon stayed near Enoch and supervised the other men's progress.

Half an hour later, with the new path completed, Simon assigned the four men to rest and refreshment while he, Sharky, Levi, and the hounds accompanied Enoch into the clearing. His eyes took in the bruised gray underbellies of storm clouds sailing in from the Southwest above the immensity of the Wall, and the ranks of motionless, hushed trees standing like wooden sentries in the windless midafternoon. The oval-shaped Window drew his gaze. It had grown. The bottom edge reached the ground.

Simon issued orders to Levi and Sharky. "Levi, see if your dogs can flush this Toad creature out in the open. I'd like to have a chat with him. If something happens to me, Sharky, you know what to do."

"Wait, what?" Enoch spun. "There's nothing to worry about. I've done this before. I need to touch the Window to contact Annabelle."

"And pigs will sprout wings and fly," Simon replied. "With all due respect, sir, there will be no more baron-knights vanishing into the netherworld. Not on my watch. For all we know, this is how Sir Thomas met his end."

Enoch stared at Simon. Had Sir Thomas crossed the Void-Bridge? Or tried… and failed, to his detriment? He hadn't considered that possibility. But then he frowned. "But Toad said nobody came through here."

Simon snorted and folded his arms across his chest. "You believe a strange creature's word over common sense?" He met Enoch's gaze. "I want to talk to this Toad fellow." The look in his eyes seemed to say: if he even exists.

Scowling, Enoch turned back to the Wall. "Doubt me all you want. I'm going to prove there's no harm. I'll even let you keep a hand on me the whole time, so I don't travel to Earth in the flesh."

"Sounds fair enough," Sharky commented in a mild tone. "I'm game, E, if Simon isn't."

Simon lifted his chin. Irritation threaded through his voice. "Now, hold on just a minute. I know what you're trying to do, Sharky."

Sharky stuck his thumbs in his belt, sighing, his brown eyes haunted by grief. "I'm not trying to manipulate you, Simon. I think if he wants to visit his girlfriend, then he has a right to do it… before it's too late."

"Annabelle is not my girlfriend!" Enoch protested, his face heating. He scrubbed his fingers through his hair. "She's like a sister to me. Fine. You know what? You can both hold on to me. I don't care. But I need to contact her. Before Commander Storm shows up and ruins everything."

"Yes, sir," Simon responded woodenly. "Sharky, keep watch."

Heart hammering, Enoch approached the Wall. Time to find out how much he controlled the wind. He wanted to petition the Almighty to protect his men from another cyclone, but he hesitated. What good would it do? The Threefold One had not protected Becky, Sally, and Janet. As the vicar liked to say, the Threefold One moved in mysterious ways. He would protect them, or he would not, regardless of Enoch's prayers.

Simon grabbed his shoulder, intoning a prayer for protection. Enoch experienced a qualm. Perhaps Yshua would listen to Simon Halloway, he thought, placing his hand on the cool, slick surface of the Window. As before, it grew warm and pliant under his sweaty palm. Silver light spiraled out from the point of contact to fill the entire aperture. Simon inhaled sharply and his grip tightened on Enoch's shoulder.

Enoch closed his eyes and bent his will on the tempest surging inside him. *You will not rage against these companions of mine. You will be calm and still.* To his surprise, the gale died back to a gentle breeze. He pressed his forehead to the portal. Yes, the slender cord still bound him to Annabelle. In his mind's eye, the silver-streaked tunnel formed. The urge to speed along its length overwhelmed him, but he restrained himself, lest he unleash the destructive force.

"Annabelle," he sent across the void. Time passed. Doubt assailed him. Previously, he'd gone to her. Would she know how to come to him?

"Enoch?" The voice sounded hesitant. Far away. A blue dot appeared.

He concentrated on the silver cord, feeling the distant joy of her sapphire kythim. Resolve pulsed from the other side of the connection. Her sending grew stronger. Annabelle was coming.

The basso rumble of a voice intruded. "What are you doing?"

And then, brutal fingers ripped him away from his contact. The blue dot winked out. Stars reeled, their brightness expanding to fill his entire vision. Shock—not entirely his own—rippled through him. The tempest inside him raged against its boundaries, pressing outward, growing stronger. Pain shattered him like a stone breaking through glass.

DREAMS IN THE MIST

"People who live in glass houses shouldn't throw stones."

Annabelle opened and closed her mouth, unable to locate words for a scathing response. Beside her, Neal grinned and emanated smugness. His green eyes danced with glee at his victory before turning back to his music.

He used to be nicer to me. What made him become such a jerk?

A mist swirled around the classroom, but Annabelle felt nothing, not even the bass clarinet clutched in her hands, only burning irritation with the baritone saxophonist on her left. She faced front. Kensi's face briefly resolved from the sight-dulling mist before fading into the obscurity of her fellow flutists in the front row.

With a sharp movement, Annabelle flipped her bass clarinet from a vertical position to the horizontal. The curved neck of her instrument struck Neal's thigh. And then, just as swiftly, she returned the bass clarinet to its original position. She kept watching the front of the classroom. Busy leading the flute section in the front row, the band instructor didn't appear to notice the war waging in the woodwind bass row.

Neal snickered. His voice dripped with sarcasm. "Oh darn, I might have a tiny bruise."

Annabelle scowled. "Jerk." Out of the corner of her eye, she glimpsed Neal's self-satisfied smirk; he pretended to ignore her in favor of adjusting the mouthpiece of his baritone saxophone. But she knew better. The band students around them appeared blurry with indistinct features, their conversations muted by the mist encompassing everything.

Annabelle welcomed the mist like an old friend. She held onto the bass clarinet, waiting for the tableau to change. It often did, in these circumstances. This is a dream, she told herself. The evidence is irrefutable. The dream mist speaks for itself. Yes, "mist" best described the eldritch film dimming her eyesight; "fog" was too juvenile.

Mist is the proper word for a sophomore to use—especially an honors student excelling at her English and Literature classes. Annabelle loved words, particularly the more obscure ones. She collected words now as avidly as she and her friends used to collect charms while they were in elementary school.

Why is it, then, that arguments with Neal so often leave me tongue-tied?

The mist condensed, and the scene shifted from the band classroom to an avenue lined with maple trees with autumn-bright foliage. She blinked, and leaves littered the ground in red, orange, and yellow splotches reminiscent of a Monet painting. Overhead, denuded tree branches like skeleton hands clawed at a blue sky tinged pinkish-gold along the horizon.

Dead leaves crunching underfoot broke the expectant silence.

Neal walked on her left, his backpack slung over his shoulders. He cast her a wry glance. "If this is a dream, it's not a very interesting one, is it? Not that I expect much out of a dream with you in it."

Annabelle grit her teeth. Screeching like a harpy always spurred Neal on to further insults. She groaned. "There's no point in arguing with you about anything. If I'm so boring, then why are you walking with me?"

The youth shrugged. "Don't know. Maybe we're just headed for the same place. We can share the sidewalk. It's a free country."

Ahead of them loomed a barrier with a colorful mosaic design she couldn't make out because it shifted every time she focused on a section. The sidewalk led straight up to it. Geometric shapes in red, purple, green, blue, gold, and milky gray formed winged, serpentine patterns outlined in ebony against opalescent white. They appeared to be dragons flying among the clouds. Were they moving, or was she imagining it?

Annabelle's feet grew heavy, and her pace slowed. She stopped in front of the wall and touched the slick surface. "A stained-glass window… wall."

Something beyond it needs me.

Neal's breath tickled the back of her head. "Go through, Ann. The way out is through." He shoved her.

Arms raised to shield her face, Annabelle crashed through the glass. It shattered. Colorful pieces rained down as gems to form new patterns around her feet. If she stopped to examine them, she knew they'd make sense. But something compelled her, and her feet carried her onward into a pinkish-gold twilight.

Glass shards crunched painlessly under her bare feet like the leaves— wait, when had she lost her shoes? Her T-shirt and jeans transformed into a white linen gown, and she clutched a lit candle in her right hand. The glass shards became sand and pebbles underfoot. She spun around to screech at Neal for pushing her, but he hadn't followed her. All evidence of the stained-glass wall was gone.

Her candle burned a steady blue in the still air. Dream mist coated the world around her and dimmed her eyesight. Tender spring foliage sprouted from bushes growing beside the twilight path. Water lapped against an unseen shoreline and the fishy and algal odor of a Northwoods lake met her nose—like and yet unlike the lake of her childhood summers where her grandparents lived.

She paused a moment and then continued walking toward the soughing sounds, holding her candle aloft to light the way in the deepening twilight. Her bare feet felt nothing of the beach grit.

It's funny how in dreams one's feet don't touch the earth.

Annabelle hardly needed the candle to see the old-fashioned wooden rowboat pulled halfway out of the water to rest on the shoreline. Beside the boat stood a tall figure wearing a black cloak. Something in the way the figure stood made her think it was a man. She couldn't see his face. A violet glow suffused the surrounding mist. She took his appearance as a matter of course; he seemed familiar.

The cloaked man beckoned her. "Come, Ahdmerel. Join me."

She didn't question or object. A haunting melody swelled forth from the stringed instrument in his hands. The mist stirred, eddying around her, and then she sat on the bow bench of the rowboat, facing the stern. The cloaked man limned in violet light sat on the middle bench. His knees brushed against hers as he played a sedate and familiar tune on the mandolin/guitar instrument cradled in his arms. The lyrics of the song rollicked through her head. "Row, row, row your boat, gently down the stream…"

Oars creaked as they moved of their own accord in time with the rhythm, propelling the boat across unseen waters. The musician's fingers increased their speed and mist rushed past on either side. Annabelle's innards stayed in place while the rest of her plunged forward. She gripped her candle with both hands as if it would prevent her from tumbling backward off the boat. She stared into the blue flame and slowly inhaled. Her gut settled.

How fast can this thing go?

Her cloaked companion chuckled. "It's called a dingy, Ahdmerel."

"Huh?"

Amusement lightened his voice. "The boat. It's called a dingy. And I can make it speed along as fast and merrily as I wish."

Annabelle did not respond at first. She raised her candle and examined the cowled face. No matter how she positioned her light, her companion's features remained in shadow. She tried another tactic. "I think I recognize your voice from somewhere. Who are you, and where are you taking me?"

He tsked. "How remiss of me. I have introduced myself, little one, after Skelsdaran banished the cyclone. However, I cannot blame you; one seldom recalls a dream perfectly—especially if it is not one's own."

Annabelle's eyes widened. *Skelsdaran? Does he mean Enoch?*

Still plucking the strings, the musician tossed his head, and the cowl fell back to reveal a handsome face framed by hair as black as the cloak he wore. His strange lavender eyes burned the same color as the eldritch light surrounding him. Annabelle's breath caught in her throat.

"I am the dream traveler," he said. "Unlike the lad, you've come along so obediently, a tame seal to the hand. I'm delivering you to… somewhere you need to be. Normally, I'd enjoy conversing the entire night through with such a lovely young maiden, but, alas!" He switched to a minor key. "I fear I will soon be deprived of your excellent company."

Did he just compare me to a pinniped?

Annabelle opened her mouth but closed it again as a new sound caught her attention. A voice called from beyond obscuring mists, off in the distance. The dream traveler strummed one final chord and then covered the strings with one hand, silencing the song. The instrument became mist and faded from view.

Annabelle clutched her candle, staring at the man's empty hands. She slowly exhaled. Water slapped against the boat.

A deep voice rolled out from the mists on her right. "Ahdmerel."

Her candle tugged her upright. With an inquisitive glance at the dream traveler, she scrambled to her feet. His eyes no longer burned but were still the same strange gray-lavender shade. He smiled and stood. Despite their movements, the dingy remained as still as a stone.

"Here is where I bid you farewell, little one." He grasped her arms and lifted her over the gunwale of the dingy until she stood on the dark, undulating surface of the water.

Oh, dear Lord Jesus, please, please, don't let him—

The dream traveler let go.

Annabelle tensed, whimpering out little gasps, expecting to plunge beneath icy waves.

She didn't. Her candle-flame flared, and she stood above the water as if on solid ground. She sighed, slumping. "Oh, thank God!"

Warm and welcoming as a tropical sea, the deep voice rang out with joy. "Come, Ahdmerel. Come to me."

The candle tugged at her hands. She cast a wild glance over her shoulder at her companion. "What? How? Who's that?"

The dream traveler's smile made her heart beat faster. "Anything is possible in the dreamscape. Now, go. Hadrien Rainblessed is calling. Your wyld shall lead you straight to him. Farewell." He bowed, then he and the dingy vanished into the mist.

This is getting too weird, even for me.

Annabelle gaped at the place they had been. The voice called again and the candle tugged. She marched across the heaving expanse of the dark lake. Her feet and linen gown stayed dry as a bone.

"Come, Ahdmerel. You must come to Tehara."

Ahead of her shone a blue light matching the candle's flame, growing brighter, undulating like Northern Lights. Before long, her eyes made out a dais rising above the water. Dark blue serpentine coils sprawled across its surface. Shackles enclosed four scaled limbs and chains pinned down a pair of magnificent, bat-like wings.

Her heart skipped a beat. *A dragon? Awesome!* She grinned and hurried forward, holding tight to her candle. *Don't worry, blue dragon. I'll break those chains and set you free.*

The creature raised its head and watched with human eyes as she approached, fan-shaped ears lifted. Fleshy tendrils like a catfish's barbels quivered around its reptilian jaws as it opened its mouth to speak…

"Ann? What the hell happened to you?"

A hand slapped her face. The image of the dragon chained to the dais shattered, dissolving into mist. Annabelle blinked in confusion at her bedroom ceiling. She rolled her head to the side. A high-pitched tone rang in her ears. Dad knelt beside her, his face furrowed into lines of concern. He was on the verge of speaking, but she beat him to it.

"Guess I'm a bit worn out from studying."

And now you're lying.

With a frown, he helped her to her feet, asking her a question she couldn't make out.

"I'm okay, Dad." Her voice was drowned out by the ringing and buzzing in her ears.

STORM'S ARRIVAL

Voices buzzed and rumbled nearby in a bumblebee's incessant drone. Or had the storm arrived? Enoch wanted to see but his heavy eyelids refused to rise. *Why can't I move?* Warm fingers pressed against his sweat-slicked throat. A thumb peeled back one eyelid; he flinched away. Hands pulled him back and forth. Snarling, he smacked at the hands, but they only tightened.

Warm breath puffed against his ear. The buzzing resolved into a familiar voice. "All's well, E. We're here."

"Steady, sir." Another familiar voice spoke, calm and soothing. "Steady. You've had a shock, but you're going to be just fine."

His eyes fluttered open. Framed by an overcast sky the color of old bruises, two faces hovered over him, one right-side up, the other upside-down. Simon and Sharky. His friends. *Praise Yshua, I didn't hurt them.* He swallowed with difficulty. His throat hurt and breathing the stifling air did not improve matters.

"Why am I lying on the ground?" he asked. "And where's Annabelle?"

Simon's head disappeared. "Let's get you on your feet," Sharky said, and then his head slid out of view. With their help, Enoch stood. What happened to Annabelle? One moment, their kythim entwined, he tasted her joy, and the next… pain.

Enoch's eyes scanned the clearing in search of the answer to his question. Instead of the petite figure he most yearned to see, a statuesque figure stood in the glade. Thoughts of the Earth maiden fled like dandelion seeds in a stiff breeze. He stiffened to attention in late mimicry of the two men on either side of him.

"Sir," he barked, his voice cracking into weakness. "Commander Storm."

"Well met, lad." The evainghir's voice rumbled its familiar basso, and he bared his teeth in an unsettling grin with far too many sharp teeth in it. Lamellar leather armor creaked as he shifted position, twitching a thick tail encircled with bladed rings. Strong fingers caressed the hilts of twin scimitars, his favored blades, but Commander Daniel Storm wielded every type of weaponry with a finesse beyond the skill of any kadorei man.

Praise Yshua that Commander Storm is the only evainghir in existence. Tehara could never handle two of them.

Steely gray eyes narrowed, as ominous as looming thunderheads in a rugged face covered with brown scales. The commander's grin faded into a soldier's wooden expression. "Despite my efforts, you discovered the Void-Bridge."

Enoch clenched and unclenched his hands. Commander Storm stood between him and the Wall, a monolith wrapped in leather with steel edges. "Void-Bridge, sir?" he echoed. "You know about the Void-Bridge?"

"Now," the warrior continued, as if Enoch hadn't spoken, "we have many things to discuss." His attention flickered to the men at Enoch's side. "Sergeant. Corporal. Dismissed."

Simon and Sharky both tensed, hesitating. Enoch experienced a spike of alarm on their behalf. "Go on," he whispered. They saluted and left the clearing.

Enoch stared at his mentor. Commander Storm, large as life, and in his private domain. The dark thunderhead on the horizon now loomed overhead and threatened an end to his plans. *I should be furious*, he thought. A ball of ice occupied the space where his resolve typically lived. His mouth tasted sour. He opened his mouth to speak and then closed it again.

"Commander Storm," he said, finding his voice. "Sir, you're here." He cringed. *Stupid, stupid, lame, and stupid!*

The reptilian warrior raised his eyebrows. "Indeed, I have returned. And not a moment too soon. You cannot fathom the peril you court in crossing the Void-Bridge." He narrowed his eyes, and his voice went soft. "You will not attempt to do so again."

Part of him wanted to cower, but he needed to face the commander, for Annabelle's sake and his own. Desperation granted him inspiration. "Please, sir. I crossed the Void-Bridge on a diplomatic mission to another world. The Darkenwood Forest and the Void-Bridge are part of the Northern Marches. And the Northern Marches are under my jurisdiction. Therefore, I have every right to be here."

The basalt gaze locked upon Enoch. "Your logic is unsound, lad," he said, his tone mild beneath those wary, stony eyes. "I see no torc of the office around your neck; it disappeared with the young knight, I heard. I have not yet invested you as the baron-knight of this realm and even then, you would still report to me. Your jurisdiction is whatever I deem appropriate. You will concern yourself only with whomever I deem appropriate; namely, the people of the Northern Marches, and not diplomatic missions to a distant realm." He frowned at Enoch. "Nay, lad. Do not argue with me."

Enoch's knees weakened. *I must say something.* "Sir, with all due respect, I disagree. My sister, Annabelle, is on the other end of the Void-Bridge. She wants to come here." He took a deep breath. "I'm going to bring her over."

Commander Storm snorted and waved a hand. "You have no sister. Besides, this woman-child can manage well enough in her own world. Until I grant you permission, you will not enter the Darkenwood Forest. You will not come near the Void-Bridge."

Enoch struggled to contain the plaintive whine in his voice. "But, why, sir?"

The commander's eyes hardened. "Need I remind you of the potential breach to realm security? Sir Frederick and I taught you better."

Trembling, Enoch bowed his head. Shame, fear, and anger whirled inside him, a tempest like the storm drawing near. *I have a sister. Annabelle is my sister. She called me her cosmic twin.* He wanted to scream, he wanted to unleash his fury, but he dared not. Sir Rick always warned him abandoning self-control was the mark of a lawless man. Such men were only beasts. Like Ravenos.

Thunder rumbled. Commander Storm glanced at the sky. "We will speak more of this within garrison walls and under a roof. Come. Your men are waiting for you. It is past the time you returned home, lad. While traveling from the Middlemarch waystone I noticed the bane-wards are down in this section of the forest. Doubtless, the predators gather on the outskirts. It will not be long before they overrun this area."

Enoch sighed. Nothing but endless combat drills and weapons training to look forward to, from Klotho-rise to Atropos-set, for the next Cycle.

What would Commander Storm do, if he knew my secret? Either add it to the training regimen or beat it out of me. Not that there's much difference between the two.

"Brass rondel for your thoughts," Simon murmured beside him.

Startled, Enoch jumped. Tinker grunted and flicked an ear back.

"Whoa, take it easy, sir." Simon chuckled. "I only asked because you've got on your thousand-yard stare. Maybe even farther."

Enoch patted Tinker's neck, soothing him. "You don't have a brass rondel."

Simon made a slashing gesture over his heart, grinning. "Point to you. Courtesy of Philip Sharkness, I have a silver rondel. I felt bad taking it from him, but a wager's a wager. Besides, it concerns you. Seems only fitting you have a share." He dug the coin out of his belt-pouch and offered it to Enoch with raised eyebrows.

Enoch waved it away. "I don't have any coin on me to change it with, Simon. I don't want your money."

And you don't want to know what I'm thinking. What I suspect I've become. If Simon knew, there'd be even more distance between them than there was now. Very few of the legendary tales cast wyldlings as the heroes. More often, they behaved as monsters.

Simon put away his rondel and they rode in silence for several moments. The forest seemed darker than usual for the time of day and the men were subdued. Enoch eyed his friend sidelong. Simon appeared pensive as he kept watch and rode as if a great weight rested on him. Commander Storm approved of Simon and the others as his guardsmen, or he'd have taken charge of the company. Instead, the evainghir commended Enoch into their care and then set off at a jog for the garrison. Enoch grimaced; he didn't want to think about the commander and the bleak future he no doubt planned for him.

Simon cleared his throat. "E, do you remember the last Harvest Festival, when Gordiman sang the ballad of Kepala Batu's Bargain?"

Enoch shivered, the hairs on the back of his neck rising. *How does he do it?*

Bart said, "Wasn't that the one his apprentice—what's his name—acted out with the puppets on the shadow screen while Gordiman sang?" He chuckled, shaking his head. "Poor lad; he missed his cue a couple times. The old fellow lit into him afterward like a panzerbar on a honey tree."

Enoch rubbed his neck and smiled at the memory. "The apprentice's name was Skylark," he said. "He juggled far better than he handled the puppets. Janet said—" The icy claws sank into his throat and the humor in him withered, coated in hoarfrost.

Simon drew his mount closer. "What I'm getting at is this: Kepala Batu made a poor decision based on his heart. His emotions. For most folks, it doesn't matter in the grand scheme of things. But he could have brought down two entire kingdoms if Sage Gilgamesh hadn't intervened and locked him away before he married the Cold Princess."

"Sarge, that's a mite harsh," Bart said. "Enoch's got better sense. I reckon Kepala Batu didn't have the good sense the Almighty gave to a rock."

Simon shrugged. "Just making conversation, trying to bring E out of his funk."

Enoch twisted the reins in his hands, the ball of ice in his stomach growing larger. His tone grew bitter as he bit off his words. "So, you're saying all wyldlings are either fools or an evil menace who should be imprisoned for the good of everyone."

Simon gave him an odd look. "No, E, what put that in your head? I'm saying Commander Storm is like Gilgamesh; he thinks he's trying to protect you from your own folly." He raised his hands. "His words, not mine."

Enoch scoffed. "For the record, I don't want to marry Annabelle; she's more like a sister."

From his position behind Enoch, Guffie chimed in. "Is this like the Bumblebee girl?"

Bart laughed. "Bumblebee girl? What're you talking about?"

Enoch stiffened. *Don't you dare, Guffie.*

"Your family didn't live in Lilac Grove yet, Bart. This happened two, three cycles ago, when he pretended he had an older sister—Bumblebee, or whatever—and swore up and down she was the one messing around with Miss Fourtier's herb garden."

"Guffie," Jim said, his voice dripping with exasperation, "that's different. He was little, then. You're comparing apples to peaches, now."

His brother-in-law retorted, "They're both still fruit, Jim. This is more of the same, except the girl's name is Annabelle this time. And Enoch was plenty obsessed with the idea of a sister. Remember, Simon? I mean, Sarge. Mrs. Mulgrove thought he was imagining things. Going bonkers. Even the doctor got worried. But like a dog with a bone, he wouldn't let go of it for ages."

"And we all remember how *that* ended," Jim said with a sigh.

"Enough, you two," Simon said, disgusted. "This isn't a matter of a smacked bottom and a stern lecture from Taggert. He's convinced himself there's a girl out there and she's his sister. I know him. He's dead set on doing something foolish and getting himself into a real heap of trouble."

"Hey," Enoch said. "I'm right here."

"Sorry, sir," Guffie said. "I didn't see it as a sore point."

The others apologized, too, even Simon. When they reached the road, the young sergeant gestured at the others to spread out. He leaned in. "Nobody thinks you're crazy, E." He grimaced. "I mean, *sir*. We're concerned, nothing more. None of us was as close to Sir Rick as you. You're going through a lot right now. Maybe you should talk to Vicar Taggert."

"I already did, on Chapelday. Yesterday." Enoch blinked. Had it only been a day ago? It felt as if seasons passed since the conversation.

"Maybe you should talk to him again."

Enoch made a noncommittal noise. *What I should do is go through my book of legendary tales. Maybe there's something in there that'll help me figure out this mess before Commander Storm runs me ragged in the training arena.*

Thunder rumbled, loud and long, almost directly overhead. Once it died away, Enoch noticed the pitter patter of rain against leaves. Soon, it trickled through the canopy.

Jim cried out, exasperated. "Bart, what happened to 'four to six hours?'"

Bart hollered back. "Cloud-reading is an art, not a science."

The men urged their mounts to greater speed as the sky opened up.

TO SOW THE WIND

A GRIEVOUS BLOW

Thunder cracked overhead. Enoch jumped, startled out of his brooding in the lamp-lit Great Hall. Wind-lashed rain pounded against the windowpanes. Intermittent flashes of lightning flickered through the tall windows, casting streaks of shadows across the vaulted chamber. Rainwater dripped from his sodden garments to patter on the marble floor.

A gnat beneath the frozen regard of giants, Enoch stared up at the line of life-sized portraits mounted along the interior wall, now barely visible in the dim storm-light. The past Baron-Knights of the Lilac Order gazed down at him in silent rebuke. He flinched, peering up at the subject of the most recent portrait. He thumped his right fist against his soggy chest to salute his late guardian, half expecting it to make a drumming sound. Inside, he was hollow as a Harvest Festival gourd.

"Sir Rick, I'm so sorry," he told the painted image of his late guardian. "More than anything, I wanted to save those girls and find Sir Thomas so he'd be the baron-knight and I could complete my training. But I failed to find them. A monster got them." He took a long breath to speak again, when a familiar voice addressed him.

"Sir Enoch, young Halloway sent me to find you here. Good gracious, you're all wet. Come along, Sylvie, dear. Don't be shy."

Vicar Taggert strode into the Great Hall. He wore a sober workday suit in shades of dark blue and gray instead of his Chapelday vestments. A small, slender maidservant followed him with a large, fluffy towel in her arms. She kept her head lowered and covered by a wimple, but Enoch glimpsed pale blond ringlets peeking out to frame her hidden face. Lightning flashed, immediately followed by a loud peal of thunder. The maid squeaked in alarm. Her ringlets bounced around her oval face as she raised her head.

"There, there," the vicar said, patting her shoulder. "You're safe and dry inside the Manor. This building has withstood worse storms than these. Go on, now."

Timid as a frightened fawn, she took a step closer to Enoch and thrust out the towel she clutched against her bosom. She slipped in the puddle from his dripping clothes. He caught and steadied her with his right arm. His thumb snagged against her blouse, pulling it askew to bare the delicate, curling lines of dark green ink traced upon her brown shoulder.

The girl cried out in the Southern Marches dialect. Cringing, she pulled loose, yanking up her blouse to cover the exposed skin. She shook like a leaf in the wind and scampered to a servant's door hidden behind a tapestry and fled the Great Hall.

Vicar Taggert shook his head. "Poor thing is frightened of thunderstorms."

Enoch wrapped the towel around his shoulders as a shawl. "I heard the Southern Marches in her voice. Don't they have hurricanes every autumn? You'd think she'd be accustomed to violent storms."

"I believe she is from Chesterton, down in Bayou County."

Enoch wracked his brains for a moment, envisioning the map of the continent his geography tutor made him memorize. He whistled. "A long way from here. The Bayou's deep in the Southern Marches, right by the Gulf. Sir Beauregard's territory." He frowned. "I've heard there's been a bit of trouble with a kadorei supremacist faction. What's it called—the Human League, or something of the kind?"

Vicar Taggert's expression grew mournful. "Yes, something of the kind." He murmured a brief prayer under his breath, and then smiled. "Sir Enoch, I'd like to speak with you, but I can see you're in no fit state to carry on a conversation. After you're clad in dry clothes, please join me in my apartment? Patsy has provided me with a fresh batch of butter tarts to go with my tea—too many for me to eat. I'd be honored if you shared them with me later." He held up his hands. "At your leisure, of course."

Enoch returned his smile. "Butter tarts sound good. I'll come by in an hour."

That should give me enough time to do my research.

The vicar nodded. "I'll look forward to it."

Once he moved from view, Enoch dashed up to his quarters, taking the steps two at a time. After peeling off his sodden clothing and toweling away the excess water, he dressed himself without paying much attention to what he pulled from the wardrobe. His fingers snagged in the snarled rat's nest of his soggy hair when he tried to comb it. He made a face.

That's what I get for being in too much of a hurry to plait my hair this morning.

He abandoned the dubious prospect of detangling his hair and turned his attention to locating his copy of *Fortulles Evaingynon Seprima*. "There has to be something in the old tome to help me navigate this mess," he muttered, looking for it in the expected places. But the old tome sat neither on his bookshelf nor on his writing desk. His hands shook as he pulled items out from under his bed. There, beneath a rumpled, cast-off tunic the maidservant hadn't found, his fingers encountered the raised sevenfold symbol of the Sages embossed on the leather cover.

He frowned. *How long has it lain here, neglected and gathering dust? At least a moon, I'd wager. I haven't cracked it open since…* His breath caught in his throat. *Since the day before I left for the Resurrection Festival.*

He'd read the first tale—the story about Gideon, the king of Goehl—but the rest of the volume remained an untapped mystery. Where should he start? A glance through the table of contents might help to make his choice, or maybe he should flip to a random page.

Enoch chuckled. "It hardly matters," he muttered under his breath. "Any of these tales could be about wyldlings. Might as well pick up where I left off."

And now you're talking to yourself. Continue on this course and you'll be back in the infirmary, right beside Red. Come to think of it, I should check on him after I see the vicar.

With a shake of his head, he opened the cover and pressed it to the blotter. Pages flopped over of their own accord to reveal a piece of cardstock stood upright in the binding's crease. A jolt ran through him and for a moment he couldn't breathe. He stared at it, frozen in a crystalline moment of subaudible humming. From somewhere in the Manor, a woman's voice rose and then fell into laughter, shattering the silence like breaking glass.

He watched his hand pluck the card from the open book and turn it over as if observing a stranger's movements. Drawings of flowers, food, plates, and utensils decorated the bottom and sides of the card. A painful pressure building in his chest, he read the beautifully rendered inscription—calligraphy executed in a familiar style.

Rebecca Cartwright, Janet Pines, and Salicia Jolson of Lilac Grove extend a cordial invitation to Enoch Northward, apprentice knight of Lilac Manor, to attend The First Picnic of the Season beginning at Jay Watch in the driest copse nearest the miller's pond.

And below this, in a different, sloppier hand: *Join us, Enoch, or be forever sundered from our company.*

Stinging heat filled his eyes. Words inked in a dead girl's hand grew blurry and swam, shaking back and forth. He ached to cry out—relieve the terrible pressure behind his breastbone—but the icy claws found his throat and bound it shut. His back met the wall as he staggered to one side. Still staring at the card, he slid until he sat on the floor.

I failed them. Lord Yshua, I'm sorry.

Enoch hugged his knees, buried his face in his arms, and wept.

Enoch trudged across the garden court to the vicar's apartments at the very end of Lilac Manor's Eastern wing. As he passed a lilac topiary in the shape of a swan with wings unfurled, Peter plummeted from the sky to land in front of him.

Enoch halted, an icy frisson of déjà vu running along his backbone. "Peter, what is it?"

Please, please don't tell me somebody else is dead.

The syrax's eyes were wild and his crest feathers ruffled. "Lawks! Dukey is running me ragged, Eenie. We needs more messengers. I wish

Silas and Timothy were here to help. I'd even take dumb Gregory," he added with a grumble, slicing up the sod with his front talons.

Enoch heaved a mental sigh of relief. "The other syraxim have their own sectors to serve," he said, frowning. "And you better not let Commander Storm hear you call him that." He crossed his arms. "Now, I'm just on my way to see Vicar Taggert. Is this important or not, Peter? If you have time to shoot the breeze, then your message must not be urgent."

Peter's tufted ears lifted. "Oh, but it is. Dukey, the commander, I mean, he sent me to summon you to the dispatch office right away." He tilted his head. "Eenie, are you sick? Your eyes are red and puffy."

Enoch clenched his jaw. "Allergies," he growled, fingering the pommel of his sword. "Never mind, Peter; I need you to take a message to the vicar: 'My apologies for not being able to make it this evening. Join me at Lark Watch tomorrow in the breakfast parlor.'"

Hopefully, Commander Storm would allow him enough time between training sessions to sit down and eat breakfast.

Peter repeated the message back verbatim and then trotted toward the vicar's apartment.

Enoch turned. The garrison dispatch office was in the opposite direction. He breathed in the fresh, earthy scent that always followed the rain and followed the flagstone garden path through a hand gate, where Bart and Thad joined him.

They exchanged nods and continued away from the Manor. As they passed the stable yard, Enoch waved at Old Harry and the other grooms. He stopped to fondle the silky ears of the goats in their pen before moving on. There were many things Commander Storm would want to discuss with him. He ticked them off in his mind as he walked, weaving around puddles in sunken places on the path; he'd have to ask someone to repair it.

When he arrived at the dispatch office—Commander Storm's quarters were above it—Thad and Bart each grabbed an arm and stopped him from crashing into Doctor Fourtier and Jessica Morton. The doctor supported the herbalist, who looked as if they had run her through a laundry wringer. She fixed him with her tawny gaze, fluttering tear-matted lashes. "I saw it in the bones," she said, her sepulchral voice shaking. "I read it in the cards. Beware, Sir Enoch. The sorcerer's hand and his hound hunt for you."

"Come, now, Jessie," the doctor said. He patted the white-knuckled hand clutching his arm. "Let's join Verbena for a hot cup of tea. And afterward, a friendly chat with the vicar. Good afternoon, sir," he said to Enoch, who greeted him accordingly.

They moved away, the doctor still soothing the frazzled woman. Bart and Thad exchanged troubled glances. "You realize she speaks nonsense," Thad said, extending his glance to include Enoch. "It is blasphemy. The future cannot be divined in such ways."

Enoch shivered. He recalled Janet Pines had been Miss Morton's protégé; the maiden often visited her little shop, learning the uses of herbs. Unfortunately, she'd picked up a few of the herbalist's less savory habits. Janet liked to think she knew more than other people and play at predicting the future. As far as Enoch knew, Janet hadn't taken it seriously, and stopped after a stern lecture from Vicar Taggert.

Not that it matters now. He swallowed past a lump in his throat.

Commander Storm stood behind a desk at the rear of the office with an unobstructed view of the entrance. A wooden chest the size of Enoch's torso sat on the otherwise empty desk. The windows were long, narrow, and set under the ceiling to admit only daylight. Glow-globes made by the dwelfnim cast a steady glow from several stands placed around the room. Posted on the walls were maps of the local districts, sectors, and the counties of the Northern Marches.

It struck Enoch, as he viewed him indoors, he'd met no one larger than the commander.

Seven feet tall, he was a giant clad in a supple leather duster, an ecru cotton shirt with long, wide sleeves, and a fitted leather vest, fawn-colored trousers, and huge black boots. Two baldrics crossed over his waist, upon which were attached two curved swords in scabbards hanging at either hip. His helm, a pewter metal bowl with leather strips fastening under his chin, still sat on his head. Even within the safety of the garrison walls, he remained armed. Enoch always wondered if his mentor slept in his armor but feared to ask.

The guardsmen saluted the commander and took up their stations outside on either side of the door. Even if yet another murderer lurked somewhere in Lilac Grove, no one would dare attack Enoch in Commander Storm's presence.

His mentor pointed at the lone chair in front of the desk. Enoch scurried across the room and sat, a child about to be disciplined.

The commander remained standing while he spoke. "Listen carefully; I'm only telling you this once. For your edification, Hesperidion Dust is a closely guarded secret of nehmwight Arkhadahns. The substance does not keep well and must be used within a few days, or its potency fades. Fortunately, the dwelfnim formulated an antidote a generation ago and the seneschal is on the mend." His eyes narrowed. "The doctor informed me of the late baron-knight's cause of death. Someone put Hesperidion Dust into his brandy hip flask. Members of the household staff are now in custody, but I do not expect to learn of a conspiracy here."

Indignant, Enoch jumped out of his seat. "Of course not. It's unthinkable. Why would anybody want to m-murder him? Everybody loved Sir Rick. Uh, sir," he added.

The commander's brows lowered. "Obviously, someone did not love him. Considering last night's events, I believe we can conjecture the traitor has fled."

Enoch's eyes widened. "Ravenos."

Commander Storm nodded. "There we agree, lad. My investigations in the Eastern Marches have turned up evidence of a similar cause of death for their baron-knight. Records indicate the traitor gatekeeper served Sir Nicolas right up to his death." The commander tapped a ledger lying on top of his desk. "Somehow, the wretch obtained a fresh enough supply of Hesperidion Dust to murder both baron-knights. The evidence of the doctor's diagnosis and treatment of the seneschal points in this direction. I understand before he collapsed, the seneschal accused the traitor of murdering three children who were missing for some time. Their corpses bear certain telltale marks I find disturbing."

Anyone would, Enoch thought, with a shudder. Aloud, he said, "Then the deaths are connected. Ravenos is the guilty party." He much preferred this theory to another murderer hiding amongst them. He frowned. "But, sir, there's something else. We still don't know what happened to Sir Thomas. If Ravenos murdered him, too, then we never found his body. He might as well have disappeared into the Aethyr."

Commander Storm gave him an odd, searching look. After a moment, he replied, "I know little concerning the man's movements beyond where the ward-bane shield used to pass through the Darkenwood Forest. I shall have to investigate this matter further." His eyes narrowed. "It is no longer your concern."

Enoch bit back a heated reply. "Yes, sir."

"I have declared martial law in Lilac Grove. Until further notice, no one is allowed in or out of the Westgate without my permission. Understood?"

"Yes, sir."

"Patrols will continue as usual along the wall ramparts. You will work out the details with Captain Faulkner."

"Yes, sir."

"Current events made it clear that you have been coddled and cosseted in my absence. It is time I took your training to the next level. Furthermore…"

While the commander droned on regarding his new training schedule, Enoch glared past his left shoulder at a district map on the wall behind the armored evainghir. His eyes fixed on the Darkenwood Forest. He always wondered what those discontinuous, cross-hatched serpentine symbols denoted—the cartographer had left some features unlabeled—but now he recognized them as pieces of the Wall.

Ugly facts stared him in the face. Commander Storm had known about the Wall and the Void-Bridge. But why forbid him from going— out of concern for his safety? He'd already crossed the Void-Bridge without mishap. Was it on account of Ravenos? *An escaped murderer poses danger to anyone, but nothing a group of armed men can't handle. No, there's something more to it.* Miss Morton's warning kept ringing in his ears.

"There really is a sorcerer in the woods," he blurted out. "Isn't there, sir?"

Commander Storm glowered at him. "I assumed this was obvious to anyone with knowledge of the baron-knight's cause of death. Your mind dwells too much on damsels from other realms when it should be concerned with the here and now. The new training schedule and your other responsibilities should soon cure you of that. Meanwhile, I shall deal with the Arkhadahn."

"But, sir, what about Annabelle? With a killer on the loose, she might be in danger."

Commander Storm closed his eyes, rubbed his forehead, and growled. "Balderdash. The woman-child is safe enough, so long as she remains in her own realm. And before you ask, the Void-Bridge has its own protections. It repels nehmwights and their spawn." He opened his eyes. "Enough of this claptrap; I will handle the sorcerer. It is time for you to focus on your duties." He smacked a fist on the surface of the desk. Metal jingled from inside the chest. "Weregild for the bereaved families," he snapped. "I trust you know what to do with it?"

Enoch saluted. Mercifully, his quivering legs did not betray him. "Yes, sir."

WEREGILD

Atropos's sanguine gloaming never seemed so appropriate to Enoch as it did that evening, riding back toward the Manor on his stag along with his guardsman. Although he dispensed the weregild to the grieving families in Lilac Grove, Enoch's heart grew heavier than ever, as if the golden rondels were pressing on it.

What price, for a human life?

He kept seeing the stricken face of Janet's father, Jedediah Pines, sitting in his wooden armchair with his splinted leg propped up on a stepping stool. Eyes glazed with an analgesic, he clutched his cap to his chest and mumbled, "It's a hard season, milord. A hard season for certain," while his wife wept in the kitchen. The Jolsons received the news—and the weregild—with calm dignity. They even thanked him for his generosity, which left his insides squirming. He'd never forget the haunted eyes of Sally's siblings.

Worst was at the Cartwright residence, where the recently widowed Mrs. Cartwright flew into hysterics, accusing Enoch—in rabidly colorful terms—of gross incompetence. And then, with a glare of withering contempt she threw the gold rondels at his feet and slammed the door in Enoch's face. As he fought back tears, Enoch fled back to the waiting guardsmen and Tinker.

Sharky elected to stay behind to soothe his aunt—and convince her to accept the money. "Don't worry, E," the medic called out from the front door, where he picked up the scattered coins. "Aunt Rose won't govern her tongue when she's in a temper. She means nothing by it. They're just words, and words can't hurt you."

Sharky's wrong. Meant or not, the grieving woman's insulting words pierced Enoch. Like expertly aimed arrows, Mrs. Cartwright's furious epithets struck too close to the mark.

Simon urged his mount up alongside Enoch. He spoke out of the side of his mouth. "What happened to those girls is not your fault. So, stop blaming yourself. Stop dwelling on it. Keep moving forward, E."

Enoch stared at the reins in his hands. "All right, Simon. But the fact remains: I still have to deal with the aftermath. I have to put things right."

"*We,*" Simon corrected him. "*We* have to deal with it. *We* must put things right. Let us help you. Lord Yshua would say we are supposed to carry one another's burdens."

Jim drew up on Enoch's other side. "Simon's right, sir. Didn't King what's-his-name write something about how two men working together is better, because if one falls down the other can help him up?"

"'For if they fall,'" Guffie quoted in a stentorian voice, "'the one will lift up his fellow. But woe to him that is alone when he falls, for he has not another to help him up.' And it's King *Solomon*, Jim, in case you were wondering."

The others laughed and teased Jim, who scowled and shook a fist at his brother-in-law. Shame smoldered inside Enoch at Simon's rebuke. As they passed beneath the boughs of the fragrant lilac trees, he blessed the crimson light and the shadows masking his flushed face. *Don't you guys throw Scripture at me*, he thought. *I get it. I'm supposed to rely on others.*

But ultimately, a baron-knight must decide. He needed to be strong and stand on his own. Sir Rick always sat in the magistrate's seat alone; the bench was only large enough for one man. Enoch must lead as Sir Rick had done. He'd do so soon, during his meeting with the officers.

A figure dropped from the overhanging branches ahead of them, cloak billowing like raven's wings, and crouched in the middle of the path. Simon's mount leaped in front and the others surrounded Enoch, forming a protective wall. The sound of drawn steel rang out in the sepulchral wood. A cowled head lifted, and green eyes flashed in a beam of dying sunslight from the East.

The seneschal greeted them as he stood up and pulled back his cowl, unconcerned at the sight of troopers drawing their swords. He nodded to Enoch and then clasped his hands behind his back.

"Jethro's black shadow!" Simon swore, slamming his sword back into the scabbard and signaling the others to follow suit. "Call out a warning next time, Milord Raeden. Someone might've hurt you."

The kaenhir lifted his chin. "Such is never likely to happen. More likely to happen is this: the man who attacked this one would be the man lying upon the ground in agonies." His whiskers twitched. "Your time to react is very good, Sergeant. One commends you and your men." In a rare show of approbation and without a trace of irony, Red dipped his head in a bow.

Simon worked his jaw for a moment before finding his voice. "Um, thank you, Milord."

"And thank you for the lesson," Bart added, followed by a hasty chorus of gratitude from the others; all had experienced the seneschal's switch on his backside during their boyhoods.

Red bowed to each of them. "You are most welcome." And then he came to stand beside Enoch. "Your servant has recovered from his—how to say it in this abomination of a language—ah, yes! Indisposition."

Enoch grinned. "Praise Yshua!"

Red touched the place where his crucifix hung. "Your servant has done so." Patting Tinker's neck, he added in his native tongue, "The captain has called a meeting for the officers in the dispatch office, and he'd be honored if you attended."

"I should go, shouldn't I?"

Red gave him a level look.

Enoch cleared his throat and raised his voice. "Gentlemen, let's go see what Captain Faulkner has to say. Duty calls."

RABBIT-HOLE

"Ann! Kensi's on the phone."

Heart hammering, Annabelle finished stuffing a pair of jeans into her bulging backpack and then shoved it under her bed. *Better to be prepared in case the wormhole comes back.* "Coming," she hollered as she ran down the stairs, taking them two at a time. Marty Balin's voice followed her from the stereo speakers.

Her mother met her on the kitchen's threshold. She raised her eyebrows as she handed over the telephone receiver. "Remember, it's a school night. And turn down the music; Amy's already in bed, and Drew will be soon."

Annabelle replied in a light tone. "Yeah, I know, Mom. I'll be off the phone by nine." As she bounded up the stairs, she put the receiver to her ear,. "Hi, Kenz. What's up?"

"Hey," her friend replied. "I'm just checking in on you, making sure you're still there."

Ann rolled her eyes as she closed the door to her bedroom. "Ha, ha," she said, without humor. "As you can see—I mean, hear—I'm still firmly planted on planet Earth." She reduced the volume on her stereo.

"What're you listening to?"

"My parents' old records." Annabelle picked up an album jacket. "Right now, I'm playing Jefferson Airplane's *Surrealistic Pillow*. I like some of their songs."

"Ooh, Jefferson Airplane." A chuckle came from the other end of the line. "My mom told me they sang about drugs."

Annabelle grimaced. "Maybe I shouldn't be listening to it, then?"

Kensi laughed. "You went through the DARE program, same as me. I think you'll be fine. Everyone sang about drugs back in the '60's, because they all *did* drugs." She continued, listing various psychedelic groups and how their song lyrics related to recreational hallucinogens and narcotics.

Annabelle listened, making noises in the correct places. *I have to tell her. But how will she take it? Kensi doesn't like Enoch; she practically pushed him through the wormhole yesterday.*

She spoke in a rush. "The wormhole appeared, and Enoch contacted me again, this afternoon."

"Really?" Kensi's tone grew cautious. "What happened? Did he... do anything?"

"No. In fact, he blinked out before I grabbed hold of him. There was pain, a massive headache. And the next thing I knew, Dad was shaking me; I must've passed out on the floor." Annabelle bit her lip. "I'm worried about Enoch, Kenz."

"You're worried about him?" Kensi snorted. Her tone strident, she added, "Wait, hold on a second. What do you mean, 'passed out?' Are you okay?"

Annabelle pulled her bag out from under the bed while bracing the receiver against her shoulder. "Oh, I'm fine. Sorry, I didn't mean to freak you out. It's more as if I fell asleep because I had a dream." Behind her, the first bass chord of "White Rabbit" pulsed from the speakers. One of her favorites. She hummed along with the melody as she rearranged items to fit better inside the backpack.

"You had another dream." Not a question. "While you were passed out."

"Asleep, not passed out. But, Kenz… Enoch wasn't in it, this time. That's why I'm worried." She told her friend about Neal shoving her through the stained-glass wall, the boat, and the blue dragon on the pedestal.

Kensi sounded interested. "Ooh, a dragon? I wonder what it means."

Grace Slick sang about a caterpillar sending out a call.

Annabelle frowned; the song's lyrics seemed disturbingly à propos tonight. "The dragon called me. I walked out on the water to him, like Peter did when Jesus called him."

"Weird."

Annabelle shoved the backpack under her bed. "Suits me, then." Floorboards creaked out in the hallway. She glanced at her closed door and whispered, "I think it means I have to go there. To Tehara."

Her friend spluttered. "Hold on, Ann. *Go* there? For what reason— because a dream-dragon told you so?"

"Not that." Annabelle bit her lip. "Or not only that. Enoch needs my help, I know it." Her fingers tightened on the receiver. "I can't shake the feeling; there's something I have to do—and Tehara's the only place I can do it."

Kensi muttered something under her breath. She raised her voice and said, "Ann, can you promise me something?"

Her chest tightened. "I'll do my best, but you know I never make promises. They're too easy to break."

Kensi sighed. "Then just listen. You're normally so cautious; I shouldn't have to tell you this. If the rabbit-hole or whatever it is shows up, don't go jumping in right away. Call me, and I'll…" She took a deep breath and exhaled. "I'll come along with you. We can figure out what happened to Enoch, together."

"You'll come with me?" Annabelle's eyes widened. "But you think I'm nuts for even *wanting* to go. Heck, *I* think I'm nuts."

Kensi laughed, but it sounded strained. "Ann, come on. Even before this dream business, I've always thought you were a little nuts. It's one thing I like about you."

Annabelle's chest loosened as warmth filled her. "Thanks. I'm glad." *Even if you don't approve of Enoch, you're still willing to help… because we're friends.*

Kensi chuckled again. "Anytime. Hey, so, can you stay after school tomorrow and practice for Solo and Ensemble? The second movement still needs a lot of work."

Annabelle bit her lower lip. *Kensi wants to change the subject. Fine. I won't tell her I plan to go if—no, when—the opportunity presents itself. She won't approve, but Enoch needs me.* Aloud, she said, "Sure."

"Great! I'll see you tomorrow."

Grace Slick wailed the last phrase of the song over the speakers.

Annabelle glanced at her clock radio. Eight fifty-nine. She managed a smile. "Yeah, see you tomorrow. Good night, Kensi."

"Good night, Ann. Sweet dreams."

DREAM TRAINING

Click.

Red consulted his silver watch. "Time for the stick-fighting training, young knight. With the chaos all around, your progress has suffered."

Enoch followed Red to the salle, twilight streaming in through tall windows to bathe the corridor of the South Hall. Black shadows stretched long in the sanguine light of Atropos-set. Enoch shivered, recalling his failed altercation with Ravenos.

Red makes a good point; I must improve my martial skills. Sir Rick would never have allowed the cur to defeat him in battle.

With his tail rigid behind him, the seneschal pushed through the double doors of the salle, holding one of them open long enough for Enoch to enter. The door swung shut behind them. As they took positions several paces apart, the lurid glow of Atropos bathed the room through the tall, south-facing windows. Pane-bars cast ebony cruciform shadows to sprawl across the floor and walls.

Red stood with his hands clasped behind his back. The kaenhir's eyes glowed in the dying sunslight as he looked down his nose at Enoch. His monocle flashed in the bloody light. "You are Acting Baron-Knight. However, you do not behave in properness as the baron-knight should. You are too concerned about maidens in other worlds." He took a step forward. "You cannot control the destruction inside you. Every time you use it, you sow the wind. If it escapes, you shall reap the whirlwind."

Enoch struggled, forcing his voice past the freezing claws in his throat. His body shook with the effort. He felt tired. So tired. Red had no confidence in him. After the cyclone tossed him from the glade like a rag-doll, Enoch couldn't blame him.

He held his hands open in front of him. "I didn't ask for this power. I don't know why I have it." He narrowed his eyes. "But I will use every tool at my disposal to protect the Northern Marches."

Red flinched, stepping back with a grunt, as if Enoch landed a physical blow. "So be it. One must beat the poison dust from you."

Huh? Enoch furrowed his brow. "What in the nethermost perdition are you talking about? I wasn't poisoned—you were! Ravenos threw it in your face before he fled."

Red whirled on his toes and stalked to the weapon rack. He removed a pair of wooden staves. His ears upright, the kaenhir tossed one staff to Enoch. Still staring at his friend, Enoch snatched it out of the air.

Red spun his staff in a blur over his head and then slammed the butt down on the wooden floor with a loud crack.

Uh-oh. Enoch's gut sank. *Maybe I pushed him too far by reminding him of his failure.* He sank into a defensive position with the staff held at a diagonal. His palms prickled with sweat.

"Prepare yourself, O mighty Baron-Knight," announced the seneschal, teeth bared in a fierce grin with nothing of amusement in it. And then he dashed at Enoch, striking with his staff faster than Enoch's eye could follow. "Your servant will beat the poison away from you, so you will be safe."

As fast as lightning, the seneschal struck at Enoch with a series of moves from several directions. *It's all I can do to block and parry, let alone go on the offensive myself.* Red's staff cracked against Enoch's weapon with each blow; he defended, but the kaenhir held nothing back this time. His hands stung from the vibration of blows against the staff.

He jerked his staff up to parry a jab meant for his throat. Their sticks blurred as they swept through the air.

Whack! Clack! Whack! Crack!

In a room bathed in crimson by the twilight and surrounded by black bars of shadow, the kaenhir advanced and Enoch gave ground.

Commander Storm emerged from the bloody light of a window. "You must separate yourself from your fear of mortality," he growled. "Any foe of flesh and blood can be defeated. Every man has weaknesses to exploit. Observe your adversary closely, always. His feet, his hands, and his eyes often broadcast clues betraying his next move."

Enoch stared into his friend's snarling visage, trying and failing to find a weakness in Red's attack. He felt a flicker of terror at the alien, wild intensity he saw in his opponent's eyes.

Has Red gone crazy?

Commander Storm kept lecturing him. "Always be aware of your surroundings. Use them against your opponent."

Maybe I'm *going crazy.*

Enoch shifted to one side, placing the entire length of the salle at his back instead of the door and adjacent wall. Repositioning bought him time to turn the bout around in his favor. In a quarter hour it would be too dark for him to see. Then, every advantage went to the kaenhir.

Red's staff cracked against Enoch's, narrowly missing his fingers.

Commander Storm snorted. "A soldier's body is a tool—but only if he's prepared to use its abilities. You must use every weapon at your disposal."

"But I can't," Enoch wailed. "If I unleash the winds, I might lose control and kill him."

His mentor said, "Balderdash. You have demonstrated control."

What did he mean? Enoch concentrated on the battle. The rosy twilight stained the white fur on Red's hands, face, and tail, in stark contrast to his whirling staff and dark clothing. Coattails unfurled behind him like a raven's wings as he shifted his hips and shoulders to bring more force behind his next attack. Enoch ducked, and the seneschal's staff whistled through the air where his head had been.

Kaspar's wings, how can he fight in those dandified garments?

Commander Storm pounded his right fist into the open palm of his left hand. "Invincibility lies in defense, lad, but the possibility of victory lies only in the attack."

I'm trying!

Sweat streaming down his face, Enoch jabbed low, aiming for Red's midsection, but the kaenhir parried the strike on the downstroke. *Beggar it all!* Enoch gasped for breath. Despite the adrenaline surging through his body, the events of the day were taking their toll. He was tired before; now, he grew exhausted. Red was not even winded. Relentless as death itself, the seneschal pressed him. Teeth gritted, Enoch scuffled back to regain his balance. Wood cracked against wood as Enoch raised his staff in a cross-defense. His limbs trembled with fatigue.

Commander Storm lowered his eyebrows and stood akimbo. "If the mind is willing, the flesh can continue despite weakness."

I can't go on much longer, sir. It's a toss-up whether I'll run out of energy, floor space, or daylight first.

Desire to win the bout shifted to concern for mere survival. His mouth grew parched as the Evergold Desert of Losaridos when a horrible thought presented itself.

If he yielded, would Red even honor it?

Commander Storm's basso rumble filled the salle. "He who knows when to fight and when not to fight, will win the battle."

The kaenhir's attacks came faster and harder now, as if he gained power as his opponent's energy waned. Enoch raised his staff to block a fierce strike and his arms quivered, giving way under the strain.

Almighty Threefold One, into your hands I commit my spirit!

"I surrender!"

Bloody light flashed off Red's monocle as he advanced, sharp teeth bared in a frightening rictus. His white-furred features rippled like a reflection in a pool of water, and then morphed into a bestial, dark-furred visage with a gaping, fanged maw.

Amber eyes flashed with hatred. "To surrender is to die, warlock!"

Ravenos came at him, twilight running like blood along his two blades. Staff held in a defensive diagonal, Enoch backpedaled, eyes rolling. *Where did Red go? And the commander?*

The long knives bit into the wood, sending slivers spinning away into the darkening salle. Somewhere in the long room, someone played "As We March to War" on a harp.

Ghostly images of Becky, Janet, and Sally flickered in the shadows by the wall. Clad in white, the girls held hands. Violet light glimmered around the edges of their translucent forms.

Three female voices blended in a chorus. "Seek justice. The innocent must be protected."

"I'm sorry I couldn't protect you," he cried, stick raised to block the kaenhir's furious onslaught. The staff cracked and split apart. He pushed back at Ravenos, screaming. A gale burst forth from his mouth, blowing his opponent the length of the salle. He crashed into the weapons-rack. Wood cracked and clattered. Polearms and staves went rolling in every direction.

I did it! Trembling, Enoch collapsed to his knees. He gazed in satisfaction at the sprawled figure of Ravenos.

Commander Storm's steely gaze pierced Enoch. He raised an admonitory finger. "Have you forgotten my lessons so soon, lad? Warfare is based on deception." He pounded a fist into the opposite hand to emphasize syllables. "Constant vigilance!"

Enoch sucked in a breath and concentrated on his fallen foe. Ravenos shivered, shimmering in a heat mirage—which then resolved into Red. Enoch's eyes widened. He shook his head. "No, no, not again. Please, Yshua, don't let me hurt him again."

Suddenly, Annabelle appeared between them, her blue eyes wide behind her spectacles. With her back to the fallen kaenhir, she stood closer to Red than to Enoch.

Annabelle peered at him, bewildered, her long hair sleep-tousled. "Enoch?"

The kaenhir clambered up from the ruins of the weapon rack, his eyes glowing with a famished light. The black suit he wore shifted to rougher soldier's garb as his frame broadened. White fur darkened to brown and green eyes turned yellow.

Annabelle glanced over her shoulder, shrieked, and stumbled toward Enoch.

Ravenos sprang at the girl, his claws extended.

Enoch struggled to rise, to summon Windblade, to do anything. "Annabelle!"

Red appeared beside him, grabbed an arm, and hauled him up to his feet. "Seek justice, young knight," he hissed in his ear. "The innocent must be protected."

Quicker than thought, Enoch's right hand whipped out and three spinning blades made of air hurtled toward the snarling rogue. The translucent blades pierced forehead, chest, and the hollow at the base of his furred throat. Ravenos collapsed, his amber eyes wide with surprise.

Red inclined his head to Enoch. "Very good, young knight."

Annabelle skidded to a stop, her eyes round with fear when she saw the other kaenhir beside him. Red laid a hand against his heart and bowed to her. "Little maiden," he said, and then disappeared. The final bit of lurid light coming through the windows faded. And yet, the strains of "As We March to War" continued.

Enoch dropped the broken staff pieces and grabbed Annabelle. He drew her in close under his left arm. With his right, he summoned Windblade. The sword hummed along with the violent marching song.

Annabelle peered into the darkness. "What the frumious bandersnatch is going on, here?"

Enoch's arm tightened around her. "Don't worry. Stay close to me. No matter what happens, I'll protect you."

Outlined in violet light, Sir Rick's ghostly form faded into view in front of them, cradling a sword in his arms. He smiled. "Walk humbly with Lord Yshua. Remember, the innocent must be protected."

Enoch's face crumpled in anguish. Windblade keened with sorrow. "But Sir Rick, I can't control the winds. What if I become a monster who hurts everyone he tries to protect?"

"Didn't seem to me as if you had a problem with control,"

Annabelle muttered.

The baron-knight turned his head and eyed him sidelong with a knowing smile—not an expression he adopted in life. "So long as you walk with Lord Yshua, Skelsdaran, you need not worry about losing control."

Commander Storm faded into view against the backdrop of blackness. He crossed his arms and glowered. "A true warrior controls himself at all times."

Sir Rick made a face. "Oh, tsk, we've had quite enough of your military blather." He waved a hand; Commander Storm shimmered and then vanished in a haze of violet smoke.

Laughter rang out, Sir Rick's vaporous image rippled with violet light, growing larger, darker, and more solid. The sword transformed into a large, hand-held musical instrument—a lytarra. Long, strong fingers moved with competent rhythm over the fretwork and strings while the amused lavender-gray eyes fixed on them. The tune changed to something light and pastoral.

The bard nodded, a mocking smile on his handsome face while he played. "You are quite welcome, Sir Enoch. Don't let my brother grind you down with his nonsense about winning battles; everyone knows the supreme art of war is to subdue the enemy *without* fighting. Good night, children." And then, he winked out of sight. The music faded.

Enoch and Annabelle closed their eyes and heaved twin sighs of relief. A gentle wind blew through their hair. A faint drizzle of rain dampened their faces, and then vanished. Enoch opened his eyes. They hung suspended by nothing, stars shining from the black depths surrounding them.

We're in the void place.

Clad in dark blue armor gleaming with sapphire light, Annabelle clung to him, looking around with a rapt expression. "You're glowing," he said.

She looked into his face and laughed. "Enoch, you're glowing, too."

He raised his right hand, still holding Windblade. Silver light radiated from his armor. The sword rippled quicksilver.

Annabelle frowned. "That bard guy sure is weird. I've been dreaming about him, too, but I can't figure him out."

"Me neither," Enoch agreed. "I wonder why he keeps showing up in our dreams." He scowled. "And why he pretended to be Sir Rick."

Annabelle shrugged. "Maybe if we keep having these dreams, we'll figure it out. Right now, I want to know what happened to you. One minute, I'm shooting through this shiny blue wormhole, and the next, I'm sprawled out flat on my bedroom floor. My dad freaked out. He was about to call nine-one-one, but I told him I just fell asleep from studying too hard." She raised her eyebrows at him in expectation.

Enoch explained what happened.

"Basically, your commanding officer has told you we can't meet anymore," she summed up, looking dejected.

"That's right," he said, his heart clenching. "From now on, until I attain my majority, this is the only way we can communicate."

Annabelle chewed on her lower lip, thinking. And then, her face brightened with a grin. "Enoch, I just thought of a loophole. Commander Storm can't tell *me* what to do."

REAPING THE WHIRLWIND

A BLACK BOX

The bone knife sliced through fur and flesh. Zakaar's back arched as he howled.

William's fingernails dug into his palms. The blade was enchanted to make every cut an agony. *Tenebris used the same knife to carve tracks for the arkhabala into my skin.*

Shuddering, he pressed his back against the door. He regretted stepping inside the spell chamber and struggled to suppress the memories of past tortures it evoked. He swallowed hard and waited for the assassin's wails to subside before he spoke. "Master Tenebris, I have news. Commander Storm passed through the Darkenwood twelve hours ago."

The Arkhadahn straightened. "Oh, shut up," he snapped at the mewling harkhurz shackled to the table. "You brought this upon yourself. Courtesy of your brilliant muck-up, we must accelerate the extraction. Be grateful I only take the amount I require and don't drain you."

William grimaced and fought against the urge to vomit. Blood welling up from the assassin's wounds flowed into the grooves of the slanted table and then into a vessel at its base. Tenebris needed to contact the Dreadlord and required blood to fuel the spell activating the Farspeaker crystal on the wall. It was also necessary to punish Zakaar for disobeying orders.

"Two enemies killed with one spear." Or so the Golorum would say.

With eyes averted from the grisly tableau, he cleared his throat. "Um, Master? According to my surveillance web—" His voice cut off. Tenebris lowered a hand dark with writhing tattoos.

William's heart went cold. *Vibrienth's garters, now I've let the snake out of the burrow.*

"Yes, yes, William; I heard you the first time." Tenebris wiped blood from his knife, set it on the tray alongside other instruments of torture, and then turned to regard his apprentice. Behind him, Zakaar whimpered prayers in his native dialect. Tenebris crossed his arms. "A surveillance web? I want to know where you learned a seventh-level conjuration." He raised his eyebrows. "You have my undivided attention, William."

He gestured, and William again controlled his own larynx. "It was accidental, Master. A fluke. I have no recollection of how I managed it— if it was me and not an emergent property of the ward-spell stone array linkages due to the Aethyric —"

His throat constricted and he went silent. He drew in a sharp breath, eyes burning with unshed tears. *Burning suns, I detest him!*

The arkhabala on Tenebris's hand wove sinuous patterns. "I warned you against babbling, William. Once I have a spare moment, I shall work on improving your memory. You've forgotten much of the approved spellworking process, and I cannot countenance this in my apprentice. It's sloppy and dangerous. But there are larger issues at stake." He stroked his beard, frowning. "The evainghir's return is a problem. I made several plans to counter him based on the Dreadlord's recommendations. Questions, William? You may speak now. Mind you don't babble. And remember to enunciate."

Fingers twitched, and William's throat loosened. Commander Storm was a problem. *Blistering blazes, how can we counter a juggernaut immune to Arkhadic power?* He licked his lips. "Master," he said, slowly and carefully, "what must I do to accomplish our mission? Doubtless, the old reptile's keeping the slaving kadorei closer than the carbuncles on his—"

"Never fear," Tenebris interjected. "I have the means of drawing the commander away from his charge." His gaze flickered to the harkhurz on the table before returning to William. "You told me he kept returning to those ruins. You two will take up residence nearby and use your newfound resources to monitor the area." He narrowed his eyes. "Unless you 'forgot' to inform me of something vital?"

William balled his hands into fists and lifted his chin, meeting his master's gaze. *There's a lot I don't tell you, Tenebris.* Aloud, he said, "Of course not. But how am I to restrain a wyldling?" He glanced at Zakaar, who'd grown calm and watched him with gleaming yellow eyes. "Without harming him."

A shark-like smile spread across the Arkhadahn's face as he strode over to the desk beneath the Farspeaker. Two boxes—one smaller than the other with a lacquered finish—took up much of the surface space. He picked up the smaller box, handed it to William, and told him what to do.

William stared at the cube in his hands. Its matte black finish appeared to eat the meager light in the room. "If the Dreadlord says it'll work…"

"I advise you to trust that assumption." Tenebris flicked a hand toward the table and the manacles fell open. Zakaar slid to the floor in a crouch, clutching his slashed forearm and snarling curses in another language. William tucked the box inside his burkheld and then wrapped a handkerchief around the assassin's arm. *He's weaker than he should be, but at least he's stopped bleeding.*

Tenebris opened the larger box, revealing his poppet collection. "Now, go. You have your instructions. I have work to finish before the suns rise and I don't need you fools underfoot."

"Yes, Master."

William hastened from the spell chamber, supporting Zakaar, who leaned on his shoulder, still whimpering. The box clinked against the whiskey flask. His stomach twisted in knots like the tattoos inked in his flesh. He dared not fail.

TRIAL BY COMBAT

"*Please, Annabelle, don't cross the Void-Bridge without me. It's not safe.*"
Earnest blue eyes blinked at him. "But... I want to help you."

Enoch stared up at his ceiling, his stomach in knots, running their dream conversation through his head. He tried to reason with her but remained uncertain whether the message went through before everything faded away into horrific nightmares about his three murdered friends. He awoke in a cold sweat, fear seizing him in icy talons: *Can Ravenos cross the Void-Bridge and get Annabelle, too?*

The clock in the hallway chimed quarter past four. Klotho didn't rise for another hour, but it was too late now for sleep—even if he could. Enoch sighed, threw off his quilt, and dragged himself out of bed. He washed and dressed in the items Red laid out for him the previous evening. He must report to Commander Storm for a skills assessment at Frog Watch. After that, he'd meet Vicar Taggert in the Southwest breakfast parlor.

He smirked. *Wait until I tell Red. He'll be so impressed; I remembered two appointments in one day.*

Nervous energy hummed through him. He climbed up to the widow's walk and summoned Windblade. After practicing a few sword forms, he dismissed the weapon and rested his forearms on the East-facing rail. Near the western horizon, stars were fading in the gray of false dawn but those making up the constellations of Gilgamesh's Shield and Balthazar's Blade glared down on him. He sighed and lowered his gaze to the dark courtyard below.

Stop judging me. I'm doing the best I can.

Below, sleepy birds stirred in their roosts, twittering peevishly. Most likely, they weren't enthusiastic about starting their day, either. Frogs peeped in the garden pond. He drew in the fragrant air and concentrated; the singing frogs sounded as if they were right there on the balcony with him.

I can do more than this.

Enoch took another deep breath and flung out tendrils of his thought—his kythim—concentrating on the surrounding air. Silver currents flowed around him, rivers in the air. They *were* rivers of air. *I need to send my kythim swimming along with them.* A pale eddy of air spun off the edge of the Manor roof and sped off toward the garrison. Quicker than an eye-blink, Enoch plunged his awareness into the silvery airstream.

The wind swept toward the dispatch office. From inside, Red's voice spoke his name and Commander Storm's rumbling voice answered. *They're talking about me.* With an effort, Enoch wrenched the airstream to a halt just outside the window. *Stay*, he told it. The breeze swirled in place.

The seneschal spoke in his native tongue. "Your servant scented the maiden on him. One presumes she is a real person. Enoch cares for her. One feels concern; the murderous rogue—the abomination—could…" Red's voice cut off, murmuring a prayer. He continued, "You are certain she is safe from harm in her own realm beyond the stars? Should one not set a guard in the Wall-place for the young knight's peace of mind?"

Commander Storm harrumphed; young females were his least favorite topic of conversation. Enoch would have smiled; had he not been so invested in the question's answer.

The commander responded in Tradespeak. He understood many dialects but often refused to speak in them. "Unnecessary. So long as she stays where she belongs, she need fear nothing out marauding in the Darkenwood Forest. Even with the ward-banes down, the Void-Bridge has its own protections and restrictions. Only a wyldling could shatter the ward-bane crystals and activate the Void-Bridge. Only a wyldling can cross it."

On the widow's walk, Enoch closed his eyes and exhaled. Annabelle was safe back on Earth. And then, his eyes widened. Had the commander said 'wyldling?'

He knows. How long has he known?

"You must tell him, Lord Commander," Red insisted. "Tell him everything. Strange things have happened, the sort of things you said would happen if he possessed the potential of his bloodline."

Enoch frowned. *What bloodline? I thought nobody knew about my family.*

"No," the commander replied. "Boys talk. I will not have a repeat of Nervashi here in Lilac Grove, or anywhere. Never again. I swore an oath to protect that boy, and I will uphold it. In my own way."

Nervashi. Enoch suppressed a shiver. *Where the commander found me when I was a toddler. And… wait.* He frowned. *Why swear to protect me?*

Red sighed. "Enoch is no longer a boy, Lord Commander. He is a stripling. Soon, much sooner than pleases you, he will be a man grown. He must be told the truth, or this one fears he will do something very foolish."

Commander Storm snorted. "He has already done something foolish. He has opened a way to another realm. Dad-rot it, he has even communicated with someone on the other side of the Void-Bridge—if we can believe what he claims."

"Do you doubt your servant's testimony?" Red sounded aghast. "He scented her on his clothes. You believe he spoke falsehoods about the maiden from beyond? One thought this habit thrashed out of him, long ago, when he told the stories of the invisible sister."

Enoch grimaced. Would he never live down his childhood folly? *Stop talking about how foolish I am and get back to the matter of my bloodline and me being a wyldling!* He sent the airstream closer to the window and strained his ears.

"No. I believe your account," the commander grumbled. "And he is not lying. I could almost desire he spoke less than honestly, but I have my ways of knowing. The lad told the truth as he knew it."

Thump! Enoch flinched; no doubt Red struck the butt of his staff against the floor, as he often did when exasperated. "Lord Commander, something must be done about this maiden; he claims she must be family, his heart-sister. From a child, he always seeks his family. He will return to her."

Red's right; By Kaspar's wings or Oberon's tail—I sure will!

Commander Storm grumbled. "Dad-rot it. I hoped he'd forget about his family once installed here. He bonded soon enough with the baron-knight and the womenfolk. I reckoned that would be enough for him."

Enoch moved the air stream closer. *What's this?*

"Over the past four Cycles, I have kept my eyes and ears open for information but have gathered naught regarding any surviving kin. The remains of his parents, the eldest son, and the eldest sister are accounted for. We never located the second sister's body—either in the ruins or for miles around."

Enoch sank to the balcony floor. Time and time again, Commander Storm asserted he knew nothing about his parents. His family. And now, here he was, mentioning not only parents, but three older siblings. *They're dead, but I always wanted to know…* Angry tears burned his eyes. He knuckled them away.

Red made a sound of surprise. "You did not tell your servant of the missing sister."

A shifting sound, and then parchment crinkled. "What was the point? The lass vanished without a trace, and I presumed her dead. I deem it improbable that a child can survive in such an environment."

Red tsked. "Improbable is not impossible, Lord Commander. All things are possible in the hands of the Almighty."

Commander Storm grunted noncommittally, as he did whenever somebody mentioned the Threefold One. "Perhaps, Raeden, the promise in her bloodline preserved the child for a season or two. But this is all I will grant you, for I have heard naught of an active wyldling. Aside from the boy—the sel Drayven bloodline is extinct."

Enoch's eyes narrowed and his grip tightened on the railing. For Cycles, his mentor had been lying to him—and Red knew about it, too! His entire frame shook with rage. He closed his eyes and clenched his jaw. *Calm down, Enoch Northward—no, Enoch sel Drayven—and breathe. Good air in, bad air out, just as Sir Rick always taught—*

He froze, eyes opening wide. Had Sir Rick known of his family, too? Had everyone known the secret and then lied to him for Cycles? Enoch's heart raced and the noise of blood rushed in his ears. No. No point in maligning the dead. Sir Rick had reported to Commander Storm;

he'd have obeyed orders to stay silent. Enoch grit his teeth. Never again would he trust anything Commander Storm said.

The blustering beggar lied to me!

Enoch's kythim slammed back into his physical body. He clenched his fists and unleashed the icy tempest howling inside him. Wind whipped and roared around him like a wild beast. He seized the airstreams and wrestled them under control. "You will obey me!" Filled with bitter anger, he rose from the widow's walk. Wind rushed past him, his view constricted to a bright tunnel with the garrison dispatch office at its end. The building drew closer until he stood outside the door. And then everything dissolved into the silver light.

Enoch wiped his bracer across his sweaty forehead. "Balthazar's blades, if I'm sweating already, then this afternoon will be a sauna." Standing half-crouched in the center of the sand-covered arena, beneath the eyes of half the garrison—the rest served as sentries along the battlements of the shield walls—he adjusted his grip upon the leather-wrapped hilt of the training sword Simon gave him. As the challenged party in the duel, Commander Storm chose the weapons. He said: no edged weapons. Training swords only.

How in perdition had Enoch ended up in this predicament? The morning was a blur, except for flashes here and there. Him confronting the evainghir and demanding a duel. Red falling to his knees and howling at the ceiling. Vicar Taggert at breakfast, pleading for Enoch to withdraw his challenge. Mrs. Mulgrove, weeping into her apron. Verbena Fourtier, silent and livid with eyes full of fear. Vicar Taggert praying over him outside the arena.

Enoch did not remember issuing the challenge, but he must have done. He imagined himself saying the words, intoning them in a coldly formal voice: "Commander Daniel Storm, I challenge you to the Machtughenna."

Trial by combat.

He eyed his much larger opponent through his new dueling goggles. The oculist had coated the lenses with a special resin to protect the wearer's eyes against the sunslight. His view through the tinted lenses was every bit as clear as when he wore his spectacles.

To his astonishment, the commander had given the goggles to him when they arrived at the garrison arena. "I ordered this made for your sixteenth name-day. I reckon, however, that current events warrant you receiving them a few days early."

It embarrassed Enoch to receive a gift from his opponent, but he accepted the goggles with gratitude.

At least, blowing sand and sweat dripping into his eyes wouldn't blind him.

Over the thunder of his own heart, Enoch heard the murmur of the men's scattered conversations in lowered voices. He wondered if any of the troopers were making surreptitious wagers on the outcome of the duel in the seneschal's absence—Red disapproved of Enoch's challenge and refused to be a spectator—and if so, how high they stacked the odds against him.

I won't let it bother me, he told himself, hefting his shield to test its weight. *I have to trust to my advantage.* To his knowledge, the commander had never battled a wyldling. Otherwise, he'd have heard a tale about it. *I'm sure the commander is unaware that* I *know I'm a wyldling.* He hoped so; he couldn't remember what he'd said when he confronted his mentor in the dispatch office.

But he vowed he'd defeat the commander.

Commander Storm looked at him with a weary sort of resignation. He wasn't even in a combat-ready stance; the training sword dangled in his hand with the tip pointed at the ground. "Cease your adolescent posturing. You shall only wear yourself out. I will give you one last chance to call it off, lad. There is no shame in walking away at this point. You have not yet reached your majority; forfeiting a duel will not represent a loss of face."

Anger flashed through Enoch. "No, Commander Storm," he said through gritted teeth. "The challenge stands. Honor is at stake."

Commander Storm snorted, his tone dismissive. "Honor? You know not of what you speak, lad. However, I shall educate you."

Enoch waved his training sword for emphasis. "I *do* know exactly 'of what I speak!' For Cycles, you've lied to me about my family. You said you knew nothing, but you *lied*. I heard you, and Red testified to it. A man ought to speak the truth. *That's* honor."

A sneer twisted the commander's upper lip to bare his teeth. "Insolent child. I hid the knowledge from you for your own protection. His Excellency testified to *that*, as well."

Deputy Korr, acting as referee, cleared his throat. "Seconds!" he hollered, and the arena went eerily silent. "Have you noted the time?"

Simon called out from Enoch's side of the battleground. "Klotho is at her zenith, sir!"

"First noon, sir!" Sergeant Matlock bellowed, standing at ease well behind the commander.

At the precise center of the arena, Korr glanced between the two combatants. "Commander. Sir Enoch. Do you both still intend to duel?"

"I do," Enoch said, swallowing a flurry of nervous panic threatening to overwhelm him now his wrath had faded. As the challenger, he chose the duel's time and the place. "The sooner this is decided, the better."

Once he won, he'd be in charge and the commander would be in disgrace. The blustering liar. He bounced on the balls of his feet.

The commander sighed and sank into a fighting pose with his weapon and shield raised. As the one challenged, he'd chosen the type of weapon. "Aye, lad. Might as well end this dad-rotted farce. This time I will not go easy on you," he added, rattling his training sword. "After all, honor is at stake."

"Don't expect you to," Enoch rasped out through a parched mouth. *Honor, and possibly Annabelle. Remember Annabelle.* She needed him to win this bout, so he could return to the Wall before she tried to cross the Void-Bridge. Just because nobody'd ever beaten Commander Storm in a duel before did not mean it couldn't be done. *As Sir Rick used to say: "There's a first time for everything."*

The referee explained the rules. "On your mark sirs. May the Threefold One have mercy on you," he added, giving Enoch one final, pitying look before taking several huge strides backwards. He flicked the burnished steel disk into the air.

The rondel tumbled through the air in an arc, flashing in the sunslight.

Enoch locked gazes with Commander Storm. The commander went still, narrowing his gray eyes. His leather armor creaked.

Breathe. Remember to breathe.

He inhaled. Silver infused his vision.

The rondel hit the sand.

Enoch and his mentor both exploded into motion. Nothing existed for Enoch, save the bundle of lashed-together strips of wood in his hands and his adversary, limned in silver light.

Damp sand flew and lacquered wood connected with a loud crack. Enoch danced back upon the balls of his feet, shield raised at the ready to intercept a blow. His mentor feinted to his left and then struck with adder-swiftness, jabbing under his guard at his right side. Enoch dodged before the blow connected, the silvery mist showing the weapon's disturbance in the air.

I must hit him soon. I need first blood. It counts double.

Enoch and the commander had sparred before, but only as an instructive game, never with such serious intent. In the past, his mentor trounced every opponent—even when handicapped. His new skill at least evened the odds; Commander Storm's complacency should blind him to the possibility of defeat.

It's legal, too, as long as I don't summon Windblade.

Both combatants prowled through the sand, boots leaving prints in their wake as they danced around one another. The commander launched an offensive, hammering a series of heavy blows. Silver mist highlighted every move. Enoch evaded direct hits. He saw his opening and scored a glancing blow upon his mentor's hip.

Halloway's exultant yell: "Point! Point!"

"First blood to Sir Enoch," the referee announced. He sounded pleased, albeit taken aback. "Gentlemen, on your mark."

Commander Storm fell back to his mark, grinning. "Well done, lad!"

Enoch blinked. *That was a genuine victory.*

Panting, he returned to his mark. Every one of his muscles had turned to jelly.

I must endure this. I must win this duel.

Simon gave him a water flask, and Enoch drank greedily. "Thanks, Simon."

The sergeant frowned at him. "You're color's off, sir. And your eyes look funny. Are you sure—"

"Yes." The world sparked with silver beyond the tinted lenses. He snarled under his breath. "I need to beat him. Prove he's a dirty liar and not worthy to be my superior officer."

"I believe you, man," his friend replied, looking concerned. "Take care, E."

The referee signaled the second round of the duel had begun. Commander Storm sprang at Enoch with a fury he seldom before witnessed—either on the dueling ground or off it. The silver light showed him the path, but his body wouldn't respond. In quick succession, the commander scored three points and the second round was over.

Mind reeling, Enoch fell back to his mark. His shoulder and chest were just smarting from the blows. His head swam from the heat.

Please, Lord Yshua, my cause is just. Be with me. I must defeat this liar.

Enoch breathed deeply and settled into the combat-ready stance. He reached deep inside. *Winds, obey me. I am your master.* The silver power rose from the core of his being in a wild tempest, filling him, unfolding like the petals of a flower crafted from shining steel.

Enoch vaulted up with a bellow, a whirlwind spinning. He struck at Commander Storm. His blow landed upon his opponent's shoulder.

Fierce exultation swept through him. *Take that, liar. I won!*

At the apex of his leap, he lost control, and he spun to face the heavens. A stinging crack across his buttocks jolted through his body. His last point meant nothing, now.

No!

Enoch plummeted from the sky and the suns flickered out.

WINDCHASER

Enoch drifted in and out of consciousness. One moment he floated in a bright chamber filled with a cacophony of noise, jostled and unable to move his body, and the next he stood near the precipice of a lofty plateau. All was silent and still. Myriad stars looked down upon him, cold and uncaring pinpoints of light in the inky sky. The moon's slight curve peeped above the horizon. Despite the cotton garments Enoch wore underneath the form-fitting, supple leather encasing his body he shivered in the chill night air. His exhalations misted from his mouth.

He adjusted his goggles and pulled a fitted leather hood over his head, buckling the fastenings under his chin. As far as he could see, from horizon to horizon, spread a sterile landscape of rolling hills covered by pristine snow, gleaming silver under the starlight. As his eyes acclimated to the dim light, however, the patchwork mounds appeared ragged and indistinct, shifting like fog. Pinnacles of rock thrust up from the silver-white sea, jagged steeples pointing to heaven. In the semi-darkness, the stone spires ranged from ebony to light gray. Their facets glinted in the light of the rising moon, which looked larger than usual. It took him another moment to adapt his thinking to his circumstances.

Here I am, perched upon the roof of the world like a real dartling jay. He blinked at the stars. They looked closer than they had from the widow's walk on top of the Lilac Manor. *How did I get up here?* He eyed one of the rocky islands and took a step toward the edge of his plateau. The pinnacles resembled watchtowers. *Who built them?* He took another step, to the very brink, and with a flexing of his legs launched himself out into the open air. A bright light seared an image of the landscape against his retinas before it blurred into shifting shadows. He fell into a world of fuzzy outlines, pain, and madness.

"— brought on by over-extension," a basso voice rumbled from somewhere nearby, echoing amid the crystalline towers of his febrile imagination. "Common enough in novice wyldlings… should have caught it sooner."

"I wasn't aware this sort of ability manifested outside of the dwelfnim community." The doctor's voice spoke from right beside his head, which throbbed with pain at every sound and movement. They propped him up in a reclining position. Something pressed against his tongue and warm liquid trickled down his throat. He gagged.

"Steady, young master. Steady now."

The voices faded away.

He stood on the plateau again; an island in a sea of silvery mist drifting in glacial fashion around the lofty spires. The moon had risen to wash the silent landscape in its pale light. Gazing at a barren world rendered in stark contrasts comforted him. He thought of Annabelle and wondered how often she stared up into her own sky spangled with alien constellations, contemplating her own moon. Did it bring her comfort, too?

He gazed in awe at the moon. *It's so huge and beautiful, but why am I here?*

A deep voice spoke. "You have retreated to your place of power, Skelsdaran."

Alarmed, Enoch whipped his head around, trying to locate whoever spoke. The whispering voice seemed to come from everywhere. He looked from horizon to horizon, but saw nobody who could have spoken to him in a human voice. Fear chilled him with the force of an arctic gale. It hadn't been the voice of the dream bard. This differed from the dreams he'd shared with Annabelle.

"Who goes there?" he challenged, his voice resounding amid the crystalline pinnacles of stone. He wore a form-fitting leather suit, gloves, and boots. His strange uniform creaked as he reached for his sword. It wasn't at his hip. *I'm defenseless.*

No. Not true. He recalled his training under the baron-knight and the relentless commander. "*A trooper might be disarmed,*" Sir Rick told him once, "*but so long as he keeps his wits he is never without a weapon.*"

The whispering voice held a teasing note as it swept past him on the wind. "How clever of you to comprehend a simple truth, Skelsdaran."

Enoch turned around on the plateau. "Identify yourself!" He summoned Windblade. It's humming sounded curiously subdued.

"In ages past, people called me Kaspar Windchaser." The voice sounded weaker now, drifting away across the expanse of shifting clouds and faceted spires. "Seek my vashryu, Skelsdaran, and I shall make everything clear… as crystal."

"Wait!" Excitement filled him, a thrill rising behind his breastbone.

Could it be? Had he spoken with one of the legendary Sages of elder days? He spun around again. The faceted spires thrust above the silver-limned clouds and the moon hung in the star-studded blackness. Windblade disappeared from his hand with a buzzing whine. He stood alone, again.

Enoch cupped his hands around his mouth. "Kaspar! Kaspar Windchaser! Why do you call me Skelsdaran? Please, come back. I need to talk to you!"

"Have no fear, little wyldling," whispered the wind. "The air is your power."

Enoch's breath caught in his throat. "Kaspar Windchaser… I truly am a wyldling?" He scanned the strange landscape. A glitter of movement. He squinted. *There*! Moonlight flashed along a ribbonlike shape coiled on a platform on the truncated summit of a distant spire. The voice came from a winged serpent with metallic silver scales—the same way his book of legendary tales described the Sage Kaspar Windchaser.

The faint voice held laughter. "What a silly question, Skelsdaran. You knew you were a wyldling. The maiden across the Void-Bridge is a wyldling, as well. I'd not be surprised if Hadrien has…" Silver scales glittered as the serpent flexed his wings against what appeared to be dark chains and then collapsed. When he spoke again, the whisper grew even fainter. "Come, child. I am bound to this dais, and this distant communication weakens me without my vashryu."

A shiver ran down Enoch's back. Annabelle, a wyldling? *If this is true, then…* His eyes widened. *She could cross the Void-Bridge on her own.* He flexed his fingers. All right, then. If he wanted answers to his questions, then he must fly over to the Windchaser's spire.

Eyes fixed on the silver ribbon, Enoch took a deep breath and leaped off the precipice.

Instead of flying toward the spire, he plummeted through the clouds.

His heart pounding, he flailed, reaching for the wind; but it refused to answer his call. As he descended, lightning flickered and thunder reverberated around him, the noise transforming into a familiar voice and recognizable words.

"—guard his door, Sergeant," the deep voice rumbled from somewhere above him, indistinguishable from thunder. "I am entrusting you with his safety in my absence. If he should awaken before firstdawn, do *not* allow him to leave his bedchamber." A gusty sigh filled the room. "When he wakes, tell him I shall answer his questions upon my return."

"Yes, sir," came the lighter-toned reply, with resolve. "No one will get through me, Commander Storm." He knew that voice, too. Simon. What was happening? He floundered, reaching for an anchor but his fingers grasped only mist.

"See to it. With the seneschal investigating rumors of the murderous traitor in the village, this attack in the South District may be a well-timed distraction, meant to divide us and scatter our strength. But I dare not ignore Trelawney's request. Send Peter to me at Southgate should anything arise outside your ability to handle. Mark my words, there is a violent storm brewing, and I don't mean the weather."

The voices drifted away. Enoch spiraled past the clouds until he plunked into a wooden chair. Now what? The buttery light of Lachesis slanted through the window of Sir Frederick's study. The baron-knight sat at his desk with a ledger open in front of him. He glanced up at Enoch and smiled. "You've done well. But you must cross the Void-Bridge again and return with the maiden. Remember to walk with Lord Yshua."

Enoch saluted his late guardian. "Yes, sir." He leaped from his chair and the sunlight vanished. Heart hammering, he plunged into a silver-spattered darkness, clawing for consciousness. He must awaken. He must get to the Wall.

Wait for me, Annabelle. Please, wait until I get there. It's not safe.

A mighty crash of thunder startled Enoch awake. He opened his eyes to the darkness of his bedchamber. Sweat dampened the pillow and his night clothes clung to him. He sat up and waited for his body to inform him of its limitations before committing himself to rising. Other than a gnawing hunger and an accompanying light-headedness he deemed himself fit enough to get out of bed.

A shielded lamp provided just enough light for him to see. He stripped out of his soiled clothing. Next to an empty mug smelling like medicine sat a bowl of tepid water and hand linens on his bedside table, which he used to wipe away the worst of the sweat and grime. He pulled on fresh undergarments and a tunic. He scowled; someone had taken away his leather armor. True, the breastplate and trousers were dirty, but the armor was still serviceable. *Only a dandy cares about appearances.* He raked his hair back and tied it with a rawhide thong he found in a drawer after pushing aside the cravats and silk ribbons. *I must hurry. I must reach the Wall before Annabelle tries to cross the Void-Bridge.*

His stomach grumbled, sounding louder than the thunder. He flung open the wardrobe and snatched a silver-gray jacket with sable stitching, a gray waistcoat, and a pair of buckskin trousers, which he tucked into a pair of the fine boots he'd once sworn he'd never wear—because a prissy maidservant decided his favorite boots needed to be cleaned. He was astonished; the fine garments fit him comfortably. *I guess I'm getting the fancy stuff dirty. That's what happens when you take away a man's work-a-day clothes.*

He strapped on his sword-belt and searched for his spectacles. After several minutes of fruitless effort, he remembered the lenses had cracked during his altercation with Ravenos at the gate. He'd sent them off to an oculist for repair. Enoch sighed and grabbed the goggles Commander Storm had given him before their duel. *I'm too beggaring hungry to think straight*, he mused as he strapped on the goggles. He knelt beside his bed and pulled out the cache of travel food left over from his trip with Red to the Wall he'd neglected to return to the kitchen pantry. As he crammed a biscuit in his mouth, he debated whether he dared to take anything with him. Would it weigh him down too much to bring the waterskin under his bed? Probably.

After he ate and drank enough to calm his stomach, Enoch crept over the door, using every skill Red taught him to avoid making a sound. He laid his ear against the wood and concentrated. A man cleared his throat. Another muttered something. Simon and another trooper stood guard outside his door. *I wasn't dreaming it; Commander Storm* did *post Simon outside my bedchamber door.*

Enoch bit back a curse. The hall up to the widow's walk wasn't an option. Praising Lord Yshua for conscientious maidservants oiling the locks and hinges, he slid the bolt home. He retraced his steps to the casement window and tied back the curtains. Rain pattered against the glass of the west-facing window as he peered out into the darkness. The storm was losing its breath; if he planned to leave, he better go now.

He opened the window and a gust of cool, damp air buffeted him. He inhaled it with satisfaction. In the distance, the weatherproof watch-lanterns strung along the curtain wall shone like lambent pearls, winking on and off as wind-tossed trees obscured and then revealed them. A flicker of lightning illuminated the grounds for a split second as he stepped up on to the windowsill. His heart raced, and for a moment he reconsidered. What would happen if he couldn't harness the wind? Most likely, he'd plummet to his death.

The floorboards creaked outside the door. "Sir, are you awake?" The door-latch rattled. "Beggar it; Sarge, he's bolted the door."

Simon cursed. "Stand aside, Vermell."

Enoch froze. *Blasted beggars. I must leave* now.

Something tugged at him, stronger than ever, just as a fresh gust of wind assailed the Manor. Every doubt vanished; he became one with the wind. From behind him came the sound of wood splintering and men shouting. As he swept up into the stormy sky, the roar of the tempest failed to drown out Simon's voice shouting his name from the open window.

West, Enoch insisted, and the gust of wind changed direction. Raindrops stung his face in his flight toward the Wall, driving away the last vestiges of sleep. Exhilarated, he shot over the curtain wall standing between the sheltered community he'd grown up in and the primeval forest beyond, leaving the lights of civilization behind him.

He whooped. *By Kaspar's silver wings—I can fly!*

Rain fogged his goggles. He flew blind. For a moment he panicked, wondering if he'd lose his way, but then he calmed himself. *Just fly West. Take it slow, or you'll overshoot it.* Though his nerves were a-jangle, he checked his speed. He went at what seemed a snail's pace and kept a palm's span the forest canopy. After several close calls when the uppermost branches of trees slapped against him, he arrived at the Wall unscathed.

The Oval Window reflected a flash of lightning, but otherwise remained dark. He landed in front of the quiescent aperture and waited while the storm dissipated into a gentle summer shower. He pushed his goggles up on his forehead; a silver glow outlined everything. He stood before the portal for a time, catching his breath. Moist, fecund earth scents filled his nostrils, a trace of an acrid odor. A strange voice whispering.

Wait. Something's wrong. His hand darted for his sword, pulling it from its scabbard as he ducked and whirled. Or, at least, he tried to turn and draw his sword. Alarm spiked through him. *I can't move.*

Something like fingers crept around his neck, something both warm and freezing at the same time. A collar closed with a snap around his throat, the sound echoing with forlorn finality. Something oozed into his skull and engulfed pieces of his mind. His insides turned to ice and grew hollow as the frigid thing devoured them. The silver illumination winked out. So did his sense of Annabelle. The cold severed her from him as completely as if a knife sliced through their connection.

Enoch screamed.

His head rang and stars flared up in the darkness. Strong arms held him. As consciousness fled, a familiar voice purred in his ear. "You're mine, warlock."

Enoch fought against a thick, consuming darkness. He must wake; something felt very wrong.

An unfamiliar voice was speaking. It sounded like a young man. "I said 'hold him fast' not 'smack him about and tear him to pieces.' Stupid harkhurz!"

His captor murmured gibberish while venting hot, foul breath into Enoch's face.

Ravenos.

Panic and disgust flashed through Enoch. He rasped out an incoherent insult. In response, the brute slammed his head against the ground. A bright flash split the blackness as his head bounced off the hard-packed soil. Something heavy pressed against his unshielded abdomen.

I can't breathe!

Enoch struggled. The traitor's grip was unshakeable. Black terror suffocated him until he gasped a mouthful of air. He reached for his sword; his arms wouldn't move.

You have another weapon. Use it!

Had not Commander Storm ruthlessly trained him for situations such as this? Enoch forced himself to focus, to repress his fear as he fought to escape, to breathe. The weight on his chest shifted. He heaved a shuddering breath. *Can I summon Windblade with my hands trapped?* No choice but to try. He concentrated.

Nothing happened.

Enoch slumped and stared up at the sky. Clouds broke apart to reveal the curve of the crescent moon sailing high over the inky black treetops. Lambent as they caught the moonlight, the baleful yellow glint of the renegade's eyes speared him from the darkness of a canid visage. He gasped. *Red was right; Ravenos is not a kadorei man.*

Fangs bared, Ravenos pinned him to the ground, one of his knees pressing against his ribs, the other levered in warning against his groin. He tried to wrench his arms out from under the powerful hands pressing his arms against the moist earth.

He glimpsed Ravenos's companion, a figure Red's height. Enoch tried for an authoritative tone, but he sounded more like a terrified child. "What have you done to me? Where have you taken her?"

The other muttered curses as he fumbled with his garments. "Eh?" he said, tugging at something under his robes. "Fiery suns! What the blistering blazes is the burning barbarian prattling on about? Ravenos, I thought you made certain there's no one else here!"

The kaenhir grunted, and his gleaming yellow eyes never left Enoch's face. "No one here; only him. No other scents but—" he raised his head and sniffed. "Animals," he concluded, returning his baleful gaze to the youth beneath his claws.

The stranger drawled in a smarmy baritone, "That settles that, My Lord

Fancy-pants. You are alone. You may plead for mercy now if you wish."

Ravenos growled. "He will receive none."

Enoch's mind seethed. *If they've done anything to Annabelle…* "Let me go, or I'll kill you. You might have my body trapped, but I can still kill you with… with my *mind*."

"Oh no!" Wide-eyed, the other youth clapped his hands against his face in mock terror. "Please don't kill me. Not with your—gasp! —mind powers. I'm so scared I'm piddling all over myself." He chuckled and then his voice grew cold. "Oh-ho, I don't think so, you slaving barbarian. Not when I have *this*." He held up on a cord gleaming a dull, dirty silver. The cord attached to the horrible collar around Enoch's neck. His captor leaned in close and whispered, "I have snared you, wyldling."

Enoch convulsed in a panic, trying to buck the kaenhir off and claw the awful thing from around his neck. He must get it off before it ate up everything. Again, he reached for the Windblade, but it was gone. The horrible collar—the wyldling snare—engulfed it.

No!

Ravenos drew back but did not release him as the other youth leaned over him. Pale moonlight glinted off a toothy leer and a pair of peculiar eyes glowing orange with their own light. "You are our prisoner, now."

The kaenhir tensed. "Someone comes," he growled. His yellow eyes pierced Enoch's gaze. His toothy grin widened. "Someone back in the trees. Someone… maybe her?"

Oh, no. The chill in Enoch's guts deepened until speech froze in his throat. Had Annabelle crossed over without them realizing?

"Go take care of it," the orange-eyed youth hissed back at the murderous beast. "I can hold this sad sack of offal while you're gone."

Ravenos squeezed Enoch's arms. "Do not move. Do not scream. Or I kill you dead."

"You'd better not," his companion shot back. "Or the master will have you on the rack, again. Until he 'kills you dead.'"

The kaenhir bared his fangs. He rose and then slipped into the darkness of the wood without a sound, drawing a pair of long knives as he went. The blades glinted in the moonlight.

No. It couldn't be Annabelle. Could it?

Enoch thrashed, a banner flapping in a gale. His mind mercifully went blank before presenting him with horrendous images of the young woman in the vile beast's clutches, the things Ravenos must have done to Janet and Sally and Becky.

The girls he hadn't been able to save from their fate.

I failed them. I failed them all!

Enoch released a wordless howl, giving voice to a hymn of miserable fury.

"Hold still. Shut up, you burning mreeshgraf!" Cloth rustled, and something smelling of leather and sweat covered Enoch's mouth. He bit down. It tasted awful. He spat, cursing.

His captor chuckled. "It's no use, Northward. Bite all you want; have a real good chew. I'm wearing bracers!" He sounded proud of himself.

The fool. He's only pinning one of my arms. Wildly, Enoch lashed out at his captor. His fist connected, and the youth looming over him cried out in pain. With his opponent distracted, Enoch wormed one leg free. He jerked up a knee. It found something soft, and there came a watery gasp followed by an unmanly whimper. The youth dropped the cord, and the pressure on his neck eased. Most of the weight restraining Enoch disappeared. He seized the cord and rolled out from underneath his captor. He ignored the clammy chill spreading through his hand. If Annabelle was here, then he must save her from Ravenos.

An agonized scream split the night.

"Enoch!"

Wait, was that *Simon's* voice?

Heart hammering, Enoch sprang to his feet and tore off after Ravenos. Over the sound of his own ragged breathing came the clash of steel against steel, the cries of multiple men's voices, and the savage kaenhir's snarling.

Enoch burst out of the tangle of brush. In the dimness beneath the trees, he saw several shapes struggling. There were two other shapes huddled on the ground, unmoving. As he approached, another shape gasped and crumpled to the ground, leaving two upright. The foul miasma of blood and perforated bowel assaulted him.

"Ravenos, you beggaring, cowardly mongrel. Let her go. It's me you want."

The smaller of the struggling shapes cried, a man's voice rising above the dark kaenhir's answering snarl, "Enoch! Run!"

Simon! And three others of his guardsmen. Shock immobilized Enoch. *How did they get here so quickly? They can't fly.* His eyes darted around, seeking another, smaller figure. *Where is Annabelle?*

"Run, Enoch. I'll hold him." Simon grunted with effort, straining to parry the kaenhir's furious double-bladed blows. "Get away… take my mount."

Indecision kept him rooted in his tracks. Enoch wanted to help his friend—under no circumstances could he abandon Simon—but Annabelle's safety concerned him. *Where is she?* He needed to find her. Why couldn't he sense or communicate with her anymore? His trembling fingers tugged at the collar encircling his neck. *This thing is the culprit. I must remove it!*

Ravenos dropped and swept the young sergeant's feet out from under him. Still on the ground, the kaenhir rocked back, raised both his legs straight up into the air, and then slammed his booted heels on Simon's thighs with the full weight and power of his lower body behind them. *Snap!* In the silence that followed, the young sergeant drew in a sharp breath and then wailed in wordless agony. Ravenos rolled into a crouch, brandishing one of his blades for the finishing stroke.

"No!"

A howling gale of wrath propelled Enoch toward his enemy. Weaponless and with his newfound power strangled, he charged across the clearing, determined to tackle the kaenhir before he killed Simon. It wouldn't bring the Maidens Three back from the dead, but he could save his friend from the same grisly death.

"Warlock." Ravenos bared his fangs. His eyes flashed with triumph. One blade hovered over Simon's throat. The other pointed straight at his heaving chest.

A giant fist seized Enoch and jerked him off his feet. His back slammed against the ground and the air in his lungs rushed out of him in an astonished whoop. He struggled to breathe, staring up into a pair of glowing orange eyes.

"Suns-cursed idiot," the other youth said. His voice wobbled. "Do you have a death wish, or something? Good thing I'm here to stop you from impaling yourself."

A blood-curdling shriek of agony split the night like an ax through cordwood. The acrid scent of singed hair made Enoch grimace.

The blazing eyes flicked away from him. "Ravenos, what are you caterwauling for? Quit howling at the burning moon and get your hairy burtokis over here. My immobilization spell won't last much longer."

Why can't I move? I must help Simon.

The cloaked youth man-handled him, wrapping him up with the flexible cord attached to his collar. A clammy chill radiated from the bindings, penetrated his clothing, its icy teeth biting into his flesh. More than anything, he wanted to wriggle free and strike out at the face leering over him; however, his limbs refused to obey him. A boulder crushed his chest and the icy mass trapping the tempest inside of him still refused to melt. He thrashed, driven mindless with terror. His mind refused to think; it grew worse with every passing moment as the strange, metallic rope bound up more of his body.

Enoch's eyes widened in horror. The collar and the rope, he thought, his oxygen-starved brain sluggish. The wyldling snare of legends. But where did they find it? Lord Evanrudhe said Sage Melkior destroyed it during the Oblivion Wars. The act cost him his life.

Air flooded into his lungs when the boulder disappeared from his chest. Enoch caught the acrid scent of singed cloth and fur. Ravenos growled, "You move, I kill the other one dead."

Hope whispered past the agony inside. Simon was still alive.

The kaenhir tipped his head to one side in a manner that reminded Enoch of the seneschal. He whined and wrinkled his muzzle with distaste, as if he'd bitten into a lime. "Dull-seeber, this rope you use. And the collar." He laid back his ears, shuddering. "I do not touch, but I can feel them when I am near. It *tingles*."

"Ignorant thug," the cloaked youth replied with a derisive snort. He rolled his glowing eyes. "Don't you know anything about *anything* important, Zakaar? The Dreadlord gave us these special restraints to keep this slaving barbarian from using his so-called 'mind-powers' on us." He pulled something out from under his robe, muttering. "Wyldling snare or not, Master Tenebris warned me not to take any chances with our esteemed guest. Ah, here's the soporific. I couldn't find it before."

A cork popped and a cloying smell filled the air. The youth leered and pinched Enoch's nose closed. Pressure built until Enoch opened his mouth and a fluid burning like spirits filled it. Enoch tried to spit it out, but his enemies held his mouth and nose closed until he swallowed it.

Glowing orange eyes boring into his. "Sweet dreams and nighty-night, barbarian."

Enoch's thoughts grew murkier as the soporific untethered his brain from its moorings. The last thing he heard as he drifted away into darkness, sliding out from underneath his enemy's taunting, was a voice from half-forgotten dreams. It told him not to fear.

THE WIND CHANGES

STRANGER IN A STRANGE LAND

Alone, Annabelle drifted in star-crazed darkness. Icicles of pain splintered inside of her, and then, nothingness.

Crickets chirped her awake, and a susurrus bringing to mind powerful wingbeats and feathers rustling in a nocturnal breeze. "Ahdmerel," a voice whispered, like something out of a dream. Her right side throbbed and a chilly dampness met her skin. Pain and discomfort were nothing compared to the absence inside her.

Enoch? Where was her silver knight?

Annabelle sent out a call: *Enoch!*

Her voice dissipated, a whisper sucked into a void.

"Enoch?" She spoke aloud. Where her sense of Enoch once dwelled, only a cold emptiness remained. It felt as if someone had reached into her viscera and torn out a node of warmth and well-being. A wail burst from her throat even as her eyelids creaked open. Her vision swam in uncertain darkness, perceiving nothing.

Come on, Annabelle. Stop being a whiny baby. You need to get up and go. You must find Enoch. He's in trouble and needs your help. She uncurled, stifling a sob, and then hissed as her abraded arm brushed against something rough. The moldy scent of damp forest bracken filled her nose. She sneezed and then moaned as painful pressure clamped like a vise around her head. As if shocked at her outburst, the crickets went silent.

Groaning, she rose to her knees and then sat back on her feet. She clutched at her throbbing skull with both hands. Her hair and clothes were clammy and cool against her skin. She gathered her bearings and tried to stem her rising panic.

Had she fallen? If so, it looked as though her arm and side took the worst of the impact and not her head. Thank God. Her brain was her greatest asset in this strange world. *So, stay calm; stay calm and breathe.*

She picked wet strands of hair off her face. *Something's missing.* She went still, alarm coursing along her nerves like ice water. *Oh, no. Where are my glasses? I swear, they were just on my face.* A fresh wave of terror washed over her and she once more struggled to stem the flood of rising panic.

Annabelle pawed at the ground, feeling for her glasses. Grass and plant stems tangled her fingers like hidden snares. The sharp scent of sap stung her nostrils. She squeezed her eyelids shut. If she could not see, then why bother to keep them open?

And then, the soothing balm of familiar words came to her.

"The LORD is my shepherd; I shall not be in want. He makes me lie down in green pastures. He leads me beside still waters."

She sucked in a great, shuddering breath and stilled her trembling hands by stuffing them under her armpits. The chill seeped from her fingers and into the surrounding flesh. If she'd arrived in the green pastures she'd sought, then where were the still waters?

Where has Enoch gone?

Something rustled nearby. She froze, gooseflesh pebbling her skin. Enoch? No, he'd call to her. The crickets remained eerily mute.

Is that wind-blowing-the-foliage type rustling, or is a sharp-toothed beast stalking me?

She hugged herself, rocking back and forth on her haunches. The motion soothed her. *Remember the words. The words will save you. They tell you Jesus has saved you. You are safe, no matter what happens, your soul is always safe.*

Annabelle looked around with wide eyes, seeing nothing in the darkness, her breathing ragged. She rocked back and forth, mentally reciting verses of Psalm Twenty-three while the crickets waited in silence. She dared not break it.

Her eyes adjusted to the darkness. She cast her eyes above the forest clearing. The stars looked blurry without her glasses, but many of them were too large, too bright, and too different. When she tried, it proved impossible to trace out any familiar constellations. No Orion the Hunter. No Big Dipper. No Cassiopeia.

Her insides went cold. Wherever she was, she no longer stood on Earth. And then, she remembered a name: Tehara.

Another world. Just as in her dreams. But how to assure she'd come to the right world? Wormholes could lead anywhere. Everything had gone wrong. Enoch was missing. Without the silver knight by her side, this place couldn't possibly be her home.

Isn't this just typical? Nothing ever turns out the way I want; I always mess things up.

She heaved a sigh. "I'd best look on the bright side of things. Enoch's disappeared; I've already lost my glasses…" Her eyes widened as another loss occurred to her. "And my backpack with my clothes and supplies… and I might be stranded here on an alien planet in a dark, scary forest—but, hey! —at least I'm not blind."

"So, kiddo, you're finally awake."

Annabelle gasped, scrambling to her feet. She backpedaled until her rump met with something cool and solid. "Who… Who…"

Foliage rustled near her feet. The voice—a gravelly, masculine voice—spoke in a sarcastic tone. "Whoo-hoo to you, too. What are you, an owl?"

Annabelle slid along the stony surface and away from the voice. "No, I'm a girl." She swallowed. "What are you, some kind of jerk?"

A ripping snort emerged from a shadowy patch of bracken fern-like shapes to her left. "Yeah. I'm the kind of jerk who's been trying for over an hour to wake you up. To make sure those freaks don't come back to nab you, too. Here, kiddo," the voice added, "you dropped these." Something glinting with starlight tumbled out of the patch of ferns.

Annabelle picked it up, delight thawing the chill on her heart. "My glasses! Thank you."

"You're welcome."

Annabelle turned the glasses over in her hands and scowled. "Hey, they're broken."

"It wasn't me, kiddo."

A frisson shivered through her. *Kiddo. That's what Dad calls me. But… whoever this guy is, he isn't my dad.* Panic rose again, and she firmly quashed it.

She put on her spectacles. Although they sat crookedly on her face and the scratched lens was annoying, she could see. "My name is Annabelle, not 'kiddo.' Who are you? And what happened to Enoch?"

Biting her lip, she knelt in the grass and stared into the shadows. Could a man hide in there?

To her surprise, a creature the size of a large tomcat hopped out from under the bracken ferns. Starlight gleamed in icy blue eyes. "The freaks took Enoch," he said, his gravelly voice thick. "I don't remember my real name, but the kid calls me Toad. Come with me. There's injured men who need help, and I don't have thumbs."

Annabelle smoothed hair back from a wound on the soldier's clammy forehead, sticky with clotted blood. It didn't appear to be bleeding anymore. She pressed the handkerchief she'd found in his belt-pouch over the cut, anyway. He breathed raggedly and his taut face glistened with sweat in the dim light of the stars. He was a large man, fit, and well-muscled. And his legs were broken. She didn't dare move him, even if she could.

Two men and three strange riding beasts lay alongside the trail in congealed pools of blood as if flung there like rag-dolls. Eviscerated and broken, they were beyond even the most gifted surgeon's skill.

Already dead.

Annabelle whimpered, her stomach fluttering after dry heaving from the stench.

Toad made a disgusted noise. "You told me you knew first aid."

Startled, she turned to glare at him. "I *said*, I read a book on first aid, once. But it was for dogs. Not people. What if I screw something up?" *Again.* She felt along the soldier's side, eliciting a groan. She winced. Broken ribs, too.

"Jiminy Cricket," Toad muttered. "Unbelievable." Louder, he said, "Look, kiddo. These guys need help. People, dogs, same difference. Don't the same principles apply to both? Staunch the bleeding, splint broken bones, keep them warm, and whatnot?"

"Yeah, but it's too dark and I can't see well enough to do anything for him."

Except pray.

"And I don't have thumbs," Toad shot back, "but you don't hear me whining about it. Follow me. There's a pile of wood over here and some sticks that might work for splints."

Reluctantly, she left the soldier and extracted the sticks from the pile according to Toad's directions. "If only I had twine," she muttered, returning to the injured man's side. But even if she found her backpack, she had packed no twine or rope. The little spool of thread in her miniature sewing kit wasn't any good for tying splints.

After a brief hesitation, she took off her T-shirt and then tore it into strips. She used a knife from his belt to start the tears. Her shirt was dirty and damp from lying on the ground, but she needed something with which to secure the makeshift splints to his legs. At least she wore a bra more modestly cut than most bikini tops.

Toad made gulping, spluttering sounds. "You didn't need to do that, kiddo. Those other guys aren't using their clothes."

"Nuh-uh. Their clothes are disgusting with blood." Annabelle shuddered at the cool touch of the night air against her bare skin. The stench of blood and perforated bowel filled her nostrils, but she was beyond gagging. She tried not to think about zombies while she worked. The man stiffened and cried out. Annabelle froze, tears stinging her eyes. "I can't do this," she said. Her throat thickened. Her hands shook. "I'm hurting him. He's going to die, Toad, and there's nothing I can do to save him."

Toad groaned with loud exasperation. He sounded so… human. "I'll go for help. Three men isn't a full squad of troopers. Someone else should have been along by now."

If he left… A nameless horror seized hold of her. "No, please. Don't leave me." She bit her lip, holding back the shameful reason. *Irascible or not, you make me feel safe.*

Toad muttered a stream of expletives, expressing his frustration with his helplessness in colorful phrases that made Annabelle flinch.

She sniffled, raining tears on the young man's splinted leg. "Please, God," she prayed, taking his limp, cold hand. "Please, give me the strength to help this poor man."

From deep within, Annabelle felt a warm energy swell and surge up in a geyser through her body. In a rush of euphoria, the warm energy pulsed through her arm and into the wounded man. Again, his entire body went as rigid as a board, and then he relaxed with a moan, eyelids fluttering. His fingers spasmed and grew warm to her touch. Bright, sapphire blue limned objects around her. She could *see.* Beneath her blue gaze the man looked familiar. Enoch had described him to her, both in words and in mind-pictures. Toad shouted something but the liquid noise of energy rushing through her in rhythmic pulses drowned it out.

The soldier's grip tightened around her fingers. His eyes rolled behind his eyelids. "Enoch," he murmured. "Hold on, E. I'm coming…"

Toad cursed again. Something bumped into her arm. "Kiddo, what did you *do?*"

"I… I don't know." *Hard to think.* Annabelle's head floated in a sapphire sea. Above her, the stars spun languidly in a stately dance against a backdrop of ebony. *Stop the world. I wanna get off.* She heeled like a sailboat pushed by stormy winds, and then the world capsized, spilling her into darkness.

THE RETURN OF SIR THOMAS

"He lives. How is this possible? The soil drank his lifeblood."

A familiar voice snorted a brief laugh. "Beats me, your Excellentness. Kiddo friggin' glowed blue, did something that made me feel…" The voice wavered and then became gruff. "His legs were broken, he was at death's door, and now he's not. She passed out when she finished doing… whatever it was."

Cloth smelling of cardamom and pepper settled on her shoulders. Warm fingers brushed her face. "She wakes."

"About time."

Pillowed on a warm surface, Annabelle's head rose and fell rhythmically. Dampness soaked her clothes. *Am I on the floor of a boat with a leaky bilge? Better get up.* She tried to open her gummed-shut eyes. Her head was too heavy to lift. From beneath her came the rumble of sleepy murmurings; a man's chest pillowed her head.

Dad? Did I fall asleep while fishing with him and Grandpa?

No, things didn't sound right. The slap of waves against the sides of the boat were absent. Wind soughed through leaves and men whispered from a distance away. She didn't recognize their voices. Brush crackled beneath heavy footfalls. It didn't smell right, either—no fishy lake scents. And the man under her cheek didn't smell like her father's Old Spice. He smelled like leather and blood. And something burnt. Gasping, she threw herself backward. Her hands skidded in damp grass and mud. Her eyelids snapped open. Steely light imbued everything with an ethereal aspect.

A croak sounded on her left where a huge toad crouched. "Jiminy Cricket, kiddo!"

That's right. I know him, sort of. His name is Toad.

A hand grasped her right arm above the elbow, steadying her before withdrawing. "Careful, Freylin. The ground is quite wet. You will do yourself an injury."

Annabelle froze. Heart raced and neurons fired, urging her to flight, but her limbs refused to work. She blinked at the strange figure crouching beside her on one knee, hands still extended from draping cloth—a cotton lace-up shirt—around her bare shoulders. The warm tenor voice suggested a man—but this man was unlike any she ever met. And yet, something about him rang a bell in her mind—as if she'd seen him somewhere.

She wrapped the shirt around herself and took a deep breath. "Are—are you a werewolf?"

The creature tilted his head and raised his eyebrows. And his wolfish ears. "Pardon, Freylin? What is this word you use?" He wore dark pants and a black vest hanging open to expose a white-furred chest.

Toad sniggered. "No, kiddo, he always looks like that. Moon's got nothing to do with it."

"Oh." Blushing, Annabelle turned her back, tugged the shirt on, and tied the laces. *Then what is he and why do I feel as if I've met him?* She glanced at the brown-skinned soldier lying on the damp ground beside her. He breathed steadily, his eyes dancing beneath their lids. *And what happened to this poor man?* Earlier, she'd helped him. In the strengthening light, he looked young and handsome despite his sorry condition.

The not-werewolf glared at Toad. He growled, "This is switching the goat in front of the wrong post." He bowed his head and placed a hand over his heart. "Forgiveness, Freylin. This one is called Raeden von Bleistaff. He regrets making the acquaintance under these circumstances." He leaned closer and peered at her with an expectant gleam in his green eyes.

She stared back at him. *What the heck* is *he?*

In a gentle tone, the not-werewolf prompted, "And how are you called, Freylin?"

Annabelle held out her right hand. Instead of shaking it, the not-werewolf tipped his head the other way and eyed it with a furrowed brow. *His name slips my mind, darn it. And why does he keep calling me 'Freylin'?* "Nice to meet you, um, sir. I'm Annabelle Leigh Wells." She withdrew her hand and licked her lips. "Uh, sorry. Is Enoch around here somewhere?"

The not-werewolf opened his mouth to speak, and the soldier groaned. "Enoch… no… run. No. Don't take E… won't let you." He whimpered. "Sweet Yshua, it hurts."

Throat sac pulsing, Toad hopped forward. He spoke with authority in a soft tone. "At ease, soldier. You're injured. We'll get you patched up." He glanced at Annabelle.

Mud squelching, she scrambled over and placed a hand on the soldier's chest. It looked so small and pale amid the leather scales and straps. She bit her lip as she bent over, examining his face. His color had improved with his return to lucidity.

I wish I knew what I did before to help you, Enoch's friend. I'd take away your pain.

Tears leaked out from underneath the wounded man's eyelids. "Failed in my duty, sir… They took E. Couldn't stop 'em… Forgive me, Sir Thomas."

Toad froze. "Uh," he grated out. "Were you talking to me, trooper?"

Raeden—*that's his name*—went still and stared at Toad.

Eyelids fluttering, the soldier grimaced. "Yes. You, Sir Thomas."

Toad's eyes went very wide. "What the… I don't remember. How?"

The soldier rolled his head from side to side, his brow wrinkled. His eyelashes twitched on the brink of opening. "Sir? You trained me… basic espionage. Know your voice… Sir Thomas."

Toad settled back on his haunches, thunderstruck. He made a gulping sound in his throat, like desperate laughter. "Huh. So, that's who I am, eh? Why can't I remember?" He stared at a point beyond Raeden, hunkered beside Annabelle. An acrid odor assaulted her nostrils.

The dog-man waved an open vial under the soldier's nose. The man flinched, his eyes fluttering open with a cry. "Sergeant Simon Halloway," Raeden said, his tone sharper than the scent. "Wake up. You must report. What has become of our young knight?"

Annabelle hovered protectively over the sergeant's head. Tears burned in her eyes. "Please, stop, Raeden—you're hurting him!"

The soldier grabbed her arm and eased her back. "It's okay, miss. His Lordship… has the right of it."

Voices called out, footsteps approached, and men gathered around them. Whispering, murmuring, asking questions—mainly, "who's she?"—that Raeden answered before issuing orders. Despite the strangeness and the mindless terror building inside, Annabelle had eyes only for the young sergeant—Simon, Enoch's friend—who may tell her what became of her adopted brother. She held his hand and his gaze. "Sergeant Halloway, I'm Ann Wells."

"Miss… Miss Wells. It's just Simon. I'd say it's a pleasure, but—" He grimaced and then managed a crooked smile. "Perdition's flames, aside from being so pale, you could be his sister. I—I'd like to get better acquainted—" Raeden loosed a rumbling growl— "but I must report to my superior officer."

"I guess that's me," Toad said wryly, hopping over. "Fire away, sergeant."

"What in Balthazar's Forge—a toad? When did Sir Thomas become a toad?"

"Button it, Guffie."

The sergeant shot a bewildered glance at the amphibian. "Sir Thomas?"

Toad leaped up on his chest. His pale eyes narrowed. "Report, trooper."

Annabelle held Simon's hand. Her heart clenched as he spoke of Enoch's abduction. The tale didn't take long, and Simon's voice soon died away into a pained hopelessness. Toad's eyes flamed palest blue as he filled in gaps, grumbling about how he couldn't remember much to be of use to them. The day brightened even as the faces of the men darkened into grimness. Raeden's white-furred visage took on a feral cast. His finger joints popped as he clenched his fists. Toad's gaze grew icy as he fell silent. He glared into the forest beyond, as if he wanted to set it on fire and burn it all to ash. Annabelle shivered. *A strange thought.*

Someone broke the silence. With a start, Annabelle realized it was her.

"Well, what are you waiting for? We have to go save Enoch."

END OF BOOK ONE

The adventure continues in Wyldling Trials!

ACKNOWLEDGEMENTS

If not for God's blessings and providence—in this case, the wonderful people He put in my life—I probably wouldn't have published this book. I believe I've written and reworked *Wyldling Snare* three times in as many years! May God continue to bless my family for putting up with me through these trying times. Ryan, Gabriel, and Michael, fair warning: it's only just begun. I'd like to thank my dear friend, Huckleberry, who was willing to read and critique my rambling story. She dragged me—kicking and screaming—into the twenty-first century and introduced me to the dubious glory of writing groups on social media. For that, I am both grateful and… Well, let's just leave it at 'grateful.' Thank you, Wes, for the critiquing and editing; you are an excellent human being. To my Writer Pals, Lawrence and Haydee: thank you for your comments and encouragement. To Kelsey, Grant, Chaos, and the rest of my Scribble Buddies: I appreciate your support and kind words. Thank you to my beta readers, Paula and Samantha, and my formatter, R. L. Davennor. Also, I'm grateful to Susanna Daniel for doing a developmental edit of my cringe-worthy first revision and Starr Davies for critiquing the second revision. For everyone else I may have forgotten to mention, whether friends from work, church, Facebook, or random passers-by, please know that I appreciate you. And last but certainly not least: thank you, Mom, for continually urging me to "finish writing that story, already!"

ABOUT THE AUTHOR

Born and raised in Wausau, Wisconsin, A.R. Grimes started writing "books" about dinosaurs in the second grade but moved on to writing fantasy after reading J. R. R. Tolkien, Madeleine L'Engle, and C. S. Lewis. She spent over twenty years trying to complete her debut novel, *Wyldling Snare*, and is living proof that any fool can get published nowadays. Several of her poems and short stories won awards in her alma mater Carroll University's literary magazine (1998-2001). She is a member of SCBWI. Other than reading and writing, she enjoys singing in the church choir, listening to music, making fused glass art, drawing, daydreaming, and going on nature hikes. She is married to a martial arts enthusiast and currently lives in Sun Prairie, Wisconsin. They share the house with two male offspring and two cats who—naturally—are the true overlords.

To see what else she's up to, please visit her website:
http://cycleoftehara.com
Get the book: https://mybook.to/wyldlingsnare
Linktree: https://linktr.ee/argrimes
Amazon author page: https://author.to/ARGrimes